PUTNEY'S SECRET

THE LEGEND OF JACK CALLAHAN

NAHUM PUTNEY
BOOK 2

D. PRESTON DAVIDSON

Putney's Secret
The Legend of Jack Callahan

INTRODUCTION

Lewis (L. H.) Musgrove (aka Musgrave) and Ed Franklin were notorious outlaws and bandits whose evil deeds spread across Utah, Colorado, and Wyoming. Their careers extended from a period during the civil war until 1868. The Musgrove/Franklin gang was probably more enterprising than any of the outlaws of the "Old West" with fame attached to their names. They probably robbed more than the James/Younger gang or Butch Cassidy and the Sundance Kid. Also, they were most likely more violent than Billy the Kid and at least as ruthless as the Cowboys in Tombstone, Arizona.

I can only speculate why their names never rose to the top of the American West's legends. It may have been that they did not have a contemporary publicist as some outlaws. They certainly did not have the Robin Hood reputation of the James/Younger gang, nor the compelling David versus Goliath story as William Bonney. Another thing they did not have was the attachment of a famous lawman or detective agency. There was no Wyatt Earp, Pat Garret, or Pinkerton Detective Agency. But I believe it was their unrepentant violence and total disregard for any standards of human decency. Simply said, they were terrible men with no redeeming qualities.

I have made them part of my novel. Some of the events mentioned did take place. Other events I modified to fit the story. For example, in my research, I found no historical information that ever placed the two in New Mexico. But it certainly would be possible. I moved the timeline of their deaths to about a year earlier to keep the story at a reasonable length. The methods of their death are as historically accurate as I could find, as referenced in the book "Hands Up or Thirty-five Years of Detective Life in the Mountains and on the Plains" By D. J. Cook.

D. J. Cook, or David Cook, was a sheriff and a city marshal in Denver, Colorado, at various times. He also owned and operated the Rocky Mountain Detective Agency. He is another person I have given prominence to in the novel. Admittedly, my descriptions of Cook are strictly from my mind.

Big Looking Glass and Quanah Parker are two other people who hold importance in the book. Many history books have documented the life of Quanah Parker. One such book is "Empire of the Summer Moon" by S. C. Gwynne. I highly recommend this book to anyone interested in the struggles between the ever-expanding United States and the Comanche Nation. Unfortunately, Big Looking Glass never became as famous as Quanah Parker. However, at a recent event, I had the pleasure of meeting Kenneth Looking Glass, the great-great-grandson of Big Looking Glass. I discovered that Big Looking Glass was an elder contemporary of Quanah Parker and that the two were not particularly fond of each other. So with Kenneth

Looking Glass' permission, I included Big Looking Glass in my story.

Other than what I have mentioned, I have thrown in a few other historical characters, but all events described are fictional and are strictly the creation of my own imagination.

This book is dedicated to my granddaughters Kaytlann and Erin Davidson.
Precious gems that fill my heart with joy.

PART I

1

Nahum Putney had been waiting on Marshal Parnell for half an hour past the appointed time, and he felt the temptation to leave just as the Marshal entered the office. Accompanying Parnell were two other men. One was the U. S. Attorney, C. T. Garland. The other man looked to be about the same age as Nahum. He was as tall, and Nahum thought they could almost pass as brothers, except the other had brown hair. This man was also wearing a deputy marshal's badge on his coat. Parnell directed everyone to sit while he planted himself behind the large oak desk.

Marshal Parnell leaned over his desk and glared at Nahum. "Do you know how many men you and Dirkson killed over just a few days?"

"None that didn't deserve it," Nahum's voice was stern.

"God damn it, son! I didn't ask for a smart assed reply! Answer me straight up!"

Nahum glared back at Parnell. "Dirkson killed two, and I killed four."

"That's right! Six men! For the love of Pete, were you just not thinking?"

"I don't believe I was thinking, sir. I was too busy trying to stay alive."

This time Parnell rose from his chair. "I did not hire you to go around gunning down every damn cowhand in Texas! I hired you to arrest fugitives and bring them to this court for justice."

Nahum knew he had overstepped and, lowering his eyes to the floor, simply said, "Yes, sir."

≈

NAHUM PUTNEY HAD KNOWN the day was coming. He just never knew the date, nor the outcome. Finally, it was time for him to learn his fate. The last time Putney had met with the U. S. Marshal Parnell was at the stage depot in Austin after they had returned from Fredericksburg. It was an arduous eighteen-hour journey from Fredericksburg to Austin, and during that time, Parnell had little to say to Putney. The same was true with C. T. Garland, who had accompanied Parnell to Fredericksburg. Their silence had not bothered Putney because he was angry, and he was concerned that he would lose his temper if a conversation started. The two officials had made a bargain with the district attorney of Gillespie County, who had Putney under investigation for murder, that Putney could remain free under the condition that he returned to Austin. Putney had to stay in Austin, under Parnell's supervision, until a grand jury convened to investigate the events at Crying Rock.

It had been over a month since the events at Crying Rock, when a gang of outlaws, headed by a former captain in the Confederate Army, had conspired with the corrupt sheriff in Llano County to falsely charge Putney with the murder of two of the brigands. Putney had been in Llano County searching for a fugitive wanted for the killing of a Seminole that scouted for the U. S. Army. While searching for the fugitive in the southern part of the county, four outlaws attacked Putney. Putney fled the gang on horseback until he reached a point where he might have some advantage. At the very moment he was turning his horse to take the battle to the bandits, someone had fired a shot, but Putney didn't know who it had been. Putney shot and killed one of the riders, and the final two fled back in the direction of Llano. So, two villains were dead, but only one death was at the hands of Putney, and that had been in self-defense. A total stranger killed the other. Ironically, his savior turned out to be the very fugitive he was hunting.

The outlaws that had attacked Putney were working for Montague Russell, once a Confederate Army captain. Working with Russell was a corrupt sheriff named Buck Oberman. When Putney returned to Llano with the two dead men, Russell and Oberman conspired to charge Putney with their murder. Putney had fled from Llano to seek help from Marshal Parnell but had only gotten as far as Crying Rock before Oberman and a posse of cutthroats caught up with him. Their intention was to murder Putney. In all Putney had killed four outlaws and survived only to be arrested by the sheriff of Gillespie County. Grand juries in Llano and Gillespie counties convened to determine whether Putney would stand trial for murder in the deaths of the brigands. Putney had no idea what lay in store for him.

≈

THE FIRST WEEK in Austin had been miserable for Nahum. He had little to keep him occupied. Nahum had no real friends in Austin, only acquaintances, and they were people with whom he did business. Every day seemed a repeat of the previous. The monotony was bleak. Nahum bought a new horse and started training it, and he bought a new Smith & Wesson pistol. He took his clothes to the Chinese laundry for cleaning. He bought new clothes. Then, Nahum picked up his order of Kinney cigarettes and ordered more. Before the week was gone, he believed he had visited every café and restaurant in Austin at least once. The rest of his time he spent reading newspapers and books.

The monotony ended one morning when he received a telegram from Deidre O'Neill. The doctor in Fredericksburg deemed her fit for travel and had recommended she go to Austin to a convalescence hospital where, hopefully, they could repair her shoulder and she could rest. She would arrive in two days.

That afternoon Nahum went to the hospital and worried the staff to distraction about preparations for Deidre. Finally, the nurse called the doctor in charge to assure Nahum that the hospital was perfectly capable of making all the necessary accommodations. On his way back to his rooms, he went by the tobacco shop and bought a box of cheroots, the kind Deidre smoked. Nahum stopped at a woman's shop and purchased two dressing gowns with frills and bows. He also bought a deep green dressing coat made of velvet and trimmed with silver brocade and a second that was red velvet trimmed with gold brocade.

The following two days went slower than the previous week. On the third day, he had breakfast in his rooms and tried to read a novel by Charles Dickens but found he couldn't concentrate. Then, a little before Mrs. Swann announced lunch, there was a light rap on his door. Opening the door, he found his landlady, Mrs. Swann, with a perturbed look on her face. "There is a, ahem, gentlemen here to see you," she said. "I told him to wait on the porch until you came down." Usually, Mrs. Swann had visitors wait in the parlor. Nahum thought it must be a messenger of some sort. Maybe from Marshal Parnell. He went downstairs to see who the visitor might be. When he walked out on the porch, he found one of the Shakespeare brothers waiting, but as they were twins, Nahum didn't know which.

"It's me, Brutus," the giant announced. "I come from Miss Deidre. I have this here wagon waiting." He pointed to the street at a four-horse team hitched to a wagon covered by canvas.

"Come with me," commanded Nahum as he led the massive man into the house past a disapproving Mrs. Swann. In his rooms, Nahum loaded Brutus with the packages from the dress shop. Nahum took off his vest, donned his best brocade waistcoat, and pulled on a morning coat. He grabbed his hat and the box of cigars and led Brutus back down to the waiting wagon. On the way to the hospital, Nahum looked in the back of the wagon to see a brass framed bed and a cushioned chair. Brutus explained that Deidre had rented the wagon and furnished it for their trip. They had stayed out on the road only one night, but Deidre and Mary had been kept comfortable.

"How is Mary holding up," Nahum inquired.

"She's doing pretty well," returned Brutus. "We buried Mr. Johnson the day after you left. Of course, the boss couldn't come, but Caesar and Billy and me were there, and so was Sheriff King. The day before we left, the stonemason brought around the headstone you ordered. It was real nice."

"Did he get it right?"

"I wrote it down," Brutus pulled a piece of paper from his jacket. It read *Charlie Johnson*. The second line was *Soldier and Indian Fighter*. Under that was *Loving Husband and True Friend.* Then it had the day he died. "That was real nice of you, Marshal," said Brutus

Nahum leaped from the wagon when they reached the hospital and asked Brutus to bring the packages. He ran up the steps and entered the building, where a severe-looking woman in a black dress stopped him. She admonished Nahum and told him that she would not tolerate such rambunctious behavior because there were ill people housed there, and she didn't want them disturbed. Nahum apologized and asked for Deidre. "We placed her in a private room, just as you requested. Follow me," the severe woman directed. Nahum entered the room without waiting to be announced. Deidre O'Neill was lying in a single bed wearing a white gown, with her arm still in a sling, and her hair flowed back over the pillows with the white streak standing out in the sea of red.

"Well, you took your own good time, didn't you," said Deidre.

"I wanted to give you time to get settled. I wouldn't want you getting the vapors," Nahum jested.

"Me the vapors? Never! Come give me a kiss, you brute!" Nahum obeyed under the disapproving eyes of the severe woman.

"Miss O'Neill, you must not over-exert yourself," she admonished.

"Woman! I just spent two days in the back of a damn wagon during this heat! I don't think a mere peck will over-exert me," expounded the Irish woman.

Nahum saw that Mary Johnson was standing to one side. "Mary! How are you," he asked? "He walked over and gave the slight woman a tender hug. "I'm so sorry I couldn't be there at Charlie's funeral."

"I'm doing well, Mr. Putney," Mary said. "And thank you for paying for everything, especially the stone. Charlie would have appreciated it."

"I was glad to do it," Nahum said sincerely. Brutus and his twin brother, Caesar, entered the room as the black-clad woman left. They were carrying packages. "These are for you, Deidre." Nahum indicated the parcels and put the box of cigars on a side table. Deidre asked Mary to open them for her. Everyone exclaimed how beautiful the gowns and dressing coats were. Brutus and Caesar then excused themselves as they needed to take care of the animals and find a place to stay for the night.

Nahum sat for about an hour as he and Deidre and Mary talked. He found out that Billy, one of Deidre's bartenders who had ridden to Crying Rock with her, had returned to Llano to run her hotel and restaurant. Caesar and Brutus would leave the next day to return the wagon and bedding to Fredericksburg and then go to Llano to help Billy. Nahum asked about Mary, and Deidre explained that Mary would be staying. She had hired Mary to be her personal secretary and companion. When Nahum asked where Mary would be staying, Deidre said the hospital would clear out a small room for her and put a cot in it.

"Nonsense," exclaimed Nahum. "There are rooms available at my boarding house. I will rent a buggy and horse, Mary. You and I can come here every day to check on our ward." Mary started to protest, but Nahum held up his hand and told her she might as well accept it because it was going to happen. Mary and Deidre thanked him.

The door to the room opened, and in walked the doctor, a nurse, and the severe woman. He introduced himself to

Deidre as Doctor Armstrong and then asked Nahum to wait in the hall while he examined Deidre. After a few minutes, the nurse told Nahum he could return.

"The doctor in Fredericksburg did a good job stitching you up, Miss O'Neill," the doctor told her. "But I could feel where a portion of the scapula is missing. I think I felt a piece of bone under the muscle tissue, but we will have to operate to see what we can find and repair things a bit better. We will set your surgery for the day after tomorrow. Until then, try and rest and keep visitations short. Miss Marcy will get a cell ready for Mrs. Johnson, and she can take her meals with the staff."

"Evidently, that shan't be necessary," said Deidre. "Mr. Putney seems to have taken care of Mrs. Johnson's needs, I hope."

"In any case, I think with your travel and all, you should take the remainder of the day to rest," Then, turning to Nahum, the doctor said, "It would be best for you to say your farewells for today. You may return tomorrow, after lunch." Then Doctor Armstrong exited the room.

After giving Deidre another kiss, Nahum and Mary left the room. Nahum hailed a cab that drove them to Mrs. Swann's boarding house. After introducing Mary and Mrs. Swann, Nahum explained the situation, and Mrs. Swann agreed to rent Mary a room. Mrs. Swann showed Mary the single but comfortable room while Nahum went to his chambers. He began reading a newspaper, but a light rap on the door interrupted him.

Nahum opened the door to find Mrs. Swann. "Mr. Putney," she started, "I have seen Mrs. Johnson to her room. She seems a respectable woman. But I want you to know, Mr. Putney, I will brook no tomfoolery in my house."

Nahum smiled at Mrs. Swann's Puritanism and replied,

"Thank you, Mrs. Swann. I assure you there will be no Tom or any other kind of foolery. I appreciate your kind generosity."

Mrs. Swann thanked Nahum even as a bit of blush rose on her cheeks from his mild admonishment.

Deidre did have her surgery two days later. Doctor Armstrong had removed some bone fragments during the surgery. He wrapped the shoulder tightly and put her arm in a tight sling when he had completed to immobilize the shoulder. "Your arm will need to stay immobilized for two weeks," Armstrong told her. "After that, we can start working on some exercise. You should be able to take your own lodgings by the end of July."

The following weeks took the drudgery out of Nahum's routine. He and Mary would have breakfast at Mrs. Swann's every morning and then take the buggy to the hospital. Nahum would read the newspaper to the women, and they would discuss the day's topics. Deidre would often have Mary write letters to Billy and the Shakespeare twins to ask how business was or answer questions they had written her. One day, at Deidre's request, Nahum brought a lawyer to make out legal documents that authorized Billy to withdraw money from the bank if he needed to and the authority to conduct business in her name. Mary always brought a book to read to Deidre. The one thing they never discussed was Nahum's situation. Nahum would stop at the hospital with Mary and then leave for the courthouse every Monday. On those days, Nahum sometimes wouldn't return until well after lunch.

Then one evening, a messenger came to Mrs. Swann's house with a note that said Nahum was to report to the Marshal's office at one o'clock the next day. That was all. It was in the clerk's handwriting and wasn't even signed.

When he rose in the morning, Nahum had breakfast with Mary as usual. Nahum said nothing about the afternoon appointment. Nahum took Mary to the hospital, but, on this day, he didn't go in to see Deidre. When they arrived at the hospital, Nahum told Mary that he had to see the Marshal, if everything went well, he would be back in the afternoon. Nahum also said that things might not end well for him, so he would walk to the courthouse and leave the buggy for her.

2

"**D**o you understand your responsibilities to this office?" Marshal Parnell asked his deputy.

"Yes, sir," Nahum was trying to be polite but silently wished Parnell would just get on with it.

"Well, I'm glad you do. Even so, Judge Duvall wants me to fire you. What do you think of that?"

Nahum looked directly at the Marshal. "Well, sir, from the way you're carrying on, I wouldn't be surprised if you did."

"Well, you're in luck because I'm not going to. Least ways not yet. Anyway, I received a letter from the district attorney in Fredericksburg. In it, he said that the grand jury had finished its investigation on you. He also told me he had received correspondence from the district attorney in Llano. Thankfully, the grand juries in Gillespie and Llano counties agreed with you that all those men probably did need killing," the Marshal announced. "They both returned a no bill on you. Also, the judge in Llano County had Buck Oberman arrested for corruption in office and suspicion of a stagecoach robbery. The District Attorney in Llano County believes that the men you and Dirkson killed were part of the robbery, but he has no evidence. Unfortunately, this so-called Captain Montague Russell has fled the area, so it is doubtful they will be able to get to the bottom of that. So, in one sense, you did a good job."

"What about Russell and Dawson?

"Oberman wouldn't say anything against Dawson or Russell. No one has seen either of them in weeks. Now that the business of the State of Texas is all cleared up let's discuss our business."

"Yes, sir."

"Fortunately for you, Judge Duvall doesn't do the hiring and firing in this office! That's my job," Parnell expounded, then to Garland, "I think you may have something to say here."

"Indeed, I do, Marshal," Garland said. " Nahum, the Marshal and I had a long discussion about you, and despite your indiscretions, you are the best person for an assignment the Marshal has."

Garland opened a case, pulled out several documents, which Nahum immediately recognized as warrants, and laid them on Parnell's desk. "There are three warrants here, and we think, with some help, you are the man to serve them." *With some help,* thought Nahum, and he understood the presence of the other deputy.

The Marshal interjected, "Nahum, let me formally introduce you to Everett Jackson. He's been working as a deputy sheriff over in Kerrville, but I talked him into coming to work for me. The Attorney General gave me another full-time deputy position. I think you two will work well together." The two deputies stood and shook hands and sat back down.

You really mean you're sending a watcher with me, thought

Nahum. This time Nahum eyed the other deputy more seriously. Jackson's hair was shorter than Nahum's but worn naturally, without all the pomade that seemed to be the fashion of the dandies those days. But Jackson did sport a mustache and chin whiskers that were becoming the fashion for westerners. Under his coat, Nahum noticed that Jackson wore a short-barreled Colt in a cross-draw holster. Nahum's overall second impression of the man was that he would do.

Garland held up two warrants, "These are for two men named Joaquin Doyle and Guadalupe Dominguez. They are Comancheros, and they are both mean and deadly men. These warrants are for selling guns and untaxed whiskey to Indians, but the main charge is for killing an Indian agent and an Army sergeant at the reservation for Comanche, Kiowa, and Apache in the Indian Nations."

"Isn't the jurisdiction for the Nations under the Western District of Arkansas?" Nahum noted.

"Normally, yes," agreed Garland, "but no judge is currently sitting there, and Washington has asked us to take this case since that particular reservation borders on the eastern panhandle and the Red River. Our district is the nearest to that reservation. Plus, the probability is that these two men are probably somewhere in Texas or maybe New Mexico. They could be up on the Edwards Plateau or the Llano Estacado."

Nahum nodded his head, signaling he understood the situation.

Garland continued, "The Indian Agency took statements from witnesses on the reservation. I'm keeping those, but there is information on the two included with these warrants. Sorry, but it's as much background as we have."

Parnell walked around to the front of his desk. "Nahum,

you have never been after more dangerous men, and they won't be alone. Doyle is the leader of a band of about fifty Comancheros if we are to believe the stories. Dominguez is his right-hand man and a stone killer. You think you and Jackson can handle this assignment?"

Nahum looked blankly at Jackson. "I reckon we'll have to."

"Good," said the Marshal, holding up the third warrant. "Now there's one other thing. C. T. held a grand jury hearing of his own. This warrant is for the murder of two U. S. soldiers and the attempted murder of a Deputy United States Marshal. The name on this warrant is William Dawson, a.k.a. Bull Dawson. And Nahum," the Marshal paused, then started again. "I – want - Dawson - brought in alive. Do I make myself clear?"

"Clear as a bell, Marshal."

Garland pulled another handful of documents from his case. "These are blank warrants. If you have to arrest any of Doyle's gang or anybody else, take them to the nearest Justice of the Peace or county judge. Have them fill out the warrants and bring everyone back here to Austin."

"I'm also sending a posse man with you," the Marshal informed the two deputies. "Nahum, you've worked with Julian Feazel before?"

"Yes, sir. He's a good man.

"Feazel's already been inspecting the jail wagon and making sure it's ready for a long trip, I want you all to leave here as soon as possible, so you need to get all your gear and the supplies you think you will need. Stop by here before you leave." The Marshal put all the documents in a leather folder and handed it to Jackson.

It was an unmistakable gesture and a slight to Nahum. Neither of the young men missed the inference.

"Yes, sir," the two men said in unison.

In the outer office, Nahum stopped at the desk of the Marshal's clerk and asked for a piece of paper and an envelope. He wrote a short note and placed it in the envelope, which he addressed to Deidre O'Neill with the hospital's address. He asked the clerk to have a messenger deliver the note as soon as possible. The clerk, who did not like Nahum, said, "Do you still have a job here?"

Smiling, contemptuously Nahum said, "Maybe I should go back in the Marshal's office and get him to endorse it,"

Knowing that Marshal Parnell expected his clerks to assist deputies with clerical issues, the clerk snapped, "Not necessary," taking the envelope, "I'll get it out in the next hour."

Nahum and Jackson left the courthouse together. Nahum paused on the steps, took a Kinney-ready-rolled cigarette out of its case, and lit up. He stood in silence, smoking when Jackson spoke. "I get the idea you don't cotton to me much," he said.

"I don't know you well enough to make an opinion," returned Nahum. "The Crystal or the Iron Front?"

Confused, Jackson just gave a blank stare in response.

"I haven't had lunch. We need to go over those papers and come up with a plan. So, do you want to go to the Crystal or the Iron Front?"

"Well, if it's up to me, I would prefer to go to Sholz Beer Garten," stated Jackson. Nahum smiled and started walking to the German establishment. Jackson kept pace beside him.

3

The two Deputy Marshals ate lunch at Sholz's Beer Garden and went over the documents Garland had provided them. Then, after discussing the outlaws, they devised a plan. Nahum told Jackson that it would be best if Jackson lay their intentions out to Marshal Parnell. Nahum didn't say so, but he believed that the Marshal would be more willing to approve it if it came from Jackson. After all, Jackson wasn't the rogue deputy Parnell thought Nahum to be.

HAVING satisfied themselves with a good meal and a plan, Nahum and Jackson left to check with Feazel to see how repairs on the jail wagon were coming. As they were leaving Sholz's, Nahum accidentally bumped into a man that had the appearance of any typical cow hand you might see in Austin, except on his vest, there was a badge that read "Texas State Police."

. . .

AT THE LIVERY, Nahum introduced Jackson and Feazel. The three men discussed the wagon and what was needed. The mechanic working on the wagon obviously disliked taking directions from Feazel since he was a former slave. Nahum asked Feazel and Jackson to check on the mules they would use to pull the wagon while he inspected the vehicle. Nahum could not abide the mechanic's churlishness toward Julian. Nahum discussed his concern with the mechanic, in no uncertain terms. When Feazel and Jackson returned, the mechanic was only too happy to work on whatever Julian told him needed to be repaired. Next, the three lawmen discussed what supplies they would need for their trip. Feazel said he could arrange for most of the stores, but the two deputies would have to take care of their personal needs, weapons, and ammunition. Feazel himself always took along a sawed-off, double-barreled shotgun and a Colt pistol. Nahum and Jackson saw that Julian had the wagon well in hand. The three agreed they would meet in Parnell's office at three o'clock the following day. Nahum asked Jackson if he would mind stopping by the courthouse and advising the Marshal, as he had other business to attend.

BEFORE GOING TO THE HOSPITAL, Nahum went to a shop to pick up a new gun belt he had designed and ordered. The saddler made the belt and holsters of sturdy saddle leather with a right-hand draw holster sewn where the grip of his pistol sat where he liked it, mid-way between his elbow and wrist. The other holster had a right-hand cross draw. If necessary, Nahum would also be able to draw it with his left. Eighteen cartridge loops were across the back of the belt and a sheath for his Bowie on the left. Nahum paid for the belt while a young helper boxed it up. After the saddler's

shop, Nahum walked to his tobacconist and picked up a
dozen packets of Kinney's he had ordered and a box of
cheroots for Deidre.

"Well, it doesn't look like they put you in jail," Chided
Deidre as Nahum entered her room, showing concern in her
voice, "Are you still working?" then, seeing the packages,
"And are those boxes gifts for me?"

"I had some things I needed to take care of, and yes, I picked
up a box of cheroots for you," answered Nahum.

Mary chimed in with her own question, "Did they fire you?"
she wanted to know.

"No, I'm still working, but how about you, Deidre? Has the
doctor said anything?
    "Aye, he did," Deidre told him. "He said I can leave here
as soon as I have appropriate lodgings. I don't suppose
there's any room in that old spinster's house where you live,
is there?"

"She's a widow, not a spinster," Nahum corrected. "No, she
doesn't have any more rooms, but you have given me an
idea. The truth is the Marshal gave me an assignment, and it
looks like I'll be away for at least two months. I have two
rooms at Mrs. Swann's. I think she would let you stay there
while I'm away."

. . .

"You mean to tell me, after they have kept you on pins and needles all this time, they expect you to go out right away?" Deidre was indignant. "When are you leaving?"

"Soon, very soon. Probably a couple of days."

"Pshaw," pouted Deidre. "I was hoping we would have time to spend together in private, if you know what I mean. Tell them I said you're not to leave until next week. We will get a hotel room, and you can leave when I'm feeling better."

"I'm after Bull Dawson."

"Oh," Deidre saw the look of hate in Nahum's eyes and knew that further supplication on the matter would be a waste. "Well, since that is so, I hope you kill the bastard."

"Yeah, I don't think that can happen. Marshal Parnell warned me not to go on another rampage. He's even sending another deputy with me to make sure."

"Oh, is that so, then you tell the other deputy to kill him, then we can all be content."

. . .

ADDRESSING Mary and hoping to diffuse Deidre's anger, Nahum said, "I never thought Deidre could be prettier, but, by God, I think the angrier she gets, the more beautiful she gets."

MARY LET OUT A LITTLE SNICKER. But the strategy had failed. "Don't you be encouraging him, Mary," Deidre charged. "I'll not be having this lout trying to mollycoddle me."

"CALM DOWN, DEAR," Mary replied, undaunted. "It won't do you any good. Besides, I think it's sweet."

"SWEET," sneered Deidre. "Hmph!"

TRYING to get her to see reason, Nahum said, "Look, Deidre, I'm not supposed to be judge, jury, and executioner. I'm the one that is supposed to see they get brought to the court for justice. I let circumstances get out of control last month. If they hadn't, you wouldn't be laying up here with a bullet wound in your shoulder. The Marshal is right. I need to do better."

"WELL, I SUPPOSE," acquiesced the Irish woman. "What about those rooms?"

.   .   .

"MARY and I will talk to Mrs. Swann when we return this evening. I don't think there will be a problem as long as I'm long gone before you move in."

～

AT FIRST, Mrs. Swann had balked at the idea of Deidre moving into her house. But after Mary and Nahum had explained the situation a third time, the old woman relented, demanding, "But you have to be packed up and out before she moves in!"

THAT HADN'T BEEN A PROBLEM. Nahum stored his gear and ammunition in his bags that night, along with some spare clothes, a slicker, bedroll, and the box of Kinney cigarettes. After packing, Nahum cleaned and checked his Smith pistols, two Colts, and Winchester. He had decided to leave his father's Walkers and the Paterson. They were hard to load compared to the Smiths, and they were old, and he didn't want weapons that might be prone to failure. Besides, with Jackson and Sorrells along, they should have enough firepower to fend off any problem that might present themselves.

WHEN NAHUM CAME DOWN to breakfast, Mrs. Swann handed him a note. The note was from Jackson. It said that he had met with Parnell, and they set the conference for three o'clock and that he had sent Julian the same message. After breakfast, he and Mary drove to the hospital. Nahum asked Mary to see to Deidre while he went to check into a hotel. He waited until Mary had enough time to get to Deidre's room, then he got out of the carriage and went to see Doctor Armstrong.

NAHUM TOLD the doctor that Deidre had a place to stay for a couple of months, and he would be taking her there that afternoon. Nahum also told the doctor he wanted to settle the bill, "You will need to talk with Miss Fleming; she takes care of all the financial matters." Unfortunately, Nahum had learned that Fleming was the name of the severe-looking woman who always dressed in black. Nahum didn't relish doing business with Miss Fleming because he thought she didn't like him. And Nahum was right. But he found her, and she guided him to a small office off the main corridor.

MISS FLEMING DIRECTED Nahum to a seat while she retrieved a ledger from a bookshelf full of registers. She fingered her way through the pages until she found the correct one. "Just a moment," Miss Fleming instructed Nahum as the woman plucked a quill pen from an ink well. She stared at the ledger for a moment, then wrote something in the register. "There," she said triumphantly to herself. "That settles it." Then looking at Nahum, "Including the Doctors fees, medicines, nursing, room, housekeeping, and meals for both Miss O'Neill and Mrs. Johnson comes to six hundred ninety-two dollars." She smiled spitefully at Nahum, believing it was impossible that a deputy marshal could pay that amount and thinking he would argue with her about the cost. Instead, Nahum pulled his wallet from his inside coat pocket and retrieved five one-hundred-dollar bills.

·   ·   ·

AFTER PLACING the notes on Fleming's desk, one at a time and counting them out loud, Nahum said, "I will need to go to the bank and get the balance. I should return within the hour. I assume you can give me a receipt for the five hundred."

The defeated Miss Fleming's smile melted into a pout as she reached inside the middle desk drawer and withdrew a receipt book. Then she precisely wrote out a receipt, carefully removed it, and handed the paper to Nahum.

"THANK YOU," Nahum smiled, stood, and left the building. Nahum drove the carriage to the Bullock House Hotel and booked a room for an extended stay since he didn't know precisely when he would be leaving. Afterward, Nahum went to his bank and withdrew another five hundred dollars. Nahum calculated that it would cover the hospital's balance, and he would still have considerable money for any needs while on the trail. So, he took one hundred in coin and the rest in various denominations of bills. Upon his return to the hospital, Nahum went directly to Miss Fleming and paid the balance of the account.

WHEN NAHUM ENTERED Deidre's room, she and Mary were sitting and discussing an article in that day's newspaper. Something to do with property prices being on the rise in Austin. Deidre had dressed in a new frock. Nahum supposed that Mary had bought it for her when he wasn't hanging around. "I was wondering if you were going to return or if you were leaving Mary and me in a lurch," Deidre poked fun at Nahum, something he had learned brought her great joy.

.   .   .

"It would have been nothing more than what you deserved after laying about for a month acting like the Queen of Sheba," Nahum returned her jest.

"I suppose all we have to do is arrange to pay the bill and leave this wretched place."

"Already taken care of."

"That is an all-mighty grand gesture you have made without consulting me."

"It was the least I could do for the woman that most probably saved my life and nearly lost hers in turn. Whether you accept it gracefully or not is up to you."

"Since you put it in those terms, I suppose I must. Just don't start making a habit of it. I made my way before I met you, and I will make my own way when you are gone; just you keep that in mind."

"I never doubted it. Now shall we go, or do you want to stay here discussing it for the rest of the day?" Nahum understood that they would both have to learn to put up with each other's pridefulness.

. . .

NAHUM DROVE the carriage with Deidre and Mary to Miss Swann's, and Nahum pulled up in front of the rooming house. He helped Mary down and, in a conspiratorial tone, said, "Tell Mrs. Swann that I will bring Miss O'Neill from the hospital in a couple of days."

MARY BLUSHED a little before saying she would inform Mrs. Swann that Deidre was staying at the hospital a few more nights. Nahum bent over and kissed Mary on the cheek. Then he climbed back in the carriage and drove to the Bullock House.

"ANOTHER OF YOUR SURPRISES," questioned Deidre.

NAHUM HAD TAKEN Deidre to lunch at the dining room of the Bullock House. When they had finished eating, Nahum led her up to their room. It wasn't as posh as the room he had used in her hotel in Llano, but it was furnished well with a dresser, two leather wing back chairs, and a low table. On the dresser was a vase filled with roses, and there was a bottle of Bushmills Irish whiskey and two glasses on the table. Deidre picked up the bottle and studied it for a moment, then said, "You realize this is protestant whiskey, do you not?"

NAHUM GAZED at her with a confused look on his face. Deidre laughed and said, "It doesn't matter, me boy! It's not

Scotch, and I haven't been Catholic in a long time, not so the church would admit anyway." She laughed again while opening the bottle and filling the two glasses.

Nahum was looking at his watch when she handed him his glass. "I hope you have a good reason for looking at that timepiece," complained Deidre.

"I HAVE a meeting with Marshal Parnell in a little bit. It won't take long. I should be back no later than five. So, you just rest until then, and the rest of the night is yours," Nahum was apologetic.

"I'VE BEEN DOING nothing but resting for the last month! So now you want me to rest some more?"

"WELL, you might need it before the night's over," Nahum laughed, then kissed her deeply before turning to the door.

4

J ulian Feazel was waiting on the steps of the federal
courthouse when the two deputies arrived, each
coming from a different direction. "Howdy, boys," he
called out as they approached. They all greeted each
other with handshakes all around.

Nahum asked Jackson if he had gotten most of his business tended to?"

"Yeah. I just have some last-minute things that need to be
taken care of," said Jackson. "Well, we better not keep the
Marshal waiting anymore."

"Before we go," Nahum reminded Jackson, "You lay out
the plan. It will go down easier with the Marshal, coming
from you."

Arriving at the Marshal's office, the clerk ushered in the
three lawmen. Marshal Parnell sitting behind his desk,
motioned the three to sit. "You boys ready to head out? Got
everything you need?" he asked.

"Yes, sir," Nahum said respectfully, believing he didn't
need to get Parnell riled up before they left. "Julian has the

rig in great shape and is getting all the supplies we will need."

"Have you come up with a plan," the Marshal wanted to know.

Jackson spoke and detailed their plan, "Yes, sir. We are going to ride to Fredericksburg together. We will split up there, with Nahum and Julian going on to Llano. They can check on Buck Oberman to see if he can shed any light on Dawson. At the same time, I will head out past Kerrville to a trading post called Harper's. There's an old-timer named Brewster that sometimes hangs around there. Word has it he deals with Comancheros from time to time. If I find him, he might have some information. He probably won't give it up easily, but I think I can shake it out of him. We have it set to meet up at Fort McKavett a few days later. We will meet up there, compare notes, and decide which way to go."

"The logic is right," agreed Parnell. " Nahum, do you think you can stay out of trouble if you go to Llano?"

"*What the hell kind of question is that?*" Nahum thought to himself, then simply said, "Yes, sir."

"When are you leaving?" Parnell wanted to know.

Before anyone could speak up, Nahum said, "We'll leave day after tomorrow. I thought we could all meet at the livery at noon and leave then. We can't make Fredericksburg in one day anyway, and I have a small business affair I need to take care of that morning."

Parnell turned his look to Julian Feazel. "Anything you want to add?"

"I went by the sheriff's office this morning and picked up a few posters on some outlaws that could be west of here. I thought we might could pick up a few bounties while we were out that way. Other than that, I think these two boys have it all covered."

"Alright, then," the Marshal said. "It sounds like a simple enough plan. Try not to run afoul of any of those new state police officers that the governor created. We don't want to ruffle his feathers. I want regular telegrams from y'all, followed up by written reports mailed in. Other than that, you boys be careful out there."

The Marshal dismissed the three men. Leaving the courthouse, Nahum noticed a Texas policeman he had seen before walking out of a café on the other side of the street. He thought nothing of it. Austin wasn't a large city, and eating places weren't that plentiful.

Walking back to the hotel, Nahum felt like a new man. He had an assignment and a plan, but best of all, he would have two nights with Deidre. Nahum was whistling as he walked through the doors of the hotel. When he entered the room, Deidre was sitting in one of the chairs, reading the newspaper.

Nahum noticed that the bottle of Bushmills was less than half full, and there was a bottle of Scotch standing next to it. "Well then," said Deidre, "Don't you look happy as a lark?"

"How could I be otherwise? I have just walked into a room where the most beautiful woman in Austin is, and it appears she's half-drunk. I'm a lucky man."

"You are a very lascivious man, Nahum Putney. Has anyone ever told you that?"

"I've heard the rumor," answered Nahum, and they both laughed as Deidre poured a glass of Bushmills.

"It's back to Scotch after this. The hotel had no idea where you got the Irish, and I arranged to have dinner sent up at six, so drink your whiskey and relax. Tonight, we don't have to worry about anything in the world."

They had just finished their dinner when there was a

rap on the door. Nahum asked who it was; a man said he was the bellman with a message for Nahum. Nahum opened the door, took an envelope from the boy, and handed him two quarters. Nahum opened the envelope and read the note, and his face went dark. "What is it, dear," asked Deidre.

"It's a note from Marshal Parnell. He wants me to come to the office right away. Says it's a matter of urgency."

"That man is becoming a pain in me arse," Deidre's anger was rising.

"Yeah, mine, too. I'll be back as soon as I can." Nahum took his gun belt off the dresser and buckled it on.

"You don't think you'll be needing those, do you?"

"Parnell said it was urgent. It's better to be prepared than not."

He bent and kissed the Irish woman on the cheek.

"You better improve on that when you return."

∾

WHEN NAHUM ARRIVED at the courthouse, he knocked on the locked door and wait for the night watchman to open it. The watchman recognized the deputy marshal, letting Nahum in without question.

Nahum went to the Marshal's Office and entered. The clerk who usually stood watch in front of the Marshal's door was absent, so he walked directly into Parnell's office.

"Where have you been," Marshal Parnell immediately asked when he saw his deputy. "I sent a message to your rooming house over an hour ago."

Nahum noticed another man was sitting in one of the Marshal's more comfortable chairs. The one usually reserved for the judge or the U. S. Attorney. The man was wearing a Texas State Police Badge with the number "one" on it.

"I moved out to let Miss O'Neill have my rooms while I'm gone," replied Nahum. "It must have taken the messenger some time to find the hotel I'm staying in."

Satisfied with the explanation, Parnell said, " Nahum, let me introduce you to Colonel James Davidson, Chief of the state police."

Davidson stood and reached out his hand to Nahum. Nahum looked the man in the eye, trying to discern the reason for his presence, while they shook hands.

" Putney," said Davidson, "That's a good Scottish name." there was a tinge of brogue in the Chief's voice.

"My father was born in Scotland. He immigrated here before the revolution," Nahum informed Davidson.

"Putney's father was a hero at the Battle of San Jacinto and later served Sam Houston as a Texas Ranger," Parnell informed Davidson.

What is this, old home day? Nahum thought to himself. *I wish Parnell would get to it.* Finally, Nahum said, "Your message said urgent."

"It did," Parnell replied as he signaled for Nahum to sit. "The Chief has brought me some information and felt you could shed some light on it."

"I'll do what I can to help," Nahum was sincere.

The Marshal cleared his throat and asked, "Have you ever heard of or known a man named Jack Callahan?"

Nahum heard the name, and his muscles tensed, but not so much as anyone would notice, he hoped.

"Yes, I knew a man named Jack Callahan," he said. "He's dead. I buried him next to his daughter."

Marshal Parnell glared at Nahum, then turned his look

to Davidson. "There you are," said Parnell. "Deputy Putney buried the man. I hope that sets your mind at ease."

Davidson rose, "It does. It does. Thank you, Marshal. Thank you, Deputy. I will say good night then and once again, thank you for your help." Davidson did not sound convincing. Nor did he sound convinced. The Chief of the state police turned and exited the office. Nahum stood as if to follow him.

"Sit down," barked Marshal Parnell after Davidson had closed the door. "We are not through." Nahum felt his neck turning hot as his anger rose, and he was trying to keep it in check. Nahum returned to his seat. Still trying to keep control, his hands gripped the arms like a pair of vises.

"This Jack Callahan," Parnell nearly spit the name. "Davidson told me that two of his policemen had seen this man in Colorado, both Denver and Boulder. They said the man was a cold-blooded killer and most likely has murder warrants out for his arrest."

"And?" asked Nahum

"And! They both said he looked a lot like you! What have you to say to that?" Parnell demanded an answer.

Nahum ground his teeth before answering, then, trying to remain as calm as possible, said, "I say they don't know what they're talking about. As I said before, the Jack Callahan I knew is dead and has been for a long time. I'm not the only red-headed man in the world. And they say we all look alike anyway. There may be a Jack Callahan wanted in Colorado, but it isn't me. But to set your mind at ease, why don't you send telegrams to Denver and Boulder. Find out if there is any paper on a Jack Callahan?"

Parnell continued to glare at Nahum. *Maybe his arrogance*, thought the Marshal, *is why I never really liked this boy. But he's smart, and he gets the job done. It isn't like we're bosom pals, anyway.* Still glaring at his deputy, the Marshal said, "Davidson sent out telegram's this afternoon, and he should have answers by tomorrow morning. I want you to go home, or wherever you are staying. I want a written report on my desk by three o'clock tomorrow afternoon detailing everything you know about Jack Callahan. Have I made myself clear?"

"As a bell," replied Nahum.

5

——

Nahum Putney walked slowly from the courthouse to the Bullock House Hotel. The meeting worried him. *What did this Colonel Davidson know about Jack Callahan? What had he told Marshal Parnell? What was Nahum going to tell Parnell?* These three questions ran loops inside Nahum's head as he searched for answers but could find none.

It was futile, he finally decided. It was time for him to pluck himself up and try to be as cheerful when he returned to Deidre as he had been when he left. Nahum tried to bolster himself and look positive and confident entering the hotel room.

Evidently, he was none too successful because the first thing Deidre said was, "What is that worried look on your face Nahum? You look like a ghost walked over your grave."

"It's nothing," Nahum lied. "The Marshal had more information about this Joaquin Doyle, and he wanted to make sure I knew it before we left." It was the best he could come up with at that moment, but Nahum knew it was weak, so he threw in, "And I guess I'm still worried about you."

"Don't you be concerning yourself about me. I will do just fine, I'm sure," Deidre reached for the bottle of Scotch, opened it, and poured whisky into a glass for Nahum. Nahum knew she would be alright; it was himself he worried about. He knew he was between the devil and the deep blue sea, and Nahum felt he had forgotten how to swim.

Deidre rose from her chair and handed Nahum the whisky. After taking a drink, she took the glass from his hand and set it on the table. She put both her arms around his waist and kissed him deeply. That kiss turned to feverish lovemaking. That night their passion for each other burned brighter than a lightning storm over the Sacred Mountains. Tangled up in sheets and each other, they fell into a deep sleep.

It was still dark when Nahum woke. A dream had awakened him, and it filled him with dread. It was a haunting dream about a grave. In the nightmare, Nahum was kneeling by the grave, looking at a flat piece of sandstone with a name scratched into it. While pondering the make-shift headstone, an arm had pushed through the grave's dirt, and its calloused hand had grabbed Nahum by the collar of his coat, pulling him into the earthy tomb. Before he descended into complete darkness, Nahum could finally read the name on the sandstone. Jack Callahan!

Nahum sat up on the edge of the bed. He was sweating like he was in the middle of a swamp, and his pulse was racing. Nahum took a few deep breaths to calm himself when he felt a light touch on his back. It startled him so that he jumped out of bed and spun to see what had touched him. Nahum had still been in that gloaming time between sleep and wakefulness. The time when a person is not sure whether they are still dreaming or not. It was Deidre's voice that finally brought him back to his senses.

"What's wrong, Nahum," she asked. "What's troubling you?"

Nahum paced in the darkness for a full minute before saying anything. Then he walked to the bed table and felt for the lamp and his matches. After lighting the lamp, he saw his cigarette case, picked it up, extracted a Kinney ready roll from the box, and lit it. Nahum walked to one of the chairs and sat down. Still naked, he reached for the Scotch bottle and poured a full glass. Finally, and without looking at the bed, Nahum said, "Deidre, there is something I have to tell you. It is a secret I have kept buried for two years, but it seems it is about to catch up with me. You should put on a gown or something because it is a long story."

PART II

6

P utney remembered the day well. It was April 28,
1865. The company had left Fort Chadbourne two
weeks earlier. Usually, the company ranged out
from the fort for about a week and would return for
resupply and give the men a few days of rest before
returning to the field. But this time had been different.
Captain Montague Russell held a briefing of his troops. The
captain said Colonel McCulloch had received intelligence
that federal forces planned an invasion of Texas. According
to Russell, the incursion would be three-pronged. First,
union forces would invade, crossing the Red River from
Indian Territory, other forces coming up the Sabine River
from the Gulf of Mexico, and the last would be federal
troops from New Mexico.

The Mounted Rangers were to stay in the field for as
long as possible, searching for the invading forces from New
Mexico. Once the attackers were confirmed, Russell would
send messengers to Fort Chadbourne.

The rest of the company would remain and harass the
federal troops until sufficient forces could relieve them and

repel the invasion from the west. To Putney, this seemed like lunacy. Their company of rangers was made up of only thirty men, and they were trained to combat small bands of Indian raiders, not a massive, disciplined force.

Once in the field, though, Russell had directed Putney to scout north in search of hostile Indians. Russell said he wanted to avoid a trap between a large Union force and marauding natives. Russell's reasoning was the first sensible thing Putney had heard, and it suited him just fine. Especially since the addition of the pardoned prisoners to their ranks. The previous year the Texas command had offered pardons to convicted criminals if they would join the Confederate Army.

Captain Russell had sent Sergeant Damien Andrews to Huntsville to recruit some of these convicts personally. The sergeant had returned with eight volunteers, two of whom were Brandon Starnes and Jessup Taylor.

Putney was astounded when he first saw the two men who had tried to rob him when he was fifteen. He was especially wary of Starnes because Putney had shot Starnes during the robbery attempt and had taken Starnes' gun, which Putney still carried. So when one of the regular rangers had told Putney that Starnes had threatened to kill him, Putney went directly to the captain.

Captain Russell told Putney that he had been made aware of the bad blood between his best scout and the recruit. Russell assured Putney that he had taken care of the situation and had told Starnes that the first time he stepped out of line, Russell would send the bandit back to the Huntsville prison.

There were other officers under which Putney would have preferred to serve. Russell was a vain man and never forgot to tell the men he had trained at the best military academy in the South, but Putney never had reason to believe the captain wasn't trustworthy. Russell ordered his Corporal to remain out, as much as possible, scouting for signs of hostile Indians, especially Comanche. He told Putney that this would ensure the least friction between Starnes and the Corporal. Putney had followed his commander's orders. He had only returned on this day because he needed to restock on provisions and to give a report.

Captain Russell had set up camp in a valley between two mesas that came together, making a slight "V" shaped canyon. It was more than large enough to host the company but small enough to be defendable, if necessary. Putney never ranged more than ten or fifteen miles from where the company had camped when he left. So, he always knew the general direction the camp would be in, and he would eventually spot smoke from the cook fire, which he used as a beacon. He was about three hundred yards from the camp when challenged by a sentry, a scrawny boy named Peter Connors.

"Hold and identify," commanded the boy who had been with the company about a year and took his duties very seriously.

"Corporal Nahum Putney, Mounted Mountain Rangers returning from a scouting mission," Putney rewarded the boy's diligence by formally complying.

"Hey, Corporal," Peter replied. "I knowed it was you cause I seen that long red hair, but I got my orders."

"You did well, private. Keep up the good work," Putney commended Peter.

"You're a heck of a lot easier to identify than the other ones that rode in here yesterday. They was a ragged-looking lot. I had to signal with a mirror to Sergeant Andrews before

I would let 'em pass. He came out and told me it was alright."

"What others," asked Putney.

"I don't really know. Reinforcements was all the sergeant said, so I let 'em pass like he told me."

"Just as you should, Private. Keep up the good work," Putney liked Peter's diligence and wanted the boy to know it.

Sergeant Andrews was the first to see Putney riding in and walked over to greet him. "Howdy, Nahum," Andrews addressed him informally. "Smith, get over here and take care of the Corporal's horse. Come on and take a load off, son. You must be tired and hungry."

"I am that," Putney told the sergeant. "After a while, I get tired of eating nothing but dried beef, beans, and rattlesnake." Before Smith took the horse away, Putney retrieved the two Colt Walker's off the saddle horn and Henry rifle from its saddle scabbard.

"Rattlesnake," hooped the old sergeant. "Boy, I think you're more Comanche than white. I believe you would eat anything."

"Then I reckon you ought to be glad that I'm not a Tonk," joshed Putney, referring to the rumor that the Tonkawa Indians practiced cannibalism.

"That's a fact, son, that's a fact," laughed Andrews. "Come on in and get some good grub. One of the boys killed a deer this morning. We got some potatoes, and these new boys brought some corn."

The additional men had not escaped Putney's notice. There must have been twenty of them. Peter had been right. They were a motley-looking bunch. Some wore gray uniform jackets, mostly patched in several places and all showing a variety of insignia. But they all wore wool pants of differing colors and shades and homespun shirts embroidered with colorful stitching. They all had one thing in common. Each one sported a minimum of two colt pistols.

"Who are they," asked Putney.

"Reinforcements," said the sergeant in an off-handed way. "Captain wants to see you in his tent after you've eaten."

Putney left the sergeant and went over to the cook wagon. There was a camp stool next to the front wheel, so he propped the Henry against the wheel and laid the saddle holsters with the Walkers over it. Putney picked up a metal plate and utensils from the back of the wagon and got his meal, then sat down on the stool and began eating. The fresh venison was a good relief from what he had been eating while out on the scout. He was glad to be eating a real meal.

As he ate, a burly man about his age wearing one of the worn shell jackets walked over. "That's a good-looking rifle you got there," said the man casually. "Mind if I take a look at it?"

"Yes," replied Putney.

The man said thanks and started to pick up the rifle.

"I meant yes, I mind if you handle it," Putney was stern.

The man stepped back a bit, then said, "That ain't too friendly of you there, fella."

Before Putney could reply, Jess Taylor walked around the wagon and said, "Boy, you don't know ole Nahum here. He ain't always the friendly type. In fact, I would say he ain't never the friendly type. Kinda touchy, too."

"Hell, I just wanted to take a look. I didn't mean no slight," said the burly man.

The conversation had drawn the attention of another of the newcomers. He was a tall, lanky man with a long scar that ran from his left eye to his jawbone. "Alphonse didn't mean any harm, Corporal. He's just naturally attracted to shiny things."

Putney nodded but remained silent.

The scar-faced man held out his hand. "Ned, Ned Blakely's my name."

Putney looked at the man's hand. He could feel the tension rising, so to keep things tamped down, he firmly took the man's hand and gave it a single pump. "Nahum Putney."

"I had me one of those Henry's once," Ned informed Putney. "Took it off a boy up in Missouri. He was dead, so he didn't mind. Trouble was he didn't have but five spare cartridges, so after I shot up what was in the rifle and those five, I just threw it away since them cartridges are hard to come by. How did you come by this one?"

"Bought it," said Putney as he stuck a bite of venison in his mouth.

"Bought it, huh? That must have set you back pretty good," said Ned.

"It did," was Putney's only answer.

"You don't talk much, do you," It was a statement and not a question.

Before Putney could answer, Sergeant Andrews barked from the captain's tent, "Putney, you done eating? Captain needs to see you."

Putney stood, drew a cup of water from the barrel, and washed down his meal. He pitched the plate and utensils in a wash tub, then picked up the rifle and pistols. "Excuse me," he said and walked to the captain's tent.

It was a warm spring day, and the captain had his camp desk set up under the awning outside of his tent. Captain Russell was seated behind his camp desk. There were also four camp stools under the canopy. On one chair sat a man that looked to be in his mid-forties. He had black hair touched with grey around the temples. His beard had nearly as much grey as black. The man wore a single-breasted shell jacket with a braid that displayed the rank of captain. Unlike the other newcomers, his uniform was complete and void of fraying or patches. He looked every bit the officer, like Captain Russell.

Sitting on the other stool was Brandon Starnes. Seeing Starnes, a bit of bile squeaked out of Putney's glands. He swallowed the bitter spit.

"This gentleman here is Captain Thomas Tidwell, from Colonel Quantrill's command. Sit down, Corporal, and give us your report," ordered Russell.

Putney sat, as did Sergeant Andrews. Putney was confused as to why Starnes was present. Starnes was a simple private and a new one, with only four months in the company. The presence of Starnes annoyed Putney greatly. The company of one of Quantrill's bushwhackers didn't do anything to make him more comfortable, either. Everyone had heard stories of Bloody Bill Anderson, Quantrill, and other Missouri bushwhackers, and the reports were none too favorable. Newspaper reports of the looting and burning of Shawneetown, Kansas, and Quantrill's massacre at Lawrence, Kansas, had been reported even in the Confederate States.

Quantrill had fled to Texas and arrived in Gainesville, located in a pro-Union County. The town newspaper had written an article unfavorable about the renegade. Quantrill ordered the paper's building burned, and the sheriff hung. No matter how well-dressed Captain Tidwell was, Putney figured the man to be a cutthroat and bandit. Starnes's presence then made sense to Putney.

As Putney sat, he placed the Walkers on the ground next

to the stool, where they would be easily accessible, and laid the rifle across his knees. He adjusted himself a bit for comfort and, in doing so, felt relieved by the touch of the butt of the Belgian revolver that nestled in a cross-draw holster. "Well, Captain, as far as Indians are concerned, there is not much to report."

"Just report what there is, Corporal."

"Yes, sir. Over the last two days, I have only seen two small hunting parties. I saw a few herds of antelope scattered about, and I suspect that was what they were after.

By their dress and the way they rode, I'm sure they were Comanche. My guess is that there may be a small band about two days' ride from this spot. They may be the first to come down from Kansas. The buffalo will begin migrating this way before long, and there will be more coming."

"Anything else, Corporal?" Russell wanted to know.

"Yes, sir. It seems like the more important thing, but it is extraordinary. About halfway between here and the head-water of the Brazos River, I saw a train of pilgrims camped. I counted thirty wagons in all. But the stranger thing is that they have a Union Cavalry escort. Nothing in the numbers we've been expecting, though. I couldn't get an exact number at the distance where I sat when I saw them, but my best guess is that there is no more than a single platoon. But I can't figure why a group of settlers would head this way during these times" A knowing glance passed between the other four men.

"Excellent, Corporal. Excellent," Captain Russell was more excited than Putney had ever seen him. Then the captain turned grave. "I have some information to tell you now, and after I have, you will have a decision to make. It will be the most critical decision of your life. I want to be sure you understand the gravity of what I am about to tell you."

"If it is all that serious, Captain, I can assure you that I will heed every word you say," Putney could not fathom what he might be getting into, but from the look of the men around him, he knew that whatever it was, it wasn't good.

"Here is the bold truth, Putney," started the captain.

"There is no planned invasion. It is what I told you and the other men to keep your spirits up and to keep you sharp. The federals have no need for an invasion because the cause is over. Two days before we left Fort Chadbourne, Colonel McCulloch told the other company commanders and me that Robert E. Lee had surrendered the Army of Northern Virginia to Grant. General Kirby, the commander of the Trans-Mississippi Army, assured us that the war was still viable, but I would be surprised if he hadn't surrendered by now. So from this point, we are on our own. You have just confirmed for me what Captain Tidwell had advised." Captain Russell was very somber. Putney was hanging on the captain's every word.

"That cavalry you saw isn't just escorting those settlers. They are using those settlers as a shield," continued Captain Russell. "The fact is they are escorting a shipment of gold bound for New Mexico. The Union has been ship-ping gold to New Mexico every quarter. Now is the first time we got intelligence on a shipment well enough in advance that we could track it here. I intend to raid that train and liberate that bullion. We have lost the war, but that does not mean that we must return home as beggars, which is what will happen to many of our comrades. Do you follow what I am telling you, Corporal?"

Putney followed, alright. He also knew that at this moment, he was in more danger than at any time he had ever been. "Yes, Captain. I believe I understand everything you are telling me," Putney's voice was flat.

"Corporal, I am telling you this because you have been a trusted soldier. You are the best I have in my command, and I say that with no fear of contradiction. You have risked your life more than once. More than once, you have been the person that has saved this company in battles against the hostiles. You are undoubtedly the bravest man I know. But" and here, the captain paused for a long moment. He began again. "But you are probably the most honest man in my command. I had two choices. The first was to do precisely as I have. That is to lay all the cards on the table and allow you to join us. The other choice was to eliminate you from the equation, which, depending on your answer, is still a viable option. But, as I told you before, you will need to decide. Now is the time for that decision."

Putney felt his face grow hot, and he knew his decision. But he also knew he needed to survive the next minute. His survival was foremost in his mind. "Captain, I have gained nothing from this war and have only earned the meager pay the Confederacy has afforded me. This war has taken half my soul, and now the Confederacy intends to give away the other half. If I am to be soulless, I chose to be so with money in my pocket." Sweat was rolling down Putney's spine, and he could feel it beading up on his forehead. He thought his heart might pound right through his chest. Putney was praying that the four now judging him would believe every word he had uttered.

Captain Russell gazed at the other three men. Sergeant Andrews nodded his approval, as did Captain Tidwell. Starnes was non-committal. Finally, Russell pronounced, "Good. Your answer settles everything. Tomorrow you will go on the scout again. I need you to keep track of that wagon

train and figure out where we can lay by for a successful
ambush. Captain Tidwell has a good man he will send with
you. What is his name, Captain?"

"Ned Blakely," Captain Tidwell advised.

❧

NAHUM PUTNEY LEFT the meeting hoping he appeared
calmer than he felt. He sought out Private Smith and asked
where he had put his saddlebags. Smith said he had left
them with his saddle, and he had placed both under a post
oak near the remuda. Putney retrieved the bags and then
went looking for Peter Connors. When he had found the
young soldier, Putney told him where he was pitching his
bedroll for the night. When Putney was in camp, Peter
wanted to be around him because Putney was helping him
to learn how to read and do arithmetic. Putney went to
where he said he would be sleeping and built a small fire for
light. Putney took his journal book and a pencil from his bag
and began writing everything Captain Russell had told him
that afternoon. After tearing the page from the journal, he
folded it four times, then got wax and a seal from his bags.
Putney sealed the note, then waited for Connors. When
Peter appeared, he was gnawing on an ear of corn. He had a
second in his other hand that he offered Putney.

Putney took the corn and thanked the boy. Then, laying
the corn next to the fire, he took Peter Connors firmly by the
arm and guided him through some trees and behind a large
boulder. There was a horse saddled and waiting. Putney got
his face close to the young Private's so Peter could see his
face in the dark and how serious he was. "I'm going to give
you an order, Peter, and I expect you to follow it without fail.
Do you understand?"

Connors nodded his head and started to speak, but Putney shushed him.

"Don't speak, just do," Putney handed him an extra Colt revolver that he kept in his saddle bag. "Take this," Putney commanded, then stuffing the note in the inside pocket of Peter's jacket Putney said, "and this. Now, Private, you are to do as I say, without fail. I'm going to check on the sentry. When I do, I want you to walk this horse around this mesa, staying between the mesa and the sentry post. I will keep the sentry's attention while you do that. Once you're past the sentry, walk the horse another mile or so. You mount up and ride for Fort Chadbourne when you're out of earshot of the camp. It's in that direction," Putney pointed. "You give that piece of paper to Colonel McCulloch or Major Williams. Tell whoever you meet that you are under order to give it to no one other than McCulloch or Williams. You're a good soldier, and you know how to treat your horse, so don't ride it to death. If you keep steady, you should reach the fort in two days, three at the most. You must do what I am ordering, understand?

"Yes, Corporal, but..."

"No buts. Just do!"

Nahum Putney never saw Peter Connors after that. Neither did he know if the young man ever reached the fort. Putney only wanted to make sure that Peter Connors was safe from the evil that was about to occur.

7

The night he sent Peter Conners to Fort Chadbourn for help, Putney prepared to leave camp, also. Putney was concerned about having Ned Blakely assigned to scout with him. Putney didn't trust Russell, which meant he didn't trust Tidwell, so there was no way he would trust Blakely. Putney had reasoned it out that Blakely's orders were to ride along only until Putney could scout up a good ambush site. Once Putney had done his job, he did not doubt that Blakely had orders to kill him. Russell may as well have been sending Starnes.

But right then, Putney was tired. He had been out five days and spending nights in cold camps because he didn't want the possibility of a fire alerting any Indians in the area. Even though it was spring in Texas, that didn't always mean it was warm. Especially in the mornings, when the temperature could get downright chilly. It had even rained one night. So, he retrieved his bed roll from his belongings and spread it out near the fire. He prepared to get a good and warm night's sleep for a change. He would worry about Blakely in the morning.

Putney was rudely awakened by someone kicking the soles of his boot. His first response was to tell whoever it was to go away and go to hell. But someone kicked his boot again. He said, "This better be important, " Without opening his eyes."

"It's important," Sergeant Andrews' voice said.

Putney opened his eyes, sat up, and looked at the sergeant. "What is it."

"You need to get your gear and saddle up. Captain wants you and Blakely to head out so you can get an early spot on that wagon train," Andrews informed him.

There was some fire light, so Putney pulled his watch out of his pocket. Quarter to midnight. He had only gotten about three hours of sleep. "What? Does he expect me to find them in the dark?"

"No, but he knows you. And he knows the dark won't keep you from getting to the last place you saw them. They won't be moving fast. You ought to be able to find them quickly. Follow the train for a day or two until you get a bearing on the direction they are going. Get out ahead of them and find a place for an ambush. Now get moving. Blakely's already up and moving," Andrews ordered.

Putney got up and stumbled around sleepily until he found a wash basin and splashed cold water on his face. Now half-awake, he stepped over to the cook wagon, grabbed a tin cup, and got some coffee from the kettle near the fire. Once Putney was fully awake, he gathered up his bedroll, saddle, and other gear and went to the picketed horses. He found the horse assigned to him and had just got the blanket on when he heard someone talking at the other end of the picket line.

He stood silent to listen. He couldn't make out the voice, and the tone was low, so it was difficult to make out everything. Putney finally caught, "That Starnes fella told me that corporal can't be trusted. I don't think Russell trusts him either." Then there was more he couldn't quite hear until Blakely clearly answered, "I got ya, Cap'n. The corporal finds the ambush spot. Then he has an accident." There was more which Putney lost, but he had heard enough to confirm what he had already thought. He would have to see to it Ned Blakley had an accident first.

Putney was glad he wore cavalry spurs instead of those preferred by cowhands. Because it was a piece of metal with a ball on the end, he could turn and walk away without being heard. He got about ten feet away, turned, and made a to-do about coming to the picket line.

"That you, Putney?" Blakely called out.

"Yep," was Putney's only reply.

"This your idea?" Blakely asked.

"Nope," Putney wasn't in the mood for a lengthy conversation. Besides, Blakely knew it wasn't his idea. It also wouldn't surprise him to find that Blakely was in on its planning. When both men had their animals ready, Putney told Blakely he was going to the cook wagon. Blakely wanted to know why.

"Because I'm not going out in the field for four or five days without some food. There will be some jerky, hard tack, and canned beans at the cook wagon."

"When we was riding with Colonel Quantrill, it weren't out of the ordinary for us to go three or four days without grub," cited Blakely,

"Good for you," again Putney was keeping the conversation short. When Putney returned, he tied a flour sack containing the food behind his saddle. "We'll walk our horses out to the sentry," he told Blakely. Blakely agreed. When they got near the sentry's post, Putney hailed him and told him who he was and that he and one other wanted to pass. The sentry called back for them to continue.

Putney led the way from the little canyon where the camp had been and headed north through a wide, flat valley. Regularly referring to his compass, Putney let his horse move at a walk, always keeping northward. There had not been more than a half dozen words passed between the two men during their trek. Finally, as dawn was beginning to break, Putney could start to see that they were about two miles east of the southern base of the Double Mountain Range, so-called because the range began with twin rounded mounds protruding from the ground that resembled a woman's breasts. Putney turned his horse west toward the mountains that rose several hundred feet from the valley they had been riding. Since it was getting light, and Blakely could now see, he rode up next to Putney, ready to break the silence.

"Where're we headed," the bushwhacker questioned Putney.

"Up," was the only answer he received.

"Why up," Blakely continued his questioning. "That looks like mighty rocky traveling up in those hills. Wouldn't it be easier riding down here?"

Putney pulled his horse to a stop. He sat for a moment, then threw his right leg up, so the crook of his knee rested on his saddle horn. Putney reached inside his uniform jacket and pulled a bag of tobacco and rolling papers out of his shirt pocket. He casually started putting together a cigarette, never saying a word to Blakely.

"What the hell are you doing now?" Ned Blakely demanded to know.

Putney finished rolling his cigarette and lit it, inhaled

deeply, and blew out a billow of gray smoke. "I'm waiting on you," he said quietly.

"What do you mean you're waiting on me? What the hell does that mean," Blakely was easier to anger than Putney had thought.

Pulling on his cigarette again and exhaling slowly, Putney finally said, "I will explain this to you once and only once. In the past two years, I have ridden all over this country. I don't know it like a Comanche, but I know it a damn sight better than you. But if you think you can lead this scouting trip better than me, I'm just waiting for you to lead." Putney took another drag off his cigarette, waiting for Blakely to respond.

"I ain't questioning your knowing of this country. I just wanted to know why we would take a trail up in those hills when riding down here has got to be easier," Blakely defended himself.

"Two reasons," Putney said, disgusted that he had to explain anything to this ignorant Missouri hillbilly. "First, the last time I saw it, that wagon train was about forty miles north of here.

They have to travel in this valley because they can't go over those mountains. I know they can't push those wagons too fast, but I figure they've made at least thirty miles since I saw them. The sun is coming up, and if they haven't already sent out advance scouts, they will soon because they're going to be looking for a pass through these mountains. Are you keeping up with me so far?" Putney was being as snide as possible?

Blakely just nodded. "Good, now if we're out here in this valley and those scouts see us, they're going to scoot on back to that train, and we'll be lucky if they don't send half that cavalry unit after us." Putney stopped to let that bit of knowledge sink into Blakley's thick skull and to draw another puff on his cigarette. "Now, the second and vastly more important reason is that while we're sitting out here yammering, it's altogether probable that there's a Comanche, Kiowa, Wichita, or some other heathens riding up above us and are shaking their heads at the two thick-headed white men just sitting and waiting for them to come and collect their scalps."

"Alright! You didn't have to go getting all high toned with me," complained Blakely. "I just wanted to know."

"Well, now you know," Putney pulled once more on his cigarette and then stubbed it out on the sole of the boot hanging over the saddle. He checked the butt to make sure it was cold and dropped it on the ground, unwound his leg, and just before he started toward the mountains, said, "As long as I'm the scout on this mission, we'll go where I say. If you don't like that, then take yourself on back to that Captain Tidwell and file your complaint with him." Putney ended the conversation by kicking his horse into a lope toward the mountains. Blakely followed.

Putney led the way up the slope to a trail he had run across on two other occasions. It was a narrow passage through the rocks and was slow going, but Putney knew it would lead them to the top of a mesa where the two would have a good view of the valley below them. It took them three hours from the base of the hills to the summit, where it was only a couple of hundred yards to the edge of the mesa.

Putney dismounted and signaled for Blakely to do the same. They walked to within thirty yards of the edge where Putney tied his horse up to a scrawny juniper bush. Blakely tied his horse up to a tree filled with long clusters of purple flowers. These were the only substantial foliage growing out of the rocky crags on the top of the mountain. "Don't tie up there," the scout said. "That's a mescal tree. The beans on that tree are poisonous. If your horse eats any, it probably won't die, but it will wish it had. Tie up over here."

With their horses secured, Putney led the way to a sandstone formation jutting a little up from the flat mountain top. Looking down on the valley, they could see for miles. Putney had brought along his spyglass and a map. Putney sat with his back to the sandstone and told Blakely to do the same.

Putney unfolded his map, concentrated on it for a while, then said, "This is where we are. When I last saw it, that wagon train was here where I marked this x," Putney told Blakely, pointing out the two locations. Putney ran his finger over the map, "This is the old Marcy trail, down to San Antonio. If you follow it north, it ties in with the Santa Fe. I can't figure out why they aren't going that way. It's a much easier trail. But when I saw them, they were heading south. If they haven't changed their minds, we ought to spot them by midafternoon, at the latest."

Putney studied the map a little more, then said, "Look, if we do see them coming this way, my guess is they plan to circle these mountains. There is a cut here," again Putney put his finger on the map, indicating a southwest portion of the Double Mountains. "This pass would get them through these mountains and out into the plains. From there, it's a piece of cake, as long as they don't decide to go south. If they do, they will run into worse mountains than this. That's the way I would go." Putney continued. "This pass is only about fifty to seventy-five yards wide. Plenty of room for them to get through but narrow enough for us to set an ambush."

"What if they keep going south and come down this way," it was Blakely's turn to run his finger over the map.

"They could, which would be good for us because they would drive right by our camp," advised Putney. "We can watch them from this perch. If they continue south, we will be able to see them for quite a distance, but if they turn west, they will go out of our view. Either way, we'll have them. We will have to ride at night again to get around them and back to camp. If they go west, it will be a hard ride for the company to beat them to the pass and set up. If they go south, we need to get to the camp as quick as we can so the captains can get set up down that way."

"That's good thinking," said Blakely.

"We're going to need some rest," Putney pointed out the obvious. "I'll keep watching a while to see if they come this way. You go on over there and put your head under that juniper and get some sleep, I'll wake you in a few hours, and you can spell me."

Blakely stood and said, "That's good with me. I didn't hardly have any sleep before we left."

About an hour had passed when Putney thought he saw something to the north. He took his spyglass and scoured over the landscape until he spotted a rider, then moved the spyglass across the valley until he found another. Two riders, keeping about fifty yards apart so as not to be clumped up in case of an attack. They had to be scouts. He guessed the wagon train was about two or three miles behind. He had been right; they would probably make it directly below them by midafternoon. It was time for him to take action. Blakely had been snoring for the better part of half an hour, and Putney knew he was sound asleep.

As quiet as he could, he moved his horse off about thirty yards and tied the reins around a rock the size of a water-melon. He returned and retrieved Blakely's horse and tied its reins to his horse's saddle. He took the Henry rifle from its scabbard and, in a minute, was standing looking at Blakely from about ten feet. Putney cocked the gun, bent down, picked up a stone, and chucked it at the sleeping man. The stone hit Blakely in the middle of the chest. Blakely woke with a start, then looked up to see Putney pointing the rifle right where the rock had hit.

"What the hell is this?" he demanded.

"It's the end," Putney told him.

"The end of what," Blakely questioned, still figuring out what was happening. "What in the devil's name are you talking about?"

"I didn't sign on with the Mounted Mountain Rangers to ambush civilians," Putney informed him. "I signed on to fight Indians and to keep from going east. I wouldn't even have minded if we had ever fought any Union troops, but we didn't"

"I don't know what you think you're doing," growled Ned Blakely. "But whatever it is, the captains ain't going to like it."

"That's alright," Putney said in a cold, stern voice. "You're going to like it even less.

Unbuckle that gun belt and toss it, gun and all over to me."

"And if I don't?"

"Then you're going to have to try and draw that pistol in hopes of shooting me before I can pull this trigger, or you can just lay there, knowing that I'm going to get tired and pull the trigger anyway. So, you can decide to throw it over here or die. It's up to you."

Grumbling something unintelligible, Blakely undid the gun belt and did as Putney had told him.

"Now strip down to your long johns and toss everything to the same spot," ordered Putney. Still grumbling, Blakely removed one of his boots and tossed it toward Putney. Then he pulled the other and, in a desperate action, threw it as hard as possible at his nemesis and jumped to his feet. But not fast enough. Putney quickly side-stepped the boot and pulled the trigger, causing a bullet to skitter along the dirt and showering Blakley's ankles with sandstone chips. Then, Putney levered another round into the chamber of the rifle. The movement had caused him to miss Blakely, but it was enough to give the bushwhacker pause.

"That was a foolish thing to do," he told the would-be assailant. "I promise I will not miss the next time." Putney knew the two scouts had heard the rifle shot. They couldn't have not heard it. But it didn't concern him. They would only ride back to the wagon train and report it, probably thinking it was the prelude to an Indian attack. His main worry now was that Blakely would try and rush him, and then he would have no choice but to kill the man. Putney backed away another ten feet. If Blakely tried anything now, he wouldn't make it ten feet before Putney could shoot him. "Now, just finish shucking those clothes."

Blakely realized he had spent his one chance and failed; He had no choice but to comply. He finished stripping and then just stood there in his underwear. Blakely was as mad as a hornet, but there was nothing the bushwhacker could do about it. But he swore he would kill Putney one day.

Putney told him to go over and stand at the sandstone outcrop. Blakely had moved away, and Putney gathered up his belongings. "I'll leave one Colt and a canteen at the top of the trail. You can do what you want from there," said Putney.

"How come you just don't kill me?" snarled Blakely. "I'd have killed you."

"Because I'm no Missouri bushwhacker that kills people for the sheer joy of it. I never killed anybody in cold blood, and I'm not starting today. Now, if I were you, I'd give myself over to that wagon train. I'm sure you can think of some outlandish lie to tell them. Maybe you can get back to Russell, but good luck with that. Those six rounds in that Colt aren't going to help you in an Indian attack, and that's more likely to happen than not before you reach Russell." Putney started backing away to the horses.

"Did anyone ever tell you you're a son of a bitch?" Blakely called after him.

"I've heard the rumor," Putney called back.

8

Ned Blakely was still cursing him as Putney rode off the mesa. Putney had been on this mesa before. Putney was always aware that he needed more than one way out of an area if the need arose and had scouted a passage off the western side of the mesa. It was so narrow and steep that Putney walked the horses down in single file. At the bottom of the mountain, he headed south-west, always keeping the hills to his right, Putney knew he would come on the wide pass, and beyond that, there were plains. The plain made traveling easy, but it was dangerous because a person was visible for miles. So, he pushed hard, switching horses every other hour, to keep both animals as fresh as possible. Putney was familiar with the area, and knew there was a spring to the west, and he wanted to make it to that point, but exhaustion was playing on him hard. He had only slept about three hours in the last two days, and he badly needed sleep.

At the edge of night, he spied a clump of juniper cedar and Osage orange trees. He decided he would take his rest there. He divvied up the water out of the canteen using his hat, so the horses got equal shares. He saved a couple of swallows for himself. By the time he finished this task, he was so tired that he didn't even bother to eat. He used his lariat to tie the horses to an Osage, spread his bedroll on the ground, and fell fast asleep.

He woke late the following day. A check of his watch showed it was a little after nine. He walked outside the clump of trees to spot a landmark. Putney circled the trees until he confirmed that he was in a bowl, surrounded on the east by the Double Mountains, and to the north, there ran another range with which he was unfamiliar. To the south laid open plain, and quite probably Captain Montague Russell. But the spring he hoped he would see was not there. He would know it when he saw it. It was more like an oasis than anything he had ever encountered before. The spring had pecan and cottonwood trees growing around it and at that time of year would provide an excellent shade under which to recuperate. There would be good water and grass for the horses. He was ashamed that he had abused his animals so. In his mind, he heard his father telling him to always take care of his horses because on the frontier a man's life depended on his animals. They had rested well during the night, and at the spring, he would allow them all day and a night to rest.

Because the terrain was rocky, he walked the horses. Loping or running could risk either of them slipping and causing injury. However, Putney knew the spring would be easy to spot once he got close. It would be ten shades greener than the rest of the area, which only had the green of cactus scattered about the country. He had ridden for nearly three hours when he thought he saw something sitting on the horizon. He reached into his saddlebags and retrieved his telescope. Peering through the spyglass, he smiled at what he had found.

The oasis was about two miles distant. In the glass, it stood out like a sore thumb. Verdant against the sea of brown grass and dirt. He took some time before moving forward. He wanted to survey the area before finding himself in a bind he couldn't get out of. He knew if he got any closer, the horses would smell the water, and then there would be no restraining them. So, he looked in every direction, both with his naked eye and using the telescope. Seeing no sign of other humans, he urged the horses forward. As expected, the horses picked up their gait as they smelled water. He was able to keep the horse he was riding at a lope, and the other tied to his saddle had to follow.

When he arrived, Putney put first things first. He hobbled his mounts so they could get to the water and the good green grass but not wander too far. He loosened the cinches but did not unsaddle. A spring in this country was prime real estate. Undoubtedly, any Indian who roamed over the Comancheria knew precisely where this spring was. The last thing Putney needed was to be caught with an unsaddled horse in the middle of nowhere and considering his actions of late; there would be no haven to where he could run.

Putney took his bag of food to the trunk of one of the cottonwoods and propped himself against it. Using his Bowie, he punctured a can of beans and pried the lid off. He ate cold beans, hard tack biscuits, and a bit of jerky. It may have been a meager meal to some, but to Putney it was a feast. After he had eaten, Putney pulled out his map. Before, he had no plan except to get away from Russell and the band of cutthroats allied with him. Now he had to develop a strategy to get to safety.

Studying the map, he knew going south was not viable. Russell was to his south, and it wouldn't take long for the captain to figure out Putney had betrayed him. For all Putney knew, Russell had other scouts out, and it would not do for them to come across him. He could go southwest to El Paso, but he would have to cross mountains that made the ones around there look like mere hills. Also, there was scarce little water in that direction. Going directly west was also out. That would only lead him to the White Sands of New Mexico. He had never seen that desert, but he had heard it was nearly impassable. He did consider that the Union wagon train would come close to where he sat at that moment. The idea had its merits, but, he reasoned, if he had just learned the war was over, it was a good possibility they didn't know either. His appearing in a gray cavalry uniform probably wouldn't bode well for him. His only option was to go north. The mountains in that direction weren't so steep or high that he couldn't make it over relatively easily. However, there was a problem with going north, it increased the chance of running into Comanches.

He was only one man, and it was a big country. Comanche usually ran in large bands or small hunting parties. So, if he kept a keen eye and his wits about him, he would probably see them before he could be spotted. He would keep an eye out for buffalo herds. The Comanche would be following the herds, and if he kept his distance from the beasts, he had a good chance. He could hit the Santa Fe Trail in six or seven days if he were lucky. From there, he could go to Santa Fe. By the time he got there, surely the word would be out that the war was over. He could get some new clothes and shuck the uniform. Putney didn't know what he would do from there, but at least he had a plan.

As he congratulated himself and folded his map, the horse neighed and seemed nervous. Then, before he could think, he heard the unmistakable click of a pistol hammer drawn back. Putney froze as he cursed himself for not being more alert.

"Don't curse yourself, Eka Toyatuku," came the voice of somebody that had read his thoughts. "I have been watching you since you left those other trees. You should have stayed there another hour. I might have passed by without noticing you."

Even though the voice was speaking good English, Putney could tell the accent of an Indian. What kind, that he didn't know. But it wasn't long before he knew. As the man came around to face him, Putney could tell that he was Comanche by his dress. "I would never have thought it would be so easy to sneak up on Eka Toyatuku, so I am as surprised as you." The man said.

"I think we will wait a few minutes; the others will catch up soon. You will want to keep your hands away from your guns and that big knife. It would be ashamed to kill you before Big Looking Glass could meet you."

Putney slowly moved his hands to the back of his head and leaned up against the tree. He didn't want this savage to mistake any move he was making. Putney looked at the man with amazement. He was obviously Comanche, except he was nearly as tall as Putney. Comanche, though fierce fighters and incomparable horsemen were usually short. Besides this and the man's command of English, his eyes were the same shade of blue as his own. For a moment, Putney thought he might be imagining things. Again, it seemed the man was reading his thoughts. "I see you are surprised. My mother was white. But do not think I am anything but Comanche. If you were any other man, you would soon be staked out to provide amusement for my men and me. But you are Eka Toyatuku, and you must be taken to Big Looking Glass so he may see you before you die."

As the Comanche had predicted, it wasn't a long wait until three more Indians arrived. They also came from behind him. "You may stand now," his captor told him. Then he spoke in the Comanche tongue to the others.

One of the cohorts came behind him and removed his guns and bowie knife from their sheaths. The English speaker said something to one of the other Indians. Another promptly grabbed Putney, spun him around, and tied his hands and arms behind him without concern for Putney's comfort.

Another Comanche tightened the saddles on the horses while the third gathered up Putney's belongings and put them on a horse. The English speaker then checked the saddle and removed the Henry rifle and Putney's twin Walker pistols. With the precautions taken care of, two men hoisted him into the saddle. They all rode away due north, with one man taking the lead about a hundred yards in front of the others. In the group that was left, one brave rode in front and one in the rear, with the English speaker riding abreast with Putney. They rode in silence. Putney prayed.

After about an hour, the English speaker broke the silence. "Do you know who I am?" he asked of Putney.

"I have an idea," Putney told him. "I think you're proba-bly, Quanah Parker, the son of Cynthia Ann Parker.

"I am. But I use only Quanah. So, you have heard of me?" Quanah inquired.

Seeing no sense in playing into the man's vanity, Putney said, "Not really."

9

Quanah did not like Putney's smugness. Somehow, this man the Comanche called Eka Toyatuku did not see himself as a captive. "How is it you say you know of me but then say you have not heard of me?" he asked Putney.

"Oh, I've heard a little of you, just not much. Your mother is much more famous among Texans," Putney told him. What Putney said was true. There probably wasn't a person in Texas that had not heard of the Comanche and Kiowa raid on Fort Parker. Five hundred Indians had raided the fort, killed five men, and carried off two women and three children. There had been several expeditions mounted to recover the captives. All but Cynthia Ann Parker and her brother John were ransomed or rescued. Finally, in 1860 Texas Ranger Captain Sul Ross led a raid on a Comanche camp on the Peas River and recovered Cynthia, and returned her to her uncle.

But Putney had heard of Quanah. He just didn't want his captor to know. From time to time, Putney had heard from Tonkawas about the up-and-coming young Comanche of the Kwahadi tribe. The Tonks had said that Quanah had a fervor in him and that, along with a young Spirit Chief named Ish-Tia. Quanah was positioned to become a war chief. It was only his age that had held him back so far.

"From the way you speak, you condemn the Comanche, but you do not condemn what the whites have done to my people."

"I condemn the Comanche for killing my parents and two sisters."

"You are a bold man, Ek Toyatuku, to speak to a Comanche in this way. Many Comanche have had their mothers and fathers, and sisters killed. Do they not concern you?"

Would it make any difference?"

"I doubt it."

"Well, since we're being so friendly and such, and before anything happens to me, maybe you could tell me what Eka Toyatuku means," Putney didn't want to continue a conversation about his impending death.

"It means Red Panther, or close to it."

"So why call me that?" Putney genuinely wanted to know.

"It is something that happens, sometimes. If a Comanche sees another man who runs fast, they may call him rabbit. For you, it is because of the color of your hair and you are almost always alone. Wolves and coyotes run together. But panthers are almost always alone. And like you, panthers do not like to be seen until they attack. Someone used that name around a campfire, and others started using it. It does not mean much." Now it was Quanah's turn to avoid playing into the other man's vanity.

Putney was making mental notes of the landscape while the two talked. It might come in handy if he got a chance to escape. A thing he doubted would happen, but he could always hope. "Since I doubt you ever lived among whites, how is it you speak English so well, better than many white men I know?" Putney inquired.

"My mother never lost her white tongue. Often, other whites were brought to our camps, and she was allowed to speak with them. My father encouraged her. He had her teach him and me. After the Rangers stole my mother, I would practice the white language with captives brought to our camps. As I grew older, white traders would come among us, and sometimes I was used to speak for them. One day I will speak for my people. I saw it in a dream. Great men from the east will come to stay in my camp and seek my advice. This will happen."

When pigs fly, thought Putney.

The Indian that had been a couple of hundred yards in front stopped and pumped his lance up and down three times. "We are close," Quanah informed Putney. "You will have a chance to become even more famous among the Comanche. It will be up to you to decide whether we sing songs of your brave death or your cowardice."

They had been riding in a narrow canyon. They came around a bend where Putney saw a camp with many teepees. People were busy with various chores. Women were working at household tasks or curing hides of buffalo and antelope. The men and older boys were training horses or making weapons. All activity ceased when the people saw Quanah and his band coming into camp with a prisoner. Shouts and whoops went up all over the village. Women and children ran to taunt Putney and throw stones at him. The men congratulated the band that had captured Putney, slapping them on their thighs as they rode past. Quanah led the group to a makeshift corral, and two men pulled Putney roughly from his horse.

Quanah barked something at the men, who then helped Putney to his feet and brushed him off as if it had all been an accident. "Those men had no right to abuse you. They had nothing to do with your capture."

"It's good to know you're looking out for my well-being," snarked Putney.

Quanah cut the bindings on Putney's arms and wrists. Putney must have looked surprised, as Quanah said. "Look around. Where are you going to go?"

Putney got the point.

Quanah led Putney to a lodge. "You will be safe in here. You shouldn't try to go out unless I am with you. There are a hundred warriors in this camp. Any of them would be proud to take the scalp of Eka Toyatuku if he thought you were trying to escape."

Putney looked around the inside of the tent. Buffalo robe rugs spread across the dirt floor, and shields hung from a wall. There were assorted bowls, but nothing Putney could use as a weapon. He continued his search, just in case, but he had no luck. He sat in the center of the lodge, trying to determine his next move. Putney admitted to himself that options were few.

Some time had passed, when a girl with dirty blond hair and ragged clothes entered. She had a black eye, and several bruises showed where her calico dress was torn. He guessed her age to be twelve or thirteen. She was carrying a bowl, which she set on the floor. "The women told me to bring you something to eat." The girl said and started to leave.

"Wait," Putney whispered. "What's your name?"

"Imogene Foster," she answered.

"How long have you been here, Imogene?"

"A couple of months, I guess. I've lost track."

"Where are you from?" Putney asked trying to build a relationship with the girl.

"I lived on a farm outside of Weatherford. The Indians killed my parents and my older brother. You're the first white person I've seen since." The girl was starting to tremor.

Putney took her arm and pulled her closer. "Do you think you could sneak me a weapon? A gun would be great, but a knife will do."

She jerked her arm away from him. "Mister, I have to go. They'll probably beat me now for staying too long. They beat me for any reason." She was crying as she hurried out of the teepee.

10

N ahum Putney realized that there could be no bleaker circumstance than where he found himself at this moment. When confronting Indians in the past, he always had a fighting chance and had managed to come out alive. But now, there was nothing to fight with except his wits, and he knew he was poorly equipped. He realized his captors had not taken the tobacco and matches from his shirt pocket. *What the hell,* thought Putney, *may as well, can't dance.* He took the makings from his pocket and rolled a cigarette. Putney was sitting crossed-legged, smoking when the flap of the lodge opened, and Quanah entered.

"It is good to see you accepting your fate with such calm," said Quanah. It was slightly amusing to Putney that the Comanche had interpreted him smoking tobacco as a sign of inner peace. The truth was Putney was scared as hell. Quanah motioned for Putney to follow him. Putney took one last draw on the cigarette outside the tent and dropped the remains, which he ground out with his boot. Quanah led Putney across the camp to another teepee, where men

sat on blankets in a semi-circle outside the lodge. All the
men were older than Putney or Quanah. Most of the men
wore simply decorated clothes, typical for everyday wear. At
the top of the arc, however, sat one man who wore ceremo-
nial attire. The shirt was ornately decorated with beads on
the sleeves. He was wearing a breastplate made of larger
beads and bone. A round, gold-framed mirror hung from
his neck on a leather cord.

Quanah and Putney stood at the open end of the semi-
circle. Speaking in Comanche, Quanah addressed the group
of men, obviously giving deference to those assembled but
especially to the man with the mirror necklace. After
Quanah finished his address, the man at the head spoke and
motioned toward the ground. "Big Looking Glass says to sit,"
said Quanah. Putney took up the invitation and sat on the
bare ground. A woman standing outside of the group
brought a blanket and laid it on the ground, close to Putney.
Quanah sat, and the woman quickly departed. Addressing
Putney, Quanah said, "I am to speak for Big Looking Glass
and you."

Big Looking Glass said something, and Quanah told
Putney that the chief had seen him smoking and wanted to
know if Putney had more tobacco. Putney reached in his
shirt pocket, produced the small tobacco pouch, and
handed it to Quanah. The tobacco was passed from man to
man until it reached Big Looking Glass. The conversation
began with Big Looking Glass saying one thing and Quanah
interpreting to Putney and then replying in Comanche,
whatever Putney said.

"I welcome you to our camp, Eka Toyatuku," said the
chief.

"If I had known you wanted to meet me, I would have
come sooner on my own," Putney replied. The men in the

group chattered in grave tones at Putney's answer. Quanah told Putney that the men thought his answer was disrespectful and that Putney should take care of how he spoke. Figuring nothing would make his situation worse, Putney decided to take a chance. Ignoring Quanah, Putney directed his following comment directly at Big Looking Glass. "If I cannot speak freely, why should I speak at all?" Again, there was chatter, but it seemed Putney's response was better received this time. Big Looking Glass looked at Putney and nodded.

"You speak boldly," replied the chief, "I understand white men speak differently than Comanche. What you say will not insult."

Putney decided now was the time to be gracious. So, holding his right hand to his heart, Putney said, "You honor me, Big Looking Glass."

"You are Eka Toyatuku. This is a name of honor for an enemy. But the panther is rarely seen and even more rarely taken. How is it that you let Quanah capture you so easily?"

"I had been riding two days without sleep. My horses were tired. I was tired and hungry. If I had not been so weary, Quanah and his warriors would never have caught me and most likely would be laying out on the plains, dead."

This comment seemed to be well-received by all the men in the group. Putney chose not to look at Quanah. He guessed Quanah had a different opinion. Finally, Big Looking Glass spoke again. "You speak as bravely as you fight. I would say you are bragging, but I have seen you fight. The other gray soldiers do not know how to fight. They try to hide behind rocks or their horses. Eka Toyatuku fights from his horse, like a Comanche."

Putney thanked the chief for the compliment, to which

Big Looking Glass replied, "Will you die as bravely as you speak?"

Putney thought for a minute before speaking. The truth was he was terrified, but he was trying not to show his fear. Putney decided he didn't have anything to lose, so he took another chance and said, "I do not know. I have never died before, but if you let me go, when I do die, I will be glad to come back and tell you if I was brave or not."

This comment got laughs from all the men. Even Quanah smirked a little, but then Big Looking Glass stopped laughing and very somberly asked, "What would you trade for me to let you leave alive?" After that, the mirth around the circle stopped, and all eyes were on Putney, who certainly wasn't laughing.

Putney contemplated the question for what he hoped was a respectable time, then said, "I have two horses. I will trade you one horse, two Colt pistols, and the Henry repeating rifle. I would keep the two big pistols of my father. They are the only things I have of his. I will also need my knife," Putney tried to think of anything else he could throw in to sweeten the deal, and it finally came to him. "Also, I have a can of peaches in my food bag."

Big Looking Glass considered Putney's words, then said, "These things you say you would give me belong to Quanah. They are no longer yours to trade. Have you nothing else?"

At a loss, Putney asked for some time to think about the question more deeply. Big Looking Glass permitted him to ponder. Putney racked his brain for something, anything, a warrior would accept if he would accept anything. *Jesus help me,* he prayed silently. *I'm too young to figure this out. I don't have the experience.* Still, he wasn't giving up. It was then a notion started to germinate in his head. The more he thought about it, the more it seemed like a good idea. It might not work, but it was all he had.

"What do I have to offer a great chief," Putney believed a little flattery could help. "Big Looking Glass is already rich. He has horses. He has followers. He has won many battles. He probably even has many wives. I am just a poor soldier who no longer even has one horse. Yet there is something I have that has not been taken from me, and no one can take it from me. It is only mine to give."

Big Looking Glass and the other Indians were impressed with the statement, even though most thought this was just a way for Putney to play for more time. The chief stared at Putney and said, "What is this thing you say you have that is so valuable and which I cannot take from you."

Well, he's taken the bait, thought Putney. *Now it's time to set the hook.* But since he was already reaching for the moon, he also decided to reach for the stars. "This is worth more than just one mere man. There is something else I must insist on having if I am to give it to Big Looking Glass."

After Quanah interpreted what Putney had said, he spoke directly to Putney. "You have overplayed your game. You may have stood a small chance, but that fruit withers on the tree as I speak." Then there were some words between Quanah and Big Looking Glass. Finally, Quanah was back in the position of an interpreter.

"Big Looking Glass says for you to tell him what more you want."

"Did you tell him what you said to me?" asked Putney. "That I was overplaying my game."

"No. I told him you are not trustworthy and that you are trying some trick," Quanah told Putney.

"Alright, then you tell him this," then looking at Big Looking Glass, Putney said. "This man," and he pointed at

Quanah, "says I am not trustworthy. What he did not tell you is that he thinks I am a trickster like a fox or a coyote that is trying to fool you. If this is what you think, I have nothing else to say. I am not ready to die, but if that is what is to be, then let's get her done. But if you think I have something, I ask you to listen to my bargain. I don't think you will regret it. If you find my trade is not a good bargain, you will always be able to kill me after you have listened."

Big Looking Glass glared at Quanah, and Putney knew he had won a point. The chief then asked, "What else would you ask for in this bargain?"

Now was the moment of truth. "I ask that you let the white girl go with me. After you hear what I have to trade and you think it is worth only my life, then at least I have tried. I think you would do the same for your sister."

Big Looking Glass nodded his head. Then he took the mirror that hung around his neck and peered into it. To Putney, the chief seemed to be in a trance. After several minutes Big Looking Glass dropped the mirror, letting it dangle on his neck again. "If what you have to trade is worth your life, it is also worth the life of the girl. No more stalling. What is it you have that you can give, but I cannot take?"

Putney let out such a sigh of relief, and he knew that all the others did not fail to have noticed. "Have someone bring my.....I mean Quanah's saddle bags. There is something in it I must show you."

Big Looking Glass gave a command, and the woman who had been standing away from the circle hurried off and came back quickly with the bags and handed them over to Quanah. Quanah passed the bags to Putney and said, "If you were hoping that pistol was still in there, you are going to be disappointed."

"Nothing was further from my mind," Putney assured

him. He first found another pouch of tobacco which he held up for all to see and motioned toward Big Looking Glass. Quanah grabbed the bag. He was obviously peeved, but he passed it around the circle until Big Looking Glass had it in his hand. Then Putney pulled out his map, bent over on his knees, and spread the map out on the ground. The chief said, "I know this thing. It is called a map, and it is what white men use to find their way. But Comanche do not need a map."

"I know," reassured Putney. "But I do." Putney sat back and said, "What I have to offer you is knowledge." This statement caused another round of muttering among the men. Putney could not tell if it boded good or ill. "Not that Big Looking Glass does not already have knowledge, but to add to that, he has."

Big Looking Glass motioned for Putney to continue, so he did. "You may not know, but the war between the blue and the gray, is over. The gray has lost, and their big chief in the east has surrendered."

"This I did not know," said Big Looking Glass. "But I do not see how this will help my people or me."

"That is what I will tell you," said Putney. "Even though the big chief has surrendered, some of his followers are not pleased with him. They want to continue to fight."

"This is not a bad thing," replied the chief. "If men want to fight for what they believe is right, they should fight."

"On this, we agree, chief," Putney told him. Putney thought he might be talking too fast and so not seem sincere, so he told himself to settle down and speak slower. "But some men want to fight to become wealthy by taking what is not theirs."

"This is the way of the white man," said Big Looking Glass.

"I know," returned Putney. "But I think Big Looking Glass wants to fight for what he thinks is right and to have respect. Am I not, correct?"

"This is so," agreed the Indian.

"What if I could give you a chance to win a victory against these greedy men and, in turn, earn the respect of the blue soldiers and their leaders in the east?"

"A victory would be good. But why should I worry about the respect of the blue soldiers?" Big Looking Glass wanted to know.

"The Comanche and other Indians have had several treaties with the government." Putney wanted the chief to understand that Putney knew this. "But the government didn't always pay the proper respect to the Comanche. I will tell you a way that you can remind the government that you provided something for them that they should respect."

"Treaties are just something that the white man writes on paper. Neither they nor we always regard these treaties," said Big Looking Glass.

"I know that, but this is something for you to have if you ever decide you want to consider another treaty."

Big Looking Glass told Putney to continue.

"There is a United States Cavalry troop escorting a shipment to New Mexico," Putney told him. "And the gray soldiers I was with want to rob that shipment. Sure, you could find these troops and attack them, but they will fight like the dickens. Even if you win, all you will find is gold. And what has the Comanche ever cared about gold?"

"That is the white man's ruin," answered Big Looking Glass.

"Exactly," exclaimed Putney. "And that is what the gray soldiers want. I can tell you where this band of cutthroats is. They are ripe for the picking. After you have your victory, you could go to the blue soldiers and tell them how you saved them from an attack by the gray soldiers and how you saved their gold and that you will let them pass to New Mexico unhindered. So, you have your victory and the respect of the army."

"Why would they believe me, a Comanche, that I did this thing you say."

"Because, I will tell you how to convince them."

"That is enough," said Big Looking Glass. "I will now think on all you have said." With that, the chief took up his mirror again and stared into it, divining what he would do. The mountains started casting shadows over the camp as Big Looking Glass sat in his trance. Putney guessed that at least an hour had gone by without anybody saying anything. Putney spent that time praying. Finally, the chief let the mirror drop. "I have thought about what Eka Toyatuku has said," he announced. "And I find it good. Eka Toyatuku will have his freedom." Then he paused.

Putney waited a full minute after Quanah had translated what Big Looking Glass had said. Finally, Putney asked, "And the girl?"

The pause held, and Putney held his breath. Then, at last, Big Looking Glass said, "Eka Toyatuku will take the girl with him. But hear my words clearly. If you have lied or tried to trick me," he stopped then began again, and to emphasize his words, he spoke in English, "I will give Quanah the mission to hunt you down and kill you like he would a mad dog. Do you understand my words?"

Putney was surprised that after all this time, the chief could speak English. Big Looking Glass must have read the amazement on Putney's face because he said, "I have understood everything you said, but these others do not. That is why I had Quanah translate."

Putney found his voice. "I am glad you heard what I have said. That way, you know I have not tried to trick you. And yes, I understand what you said and more, I believe it."

"Good, then tell me more about how I trap these gray warriors and how I convince the government soldiers how I have helped them." Quanah continued his interpretation for the sake of the others.

Putney bent over the map and explained where Russell and his men were. He showed that they were in a blind canyon, and though it was defensible from a frontal attack, it was a death trap if the Comanche came over the hills and attacked. "This last thing I must tell you," Putney said. "The men that wear complete uniforms, like me, are mostly good men. I understand that some of them will die, but chances are, if they attacked the government troops, they would die then, too. I only hope you will understand they are not all bad. But there are others who only wear parts of uniforms or none at all. There is not a good man among them," Putney paused to let his meaning sink in. Then began again, "There are two men who will be in fancier uniforms with gold braid and epaulets."

Quanah paused Putney and asked him to explain the adornments of the captains' uniforms, then signaled Putney to continue. "You must capture at least one of them. These men will tell the Union captain about what you have done and why. They will try to deny it. You must tell them, and the Union captain my white name, Nahum Putney. Tell them that you learned all this from me. That way, the gray captains will not lie, and the blue captain will know that what you say is true."

"This is good advice," Big Looking Glass acknowledged.

"I won't try and tell you anymore of your business, but I will suggest that it would be a good gesture if all those you

do not kill are taken to the Union captain, too. It will show `
goodwill."

"I will consider what you say," returned the chief. Then,
signaling to the woman, he spoke to her in their language.
In a few minutes, the woman returned with the Walkers,
Putney's canteen, the bag with his food, and dragging
Imogene Foster behind her. She handed the guns and
canteen to Quanah and the sack to Big Looking Glass, and
she shoved the girl to the ground at Putney's feet.

"Quanah, you take Eka Toyatuku to the north of the
camp," Big Looking Glass directed. "There, give him his
father's guns and the water." Big Looking Glass then
emptied the contents of the bag onto a blanket, then picked
up the can of peaches and placed it back in the sack. "And
give him this can of peaches. He places great value on it."

11

———

Nahum Putney stood at the north end of the Indian encampment looking into the hard blue eyes of Quanah. Quanah glared back. Quanah handed Putney the canteen; from the heft, Putney knew the vessel was full. Putney hung the strap of the canteen holder over his right shoulder. The Comanche handed the flour sack with the canned peaches to Putney. Lastly, Quanah hung the rig holding the two Walker pistols over Putney's left shoulder with one gun hanging in the front and the other in the back.

Quanah glared at Putney with blue eyes that were cold as ice. "We will meet again, Nahum Putney," Quanah informed the former ranger. "And when we do, Big Looking Glass will not be there to protect you. It is then that I will hold your life in my hands."

That was the extent to their farewells. There was no condemnation of Putney, no further harangue or lecture, just that veiled threat. For Putney's part, he had nothing to say. He took the girl by the hand, turned, and started up the incline to the mountain top.

The summit looked to be about 300 feet above where Putney stood, and it was starting to get dark. It was a steep hill with large boulders scattered over its side. It would be a hard enough climb in broad daylight, but with the light failing, it would be difficult, and by the time dark fell completely, the ascent would be almost impossible. Also, it would be tough dragging a young girl with him.

Holding Imogene Foster's hand firmly in his grip, Putney began the ascent. Loose gravel and sand caused his feet to slip, and more than once, the girl stumbled. But Putney kept the pace as fast the girl could move. There was always the possibility that one of the Indians would disapprove of Big Looking Glass' decision and come after the fleeing duo. Putney wanted to be on the flat top of the mesa if that happened. At least he would have a fighting chance.

Imogene didn't know what was happening, but she did not speak or question. Her time in captivity with the Comanche had taught her that if silence was not golden, it at least kept a person from getting a beating. To the best of her understanding, Imogene was the property of the warrior that had seized her. In turn, he had given Imogene to his wife if they had such a term. The woman would beat Imogene anytime the girl uttered a sound. Imogene could say, "My, what a beautiful day." But because the woman didn't understand English, Imogene would get beaten. It didn't even matter if the woman wasn't around. The other women in the tribe would beat her. Even the little girls, younger than she, would pelt her with stones or whip her with thin branches just because they could. That day, she had received a beating because someone had heard her speak when she was inside the lodge with the white man that was now dragging her up the side of a mountain. She didn't know what was happening, but Imogene knew one thing. She would remain silent.

Surrounding the top of the mountain was a ribbon of sandstone butte from twelve to twenty feet high. The pair reached the foot of the butte as the final rays of sunlight were lost in the enveloping darkness. Putney thought he might make the climb in the dark, but he worried the girl wouldn't be able to make it. Dejected, Putney sat down with his back against the rocky cliff. Imogene followed his example and sat down beside him.

The moon had not risen, and the face of Imogene was dark. Looking at her, Putney imagined the faces of his twin sisters, Susana and Angelina. His sisters were about the same age as Imogene when the Comanches had killed them and his parents. Even if he had been there when Comanches attacked his family, he could have done nothing to save them. But he had saved this girl, at least for a while. Putney pulled the horse pistols off his shoulder and the canteen strap. He took the cork from the canteen and offered it to Imogene, who was reluctant to take it.

"Go ahead, girl," Putney urged her. "I'm thirsty, so I know you must be. But just a mouthful. I don't know how long this water is going to have to last us." Imogene was tentative about taking the canteen, but the man had been so kind in offering it to her that she finally put it to her lips, filled her mouth once, and swallowed. Then, she returned the canteen to Putney, who replaced the cork and said, "I'll get a drink later." Putney reached up and brushed stringy blonde hair from the girl's face. "You're going to be alright now," he assured her, even though he didn't know if he believed it himself.

Imogene was in a daze. She felt she was dreaming, yet she knew she was awake. Imogene couldn't believe she was

finally free after all the weeks of near starvation and beat-
ings. It was a nearly impossible thought. She didn't know if
this man would beat her, but she had to know if this was a
dream or if she was truly free. "I don't understand, mister.
What's happening?"

It hadn't occurred to Putney that the girl would be
confused about the day's events. "Well, Imogene, I traded
the Comanche for our freedom, so here we are, free as birds,
except we haven't got wings."

"You ain't gonna whoop me for talking," Imogene was
worried he might treat her just as the Indians had.

"No, girl, I'm not going to beat you. You can set your
mind at ease on that," said Putney.

"Will they come after us," asked Imogene.

Putney saw no sense in trying to give Imogene false
hope, so he told her, "I don't know. They may get to thinking
about the trade and get it in their minds that it was a poor
one for them. I hope not. All I have are these two horse
pistols, and once I run out of ball, they won't be good but as
clubs."

"I got a knife." Imogene suddenly boasted.

"You what?" Putney was surprised at her revelation.

"I stole it. Just like you asked. I was afraid all day they
would find it gone, but I done it cause I reckoned if it helped
you, then you would help me."

"You are a brave girl, Imogene Foster. Where is it?"

"Here under my dress. I got it tied with a leather string,"
Imogene said proudly, pulling up her skirt.

Putney stopped her. "That's alright. You just hold on to it
until we need it or until it starts wearing on you."

12

As the moon rose, Imogene started crying. Putney didn't say anything to stop her. Putney couldn't imagine how tired she must have been after weeks in captivity, so he let her cry. He put his arm around her and nestled her close to him. He had intended to stay awake through the night and watch in case some Comanche had taken it on himself to come after the two. However, Putney hadn't reckoned how on tired he had been, and he had drifted off during the night.

When Putney woke with the morning sun, he found that Imogene was still leaning against him. He guessed that when she had stopped crying, she had fallen fast asleep. He stirred some, and when he did, the girl had awakened. She stretched when she woke, then suddenly announced, "Mister, I gotta pee." Again, her lack of modesty had caught him off guard, but then he thought she hadn't been living the last few weeks in a civilized society, and he let his amazement pass.

"Go over there a few feet," he told her. "I'll keep my back turned until you're finished."

When Imogene returned, she told Putney that she was hungry. "I ain't had nothing but scraps to eat since they took me. Sometimes they fed the dogs before they fed me."

The only things they had to eat were the peaches, and Putney wanted to hold off eating them as long as possible, but the girl was so pathetic he could not help but give in.

"Let's get up on top of this mesa, then we can eat," he told her.

Putney spent about fifteen minutes looking for a passable way up the bluff. He finally found an area he believed would have some footholds that Imogene could reach. With his height, Putney knew that if he boosted her up, Imogene would already be halfway, so it wouldn't be much of a struggle for her. Putney didn't want Imogene to hurt herself during the climb, so he suggested she give him the knife she had taken. Once she started up, Putney stayed close behind, prepared to catch her if she lost her grip. It had been an easier climb than what Putney had figured, and they were on top of the mesa in ten minutes. They both sat down after moving a few feet from the edge. Putney pulled the knife out of his belt and finding a large enough rock hammered the blade into the top of the can. He repeated the process a few times until he had a way to pry up the edge of the lid, so they could get to the treat inside.

Once he opened the can, Putney said, "There ought to be four or five peaches in this can, so we're only going to eat one a piece for right now. Is that alright with you?"

Imogene nodded her head, smiling. She never thought she would ever get much to eat, and now, to get a whole peach for herself was nearly unimaginable. Putney fished out a peach with the knife and handed it to Imogene. She held it in her hand as if it were a precious jewel.

Then cautiously, she took a nibble, then giggled. "Mister, this is the best thing I ever ate."

Putney laughed a little himself. "Look," he said, "you calling me mister all the time is making me feel old. I'm not more than twelve or thirteen years older than you. Start calling me Nahum. That's my name." he fished another peach out for himself. "And save that pit. You can suck on it later when the hunger comes again."

"Alright, Nahum," she said.

"I guess we are going to have to drink up this syrup. We don't have anything to put it in, and it will just slosh out if we try to carry it. That will save us some water." Putney told her, handing the can over. "Drink a bit now, and you can have some more in a little while." Imogene held the can with both hands, took a drink, and passed the can back to Putney. She wiped her mouth on a torn sleeve of her dress.

She looked at Putney as he drank his share. "Nahum," she started, "how come you took me along with you? I mean, you might coulda got a horse or something and not have me to take care of."

"That's just crazy," he told her. "I would much rather have you with me than any old dumb horse." Putney was ashamed to say to her that if Big Looking Glass had not accepted the deal, he would have left her. "I had to try. I would never have forgiven myself if I had to leave you with them." That was the truth. Putney's torment would have haunted him for the rest of his life. "You see, I had two sisters, Susana and Angelina. They were twins, about your age. The Comanche raided my parent's ranch and killed my mother, father, and beautiful sisters. So, I couldn't leave you. That's all there is to it."

"I'm sorry, Nahum," Imogene was almost in tears again.

"We're kind of alike, seeing as we both lost our family to Indians."

"I reckon so," Putney agreed. "Finish that peach and take another drink. We need to get moving." Imogene did as she was told and then licked the syrup from her fingers.

They both put the pits in the can, and Putney closed the lid as best he could. Finally, he put the can in the sack and tied a knot in the neck. "Here," Putney handed Imogene the bag, and she understood she was to carry it, which was alright because it wasn't heavy. "Before we go, I want to tell you my plan. You need to know this, so you can keep going if anything happens to me. Do you understand?" Imogene nodded. "If these Comanche follow through with what I told them, we shouldn't have any more trouble from them, but they aren't the only Comanches or Indians out here, so we must be on constant watch. If something goes wrong with the plan I laid out for them, then they are going to come after us, so we need to put as much distance between them and us as we can. That means today we are going to get precious little rest." Putney stopped to make sure she understood. "If we work at it and stay lucky, we should be able to make fifteen to twenty miles a day once we get out of these mountains. Probably less until then. There is a buffalo hunters' station north of here called Adobe Walls. My guess's a hundred or so miles. I'm just going to be guessing where it is exactly. I have never been this far north. But if we hit the Canadian River, we should be able to find Adobe Walls, and we will be safe there. So, we need to keep north as much as possible. We will go around the base of the mountains. That will take us out of our way once in a while. The best thing is to travel at night and hide as best we can during the day. But today we are going to have to chance it. I doubt there are other bands close by this one, so we have that working for us. It's going to be a long time before we get to rest tomorrow morning. It's going to be hard. You have to tell me if you get to where you just can't keep going."

"I'll keep up, Nahum, I promise," Imogene meant what she said.

"I can't use these guns to shoot any game because if Indians or worse, bandits do come on us, I will need them. If we get lucky, we might run across a rattlesnake I can kill with the knife. They're not the best eating in the world, but they beat starving. I'm sure there will be some creeks or something along the way, but I've never been in this country. I don't know where they might be, so we will have to be sparing with the water. A drink every few hours at the most. If something happens to me, you need to keep moving north. I will teach you how to do that as we go," Putney finished with, "That's a lot for a child your age to understand all at once, so we will go over it again as we travel."

"I know you're going to take care of me, Nahum," Imogene said.

$$\approx$$

LIKE MOST MESAS, this one was long, and luckily it ran north-south. By Putney's estimation, he and Imogene had walked a couple of hours when they came to a point where another mesa running east-west joined with the one they were traversing. Putney had been surveying the landscape as they walked and noted that below them, a valley had formed several miles wide and ran north-south. Where the two mountains met, a cut formed where there wasn't a butte, and the slope was less steep than where bluffs had formed. The pair took the decline and were at the base in just a few minutes. They had to go a couple of miles east to be on the edge of the valley, which allowed them to walk on flatter ground but didn't move them too far from the mountains and the large rocks and boulders scattered on the sides. That would be where they would go to hide from anyone they saw. Putney knew that anyone they saw out in this wilderness, whether they were Indians, whites, or Mexicans, would be someone from which they must hide. Once in the valley, there were tufts of grass, some growing sparsely and some in mass. Putney kept them bearing north all that day.

They had already stopped and rested twice, each time taking a drink of water, but now they were in mid-afternoon, and the May sun was bearing down on them. Putney looked at Imogene and saw her face had grown red from the sun and exertion. Putney told her they needed to stop for a more extended rest. Imogene protested and insisted she wasn't too tired and could keep moving, but Putney could see she was on the verge of collapse. There wasn't even a scrawny mesquite tree for them to find shade under, so Putney finally stopped and sat in a large patch of grass. Imogene had no choice but to join him. Putney had his hat that kept the sun from bearing down on him, but Imogene's head was bare, and Putney knew he had to do something about it. Putney removed his jacket and then his shirt, exposing his long john top. He scooched close to Imogene and fashioned a sort of turban around her head with the shirt. Putney cut the sleeves off his jacket and made leggings to keep the tall grass they would be walking through from cutting her. Then, He rolled up the jacket into a pillow and told Imogene to lay down for a few minutes. Even though she protested, Putney saw she was glad to do as he told her. To block the sun from her, Putney placed his hat over her face. By the time he had placed the hat, Imogene was asleep.

Putney looked back in the direction they had come from

and guessed they had walked about seven or eight miles. It was better than he had thought they would do. Putney spent the time looking around the area where they rested, hoping to find a snake of any sort, but he had no luck. Finally, after what he figured to be an hour, Putney gently woke Imogene.

Imogene sat up and apologized for going to sleep. "How long was I asleep?" she asked.

"Not more than a few minutes," Putney lied. He didn't want her to think she was slowing their progress. So, Putney gave Imogene the water and told her to take a couple of drinks. When she had some water, Putney took the canteen and took a long swig. He thought, *If we keep drinking at this rate, the water won't last more than a couple of days.*

Imogene said she was ready. Putney helped her to her feet, and the duo resumed their trek north. They walked until late afternoon when Putney spied what looked like a clump of trees a mile or so northeast. If there were trees, that meant a possibility of water. Putney pointed out what he had seen to Imogene. At this distance, though, it could just be a grassy knoll. Putney couldn't tell. It wasn't taking them out of their general direction, so he adjusted their course.

As they came closer, it was evident that it was a stand of trees. From the shape of them, they looked to be black willows. If they were, Putney knew the chances of water being close by were good. Back home, there had been black willows on their ranch, and they always grew near a stream. The closer they walked, the surer Putney was about his guess. There was no doubt when they were within a couple of hundred yards. They were black willows.

Putney couldn't prevent himself from stepping up his pace when Imogene spoke. "I can't go this fast. I don't know

if I can even make it to those trees," she informed him.
Putney was remorseful about his greed to get to the trees
and hopefully water.

"I'm sorry, Imogene, I wasn't thinking." Then, without
saying anything more, Putney picked her up and held her
like the young child she was. He carried her the rest of the
way to the trees. When they got to their destination, Putney
laid her on the ground so that she was leaning up against a
tree trunk. Then he looked and saw they had indeed found
water. A small stream no more than five feet across and a
foot deep ran beside the trees. Putney felt the thrill of
elation run through his body. He felt God must be looking
after them.

Putney opened the canteen and told Imogene to drink
what she needed but to drink slowly. She lifted the canteen,
took a long drink, then set the canteen down beside her.
Putney took the turban from her head, went to the creek,
and soaked his kerchief in the cool water. Then he went
back to Imogene and laid it on her forehead.

"That feels wonderful," the young girl said and sighed.

Putney returned to the stream and, kneeling, stuck his
whole head in the water, taking care not to drink. He jerked
his head back when he brought it out of the water. His long
red hair dangled down the back of his neck to his shoulders,
causing a stream of cool liquid to run between his jacket and
undershirt. It was glorious. When Putney looked back at
Imogene, she was fast asleep. *Poor child,* he thought.

Black willows are unlike other willows, with long
flowing branches that wave in the wind. The reed-like limbs
of black willows are shorter and more brittle than the other
species, so any good wind will always break off a few and lay
scattered on the ground and dry quickly. Putney gathered
up dry limbs and twigs. They weren't large, but they would

serve. Then he gathered a few stones and placed them in a circle. The next thing Putney did was get the sack with the can of peaches. He untied the bag, smoothed it on the ground, then laid the remaining three peaches and pits on the bag. Putney took the can to the water and filled it. He had given Big Looking Glass his tobacco but not the matches still in his shirt. Putney built a small fire in the circle of stones and put the can of water over the fire. It would take some time for the water to boil long enough to purify it, then it would have to cool before he could refill the canteen. Once the water was on the fire, he got the canteen and drank long and deep.

Putney had boiled one can of water and was waiting for it to cool. He was hungry and tired. Putney thought about how much harder it must be for Imogene. He had not been around young children since his sisters were killed and had thought that Imogene couldn't possibly have the stamina to follow the pace he wanted to set. Putney had wanted to travel that night, but he knew Imogene needed the rest. The truth was he needed the rest as well. So, Putney decided they would stay here in this small oasis until late at night to get the needed rest. Then they could walk until daylight and hopefully find a suitable place to stay hidden from whatever danger they might otherwise incur.

It took some time to boil enough water to fill the canteen. Putney then boiled another can full for them to drink before heading out. Traveling at night would reduce their need for water. Putney rested against the same tree as Imogene. He knew there was no chance of him staying awake, so he unholstered one of the Walkers, held it in his lap, and hoped nobody would sneak up on them as they rested.

Since Quanah had taken his watch, Putney had no idea

what time it was when he awoke. He only knew it was still dark, and that was good. Putney gently woke Imogene and told her it was time to leave. He gave her the peach can and told her to drink what she wanted and eat one of the peaches. He hoped the fruit hadn't gone bad. "Thank you, Nahum," said the girl. For an answer, Putney gave her a long hug, and she hugged him back.

It was a clear night, but there wasn't much moon, and the darkness was going to slow their journey, but Putney knew this was good because the pace would be less difficult for Imogene. Putney looked for the North Star and pointed it out to Imogene when he found it. "If anything happens to me, you keep going but travel only at night," he told her. "Keep that star in front of you, and it will keep you in the right direction. With any luck, we will come across the Canadian River. I figure Adobe Walls will be east of wherever we land on it. Tomorrow I will show you how to use these pistols."

To make their trek easier, Putney tried to keep them in the center of the valley. Putney had experience in this type of terrain. He could barely make out the shapes of the mountains, but if he kept them to his right and left, he could center between them. Unfortunately, there was no vista traveling at night for Putney to judge their progress, so he couldn't determine how far they had traveled.

The pair walked in silence, only speaking when it was time to rest and have a drink. Putney always kept Imogene's hand in his when they were moving. As dawn started creeping over the easterly mountains, Putney could see that the range ended about three or four miles from their location. They would have to walk up a steady slope to get to whatever lay on the other side of a ridge. But for now, they need a place to lay up.

There were a few scrubby junipers scattered along the hillsides but no grouping of rocks that would provide a defensible position. Putney led them to one of the larger clumps of juniper cedars. It would at least give them a place to hide and shelter them from the sun. They pushed their way into the cedars and ate the last of the peaches, which had badly shriveled. Putney stretched out, and Imogene nestled under his arm. In no time, they were both fast asleep.

When they woke, Putney had Imogene stay hidden while he climbed up the side of the hill to see what lay beyond the ridge in front of them. What he saw didn't fill him with confidence. There was nothing over the ridge except a flat, grass-filled plain that undulated north. Putney had been to Galveston on a few occasions and had looked with awe at the vastness of the sea that stretched out seemingly forever. The sight he now took in filled him with the same wonder and dread. It

was a sea of grass that went on forever. There were no landmarks, no trees, no anything except grass moving back and forth with the wind like the waves on the Gulf of Mexico. Nevertheless, this was the path Putney had chosen, and there was nothing to do but to continue forward. They couldn't turn back now.

Returning to Imogene, Putney told her what he had seen, but in such a way as to try and keep her spirits up. He told her the plains were mostly flat with only a few easy rises. So, it would be easy walking, especially at night. Imogene was pleased they would not have to wind through rocky valleys anymore and was anxious to get started. She wanted to see this incredible sight before the sunset.

Putney told her they had some time yet but promised they would be on top of the ridge before sunset. Right now was a time for instruction. Putney removed one of the heavy Colt Walkers from its holster and handed it to Imogene so she could feel how the weight of it. Then he instructed her on how to use it. "The most important thing is to remember to pull the hammer back," Putney told her. "This is a big gun, and it may be hard for you to get your hands around the grip and reach the trigger," He told her to hold the gun up using both hands and see if she could manage to reach the trigger. The gun was not cocked, but he saw she could reach the trigger, but just barely. With it cocked, she wouldn't have any trouble. "If I can no longer help you, you must remember this. Do not try to shoot anyone more than a few feet from you. You don't have the experience to shoot anyone at a distance. Wait, pull the hammer back, and when they are close, all you have to do is point the gun. You won't have to aim. Just point the gun, pull the trigger, pull the hammer back, and get ready for the next shot." Putney asked her if she thought she could handle it. Imogene told him that she would try with all her might. "We can't afford to let you practice, so you're just going to have to rely on what I tell you. We will go over it several times, so you are as sure as you can be."

"I understand, Nahum," Imogene told him. "I'm not worried, though, because I prayed to God like my momma taught me. He will keep us safe."

Putney had no response.

Putney told her it was time to go, and she could see the prairie before the sunset. It took about an hour to get to the top of the ridge. The sight of the endless plains struck Imogene with several emotions. Its vastness filled her with fear and wonder at the same time. The green and brown grass waving in front of her all the way to the blue horizon, streaked with shafts of orange from the setting sun, amazed

Imogene as she thought there could be no end to their
journey.

~

To Putney, it also seemed like the journey wouldn't end.
They walked night after night with only the stars and the
ever-dimming moon to light their way. Putney had insisted
Imogene eat the last peach. She needed the nourishment
more than him. As the days passed, Imogene grew weaker.
Putney realized that she wasn't going to be able to walk at a
pace that would get them to safety as quickly as he wanted,
so when she seemed to be flagging, Putney would carry her
on his back. As light as she was, the extra weight still slowed
him, and he found he was taking more rest breaks.

Fortunately, the vast prairie wasn't all it seemed, all the
time. The pair encountered a few arroyos and gulleys as
they traveled north, and in some of them, they found small
streams or creeks. Putney was good at predicting, by the
movement of the stars, when the sun would rise, so when
they came to a gulley and dawn was not far off, they would
stop and rest for the day.

Twice they found themselves in draws that had some
small shrubs and brush. Putney had gathered enough twigs
and sticks to boil a can of water each time. The rest of the
time, there was no material to build a fire. The knee-high
grass was mostly green and wouldn't burn, but even if it
were dry, it would burn too fast to maintain long enough to
boil water. And Putney wouldn't let them drink unless he
could boil the water. He insisted to Imogene, but primarily
to himself, that they not drink from streams until they had
no other choice. Putney thought it a damnable thing that
animals could drink raw water without problems, but

humans couldn't. He had seen the effect it could have when men in his military unit drank water that wasn't clean. But they could use the water to wash with, which provided some refreshment. But Putney was worried. He had rationed out the water carefully, but now on their eighth day, they were down to a few mouths full. One more night and the canteen would be empty.

Fortunately, the cuts in the plains provided good cover to keep them from being seen during the day. So they could rest in peace without worrying that an Indian or a bandit would see them from a distance. The chances of someone happening on them were slim, which was a comfort. Still, with his back to an arroyo wall, Putney always slept in a sitting position and always with a pistol in his hand.

One morning, just before dawn, they had come across an arroyo. So, they had settled down in it for their day's rest. Putney took his usual position, and Imogene took hers, snuggled under Putney's left arm. Putney let his right hand rest with the gun in his lap and felt the rising sun's warmth hitting his face and lowered his hat to keep from getting burned. As he was about to drift off, a noise assaulted his ears. Suddenly, Putney was as alert as he had ever been, and his heartbeat picked up. He cautioned Imogene to stay still and quiet as he crawled to the opposite wall of the ditch. Then, with pistols ready, he raised his head until his eyes were above the height of the grass. Then, he lowered himself slowly back into the gulley. What he had seen was impossible to believe.

13

Sheepherders! Nahum Putney had seen sheepherders together with three wagons. Putney rose again to make sure he wasn't hallucinating.

There they were, about fifty sheep, a few men and women, and three wagons.

"What is it, Nahum? What's wrong," Imogene was curious about what he had seen.

"I don't know if I believe it," Putney told her. "I think I saw a bunch of sheep and some people."

"Does that mean we're saved?" Imogene's face had a look of hope and desperation on it.

"I'm not certain what it means. I don't know how anybody could make it out to this wilderness with a bunch of sheep." Putney told her.

"What are we going to do?" Imogene's head was full of questions.

Putney motioned for Imogene to sit next to him. "This is what I know. We have been without food for five days and what we had up to then was next to nothing. I don't know if these people are good or bad. What I do know is we will have to take a chance on them being good. But that doesn't mean we have to be stupid about it."

Putney undid his belt and slid one of the holsters and the pistol off his belt.

"Take the can out of that flour sack and put this gun in there," he told her. "We have gone over and over how to use the gun. You must remember everything I told you. We are going to meet them. You stay behind me, if anything bad happens run back here. If you can, wait until you are in this ditch, shoot anyone who tries to comes in after you."

"Nahum, you're scaring me," Imogene looked like she was going to start crying,

Putney drew her close to him and hugged her. "I know, sweetie. But you must understand. Bad white men are an awful lot worse than Indians. Likely as not these will be peaceable folk." Putney hugged her again and asked if she were ready. Imogene smiled and nodded her head.

Taking the knife, Putney cut off a sleeve of his under-shirt. Then, holding the white cloth, he climbed out of the gulley, Imogene tagging right behind him. Putney stood and waved his peace flag until he had the shepherds' attention, then began walking slowly in their direction; the flag held high in his left hand while Putney's right rested on the handle of his pistol. One of the men near a wagon ran over, pulled a long gun out of the front of the vehicle, and pointed it in Putney's direction. From the distance, Putney couldn't determine if it was a rifle or a shotgun, but he hoped it was the second since they were still out of range of a scatter gun.

"Whoa, mister," Putney hollered. "I don't mean any harm! I just want to parlay with you folk. I have a little girl with me, and she needs help!" Putney signaled for Imogene to show herself, then waved for her to get back behind him.

"Then why do you have your hand on that gun?" Came a reply.

Putney now had two pieces of information. The first was the man had a foreign accent. It was either Scottish or Irish, but Putney couldn't tell due to the distance. He also knew that the man was probably holding a shotgun and wasn't an outlaw. If he were an outlaw and had a rifle, he would have already shot Putney if he were any good with it. "Same reason you're pointing that rifle at me! It's dangerous country, and I don't know you, just like you don't know me. But I'll take my hand off my pistol if you lower that rifle."

The man lowered his gun as Putney raised his other hand. "Sure, and it's no rifle, only a shotgun. What are you doing out here afoot with a wee waif-like that?"

"It's a long story! Let us approach, and I will be glad to give you the short version! Besides, all this yelling is making me hoarse," Putney hollered out.

"Come forward then, but just you take care," the man called back. Putney kept the pace slow as he and Imogene walked toward the group. Putney could now see that there was another man half-hidden by one of the wagons. As far as Putney could tell, he wasn't armed, but Putney would keep a wary eye on him.

There were two other men another fifty yards away with the sheep. The three wagons had women holding the reins. The man with the shotgun lowered the barrel until it pointed at the ground. Putney was confident that, if need be, he could draw and shoot before the man could raise his gun. Putney stopped ten feet from the man with the shotgun and, with his left hand, made sure Imogene was still standing behind him.

"My name is Nahum Putney. This girl and I were captured by Comanche but managed to escape. We've been walking eight days since" Putney didn't see any sense, at this point, trying to explain all their situation. "May I ask who you are and how you folk found yourself in the middle of nowhere?"

"That would be another long story, as well," the man told Putney. "Me name is Jack Callahan. The woman in that first wagon is me wife, Sinead. If I find you to be an honest man, I will introduce you to the rest."

"Mr. Callahan, my problem is, if I weren't an honest man, I wouldn't be here today," Putney admitted. "We haven't had anything to eat in six days, and we're nearly out of water. So if you could spare us even a couple of biscuits and a cup of water each, I'll tell you our story, and I'll listen to yours. Then, just maybe, we could help each other."

"Sure, I think we can provide you a crust and some water," Callahan told him, then over his shoulder, "Mother bring a few pieces of bread and some water for these people."

Then speaking again to Putney. "I might be willing to shoot you, Mr. Putney, but I would not begrudge a starving man and a wee girl a morsel and some water."

"You will never know how much we appreciate it, Mr. Callahan," Putney said with a sigh of relief.

The woman got down from the wagon and went to the rear. In a few minutes, she brought a tin plate with some slices of bread and a canteen. Sinead Callahan was a slight woman, maybe a little over five feet tall. She was slender, and the hair showing from under her sun-bonnet was dark, the color of pecans with streaks of gray. She handed the plate and canteen to her husband, then hurried back to the wagon and stood watch. Callahan passed the items to Putney.

"Do you mind if we sit, Mister Callahan?" asked Putney.

"We've been walking all night, and I doubt little Imogene can stand much longer." Putney sat down without waiting for an answer, and Imogene followed him to the ground, still not showing herself from behind Putney's shelter. Putney placed the plate beside him and then took a drink from the canteen. Imogene reached around Putney and took a piece of bread. Putney set the water down so she could get it. "Not too much at a time," he told her. Putney took a piece of bread and worked on following his own advice, eating as slowly as he could.

Jack Callahan waited politely while Putney and Imogene ate and drank some more water. After they had eaten some, Callahan asked Putney to explain more how he and the girl came to be in the middle of the grassy desert, with no food or water.

Putney tried to keep the story short but without omitting any important details. When he had finished, he asked Callahan for his story.

Callahan said that their leader, a man named John Kavanaugh, a family friend, had come from Ireland first and found some land in Northeastern New Mexico, not far from the Santa Fe Trail on the Cimmaron Cut Off. Kavanagh had written and said it was green and lush as Ireland. He also talked about the gold and silver mining in Colorado and how people up there needed meat and wool. So three families agreed to come to the United States and meet him in Independence, Missouri. Once they were there, Kavanaugh would go to Santa Fe and file a claim on the land. The others would purchase sheep, wagons, and supplies and meet him at Fort Dodge.

Callahan and the other two families purchased one hundred sheep from a farm in Missouri. They then traveled to Fort Dodge with a guide and kept north of the town to avoid mixing the sheep with cattle. Kavanaugh met them there with a claim to homestead two sections of land. They would divide the land evenly between Kavanaugh and the three families but would own the sheep as a cooperative. Rather than go with an organized group of settlers, the Irish sheepherders had agreed that, since Kavanaugh had already traveled the route twice, he would lead them all to the promised land.

They had gotten five days from Fort Dodge and crossed the Beaver River before camping. Kavanaugh told them to stay alert because they were in the Indian Nations. However, Kavanaugh had not warned them about the unpredictable storms that passed through that part of the country in May. On the sixth day of their trek, a tornado hit their train of six wagons while they were packing up to leave. The cost of the storm was devastating, killing Kavanaugh, three other men, a woman, and three children. The storm wrecked three wagons completely and badly damaged a third.

The sheep had made it to a low-lying area of land and mainly had been saved, but the shepherds had lost ten head of their sheep stock and three wagon mules. In addition, two other mules had run off, as did Kavanaugh's horse.

They spent the next three days burying the dead and reorganizing the wagons. They repaired the damaged wagon using parts and pieces from the destroyed wagons. They used the remaining mules to search for the draft animals that had been lost and were able to recover both mules and the horse.

On the fourth day after the storm, they encountered their next obstacle. Three Indians rode up to within a hundred yards of their camp. The Irish had no notion of what to do, so they did nothing.

They only had two shotguns and three pistols they had

purchased in Independence. But none of them were frontiersmen and had little knowledge of how to handle the
circumstance they had found themselves. Finally, one
Indian moved closer to the camp, and Callahan, being the
oldest, took it on himself to go out and meet with the man.
The Indian spoke a few English words, and with that and
some struggling communication with hand signs, Callahan
understood that the Indian wanted half the livestock.
Callahan spoke with his group, and they agreed to give up
30 sheep and two of the mules. Callahan relayed this to the
Indian, who refused the offer. Instead, he wanted the 30
sheep and the horse, to which Callahan agreed. Callahan
was surprised that the Indians knew how to herd the sheep
they had taken.

After their encounter with the Indians, the Irish folk had
another meeting. They officially elected Callahan as their
leader. The group also agreed that since they didn't know
exactly where they were, they would travel five days south
and then go west, hoping to find someone who could help
them get to their land. They were about to begin their
fourth day when Putney had popped out of the grass.

Putney asked Callahan if he knew whether they had
crossed the Canadian River. Callahan told Putney they had
only crossed a few shallow creeks, but nothing any of them
would consider a river. Moreover, the only map they
possessed was Kavanaugh's, another thing the storm carried
off.

Putney asked about the land claim and if there was a
surveyor's map of that area. Callahan told him they had kept
the deed and a parcel map in a strong box, along with other
valuable records, such as births, weddings, and family
bibles that recorded those events. From what the Irishman
had told Putney, he believed that he and Imogene had been

further west than he thought when they started. Otherwise, the settlers would have crossed the Canadian. Also, Putney figured that he and Imogene had trekked further north than he had thought possible, by maybe a day.

"Mister Callahan, if you would let me take a look at your parcel map, I may be able to tell you how close you are to your mark," Putney told the Irishman.

While Callahan went to get the map, Imogene and Putney finished the bread and sipped the water, taking care not to get bloated. Then, Putney spread the map out in front of him. It was challenging to decipher exactly where the land was, but there were two items on the map that could put them in the general area. The first was a line on the map labeled Seneca Creek. This creek ran west to east and divided the claim in two. One section was north of the creek, and the other was south. The other was an arrow that pointed east and was labeled Rabbit Ears Mountain. Putney didn't know exactly where they were at present, but he bet they were much further south and east than the pilgrims had suspected.

"Mister Callahan, understand that I'm not sure, but I believe you are several days south and a few days east of where you want to be. I'm not familiar with this part of the country, but I had a map that included parts of New Mexico and the Nations. I recollect that this," Putney pointed to the name of the mountain, "is nearly due west of Beaver River. But, as I said, I'm not certain because the Beaver starts somewhere in the Nations, and Rabbit Ears is in New Mexico. If you had followed the Beaver River, my bet is you would be to your destination by now. Imogene and I are lucky that you came the way you did."

"Well, then, we'll be thanking you for that bit of information, Mister Putney," said Callahan. "I wonder, Mister Putney, since you know more about this vast land than we do, what would be the chances of you guiding us to our land."

"Mister Callahan, I believe there is safety in numbers, and little Imogene here could certainly use riding in a wagon. So I think we can strike a bargain, "said Putney. "But you need to know I won't be able to get you exactly where you need to be, only close. Here is what I think I can do for you. I have a lot of experience scouting for Indians. I'll scout for you and get you as close as I can. In return, you furnish Imogene and me with some proper clothes and feed us. Once we get you near where you should be, we can discuss what we will do from there."

Callahan thought a minute, then said, "Generally, I am willing to accept your terms, but I will need to discuss it with the rest of me folk."

Putney looked at the man as if measuring him, then said, "If Imogene can sit in the shade of one of those wagons, I have no problem with that, Mr. Callahan."

14

Callahan had called together all the adult members of their party, including his twin seventeen-year-old sons, Matthew & Mark. After a few minutes of discussion, all the pilgrims gathered around Putney and Imogene. "We have agreed that you can scout for us," announced Callahan. "This here is Mary Dorsey and Eileen Gallagher. They both lost their husbands, and Mary lost two children. Eileen has a son named Alan. They've taken one wagon, so they have plenty of room. Your Imogene is welcome to ride with them, and she can get the rest she needs."

"That's just fine," said Putney. "Thank you."

"I'll introduce you to the others now," said Jack. First, he introduced his wife, two sons, and then his daughter, Erin. "Erin is fifteen," he informed Putney. "Now, this strapping young man is Phineas Forsythe and his wife, Brigid," Callahan placed his hand on a blond-haired man nearly as tall as Putney. "These two lovelies are their daughters, Alanis and Caitlin. They are two years apart but, by my guessing, about the same age as Imogene. They have agreed to share some clothes with her. Last is William and Margaret Fitzgerald and their son Brendan, about Imogene's age, and their daughter, Breanna, probably a wee bit younger."

Putney shook hands with all the men and boys and gave a short bow to the ladies and girls.

"My name is Nahum Putney, and I'm honored to meet you all." During the introductions, Imogene had remained behind Putney like he had told her. Finally, Putney reached behind him and pulled her out so everyone could get a glimpse of her. "This is Imogene Foster. She has had a rough time, and it may take her a while to warm to you, but I'm sure she will, given some time."

Brigid Forsythe, a slender young woman with dark auburn hair, came and knelt in front of Imogene.

"Ah, you could pass for one of me own daughters," she told the young girl. "I'll tell you what, why don't you come with us, and we will fit you out with some proper clothes. It looks like you've worn those to a frazzle."

Imogene looked up at Putney for approval. "You go ahead, sweetie. These are good people, and they are going to help me take care of you." Mrs. Forsythe held her hand out. Having gotten Putney's blessing, Imogene took the woman's hand and walked with her to a wagon, followed by the three young girls.

"Mary," said Sinead Callahan, "why don't you and Eileen get a fire started, and I'll get out a pan and cook up some bacon for our newly acquired traveling partners?"

With the women all off attending to matters, Jack signaled the men to follow him over to his wagon. The boys and Erin followed. Jack took two chairs, a stool, and two boxes from his wagon, for the men to sit. "Well, Mr. Putney," Jack began the conversation. "Since we're putting ourselves in your hands, what are you suggesting we do, now."

"The first thing is for you men to start calling me Nahum. I'm well younger than any of you, and it kind of puts me ill at ease."

"Nahum it is, and you call us by first names as well," said Jack

"Alright. Since we've already burned up some daylight, I think you should turn your wagons to the northeast," Putney pointed, indicating the direction they should head.

"We will only make about ten miles today. But I'm only guessing. I don't know how fast sheep move."

"Oh, they'll outpace us if we let them," Phineas Forsyth answered with a laugh.

"Good," praised Putney.

"How about weapons? Other than that shotgun. What else do you have?"

"Between us, we have three pistols, all forty-four caliber, a carbine rifle, and the shotgun," answered Jack.

"Is the carbine a single shot, and is it a cartridge gun? How about the shotgun?" Putney knew the shotgun was a double barrel, but he wanted to see if it took shells or was a powder gun.

"Aye, the rifle is a single shot and takes cartridges," answered William Fitzgerald. "The shotgun takes shells."

"That's good," said Putney. "How about ammunition?"

"In that, we were lucky," continued William. "We kept all the guns and ammunition in Jack's wagon. We have plenty of powder and ball for the pistols. We have fifty cartridges for the carbine; for the shotgun, we have twenty bird shot shells and twenty-five buckshot."

Putney nodded his approval. "How many of you have used a gun before?"

Phineas spoke up. "We all know how to use the shotgun; we did some bird hunting in Ireland. Kavanaugh showed us how to use the rifle and pistols, but we never shot them. Those sorts of weapons were only to be used by the gentry."

"Kavanaugh didn't have you practice at all?" Putney's eyes opened wide in amazement.

"No, he said if the time comes, we would figure it out quick enough," replied Phineas.

Putney shook his head in disbelief. "Get all your ammunition and bring it here," he commanded. "Before we move another wagon wheel, y'all are going to get some lessons."

Putney conducted an inventory and found they did have plenty of ball and powder, so that wouldn't be a problem. The shotgun shells and carbine cartridges were as Fitzgerald had said. When Putney inspected the handguns, they looked brand new, and not one was loaded. "Do you mean to tell me you've traveled all this way and never loaded these weapons?"

"Well, sure, and you're right there. John said he would show us but never got around to it," Jack said as he began to realize their folly.

"You're damned lucky all you came upon was a tornado," Putney scolded. "Didn't anybody ever tell you there were hostile Indians and murderous outlaws out here?"

All those assembled looked at the ground, and the boys kicked at the dirt. "Alright, forget what I said about us making ten miles today," said Putney, "Y'all need some training, and you need it now. And that goes for everybody twelve or older, so you may as well set up camp again." Everybody kind of looked to one another and then back at Putney. "Well, get to it," Putney barked like he was instructing the privates in his company. The men started to stir slowly and with no enthusiasm. "Look," said Putney, softer this time. "I apologize. I know I was rude, but I'm frustrated that this Kavanaugh would bring you out here so unprepared. I just want to give you people a chance at survival."

"Sure, we know," said Jack. "I think maybe we are all a wee bit ashamed for being out here and not having any real idea what we're doing."

"I know, and again I'm sorry. It's been a long couple of weeks for me, and my temper is short," admitted Putney. "Just go ahead and set up camp."

The men went to the wagons and started pulling various items out. Putney could only stand and shake his head in amazement. Finally, he said, "Stop, just stop. What are y'all doing?"

"Setting up camp, like you said," Phineas looked at Putney like he was daft.

"Christ, how did y'all survive this long," Putney asked in wonderment. "I think I'm going to find myself apologizing for my demeanor, over and over. But truly, I am amazed. Drive the wagons around, so you make a square. Then unhitch the mules, and let the older boys take them out to graze for about an hour. Then bring them back and tie them up to the wagons. I'm going to check on Imogene and eat some of that bacon the ladies cooked up."

Brigid and the girls had done wonders for Imogene by washing her face and brushing her matted hair. Alanis and Caitlin had dressed her in a light blue dress with lace at the collars and cuffs. Breana had fetched an extra pair of her brother's shoes and tied a blue bow in Imogene's hair. She looked nothing like the wretch he had first seen in the Comanche camp. "Excuse me, girls," said Putney in a joshing manor. "Have y'all seen a scrawny little squaw girl around here? I seem to have lost one."

All the girls giggled, except Imogene. "It's me, Nahum.

I'm right here, and I ain't no squaw girl," her voice cracked, and Putney could tell she was about to cry.

He knelt by her and took her in his arms. "Of course, you're not, sweetie. I'm sorry it was a poor jest," Then, holding her at arm's length, he looked her in her eyes. "The truth is that I was just bewildered at how pretty you are. You got to admit we both looked pretty rough."

"Yes, and you still do, you old horse," It was Putney's turn to be joshed.

"I reckon you're right, and I'm going to take care of that as soon as I eat me some bacon. Would you like some bacon?"

"Oh, God. Yes," exclaimed the girl.

After they had eaten and the men had the wagons in position, Putney walked around and inspected everything. Then, he told them to set out any crates or boxes they had between the wagons. Putney said they probably wouldn't be able to fill all the gaps but to do the best they could. When they had accomplished that task, he got everyone together. "Alright," he said to everyone. "My two Walkers are loaded, and I loaded the one Colt, so we're going to have everyone take one turn shooting, one time each. Then I will show you how to load these pistols. They all load pretty much the same, so everyone will get a chance to do it." He took them outside the wagons and away from the sheep. "These Walkers are heavy. Much heavier than your pistols," he told them. "Don't be too concerned about it because I will be carrying them, and unless something happens to me, y'all won't be using them. I'll save the other pistol for the young-sters to fire. It will be easier for them."

He arranged everyone in a single line. Men first followed by the women, then the teenage boys, and finally the girls. "I'm going to hand Jack here a gun first. He'll shoot it, pass it down until it's empty, then we will start with the next. This is not target practice. We don't have ammunition or time for that. I just want you to know how to work the pistols and see how it feels when they go off. Use two hands because they are going to kick like mules, and if you're not used to it, you will probably drop the guns, especially you younger ones."

Putney showed them how to aim and hold the gun using one of the unloaded guns. Then he showed them that they had to cock the hammer back, all the way, before trying to pull the trigger. Make sure it cocks back all the way," he reiterated. "If you only bring it to the half cock, the hammer won't come down with enough force, and the gun either won't fire or will misfire." Then handing the gun to Jack and stepping behind him, he told Jack, "Cock the hammer. Good, now fire."

The Walker went off with a loud boom and jerked Jack's hands up. "Does that mean I shot the gun in the air?" Jack wanted to know.

"No, not at all," said Putney. "That ball has already left the barrel before the gun kicks up. The thing you want to remember is to bring it back level before you shoot again."

They repeated the exercise until everyone had a chance to shoot the guns once. There was one round left. Then, Putney asked if there was an empty can or bottle in one of the wagons.

Everyone looked at each other, shrugging their shoulders and shaking their heads. Then Mary Dorsey spoke up, saying she had a hand mirror broken in the storm if that would do and Putney said it would do fine. So Mary got the mirror out of her wagon and brought it to him.

Putney paced off about twenty-five feet, stuck the handle in the ground, and returned. Using one of the spent pistols, he showed them how to aim, lining up the sights. Then

Putney had everybody step behind him. He aimed and fired. The mirror frame flew up in the air several feet and landed another ten feet further than where he had initially placed it. Putney retrieved the busted mirror and brought it back. The glass was all gone, and there was a hole in the center of the metal back. Everyone was duly impressed.

"Now," he addressed everyone. "That is going to be as far as any of you can shoot and hope to hit anything. But even at that range, chances are you're going to miss, so it is best not to try. Wait until the person you are shooting at is about half that distance. At that range, you ought to be able to point and shoot and hit some part of him."

Eileen Gallagher held up a hand, and Putney looked her way. "Do you mean to say you are expecting us to shoot a person with these?"

"Yes, ma'am," Putney looked at her firmly. "That is the only thing these pistols are good for. You can hunt with the rifle and shotgun, but unless you're just plinking at targets, these pistols are for killing human beings."

"Well, that's against God's commandments," she expounded.

"Ma'am," a frustrated Putney began. "I doubt any Indians have read the Bible, and if they have, it wouldn't mean anything to them," Putney tried to tamp down his ire. "As for bandits, they probably had Bible teaching. They just don't care. If we get attacked by either kind, somebody is going to have to kill them. If you don't, they will kill you. Or worse. And then they'll kill you when they're done. And these young girls, just you ask Imogene what will happen. She will tell it to you plain."

"Aren't you exaggerating just a little, Mr. Putney," she questioned him.

Putney became angry and took two quick strides to

come face to face with the woman. "I would let you ask my mother, father, and two sisters, but I buried them after Comanche had butchered them. Or maybe you should talk to Imogene. Do you know what they had planned for her? They were going to give her to one of the men of the tribe. And that would have been if she were lucky and they didn't sell her off to the Apache. Or worse, they would have sold her to Comancheros. Those animals would have raped her and then put her to work as a whore. So, no, ma'am, I'm not exaggerating, not one little iota."

Eileen Gallagher burst into tears and ran back to her wagon. Putney turned and walked into the grassy plain, then dropped to his knees, angry at himself for the way he spoke to the woman. Imogene ran after Putney and put her arms around his neck. "Nahum, don't cry," said Imogene, mistaking his self-loathing for sadness. "She had to be told. They all have to know."

"It was wrong of me," said the weary scout. "She is a good, God-fearing woman, and I should never have spoken to her that way. These people are already scared, and I didn't help them with that outburst. It was the worst thing I could have done."

Putney opened his eyes and noticed a hand holding a bottle in front of his face. It was Jack Callahan, and the bottle held whiskey. "Here, lad," said Jack. "You may need a wee bit of this." Putney looked over his shoulder into the kind eyes of Callahan and shook his head.

"No," said Putney as he stood. "That's not what I need right now." He turned and walked toward Eileen Gallagher's wagon. Mrs. Dorsey was trying to console the sobbing woman. Excuse me, ma'am," he said to Mary Dorsey. "I need to speak to Mrs. Gallagher."

"I think maybe you have already spoken too much," Mary Dorsey scolded him.

"I know," Putney's eyes showed the remorse in his soul, and Mrs. Dorsey stood aside. "Mrs. Gallagher," Putney said. "I should have never spoken to you in that manner. It was wrong, and it was disrespectful. I will regret it for as long as I live. I want you to know how sorry I am."

Through her sobs, Eileen Gallagher said, "It's not just you, Mr. Putney. I told my husband we should have stayed in St. Louis. Things were safe there. Now here am I with no husband and only a son not yet full-grown to look to for protection. I have lost all hope."

"Mrs. Gallagher," Putney reached out and touched the woman's shoulder. "I promise I will do everything I can to protect you and keep everyone in your company safe."

Eileen Gallagher reached out, drew Putney close to her, hugged him firmly, and spoke softly in his ear, "I know you will." She kissed him on the cheek and, with enthusiasm in her voice, said, "Let's all get back to our lessons." The three walked back to where the rest of the group were standing around, speaking softly and looking embarrassed. "What are you all gawking at?" said the Eileen. "We have work to do."

Putney instructed the older boys to bring over a box and a chair. He then sat and began demonstrating how to load the pistols. Once he finished, he had everyone take a turn, patiently guiding them when they were uncertain or looked to be about to make a mistake. Once all the pistols were loaded, Putney asked for someone to bring him the carbine. Putney was pleased it was a Starr model two because it took brass rim fire cartridges. Putney showed them how to open the breech and load the cartridge. It was a relatively simple operation, and everyone took to it quickly.

Putney then examined the shotgun. It was a durable double-barreled, twelve-gauge gun.

After Putney had instructed them on the weapons, he decided they needed to know a little about tactics. "When you're moving, keep your wagons tight together, don't allow too much space between them," He advised. "You don't want to take the chance of someone separating a wagon from the others. One advantage you will have in these flat plains is you can see an attacker from a great distance. Always have someone looking to the rear, the front, and both sides. You can't be lax because they could pop up any time." He looked to make sure everyone was following what he told them.

"If you do see someone, don't wait for them to attack. Go ahead and form your wagons like we have here, except you won't have time to unhitch the animals, so move them to the inside of the wagon in front of you." Putney called for a pencil and paper so he could draw a diagram of what he was saying. It's essential to keep the mules inside the circle. Indians and outlaws want to steal your animals, and they would rather do it without risking themselves. Also, forget what you may have read in dime novels about Indians never attacking at night. Indians, especially Comanche, will take every advantage they can. That goes for outlaws, too. So, at night always have two people on watch. Rotate them so nobody falls asleep."

"What about the sheep," asked Phineas. "Do we need to put a guard on them at night?"

"I'm afraid the sheep are going to be on their own at night," said Putney. "You don't have enough people to watch the camp and the sheep, then drive the wagons the next day. But during the day, herd the sheep to one side or the other, not far from the wagons.

"The last thing is your guns. Always keep the shotgun

loaded with the buckshot unless you are hunting birds or rabbits," Putney told them. "But always have buckshot shells with you. The lead wagon will always be Jack's, and the shotgun will always be with him. The next will always be Mary and Eileen, and they will have one of the pistols. It doesn't matter which one. They all operate the same. You decide the last two wagons amongst yourselves. Each will have a pistol, but whichever is last will always have the carbine."

Satisfied that everyone understood his instructions, Putney closed with, "I will leave on one of the mules before light every morning. I should be able to make it out about fifteen miles in front of you and return before dark. Every day you're going to need someone to ride out a few hundred yards in front to make sure the high grass isn't hiding a ditch. We don't need any broken wheels. When I return in the evening, I will have a map and directions that will show any obstacles, creeks, landmarks, and the such."

When he finished, everyone agreed that it had been a productive day, and they were glad that Putney was there to help them. Putney approached Jack and said, "I'll take that drink of whiskey now if it's still offered."

15

Matthew Callahan woke Nahum Putney around four-thirty the following morning. It was a long, restful sleep that he needed. Mary Dorsey was already awake and had bacon and beans ready.

For Putney, it was better than any meal he had eaten in Galveston or San Antonio. The day before, Putney had found out that Kavanaugh's saddle was in a wagon when the Indians had extorted his horse from the pilgrims. Jack Callahan had given Putney a shirt and a jacket that almost fit. Phineas Forsythe had provided Putney with a pair of corduroy pants about 2 inches short, but Putney didn't complain. The only thing that showed he had served in the Confederacy was his hat, but he could live with that. Before he left, Putney went to the wagon where Imogene was sleeping. He kissed her lightly on the forehead so as not to wake her. Then he left to scout out a path for the settlers.

The day before, he had told Jack to head the group to the northeast and that he would return before dark. So he could make maps, Putney had folded up several sheets of paper and placed them with a pencil in the pocket of Callahan's jacket. Eileen Gallagher ran to catch up with him as he was leaving the camp. "Here's me husband's watch. You might be needing one. It's not expensive, but it's been a good watch." Putney patted Eileen on the hand and thanked her for the gift. It was a watch he would carry for a long time.

Putney rode until noon before he started drawing a map. There was no sense in drawing one before that because the sheepherders would already have passed any point that would make the map practical. When he saw a good landmark, creek, gulch, stand of trees, or anything that would help Callahan guide the wagon train, Putney would note the time it had taken him to get to that area. He pushed the mule to get out ahead of the rest of the group as much as possible, but he did encounter a small creek where he let the animal drink. He would do the same on his return. Then, considering the progress the others should make, and the time it would take him to get back to them, Putney turned the mule and started back. Putney hadn't worn the mule out, so Putney pushed hard to make sure he got back before dark. The sun was getting low when Putney spotted the wagons. The Irish had already formed a camp like Putney had told them, and he felt a small swell of pride that they were learning.

The first person to see Putney return was Imogene. She ran to meet him when as he rode toward the camp. Putney reached down for her hand and pulled her up behind him. "I missed you when I woke up," she told him. "You didn't say goodbye or anything," she whimpered.

"I didn't want to wake you. You needed the rest, "Putney replied to her rebuke. She hugged him tightly around his waist as they rode into the camp.

Callahan came and greeted Putney on the outside of the camp. The two men discussed how the day had gone. "We had no problems and didn't see anyone," Callahan reported. "And we kept careful watch, just like you told us. How was your day?"

"I saw nothing but more of this grassland. I did cross a small creek, but it's shallow, so you don't need to worry about it. It's only a foot or so deep and not very wide. But the bottom is muddy, so when you go to cross it, don't hesitate. Ford it as quick as possible, or you'll bog down in the mud. I have a map that I will go over with you and the others later."

Callahan told Putney to come to the camp and eat. That evening they ate mutton stew with potatoes and carrots. There was also bread that the women had made in a Dutch oven. Putney had never eaten mutton before, and he found he liked it. The bread reminded him of his mother's bread when he was a boy. It was a good memory.

Out of politeness, nobody asked Putney about his day until the meal was over. When everyone had eaten, Jack gathered everyone to hear Putney's report. The entire group was eager to know what, if anything, their scout had seen. "I didn't see any sign of Comanche or any other people for that matter. I found no tracks or remains of campfires. I think you will be alright tomorrow," Putney told them. "Here, Jack. Take the map I made. I couldn't be sure of the distances, so I marked the time it took me to come to each landmark. That should give you a good estimate of where you are or if you veer off course."

"Sure, and we'll be sure not to stray," Callahan assured Putney and everybody else.

"How many water kegs do you have, and how full are they?" Putney inquired.

"Two and they are both about half full."

"Good," said Putney.

"I know you have one big pot; do you have a second?"

"We have three, actually," Jack was wondering why Putney had asked.

"Even better. Do you know about boiling water to purify it?"

"Sure, we do," replied Jack. "We're not completely daft, you know."

"I figured, I just wanted to make sure. When you get to the creek, don't cross it right away. You want to stir up as little mud as possible. Fill one keg with the water from the other. Fill canteens with any left over. Once you have the water boiled, let it cool. You don't want to fill the keg with hot water. That will make the wood swell, and when it cools, the wood will shrink, and the keg will leak."

"That's good to know.

"It's going to take a while, and you won't get as far, but we don't know if we will run into any more water. Better to have some and not need it," Putney told Jack.

Afterward, Putney listened to stories about Ireland and their trip across the ocean and the continent. To Putney, it almost felt like home. Their accents weren't very much different than his father's Scottish brogue. Maybe a little more musical. Putney took to Jack more than the others. Jack was probably near the same age as Putney's father when The Comanches had killed him.

When the conversation hit a lull, young Brendan Fitzwater asked Putney if he had killed many Indians or had fought robbers like the books he had read.

Putney looked straight at the boy. "A man shouldn't brag about killing another person. It doesn't matter if they are red or white. My father once told me that sometimes, out on this frontier, a person may have to kill another. It's either kill or be killed. But he also told me that a little bit of your soul dies every time you kill someone. So, I won't tell you about that, but I will tell you about a time two bandits tried to rob me, and I fought them off."

"Will you, Mr. Putney?" the boy was excited, and it sparked the interests of the other youngsters. Some of the adults were also quite interested.

"I was about the same age as Alan, there," Putney continued to tell the story of when Jessup Taylor and Brandon Starnes had tried to rob him. His story enthralled the children and the teenagers. Even Imogene, who had not heard the story before, was impressed. He finished his story without going into the next day when he found his family murdered by Comanches. When he finished, the women started herding the younger children to bed. Erin helped wrangle the young ones. The three older teenage boys were rotating the watch.

The following five days consisted of the same routine. Putney would go out early in the day and return in the late afternoon. First, everyone would eat, usually the same mutton stew and bread, but twice just a vegetable soup made with the bones of a butchered sheep. Then they would swap stories. On the third night, Imogene told them about their escape from the Comanches and how they had survived on only water and five peaches.

When he headed out the sixth day, Putney figured they had traveled about one hundred fifty miles. He believed they were getting close, and it would only be two or three more days before they would spy Rabbit Ear Mountain. This day had been no different than the previous. The landscape was mostly flat plains with a slight rise or hill every so often, a narrow, shallow creek, and a rare stone formation.

He crested a slight rise just after twelve, and the sight made his heart sink. Below was a herd of buffalo. They covered acres upon acres. There was no way he could estimate how many there were. A herd of buffalo was not a good omen. Where there were buffalo, there would be Indians. Most likely, there would be Comanche or Kiowa or maybe both. Kiowas and Comanche were allies and the only tribes that got along with each other. But Putney had heard that even the Cheyenne were known to range down as far as this. So Putney turned his mule and headed back toward the settlers.

Jack Callahan saw Putney coming and knew something was wrong. It was too early for him to have come back. Jack pulled up his mules, jumped out of the wagon, and signaled the others to stop. Putney rode up to Jack and dismounted.

"We have a problem, Jack," said Putney. He explained about the buffalo and how Indians could be nearby. "This is a big herd migrating north after winter. It could be a couple of days before they clear."

Callahan was familiar with domesticated cattle and sheep and asked, "Can't we ride through them like we would cows," he asked.

"Buffalo aren't like cattle," answered Putney. "They are wild beasts and apt to charge. A bull could probably knock over a wagon. And if there were Indians around and they saw us trying, it would cause them to attack.

Your people aren't prepared for an attack when they're on the move. I think we have two choices. We could camp here, wait for the herd to move on, and fort up against a possible attack or we could try to go around."

"How long would those options take?" Jack was anxious to get to their land and start settling in.

"It's hard to tell. If the herd is migrating, I think it might take the buffalo two or three days to clear the area. Then as big as the herd is, it could take the same amount of time to skirt them." Putney advised the Callahan.

"Alright then, let me speak with the others, and I will make a decision," Callahan told Putney.

Imogene had seen Putney and had gotten out of her wagon but waited politely while the two men talked. Then, when Callahan left to speak to the others, she walked to him. "Do you think Indians might attack us, Nahum?" the girl was shaking with fear.

Putney knelt and held her firmly by the shoulders, hoping to stop the tremors. "If we make a good plan, I think we can avoid that happening. If there are Indians around, they will be more interested in the herd of buffalo than us."

"I hope you're right, Nahum. I would rather die than be captured again

Putney hugged her closely and said, "Don't worry, sweetie. I won't let anything happen to you. I promise."

When Jack had informed the others of what Putney had told him, Jack and the other men came to confer with Putney. "What do you think we ought to, Nahum," asked William Fitzgerald.

"Since you asked, here's what I think. We have a good shot at being in direct line with your claim, and we're only two or three days away at the most. If we try to go around the herd that will take us further southwest, then we will have to recover ground lost, just to get to a point where we would be a day ahead of where we are now," Putney paused to let that sink in. "Also, if Indians attack while you are moving, you would have to square up the wagons in a hurry, and honestly, it will be chaos. Since I would be out ahead on the scout, I wouldn't be here to help."

"That seems a bit dismal," said Phineas.

"It is," agreed Putney. "On the other hand, if we go ahead and square up the wagons now, we can fortify with crates and whatever else you have in the wagons. We can prepare in case of an attack, but I think that would be unlikely because any Indians in the area will be following the buffalo. I haven't seen any sign showing they're in this area, so their camp is probably further north from us. But if there is an attack, I would be here to help. That adds an extra man and two guns to the fight."

It was Jack Callahan's turn to speak. "Nahum's given us his best advice, and since he's the only one of us that has experience fighting Indians, I think setting up camp here is our best option. And since you elected me as leader, that's what we will do."

The other two men agreed that it was the best decision, so Jack started directing them to set up the wagons in a square and start off loading to provide an additional barrier against attack. Everyone got to work and started forming up a camp. Once the wagons were in place, Putney hobbled the mules so they could graze outside the camp. There would be time to move them to safety if there were signs of any hostiles.

While everyone else worked, Imogene walked a little way out in the prairie. Getting on her knees, she fervently prayed.

16

K nowing the size of the herd of buffalo, Putney
had decided it was unnecessary to look to see
how far they had moved, if at all, for the first two
days. So instead, he stayed at the camp, but he was getting
restless, as were the settlers. On the other hand, he did
enjoy getting to know them better, especially Jack. Callahan's charism and personality were so large they negated his
physical stature.

He was nearly a foot shorter than Putney but carried
himself with such confidence that he seemed taller. When
he was a boy, Putney had a book with pictures of
leprechauns, and Jack reminded him of those funny, little,
mythical creatures except for the color of his hair. Callahan
had a mass of coal-black hair instead of the bright orange in
the picture book that they almost always covered with a
high crowned hat and a short brim which added to the
image. Jack quickly became the man that Putney liked best
out of the group. Jack always had a story to tell about
Ireland's long-ago history. One time he would speak about

Queen Maeve and the next about Finn McCool, or he would thrill the children with stories about kelpies and banshees.

Jack was also a natural leader. The kind that men looked to when crucial decisions needed making. It was the apparent reason the others had elected him to head up their little band. Jack was the kind of leader who wouldn't shy away from making the hard decisions, but he almost always shared the problems with the group, listened to what they had to say, and then made the final decision. That decision was not always the most popular among the others but once made, Jack stood by it. On the other hand, when a decision resulted in a less than favorable outcome, which was a rare event, Jack would admit to his error and not try to shift blame to anyone else. It was the quality that Putney respected the most.

Jack had also come to like Putney a great deal. Theirs was a complex relationship. Putney was only a few years older than his sons, and because of that youthful spirit, Jack often thought of Putney as a son. Putney had told Jack of the events of his life and Jack could tell they had aged the young man. Because of those tragic times, Jack sometimes thought of Putney as a brother. Putney's experience as a soldier and a scout, his knowledge of the land and the culture, and his strong belief in right or wrong caused Jack to consider Putney as his mentor, like an older brother or an uncle.

Over the few days they had known each other, Jack and Putney had become more than friends. They had become companions, or as Putney thought of it, compeneros. Men who stood together against the odds. Men who, if called on, would spill their blood for each other.

Besides getting to know Jack better, Putney liked being around all the Irish. Men and women, girls and boys. Despite their desperate circumstances, they were cheerful.

Sometimes at night, when they had finished eating, William would get out his fiddle and play some tunes, usually lively reels. The children enjoyed teaching Imogene their native dances. Generally, as evenings wore on, the pace would slow, and Sinead or Eileen would sing ballads in their native Irish. They were slow and mournful tunes. Putney loved the songs. Even though he couldn't understand the words, they flowed into him, giving him a forgotten inner peace.

Another thing everyone relished was listening to stories. Of course, Jack's stories were always the favorites. But even the children had little tales they would relate about fairies and brownies and other mythical creatures. One night Imogene was inspired to tell a story of her own, and she was a natural. Everyone was sitting in a circle around the cook fire when Imogene decided to spin her yarn. It was all about how Putney had fought with Quanah and bested him. Then she told how Putney had tricked Big Looking Glass and made him such a fool that the chief could do nothing but set Putney free and give him his choice of anyone he wanted to take with him, and he chose her. All during the telling, Imogene would walk around the fire, increasing the drama by getting low and spreading her arms, and then when a climax would come, she would stand up tall and wave her hands in the air to the excitement of everyone. Of course, almost none of it was true, but Putney didn't correct her. *Let her have her fun*, he thought.

On the third day, after spotting the buffalo herd, Putney decided it was time to see what progress the buffalo had made. He didn't start before dawn, as had been his practice, because he wanted to be able to see if there was any sign of Indians near the camp. Putney knew that if anything happened with the settlers, he wouldn't know about it until he returned, and by then, it would be too late. It was also an excellent time to teach some of the company about what he did and how he did it. His time with them would eventually end, and they needed to start learning the ways of this wild land.

He decided he would take one of the twins. Both wanted to go, so Jack decided to flip a coin to see which one it would be and that the other would go the next time. Matthew won the coin toss. Putney offered him the mule with the saddle, but he wouldn't have it. Putney knew Matthew would regret it but let him have his way. Before they left, Putney cut pieces of rope to make hobbles for the mules. Along the way, Putney showed Matthew the old tracks the mule had made in the previous days and how the tracks coming and going differed. Putney told him on the return trip that he would show him the difference between old and new tracks. The lessons did not distract Putney from watching for any sign of Indian, white, or Mexican hostiles. The plains looked as empty as the day God made them.

They stopped when they neared the rise where Putney had first seen the buffalo. Putney told Matthew they didn't want to go over the hill on the mules because anyone looking would see them coming over the rise. So, instead, he hobbled the animals and said they would approach on foot. As the pair neared the top of the hill, Putney signaled to crawl on all fours until they could see over it. Once at the top, they lay in the high grass and looked at the shallow valley below.

There was still a long line of the beasts, but they were looking at the end of it. The trailing buffalo had thinned out with the older animals straggling behind the herd, which was a good sign. Putney figured the pack could be out of eyesight by the next day. But then Putney caught sight of something that dashed his hopes. On the far horizon, he saw smoke. What he saw wasn't a narrow column of thin white smoke that would indicate a campfire. This smoke was darker and came in puffs of different lengths. Putney was looking at a smoke signal. Putney had no idea what the smoke meant. There were some basic codes, but signals varied between tribes, and even different bands within a tribe had their own codes. The signal could mean anything from there was good hunting to there were enemies in the area. Putney looked around himself in every direction but did not see any other smoke. That provided some relief. It meant the signals he had seen were informational, and whoever sent them did not expect an answer. However, it wasn't all good because it said there were at least two bands in the same general area as they were. Putney hoped that because the signal was ahead of them, it probably was nothing about the group of Irish settlers. But he couldn't take a chance.

"Let's go, Matthew. We need to get back and make sure everything is alright there," said Putney. "We don't have time to dawdle, so we will have to pass on any tracking lessons on the way back. But if you happen to see tracks you didn't see before or that cross ours, let me know."

Putney insisted that Matthew take the saddled mule because they would have to push the animals hard, and Putney could sit a barebacked animal at speed. It took them two and a half hours to return to the camp. Putney went directly to Jack to report what he had observed, while Matthew went to the other young people and told them all about their adventure.

Jack wanted to know what it meant and what Putney thought they should do. "I don't really know for sure," Putney admitted. "It could be just a hunting party signaling something back to their main band. The smoke couldn't possibly be about this camp because of the distance. I don't think they could have seen Matthew and me, but you never know."

"We're running low on water," Jack said. "I don't think we can stay here much longer. There is no water around here. I'm thinking we need to take the chance and move on."

"Your call, Jack," Putney said. "If that's your decision, I'll find some water."

Jack went to confer with the other men and the women. Putney took the opportunity to rest a bit. Imogene had heard everything Matthew had told the children, so she ran to Putney. "Is it true, Nahum? Did y'all really see Indians?" she asked. Putney heard the anxiety in her voice.

"No, sweetie," Putney reassured her. "We only saw some smoke. Whoever they are, they're a long way off. Don't worry, sweetie. I'll take care of you." It dawned on Putney that he had started calling Imogene by the endearment and realized it was what his father called Putney's twin sisters when they had bruised an elbow or scraped a knee.

When Jack returned, he told Putney that the adults had split evenly on whether to stay or move on. "What's your mind on it?" asked Putney.

"We move on tomorrow. If the buffalo herd is still there, from what you say, we should be able to go around them without taking us too much out of our way," Jack said.

"Good, I'll be ready to start out early. "I'm not taking Mark with me. If I run into trouble, I can take care of myself easier than trying to take care of another person and me," Putney advised the leader.

The next morning, Imogene came to Putney before he had finished breakfast. "I had a dream in the night," she informed Putney. "I dreamed you ran into Indians, and they killed you," as soon as the words were out of her mouth, she began crying.

Putney took her in his arms and let her tears run into his shoulder. "Now, now, sweetie," he tried to comfort her. "Didn't I tell you I was going to be around to keep you safe?"

I – know - but," Imogene stuttered out between sobs.

"No, buts," Putney's voice was firm but soft. "I said it, and I meant it. I mean to be around for a long time."

Still whimpering, Imogene said, "I hope so, Nahum. I hope so."

Putney patted her on the back, "Go on now and help Mrs. Dorsey get packed up, y'all are going to leave after dawn, and I need to be gone now."

Imogene kissed him on the cheek and ran to Mary Dorsey. The sun was starting to break in the east when Putney left. He pushed his mule to get to the rise as quickly as possible. Putney knew there was no water between the camp and where he had seen the buffalo, and he wanted as much time as he could give himself to find water. When he got to the rise, he decided to go ahead and ride the mule to the top. It turned out to be a hell of a mistake.

Just as he reached the top of the hill, he saw a line of Indians traveling to the northwest in the distance. Hoping they had not seen him, Putney began to turn the mule back, but it was too late. He heard whooping and hollering coming across the plain. Even though the Indians were distant, Putney knew they could easily outrun his mule. So instead, he kept his right side to Indians, drew the pistol on his left, and let it hang to his side so that they couldn't see it. Putney's father had taught him that there was no fast draw like a gun already in your hand, and he meant to take advantage of that wisdom if necessary.

Putney saw that the Indians had three travoises loaded

with what were probably buffalo carcasses, and women and children were walking beside the loads. That meant he had run into a hunting party, not a war party. But it would have only made a difference if Putney had a dozen more men with him. One lone white man wasn't going to scare these people.

Putney stood his position. The hollering died, and then a single man rode toward him at full speed. Putney waited. He knew he had only one chance, and that was to take this man out with the first shot, so Putney would wait until the Indian was so close that it would be almost impossible to miss. But Putney was wrong again. The rider reined in his horse, came to a complete stop about fifty yards away, threw a spear into the ground, and waited.

Other than fighting Indians and being captured by Quanah, Putney had no further interaction with Indians, so he was not sure what the gesture meant. The man sat on his horse and waited. Putney hoped the man only wanted to parlay, so he holstered his gun and rode slowly toward the Indian. As Putney rode close, he could tell by his clothes that the man waiting for him was Kiowa. Putney stopped when there were a few yards still between the two men. The Indian held up his right hand with the index finger pointing up and the other fingers facing himself. Then he turned his hand around and held up two fingers.

Putney hoped the hand signs meant something like peace or friend, so he mimicked the gesture. The man then patted his chest with an open hand and said something that Putney didn't understand, but he reckoned the Kiowa was introducing himself by saying his name.

Putney decided to introduce himself in the same manner, hoping he was right. Putney patted his own chest and said, "Eka Toyatuku."

Holding his palm up near his mouth and gesturing forward, the man said, "Comanche."

Putney said, "No Comanche. No Kiowa." while shaking his head, hoping the movement was universal.

"I talk white man," The Kiowa said. Then, again, he patted his chest and said, "Leaping Antelope." Then pointing at Putney said, "Eka Toyatuku, I know your name. Brave gray warrior."

Putney nodded his head and said, "Red Panther, yes."

All the while making gestures that Putney did not understand, Leaping Antelope said, "What Eka Toyatuku pay cross Kiowas land?"

Since he didn't have anything, he was willing to part with Putney looked Leaping Antelope in the eyes, "Nothing. Only friendship."

"Not good," returned Leaping Antelope. "You give gun, you cross."

Putney knew this conversation was going downhill fast but decided to stand his ground. "No," he said, "I will not give you a gun. I pass free or return. It makes no difference to me."

Leaping Antelope paused. Putney guessed he was trying to understand what Putney had said. The Kiowa then said, "No pass, no go back. Eka Toyatuku no pay, Eka Toyatuku must fight."

Pointing at all the men that were in the band and shaking his head, Putney said, "There are many Kiowa. Only one Eka Toyatuku. A fight would not be fair."

"Eka Toyatuku fights only me," Leaping Antelope said, patting his chest.

Putney patted his chest and said, "I only have guns, and I do not want to kill Leaping Antelope or anyone else today."

With his palm facing down and then moving his hand

up in an arc, Leaping Antelope said, "Wait." He turned his horse and rode back to the waiting band. He was handed something by one of the other men then he sped back to Putney. The Kiowa had returned with a club in each hand. Leaping Antelope stopped at the spear, held up the clubs, and said, "Choose."

Putney figured out that the Kiowa was challenging him to a duel like jousting he had read about in "Ivanhoe" when he was a boy. Jousting was not a skill Putney possessed, but he knew the Indian did. Putney had read how the Kiowas, the Comanche, and others practiced counting coup with clubs or paddles. Putney was reasonably sure this was a fight he could not win. Putney tried one more attempt to convince Leaping Antelope that he did not want to fight. "I have no cause to fight Leaping Antelope. I will leave in peace."

This time Leaping Antelope was emphatic. "No! You fight Leaping Antelope, or you fight all Kiowa." And he waved one club at the waiting band in the distance.

Understanding that there was no way out of the contest, Putney finally said, "Fine! Give me that one!" he pointed to a club that was not decorated with feathers but studded with hobnails driven into the upper part. No nails were sticking out, but it still looked more dangerous than the one with only feathers. Leaping Antelope tossed the club to Putney and spun his horse around. As he rode back toward the band of expectant Kiowas, he pumped his club up and down and howled. The crowd of spectators answered his whooping. Finally, when he had ridden about a hundred yards from Putney, Leaping Antelope stopped.

Putney suddenly remembered Imogene's dream. "Shit," he said out loud to no one.

Leaping Antelope turned his horse and gave a few more

whoops, then kicked his horse into a gallop, waving his club. Putney didn't know anything to do but to spur the mule as fast as it would go toward the charging Indian. He held his club up and across his chest, hoping to get one good swing.

The two men were moving so they would go past the other's right side. As they passed each other Leaping Antelope swung his club at Putney's head. Putney was able to duck the blow and thought he had faired alright. But Leaping Antelope knew what he was doing and, having missed with a direct impact, had come with a backhand swing of the club. The blow landed in the middle of Putney's back and almost knocked him from the mule.

By the time Putney had gathered his wits and turned his mule, Leaping Antelope was already charging back. Putney knew he needed to change his tactics, or this joust would be over in this pass. This time Putney steered his mule so that he would pass on his attacker's left side. He wasn't sure what to do, but he hoped it would throw the Kiowa off. But Leaping Antelope deftly moved his club to his left hand and held it high. When the two met this time, Leaping Antelope's club made a glancing blow off Putney's left shoulder, but the impact was nothing compared to the one Putney had received in his back. Since the mule was slower than the horse his opponent was riding, Putney was able to turn before the warrior had. Then, with only a flashing moment to think, Putney made a decision.

Kiowas and Comanche had always opted for the faster but smaller ponies over the large but slower breeds. Putney's mule was slow but was much heavier. Nobody had ever trained the mule for combat, and Putney didn't even know if he could get the animal to do what he wanted, but he was going to try. The idea might not work, but Putney figured it might be the only chance he had left. As Leaping Antelope began charging toward him, Putney urged the mule to go as fast as it would. The combatants were again going to pass each other on their rights. Putney waited until the last moment and then reined his animal to his right, causing it to collide directly with the much smaller horse.

The impact threw the pony into the air, knocking it entirely backward. Leaping Antelope went flying off his steed and lost his club. Putney turned the mule quickly. Leaping Antelope was getting to his feet, but his legs were shaky. Putney rode down hard on his opponent, ready to deliver a killing blow. Just as he was about to strike with his club, Leaping Antelope held up both arms crossed over his head. Putney's strike was severe but not enough to penetrate the crossed arms and crush the skull. Leaping Antelope was on his knees when Putney came back around. The Kiowa stood to face his attacker. Putney rode toward the Kiowa but reined in as he got to him. Leaping Antelope's head was bleeding. Putney didn't know if it was from his strike or the Indian's fall from his horse. Putney also saw Leaping Antelope's right arm had a bone protruding just below the elbow, and his left arm was dangling, lifeless at his side. It didn't matter whether Putney had broken the man's collar bone or dislocated his shoulder. Leaping Antelope was defenseless. Putney urged the mule forward at a walk and stopped in front of Leaping Antelope. He dismounted and walked up to the Kiowa with the club in his hand.

Leaping Antelope grunted something in Kiowa that Putney interpreted as "Finish me."

Putney threw his club on the ground. "No," he said. "I told you I did not want to kill anyone today."

"It Eka Toyatuku right," Leaping Antelope told Putney.

"No," Putney spoke with the force of conviction and tapped his chest, "It is the right of Eka Toyatuku to cross

Kiowa land forever! And anyone he is with can cross freely! And I will take your horse. That is as much as your life!"

Leaping Antelope bowed his head. "It is as Eka Toyatuku says." Putney signaled to the band of Kiowa to recover their combatant. Two men rode out with a third horse. Leaping Antelope said something in Kiowa. The two men dismounted and gently lifted Leaping Antelope on a horse. Before they rode away, Leaping Antelope looked Putney in his eyes. "Eka Toyatuku brave warrior," he said. The three men rode back to their band, leaving the Indian Pony behind.

Putney checked over the horse. It had some scrapes and probably some bruises that Putney couldn't see, but there was nothing that wouldn't heal. Then he checked over the mule, petting and complimenting it as he did. Then Putney stood and watched as the band of Kiowa rode away. He watched until they were no longer in sight.

17

P utney rode on for two more hours with the pony
tied behind him, but his shoulder and back were
throbbing so bad he decided to return to the
wagons. As soon as Jack saw Putney coming, he held up the
wagons. Putney rode next to the wagon and explained to
Callahan that he had not located water but would try again
the next day. Jack asked Putney how he had come to have a
horse. "I'll tell you later. Right now, I need to lie in that half
bed in the back of the Dorsey wagon." Putney rode to the
Dorsey wagon and asked if he could lay down in her wagon,
and she granted permission. Tying the animals to the back
of her wagon, Putney asked if she or Eileen had any arnica.
Mary told Imogene to get the box from under the wagon
seat. In a moment, Mary had retrieved a bottle of arnica
cream. Putney removed his shirt and undershirt and asked
Imogene to rub some cream on his back.

SEEING the huge bruises on Putney's back and shoulder,
Imogene shouted, "My God, Nahum! What happened? Did

you fall off your mule?" the anxiety in Imogene's eyes was clearly visible.

"Something like that," Putney replied. "I'll tell you later. Right now, I need some rest."

WHEN IMOGENE HAD APPLIED the ointment, Putney laid face down and instantly fell asleep.

THE IRISH HAD FORMED a square and had a cook fire going before Putney woke. When he crawled out of the wagon, he was pleased and a little proud at how efficient the Irish were becoming out in the wilderness. Having donned his shirts and picked up his guns, Putney walked to one of the camp stools and took a seat. He was still surprised at how tired he was.

IMOGENE WALKED over to Putney and, to show her aggravation with him, placed her hands on her hips and tapped one toe. "Now, are you going to tell me what happened or not?" she demanded.

"GO GET JACK. I only want to tell this once," Putney instructed his half-sized scolder.

WHILE IMOGENE WAS HUNTING for Jack, the women and Erin Callahan had begun to prepare the evening meal and required that Putney move out of the way. "Da, slaughtered another lamb today, Nahum," Erin told him. Erin's beauty suddenly struck Putney. He had been so busy with other tasks he had hardly time to give her but a passing glance. She had Jack's black hair, but it was shinier, like a piece of obsidian and her eyes were the green Putney imagined when Jack would describe Ireland. Even having been out in this prairie sun for so long because she always wore a sun bonnet, her skin was the color of ivory. She was only fifteen. Putney knew that, but girls in the west married at such young ages. He pushed the thought to the back of his head but did not forget it.

IMOGENE RETURNED with Jack and the men that weren't on watch. Everyone gathered around to learn what Putney had to report. "The bad news is I didn't find any water today, so we may need to start rationing," he told them. Of course, everyone clamored to hear the good news. "Well, the good news is that we may have to worry about Comanche or even Cheyenne, but we don't have to worry about Kiowas. At least as soon as the word gets out." Again, everyone wanted to know what he meant, so he held them in suspense no longer and told them of his duel with Leaping Antelope.

After he finished his tale, for a moment, everyone was silent, as if dumbstruck, until Erin spoke up. "Oh, Mr. Putney, you're so brave! I cannot imagine even Finn McCool being as brave as you!" Erin danced to Putney and gave him a peck on the cheek, which caused them both to blush, and everyone laughed. Everyone except for Imogene, who scowled at the Irish teenager.

FINDING he was still tired after eating and not wanting to answer more questions about Leaping Antelope, Putney got his bedroll and spread it under Dorsey's, where he always slept. The arnica had done an excellent job, but he was still sore, so he laid on the unbruised side and was about to fall asleep when Imogene crawled under the wagon. "Is your back still hurting, Nahum?" concern like a mother's was in her voice.

"IT'S NOT SO bad now, Sweetie. Thanks for asking. I'll be fine in the morning," he told her.

"NAHUM?" she asked.

"YES, SWEETIE, WHAT IS IT?" Then, with earnestness in her words, Imogene asked, "Do you love her?"

PUTNEY ROSE UP on one elbow. "Love who," he asked.

IMOGENE BECAME A LITTLE HUFFY. "Erin! You know who I mean!"

"WHAT A NOTION, girl. I hardly know her," it was Putney's turn to scold. "You get that out of your head."

"WELL, she kissed you, didn't she?" Imogene continued her interrogation.

·   ·   ·

"THE POINT IS she kissed me. I didn't kiss her. Now you either go help the women or go to bed."

PUTNEY SOUNDED like her father when he said this. "Yes, sir," she replied. But before leaving, she said, "Nahum, I think you're the bravest man that ever lived." Then she kissed him quickly on the cheek and scurried from under the wagon before he could say anything else.

THE NEXT DAY, Putney rose, ate his breakfast, and saddled a mule. He wouldn't ride the horse until it was good and healed. After his run in with the Kiowa, Putney chose not to take Mark with him. It was, too, dangerous for a novice. He had ridden about four hours when he found a tree-lined creek. *This will be a good place for them to camp and replenish with water*, he thought to himself.

BEFORE HEADING BACK, he crossed the creek and pushed through the trees to see what the next day would have in store for him. On the horizon, he saw a mountain rising from the plain. Rabbit Ears Mountain! "*It has to be*," Putney said to himself. The twin peaks were barely visible at the distance. It was still at least a day's ride, but their destination was nearly at hand. His heart picked up a few beats, and he felt he could hardly wait to get back and tell them.

That afternoon Putney again returned early. When asked why, he only told them there was water ahead, and he wanted to make sure they didn't stop before they got there. They would have the night to boil water and replenish. He didn't tell them what he had discovered.

. . .

THAT NIGHT WAS much like the others. Dinner, a couple of stories, a song or two, and then to bed. In the morning, Jack found the sun was up, and Putney was still sitting by the fire. "You're getting out a little late, aren't you, Nahum," he asked his scout.

"COME WITH ME, Jack. I wanted you to be the first to see it," Putney took Jack by the arm as they splashed through the narrow waters and went through the tree line on the opposite bank. "Look there, Jack," Putney pointed to the mountain in the distance. "A mile or so beyond that should be Seneca Creek, Jack!" Putney could barely contain his excitement.

JACK STOOD in awe at the sight for several minutes, then, taking Putney by the shoulders, said, "That's it, son! That's where we will make our new home!"

IT GRATIFIED Putney that Jack had included him with his words.

18

Seneca Creek was a good size stream. Not near as deep or wide as the Guadalupe or Llano rivers, but it was a good, flowing, constant water source. They had arrived at Seneca with enough light to set up a camp. Putney had found a good-sized bend in the creek and had them set up the wagons in a straight line spanning from bank to bank. That way, they had a barrier on all four sides, larger than they had on the open plains. They also had trees to provide shade in the daytime. They had exceptional lamb stew that night, and music and stories went well into the night.

After breakfast the following morning, Jack called everyone together for a meeting. "First things first," he started. "I want us all to thank young Nahum here for guiding us to this place. Without him, no telling where we would be or even if we would be anywhere at all." All the Irish clapped, and a few whistled and howled. Putney sat with his head down, embarrassed by the adulation, wishing Jack hadn't made a big deal of it. Then Jack called for Putney to say something.

Still embarrassed, Putney rose from his camp stool. "Look," he said, "It was y'all that saved Imogene and me. If we hadn't come across you, it's likely we would be the ones dead by now. I just want to say thank you for letting us join you and being part of your family. Putney sat down while everyone clapped again.

Taking over, Jack asked everyone, "Now, then where do we start?" Everyone started throwing out ideas at once, and Jack held out his hands, motioning for them to calm down, and he would call on them for their thoughts.

Phineas spoke first. "Well, then. I think we should start with building shelters of some sort." Everyone agreed that was a good idea, but when Jack asked what sort of shelters they were to build, none of them seemed to have an opinion. Finally, Jack turned to Putney and asked if he had any thoughts. Putney stood again, saying, "There are plenty of good trees along this creek. There are good-sized cotton-woods and black willows as well as a few Osage orange and others. I would start by felling some of those trees and build one large cabin, big enough for everyone to find shelter in bad weather and against attacks."

All the people wanted to know how long it would take to build a cabin. William said he knew how to build a stone house but not a log cabin. He also could do a thatch roof. "I've never built one, but I've seen plenty, and I don't think it will be too hard," Putney told them. "But I don't think a thatch roof is a good idea. Too easy to burn, and Indians nor outlaws are not above that. No, I think you should also make the roof out of logs, but smaller ones."

"Alright, then," said Jack. "What's next?"

Sinead spoke up. "We need to get some things planted. Potatoes and onions and such. We also have some seeds for other vegetables, and we need to get started, so we have something other than mutton to eat during the winter."

Again, everyone agreed. "We are going to need other supplies, too," Margaret Fitzgerald said.

"Aye, we are," said Jack. "But let's put that to the side for a bit. Does everyone agree that shelter and planting are the most important to work on for the time? Is there anything else we need right now?"

It was Putney's turn to speak out. "You need to build a good sturdy corral for the animals. It needs to be something the animals can't easily bust and outlaws and Indians can't pull down without some effort. Otherwise, before you know it, these animals will be gone."

"Good thinking, boy," said Jack. "Alright, then, the women and small children will find a good place to plant, clear it out, and get started. Nothing too large, mind. Just big enough to see us through this winter. But let's figure out where we will be building the cabin and corral because we want to plant nearby."

"I say we find another bend in the stream, like this one, and build there. To give us the same protection and all," suggested William.

"That's good, thinking," agreed Jack. "You and Nahum find us a good place. Alan, you, and Brendan watch the sheep. Me and me boys and Phineas will start cutting some of these large trees."

The men got to work on the heavy labor. The women divided into three groups. Brigid and Sinead began unpacking wagons to get to the potatoes they had saved for seed, the various vegetable seeds they had, and prepare onions for planting. With the two youngest girls, Eileen and Mary began preparing a mid-day meal. They knew everyone would be hungry after their hard work. Erin,

Alanis, and Imogene were assigned to boil water and fill the kegs.

William found another bend in the creek about two hundred yards upstream from the camp.

Stepping it off for measurement, they agreed it would be large enough for a twenty by thirty cabin, a large corral to hold all the animals on one side, and a nice sunny area for the vegetables in the front. They reported back to Jack, and he said they would need a fireplace and chimney.

Putney suggested that he and William take one wagon to the mountain. He said rock would be plentiful there and river rocks were apt to explode when heated. Jack gave them the assignment.

Every morning Jack would pass out work assignments, and the Irish jumped to their jobs happily. The women cleared a place for the planting, and the men chopped or sawed trees. When they finished the planting, the women helped by removing the limbs and branches off the larger trees. Sometimes the women would watch the sheep so the boys could help haul wood or stones. None of them ever complained about their task being more difficult than another's or about the work at all. One day Putney asked Jack how they could all be so happy when the work was so grueling. "It's like this," Jack told him, "Back in Ireland, all our work profited only the squires. We got precious little for our labors. Then they started the evictions. We didn't own our homes. We lived at the will of those that lorded over us. Here, we own the land. We are our own masters, and we are building something for ourselves. Whether we get rich or we go bust, it is up to us. That is what is so great about this land." Putney had never felt that sort of oppression and thought to himself that these people had been little better off than the black slaves before the war.

Each day was a repeat of the one before, hard work and plenty of it. At night they would have a good meal and sometimes have a little music, but most would retire early to get up the next day and continue the work. The younger people would sometimes stay up a little longer, telling ghost stories or other sorts of tall tales. Putney would be among them and tell them stories of Daniel Boone, Davy Crockett, Big Foot Wallace, or other frontiersmen.

As the campfire would start to dim, Putney would find a reason to sit and talk with Erin. The two became close quickly, even at the disapproval of Imogene. Putney was growing more and more fond of Erin. But more, Putney had grown fond of the entire group. They became like a family. Like the one, he hadn't had in over ten years He had lived with the McKinneys, after his family's deaths, and they had treated him well, and Putney had become reasonably well to do because of T. J.s investments and buying Putney's parent's ranch before he had to join the Army. But they were more like caretakers. They never felt like family. Putney would never have thought about raising sheep, but now here he was. There was a peace and calm he hadn't felt in years.

Putney had drawn up plans for the cabin. He made sure they understood that it was necessary to have two doors, front, and back. He told them they needed to find some oak or elm for the doors. "No windows," Putney had said. Only gun ports in the shape of crosses. At least two on every side." Putney showed them how to cut notches in the tree trunks so that they would fit as tight as possible against each other. Then the cracks needed to be filled in with a mixture of mud and grass. Finally, thinking about how winters might be, Jack and William decided to build a fireplace on each end of the cabin.

One morning Jack and Sinead took Putney aside and

told him they were worried about their supplies running low. Putney said he had recognized the problem as well, and he had wanted to talk to them about something as well. "I have money in the Galveston Commercial Bank," Putney confided to the couple. "The last I checked, it was one of the only Texas banks that hadn't failed during the war. I could go to Santa Fe and send a telegram to the bank. If my money is still there, I could buy all the supplies y'all need." Jack began to protest, but Putney stopped him. "Jack, all of you have become like family to me, and I would like to use that money to invest in your sheep ranch. I want to make my home here. With y'all."

"We would certainly welcome you, Nahum," Jack told Putney. "But you've done a great deal for us already. We wouldn't want to take money from you as well."

"You won't be taking money from me. You can't take what I freely give," Putney argued. "In return, I'll be getting a real home. Something I haven't had in years."

"Well, done then," agreed Jack. "But what if there is no money in the bank?"

"That won't be a problem," Putney assured him. "When I sold my parent's ranch, I got all the money in gold and silver that I have locked away in a safe deposit box in San Antonio. It would take a little longer to get. I would have to get a wire to T. J. McKinney. He has my key and would have to get the money for me. The point is I have the money."

"Well, if we had known we were traveling with a tycoon, we would have just gone to San Antonio," Jack laughed hard at his own jest.

Putney laughed, too, then said, "I can prepare to leave today. I think it will take about a week to get there and a few days to get the money transferred and supplies. Then it will take another week to return. You think you can last that long?"

"Oh, sure, what else are we going to do?" Jack was pragmatic.

"There is one last thing I would like to ask of you and you, too, Sinead," Putney's voice was solemn.

"Well, ask it, Nahum," Sinead Callahan told him.

"I know there is no preacher or anything out here, but y'all have a bible to record things in, right?" Putney asked.

"Yes," Sinead wondered why he was asking.

"Well, when I return, I would like your permission to marry Erin," said Putney.

"Saints be praised!" exclaimed Sinead. "If you only knew how many times she has asked me if I thought you might want her for a wife! She has worried the daylights out of me!"

"By Saint Patrick's beard, son! It would be our honor!" Jack was as excited as his wife. "But I think you should be asking her before you leave."

"You can bet I will," Putney could not remember a time he had been happier. "And I will do it right now!"

"Well, you be sure and let us know what she says," Jack told Putney. "Meanwhile, we will make a list of what we need. I'm sure you will add some things. And I'll give you some money for your trip to tide you over until you can get that from your bank."

Putney left right away to find Erin. He took her a little piece away from the camp. At first, he hemmed and hawed, but after some coaxing from Erin, he finally came out and said, "I'm going to Santa Fe to buy some materials and supplies," he told the girl. "I've talked to your mother and father, and they said when I return if it's alright with you, we could get married."

She let out such a squeal of delight that Putney would have sworn they had heard it all the way to Uvalde County, Texas. "From that outburst," said Putney, "I doubt the others won't be figuring things out for themselves, but don't say anything until I talk to Imogene. I think she may take it hard."

"Of course not, darling," Erin told him, and she grabbed him around the neck and gave him a long hard kiss.

It was too late. Imogene, Alanis, and Caitlin had been lying under a wagon watching them. When Imogene saw Erin kiss Putney, she ran away, crying. Putney looked for Imogene for quite a while before finding her sitting by the creek, sobbing into her folded arms.

"There you are," said Putney. "I've been looking all over for you."

"I don't want to talk to you!" she yelled at him.

Putney sat beside her, picked up a pebble, and tossed it in the stream. "I guess you figured things out," he said.

Imogene looked up at him with red eyes. "You said you didn't love her! You lied."

"No, I didn't, sweetie, not really," Putney explained. "When you asked me, I didn't. But over time, I did fall in love with her. But it doesn't change what I feel for you. You will always be my sweetie."

Imogene unfolded her arms, balled her little fist up, and swinging as hard as she could, hit Putney on his arm. "I hate you!" she yelled, then buried her face in his chest.

Putney let her cry herself out.

Finally, she looked up at him, her little face was red, and her hair had matted with tears. "I don't really hate you, Nahum. I love you."

"I know, sweetie, I know."

19

P utney wanted to go over some things with Jack, so it was mid-morning before he left for Santa Fe. "I'm only taking one pistol, Jack," he had told his soon-to-be father-in-law. "I'm going to head north first and see if I can hit the Santa Fe Trail and maybe meet up with a train of pilgrims or traders. It ought to be pretty safe on the trail, so I'm not going to need more than one gun. Hopefully, you won't have any need for any, but an extra won't hurt." Jack told him he appreciated the offer. "The walls are nearly high enough to start the roof on the cabin. If anyone happens by, make sure everyone gets behind the walls. There's a thicket down by the creek. If anything starts, tell the women and children to go there and hide.

He then went to check on Imogene. "Are you going to be alright, sweetie? Putney asked her.

"I think so, Nahum," she said, her voice still had a twinge of anger. "It wouldn't hurt any if you promised to bring me some candy when you come back."

The comment brought memories of when his sisters had asked him to bring back rock candy and peppermints from Uvalde the day before Comanches killed them. It was all he could do to keep from crying. "Sure, I will, sweetie," he said.

Putney then found Erin in the camp. All the women and girls had surrounded her and congratulated her on her upcoming marriage. Putney almost had to drag her away from the clutch of women. They walked to where he had tied up the pony he had won from Leaping Antelope. "Please be careful, Nahum," Erin had begged him. "Come back as quick as you can. I will be on pins and needles until you return."

"Nothing could keep me away one minute longer than I have to," Putney assured her. Then, the two kissed, and Putney told her, "You take care, and take care of Imogene, too." Erin assured him that she would look after Imogene like her own sister.

The two walked back to the camp where Jack and Sinead met them. Jack gave him a list of what he and the others thought they needed and fifty dollars. "That's more than I'm going to need," Putney told Jack.

"You take it," said Jack, then asked, "What are we going to spend it on out here?"

As Putney stepped into the stirrup, Erin pulled him back down and gave him one more long kiss. Putney was a little embarrassed she had done that before her parents, but then kissed her back one last time. Putney crossed north over the creek and headed to where he hoped he would find the Santa Fe Trail. Putney looked back once to see everyone waving at him. He gave a big wave of his hat and spurred the pony northwest.

Putney slowed his pace after getting out of sight of the group of immigrants. He figured the horse was used to hard riding, but there was no need to wear it out, it might be some time before he found water, and he had days to go before he reached his destination.

It was two o'clock when Putney spotted dust ahead of him. That must be the trail and a train traveling one way or the other. Putney hurried his pony until he he could see what was making the dust. Sure, enough, it was a wagon train, and it was headed west.

Putney sped his horse so he could overtake the train, but slowly. He didn't want to ride in full steam and be mistaken and get shot for his effort. When he was about half a mile from the wagons, a rider on a black horse at the train's rear rode fast to the front. Putney could just make out that two men were talking. The man on the black horse kept his position, and the other man on a big roan came galloping toward him. Putney stopped and waited. He didn't want to give the man coming at him any cause to do something rash.

As the rider came nearer, Putney could see that not only was the horse big, but the man was also large. When the big man got within fifty yards of Putney, he called out, "Who are you, and what the hell do you want?"

"My name is Nahum Putney, and I mean no harm. I'm just hoping to tag along to Santa Fe." Putney hollered back.

"Nahum Putney?" returned the big man. "Are you any kin to Charlie Putney?"

Putney answered back, "He was my father!"

"Well, I'll be God damned!" the man on the big roan hollered and started walking his horse toward Putney. "I knew your father well." He said as he got nearer.

Putney could see the man was big and tall. He was probably four or five inches taller than him, which would put him at about six feet, seven inches. Even though the man was older, Putney guessed who he was. "Are you Bigfoot Wallace?" Putney called out.

"That's right, boy. William A. A. Wallace. A legend in my own mind." The big man gave a hardy laugh as he rode up to Putney. "By God, you look like your mother, except you have your pa's red hair!" Wallace reached over and nearly pulled Putney off his horse to give him a hug. Then, releasing him, Wallace said, "I was mighty sorrowful to learn what happened to your family. I scoured that part of the country for three weeks looking for those bastards, but they were mighty slick. I never found hide nor hair of them. I'd have scalped 'em all if I had!"

Putney didn't know what to say except thank you. Wallace then asked, "What in the world are you doing out here? You're a long way from Uvalde, or did you already know that?"

"It's a long story, Mr. Wallace, and I would rather tell it over a cup of coffee tonight," answered Putney.

"Hell, yes, boy. And a spot of demon rum to boot. C'mon," Wallace turned his horse back to the wagons, then called over his shoulder, "And Mr. Wallace was my daddy. You just call me Bill."

That night, when all the wagons had circled, and the people made camp, Wallace gathered some of his hands around. "Boy's, I want y'all to meet Nahum Putney, son of the damnedest Scotsman I ever rode with in the Rangers. Of course, I only rode with one." Wallace gave out a roar of laughter, and all his hands roared, too. "Come over here, Putney, and get a piece of this beef steak, then tell us your tale."

It had been weeks since Putney tasted beef. He had eaten mutton for so long that he had almost forgotten how beef tasted. And it tasted good. Between bites, Putney told those gathered how he had joined the Mounted Mountain Rangers and what had happened to him and Imogene.

When he finished, Wallace bellowed out, "Boys, when we get this train to Santa Fe, I'm going back to Texas just so I can find Captain Montague Russell and kill him myself," Putney felt like he meant it.

It was good to ride along with a friend of his father's. Wallace told him many stories about their days as Rangers and then about his days during the war. "Damn stupidest thing I ever done." He would repeat several times during the trip.

Wallace drove the train hard but no faster than could be tolerated by the people and the equipment. On the evening of their fifth day, they were on the hills overlooking the old town of Santa Fe. Wallace told Putney that this was as far as he was taking this group. Some were headed to southern New Mexico, while others were going to Arizona and California. He said they would have to find other guides because he was returning to Fort Dodge. He said he might start buffalo hunting, but he wasn't sure.

The following morning, Wallace told Putney to meet him at the Cantina del Canyon for a meal and some drinks when he was through with his business. Putney said he would. "By the way, Putney," said Wallace before they departed company, "The Army post in Santa Fe has a registry of folks that have lost family members to Indians. You should check there and see if that girl has any family looking for her. She don't need to be out in that wild country if she does. For that matter them Irishmen don't have no business being out there either. Too damn many Indians and outlaws. And that's not even talking about cattlemen that are free-ranging out there. They ain't likely to take kindly to sheep herders."

Putney said he would check with the registry and tell the others what Bigfoot had advised. The first thing Putney did

when he got into the town was to seek out a bank until he
found one that would accept a transfer from his bank in
Galveston. The president at the Stock Growers Bank said
they would extend him credit upon receiving a telegram
from Galveston if he left a deposit of one thousand dollars
from which they could draw interest until the actual money
arrived. His next task was to find the telegraph office and
send a telegram to the Commercial Bank in Galveston. He
asked his bank to wire the Stock Growers Bank that it held
his money and to send him three thousand dollars. Putney
added the account number and the password the bank president had given him. He told the telegrapher he would stop
by later in the day to see if there was a reply. His next stop
was a boarding house where he got a room at a dollar a day.

With time left on his hands, Putney went to a livery to
stable his horse and see about hiring some wagons and
teamsters to drive them. The livery owner said he had three
wagons for hire, but Putney could arrange for the drivers.
The wagons and mules would cost seven dollars a day, plus
feed, upfront, but Putney would have to deal with the
drivers on their wages.

From the livery, Putney went to a gun shop to look at the
weapons available. Then Putney visited various stores and
shops to arrange for provisions. He wanted to arrange as
much as possible so he could return to the Irish settlement,
quickly.

Putney sought out the territorial land office. He showed
a clerk the copy of the plat map Callahan had given him and
asked exactly where the land was. The clerk copied
numbers from the map, went to a cabinet with several small
drawers, and searched through the file cards. Then,
selecting one, he looked in another cabinet with long flat
drawers. Searching there, he pulled out a surveyor's map.

At last, the clerk went to a map of New Mexico territory covering an entire wall. After studying the map, the clerk called Putney over and showed him exactly where the property was located. Putney had been lucky because he had guided the immigrants to the eastern portion of the property grant. "I can get you a map that shows the exact position of the property for three dollars," the clerk told him. "That ought to convince skeptics about the land. But, of course, you're going to need to hire a surveyor to stake it out." Putney paid the man and said he would return. The clerk gave him a list of certified surveyors he could use.

Finally, Putney went into a small general store to buy some tobacco and rolling papers. The man behind the counter turned to the shelf behind him and got the items. "You know most men smoke cigars or pipes. I don't get many sales for cigarette tobacco. But before you get this tobacco, do you think I could interest you in this?" He reached under the counter and pulled out three square packets. "These are Kinney Ready Rolled Cigarettes, specially made in New York. There are twenty cigarettes in each packet. And I have this nice tin case you can put ten at a time in to keep them from getting crushed." The cigarettes were more costly than a bag of tobacco and papers, but they appealed to Putney, so he bought all three packs, the case, and the loose tobacco and papers.

Putney stepped outside, removed the outer wrapper from a pack of Kinneys, removed a cigarette, and lit it. He liked the milder tobacco, and the more fragrant smell. He decided to only smoke these when they were available.

He returned to the telegraph office an hour before the bank closed. The clerk handed him a sealed envelope. "Just got this in a few minutes ago," said the clerk. "I got another that I just sent to the Stock Growers Bank. Hope it's good news." Putney told the clerk he hoped the news was good also and thanked him.

Putney walked outside and opened the envelope. It was good news; the bank was arranging to send the requested money and had sent a separate telegram to the Santa Fe bank authorizing a line of credit for Putney that would be satisfied when the cash arrived. Putney went directly to the bank.

He was thrilled that the process was moving so quickly. He would be able to buy the supplies he needed the next day and have the wagons loaded and ready by the following. The bank manager said they had received the telegram authorizing the credit, and funds were available to Putney. He didn't want to carry wads of cash with him until he had secured the supplies and services he needed, so he only withdrew three hundred dollars for some personal necessities. Putney thanked the manager, saying he would return when he had matters lined out.

Putney needed clothes that fit him, so leaving the bank, he went straight to a men's clothier he had seen earlier. For his wedding day, he purchased a blue suit, vest, frock coat, and two white shirts. Putney added two twill bib-front shirts and two pairs of corduroy pants for everyday wear. Along with underwear, he finished off with a pair of high shank boots and a Stetson hat made of good beaver felt that was called Boss of the Plains.

Next, Putney went to one of the gun shops he had been in earlier. The shop had two French-made revolvers. These were cartridges pistols similar to the Belgian pistol he had lost to Quanah. They were expensive, but in addition to the firearms, Putney could get a cartridge belt, two holsters, and three boxes of cartridges for one hundred dollars. He paid another ten for a well-made Bowie knife with sheath.

Putney was pleased with his purchases. Like the cigarettes, they fit his vanity.

He toted all his purchases to the boarding house, where he asked if it was possible to get a bath. The bath was available and would be filled and ready when he came down from his room. When he had finished bathing and dressing, he looked at his reflection in the mirror of the dressing table in his room. It felt good to be out of borrowed clothes. Then, he left to meet Bigfoot Wallace at the cantina.

Standing at the bar, Wallace noticed Putney as he entered. "Why look there, gentlemen," he announced to the men in the room. "Yonder is Nahum Putney. The damnedest Indian fighter to ride the Texas and New Mexico plains!" The boast embarrassed Putney because he surely didn't deserve the accolade. Several other men gathered around to pat him on his back or shake his hand. There was no telling what outrageous things the old Ranger had said about him, but Putney took it in good stride. After a drink of whiskey with Wallace, the two men sat at a table and ordered a meal with tamales, enchiladas, and frijoles.

During the meal, Putney told Wallace that he had been able to get the credit he needed to buy the supplies he would take back to Jack and the others. Putney told him he wanted to return to the Irish as soon as possible.

"I tell you what, boy," said Wallace. "I'll meet you first thing in the morning, and we'll start gathering up what you need. Two men can work faster than one. You gather the dry goods and such, and I'll get those horses and tack you need. I'm well known around here, and I can get these old misers down on their prices a bit."

"Thanks, Bill," Putney told him. "I already lined up some wagons, but if you could get me three good skinners, I would appreciate it."

"Anything for Charlie Putney's son!" Wallace patted him on the back. "And on top of that, I'm gonna ride back with you. I want to meet these people. But mostly, I want to meet this pretty young gal you're gonna tie yourself to. If she's half as pretty as your ma was, she'll be a stunner!"

Putney reddened a little at Wallace's crass way of speaking of his mother and Erin. He knew the old frontiersman meant it as a compliment, but it still rose his hackles. He thought that if his mother had heard Wallace talking like that, she would have boxed his ears. But Putney let it go. It was good to have a friend like Bigfoot Wallace.

The following day the two men met at the Stock Growers Bank, where Putney withdrew twelve hundred dollars. Wallace told Putney that when he had deals made for the horses, he would find Putney so he could settle up. Putney went to the largest general store in town and went on a shopping spree. He had never bought so much at one time: clothes, blankets, tools, a single shovel plow, two cook stoves, fresh vegetables, dried beans, canned and dried vegetables, and fruits, six hens, two roosters, three kegs each of salted beef and pork, several slabs of bacon, some hams, canvas tarps, a tent and bed and wood stove for him and Erin, and candy for the youngsters. The list seemed to go on and on. When he finished, he paid up. Putney didn't think the store owner and his wife would ever quit smiling. Putney said he wanted everything crated up and ready to be picked up the next morning. The store owner was happy to comply.

When he had finished at the general store, Putney went to three gun shops and ended up with two Sharps repeating carbines, a Henry repeating rifle, six Colt revolvers, and ammunition for them all. He told each shop owner he would be by in the morning.

Bigfoot had caught up with him at the last gun store. He had made a deal on two saddle broke mares and a stallion, plus saddles and tack for five hundred dollars." Putney couldn't believe he had made such good bargain. I also got you three good teamsters for those wagons at two dollars a day, plus grub. And I got something else for you, Putney," Wallace told him. "Meet me outside when you finish here," Putney said he would and finished up his purchases.

Outside Wallace was standing talking to two Mexican vaqueros. When Putney walked up, Bigfoot said, "Putney, I want you to meet the Mendez brothers, Javier and Jesus Mendez." Putney shook the hands of both men, and Wallace continued. "From what you told me about those immigrants, I figured they could use some extra help. These boys worked herding goats for their father when they were young. They're top cow hands and know their way around a gun. So if you think you could use them, they agreed they could work for you for six months. And only twenty-five dollars a month. Each, of course."

"I don't know, Bill," Putney said. "I didn't discuss this with Jack."

"Don't worry," Wallace said. "I told them that might be the case. But they said they weren't doing nothing right now and would just ride out and take a look-see. I can vouch for 'em. They worked for me a few times. They're good men."

"Well, if they want to come along, I won't stop them," Putney said. "Welcome, men."

"Gracias," they both said.

"I'm hungry," announced Wallace. "Let's head over to the cantina."

"I have one more stop to make, and I'll meet y'all over there," he told the trio.

The men parted ways, and Putney headed to a dress

shop he had passed a couple of times. He stopped and looked in the window at the dress on display. It was white with little blue birds embroidered on it. It had a high collar with a little ruff at the top and long sleeves to match. When he entered the shop, a prim little woman greeted him. "Yes, sir. What can I do for you?"

"That dress in the window. I want to buy it." he told her.

"That dress is all silk, sir. It's a bit expensive," Putney thought she was a bit haughty.

"What do you consider expensive, ma'am?" Putney asked.

"Well," her voice was nasally. "That dress with a matching hat and parasol is thirty dollars."

"Can you wrap it up and send it over to my room?" Putney pulled what remained of his cash from a pocket and peeled off thirty dollars.

"Certainly, sir." She was no longer haughty or nasally. Putney wrote where he was staying on a receipt book and left the shop. Outside, he lit one of the Kinney's and inhaled deeply. *That's a good day's work,* he thought. *Erin will be beautiful in that dress.*

Putney was at the livery early the next morning and already had his horse saddled when Wallace and the Mendez brothers showed up. The livery owner came from the back and brought with him three burly men. "Here's your skinners Mr. Wallace. They got the wagons hitched up and ready to move." He said. Putney went and met the men and told them to meet him at the general store.

They were loaded and ready at the store by nine in the morning. Putney had one wagon follow him to the gun shops and told the others to meet him on the east side of town. After picking up the guns and ammunition, Putney stopped at the bank and withdrew another four hundred dollars. He wanted to ensure he had enough to pay the Mendez brothers if Jack wanted to take them on. Putney told the teamster to drive on and that he would catch up to them.

He had one last errand to run. So Putney rode out to Fort Marcy. Stopping at the sentry post, Putney asked where he could find the registry of people looking for their kinfolk that Indians had captured. "Over at the Post Liaison Office," the soldier told him. "You'll have to leave your pistols and that big knife here. People get kind of upset over there. We had one shoot a civilian clerk two months back." Putney handed over his guns and knife. The soldier wrote out a chit for the weapons and then pointed out where Putney should go.

Putney walked through the office door to find a corporal standing behind a counter opposite a man and woman. He was trying to explain that they didn't have any captives there at the time and that the fort would be notified by telegraph if their daughter was recovered. Then he told the couple if they were staying in Santa Fe to write down the name of their hotel. If any news came in, he would get a message to them.

As the couple walked past Putney, the man was trying to console the crying woman. "Mister, like I told that couple, we ain't got nobody here right now. If you sent in a name, it would be on one of the posters hanging on the wall." Putney thanked him and turned to the wall the corporal had indi-cated. Tacked on the wall were several rosters, each one with a large label above it, showing the state where a person was captured. Under the one labeled "Texas," several papers were tacked together. He scanned the pages one by one. On the third paper listed as number 7 was "Foster, Imogene – 13 years old – Weatherford, Texas – Parents dead." Under that was another line that read, "Relative – Uncle-Foster, Benjamin-McKinney, Texas.

Putney turned back to the counter. The corporal looked up from a logbook he had been writing in. "You have one named Imogene Foster on the Texas list," he told the soldier.

The soldier, making his boredom obvious, reached under the counter and pulled out another logbook labeled "Texas" "Foster, you say," muttered the corporal as he ran his finger down the entries in the book. Then, finally, he turned the page and said. "Yeah," he said. Imogene Foster. If you're her uncle, like I said, we ain't got nobody here."

"I'm not her uncle," Putney said. "I know where she is."

That perked the corporal's interest. "Oh, you do? You got her here?" he asked.

"No," said Putney, "But I know where she is. She's safe. If you give me her uncle's address, I will write and tell him where she is."

"It's illegal to ask a ransom," the corporal's voice had lowered. "But I could let you look at the logbook if..." then he tapped his finger on the counter. Putney gave the soldier a disgusted look but reached in his pocket, pulled out a silver dollar, and laid it on the counter. The coin disappeared with the speed of a conjurer's trick. The corporal turned the log around. Imogene's name and her uncle's name and address were the only entries on the page. Putney tore the page out of the book. "Hey! Mister, you can't do that!" barked the corporal. Reaching his pocket, Putney produced another dollar and flipped it over the counter, aiming for the back wall.

20

By ten-thirty, they were rolling west. The teamsters said they knew another route to the area that could cut a day off their trip, so Putney let them lead the way. The men spent four days on the trail when they spotted Rabbit Ears Mountain in the distance. On the morning of the fifth day, Putney was anxious to return to his friends. But he was even more anxious to see Erin and Imogene. As soon as he had wolfed down breakfast, he told Bigfoot that he didn't want to go at the pace of the wagons and was going to ride ahead. "You get on in there and give that pretty girl a kiss," Wallace told him "We will find you in late afternoon."

Putney wasn't exactly sure how far the settlement was, but he reckoned it to be about thirty miles. He relied on his hopes that the Indian pony was used to long rides at a steady pace and figured he could make it there by noon. Putney spurred the pony to a canter and rode steady all morning. It was eleven o'clock when he came across a small stream and decided to let his horse take a short break and get some water. Putney himself was taking a drink from his canteen when sounds came across the valley that sounded like gunfire. He strained to see if he heard anything else or had just imagined it. There it was again, and it wasn't his imagination. A gun battle was going on, and it couldn't be anywhere but the Irish settlement. He pulled the horse's head out of the water and spurred it towards the horizon. His senses were on alert, and he kept a strong eye on his destination. Then in the distance, he saw a pillar of black smoke rising and heard more shots. Putney slapped the pony with his reins to urge it to run faster.

He first saw the white shape of the sheep herd and thought the sheep were too far out from the camp. Thundering down on the flock, it split in two, like the Red Sea, and he rode through. Riding faster, he passed a half dozen dead and bloody sheep. Just past them was a man or boy lying face down on the ground. He pulled the horse up hard and, hanging on to the reins, jumped off just as he approached the figure. It was Alan Gallagher, dead, shot twice in the back. Putney jumped back on the horse and, this time, spurred it hard. In about a hundred yards, he saw Matthew Callahan sitting in the grass. Jumping off his horse again, Putney grabbed the boy by the shoulders. "Are you shot?" he didn't know why he was yelling.

"In the leg," the boy was crying. Putney looked at the wound and saw he was shot in the thigh. He pulled the large scarf from around his neck, wrapped it around Matthew's leg above the wound, tied it tight, then slipped the handle of his knife under the scarf and gave it a full twist. "What happened, Matt?" Putney's volume had dropped.

"Bandits, Nahum!" said young Callahan. "They just came riding at us, shooting the sheep. We tried running, and they shot Alan, I looked back, and he was lying on the ground, so I kept running, and that's when they shot me. I fell, too, and

I guess they thought I was dead because they just kept riding."

"Keep that bandana tight to keep from losing more blood," he ordered the boy. "I or somebody will be back as soon as possible."

Putney didn't wait for a response but jumped back on the pony and, slapping it hard, pushed it toward the camp. There was no more shooting, but the smoke had gotten thicker and darker. Putney was shocked at the sight when he arrived at the settlement. Margaret Fitzgerald was sitting on the ground, slumped over her dead husband as she cradled him. Blood oozed from a bullet hole in her head. She was dead. Mary Dorsey had been stripped down to the waist and was wandering aimlessly. Eileen Gallagher lay with a bullet hole in her head and a pistol in her hand.

Putney could not see anyone else. He leapt off the pony and yelled for Erin and Imogene. "Over here, Nahum! Over here!" he heard Sinead calling mid-way between the camp and the half-built cabin. Running to her, she fell in his arms, crying. Putney asked where Erin and Imogene were. All Sinead could do was point toward the cabin.

Putney rushed to the cabin to find a body lying just outside of it. The man was wearing a brown slicker. As he entered the cabin, there was the body of another slickered man.. Leaning up against one wall was the body of Jack Callahan, riddled with bullet holes. Standing in the middle of the cabin, Imogene stood with the big Walker pistol hanging in her hand. She was standing over a blanket-covered figure. "Imogene," Putney's voice was almost a whisper.

The girl looked up, and when she saw him, she burst into tears and dropped the gun. Imogene ran to Putney and threw her arms around his waist. "I stopped him, Nahum," she said over and over.

Putney knelt and, looking her in the eyes, asked, "Stopped who, sweetie?"

Imogene pointed out the door at the dead man next to it. "You did good, sweetie," he tried comforting her.

"No!" screamed Imogene. "I didn't stop him soon enough!" She began bawling uncontrollably.

Putney held the young girl tightly, telling her she was alright and smoothing her hair. Her sobs finally subsided enough Putney could ask her. "Where's Erin?"

Her chest heaved, and the sobs began coming faster again as she pointed to the blanket-covered figure. "I'm sorry, Nahum. I wasn't soon enough," Imogene's voice was hoarse from the crying.

Catching some movement from the corner of his eye, Putney spun, pulling a pistol. Brigid Forsythe stood stark still. Putney saw her dress had a torn sleeve. Putney apologized, holstered his gun, and gently handed Imogene over to Brigid. Then he stepped over to the blanket and pulled back a corner. There, with her throat cut, lay Erin Callahan. Putney covered the girl's face, stood, and walked out of the cabin. The massacre was over, and there was nothing he could do about it. Despondent, Putney leaned against the wall, pulled out the tin case, lit a cigarette, and blew out a plume of smoke.

It was then Putney heard a woman scream. He couldn't tell which one. Putney pulled a pistol and looked up, then saw Bigfoot Wallace and one of the Mendez brothers riding in, fast. Putney realized the scream had come from Brigid, so he reached out and took her hand. "Don't worry," he told her calmly. "They're friends."

Wallace and Javier Mendez stepped off their horses and

came over to Putney. "What the hell happened here?" asked the big man.

Putney just shook his head.

Putney didn't know how much time had passed when he felt the big man shaking him. "Snap out of it, son!" Wallace was telling him. "These people need our help." There was some more shaking again. "Snap out of it, you hear!"

Putney blinked a few times and looked around, but nothing had changed. It was all still there. The carnage had not disappeared. He knew it sounded stupid, but he said, "What do you mean?"

"C'mon, boy," Bigfoot put a massive paw on Putney's shoulder. "I got a pint of whiskey in my bag. You could use some. So could I, for that matter."

Putney let the giant guide him to a horse and then found himself taking a big gulp of whiskey straight from the bottle. Putney felt his senses coming back, and he took another swig. Putney looked around again. He saw Jesus walking his horse with Matthew hanging on in the saddle. Sinead had seen them and ran to her son. Looking down, Putney saw that Imogene had followed him and Wallace out to the horse. Putney picked her up and hugged her again, saying, "I'm sorry, sweetie. I should never have left y'all alone."

There was a short scream, and then Putney heard Brigid calling, "Nahum! Nahum, come quickly! This one is still alive!"

Putney put Imogene down, and both he and Wallace ran to the cabin. The bandit laying inside had rolled over and was groaning. When he saw Putney and Wallace, he tried to go for a gun, but there wasn't one in his holster. However, a pistol lay nearby, and Putney quickly kicked it away. The man groaned again, then said, "Help me, mister, I think I'm done for."

Putney pulled a pistol and said, "I'll help you, you son of a bitch! I'll help you straight to hell!"

Wallace grabbed his arm before Putney could pull the hammer back. "Hold on there, boy," he said. "We're gonna need this guy to do some talkin before we put him out of his misery." Javier and Jesus had come to the cabin on the heels of Putney and Wallace. "Boys, y'all drag this dog over in a corner and see if you can patch him up any. But don't let him get too comfortable." Wallace then took Putney by the arm and dragged him outside. "Look here, Putney. I know you're madderin a rabid dog, but you gotta start thinking. That man in there knows who done this, and we need to keep him alive so he can tell us. Understand?"

"Yeah, yes, I do," stammered Putney

"Alright, these folk need you more than they need me." Wallace directed him. "You get the ones walking around to settle down somewhere and tell you where everybody else is. I'm gonna drag that burning wagon out of the way before it catches them others on fire."

Putney looked around and saw Mary Dorsey still bumbling around half-naked. He hurried over to his pony, took his roll off the saddle, and unfurled it. He took his slicker out, caught up with Mary, covered her with the coat, guided her back to the camp area, and sat her down on a stool. That was when he heard some rattling in the brush. he quickly turned, gun in hand. But there was no danger. It was Phineas, and he was hurt. Putney felt a tug on his arm. It was Imogene. he hadn't noticed she was still following him around. "I'll take care of Mrs. Dorsey," she told Putney. "You go get Mr. Forsythe."

Phineas was on his knees when Putney got to him. He helped the man to his feet and saw he was bleeding from the shoulder. Putney helped him to the fire and sat him on a stool near Mary. Putney tore away the shirt sleeve and saw that Phineas had a bullet wound in the fleshy part of the chest just under his arm. The bullet had gone through, but it ripped Phineas up good. He was lucky it hadn't hit an artery because he probably would have bled out. Still, he was bleeding badly. Putney pushed the shirt sleeve into the wound to slow the bleeding, and Phineas gave out a howl from the pain. Putney found a knife with the cooking utensils and put it in what little of the campfire was still burning. Using his hat, he fanned the fire up and grabbed some more wood, and got it roaring as quickly as he could. When Putney thought it was ready, he pulled the knife out and turned to Phineas. "This is going to hurt like hell, but I have to do it," he told Phineas and, without waiting for a response, pulled the rag out and stuck the hot knife to the wound. Phineas tried to pull away, but Putney held on tight until he seared the damage in the back of the injury. "I'm going to have to do the front, too," he said. "You just hold on to this rag and keep pushing on the wound to stop the bleeding. Putney repeated the procedure. This time, knowing what to expect, Phineas didn't fight him as bad, but he slumped over, and Putney had to hold him to keep the man from falling into the fire.

By the time he finished caring for Phineas, Wallace had come to the fire with Sinead and Matthew. Wallace laid the boy on the ground and pulled out his knife to cut away the pants. The tourniquet had slowed the bleeding, but Bigfoot couldn't see the severity of the wound. Wallace went to a water barrel, soaked his kerchief, and came back and cleaned the wounded area.

"Putney, the bullet missed the bone. So we're going to need to do the same as you did over there," the big man said.

· · ·

PUTNEY SAT PHINEAS UP. Once he was certain, Phineas could stay upright, he took his knife and Wallace's and stuck them both in the fire. "Ma'am," Wallace said. "We're going to have to roll him over on his side so that we can get at the entry and exit at the same time. You're going to have to hold him tight." Then looking at Matthew, he said, "Boy, this is going to hurt worse than the bullet did, but when it's over, you'll have a beautiful scar to show all the girls. You just think on that." When the knives were ready, Putney and Wallace each took one and, at the same time, stuck them on both sides of the wound. Matthew passed out from the pain.

"Sinead," said Putney. "Where's Mark?"

"I don't know," she said. "Mark was here when it all started." Then she began calling his name.

Phineas had become more alert and spoke up. "He's over in those bushes. I was trying to drag him up here. Those men beat him terribly when he tried to help Mary."

Putney and Wallace searched through the brush and found Mark lying near the bank of the creek with his pants pulled down. Bigfoot hoisted the boy up and, looking at Putney, said, "Pull them britches up. Nobody needs to know anything about this." Putney did as Wallace said, then helped carry Mark to the camp.

Brigid came walking into the center. "I think those two other men may be cutting that bastard's throat," she announced and sat calmly on a stump.

Wallace and Putney ran to the cabin to see Jesus with the man's head in his lap. Jesus had one hand on the man's forehead holding it still, and his gloved hand over his mouth to keep him quiet. Javier was sitting on the man with a Bowie knife at the man's throat. "Hold on!" yelled Bigfoot. "Y'all are supposed to be fixing him up, not giving him another mouth!"

Javier looked up and flashed a big toothy smile. "Oh, we're not killing him, Bill. We're just giving him a shave," said Javier and laughed. "We thought he needed cleaning up before we talk to him. Then when he has told us what we want, we can see better where to cut his throat."

The man was struggling to get loose, but Jesus held tight. "Si, Bill," he said. "This man is not so hurt. He only has a bullet in one hip and a small one across his head. I think a bullet must have skipped across it. See here." Turning the man's head, Putney and Wallace saw a gash about an inch wide through the man's hairline.

"You boys quit playing around," Wallace ordered. "Build a fire and burn that wound, so he don't bleed to death. Then tie him up."

"Si, Bill," said Javier. "That will be more fun anyway."

As Wallace was walking back toward the camp, Putney stopped him. Wait a minute, Bill," Putney told him. "Four youngsters are missing. Come with me." Wallace followed Putney out of the back passage and down a little trail toward the creek. Just before they got to a thicket of brush, Brendan Fitzgerald jumped out with a knife in his hand, looking like he was ready to do business. "Nahum!" he cried out. Then turning to the thicket, "You can come out, girls. It's Nahum."

All the children rushed out of the thicket. Seeing Putney, they gathered around, all hugging him at one time. Little Breanna looked up and said, "I knew you would come, Nahum. We all prayed for you to come."

Putney knelt and gave each of them a kiss on their foreheads. "Y'all come with me," he said. Putney guided them around the back so they didn't have to witness the slaughter in the front. When Brigid saw the children, she ran and threw her arms around her daughters. Brendan and Breanna walked toward everyone else, looking confused.

Sinead saw them and their state and went over to them. "You come with me," she said softly and guided them to the fire. From somewhere, she produced a blanket, put it around their shoulders, and hugged both.

Wallace pulled Putney aside, "That everyone?" he asked.

"Yeah, with the dead ones, everyone is accounted for," Putney told him. "I guess it's time to find out how all this happened."

Putney and Bigfoot heard a loud whistle and looked to see the wagons coming. Wallace waved and directed them toward him. Once the wagons had stopped, the man in the lead wagon, that went by the moniker Chappy, jumped down and walked over to the two men. "What in Billy blue blazes happened here?" he asked.

"That's what we're about to find out," said Wallace.

"We saw a dead boy out past them sheep and picked him up," said Chappy. "Jimbo and Kenny are getting him out of the wagon."

Wallace told the teamsters to lay the body in the cabin. Then turning to Putney said, "We've been taking care of the living. It's time now for us to respect the dead. Before we do anything else, we ought to lay them, folks, out in that cabin and cover 'em up. Except that bastard there," pointing out the dead outlaw near the door. "Put him to the side of the cabin 'cause he don't deserve to be laid out with honest folk." Putney agreed, and with the help of the teamsters, the men collected the bodies and did as Wallace had said.

"Javier," Putney said. "Will you and Jesus move that piece of trash out there by his compadre? He doesn't deserve to be in here with these people." The brothers heaved the man up and dragged him outside. One of the teamsters had gotten into the crate of blankets and brought several to the cabin. The men were conscious of the solemnity of their duty and laid each person in a neat row and covered them. Putney helped place Erin's body, gently folded her arms across her breasts, and spread the blanket over her. Putney asked Jimbo and Kenny to lay Jack Callahan next to his daughter. Putney looked at his dead friend's face, "Jack," he whispered. "I swear the men that did this are walking their last days on this earth." Then pulled a blanket up over his face. Their morbid duty completed, the men walked over to the camp and faced the wounded settlers.

Putney introduced William Wallace and the teamsters to his friends. He then thought back to the day T. J. McKinney had told him that his family was dead, killed by Comanches. Mr. McKinney had spoken to him kindly but firmly, comforting him as best a rugged rancher could.

Putney needed to fill that role now. "Friends," He began. "Today has been awful, and you all are mourning and hurting. These men and I are going to do the best by y'all that we can. We will get the wounded bandaged up properly and get the rest of you as comfortable as possible. But the men that did this horrible thing must be held to account. We need to know what happened so we can know what we need to do. So, tomorrow we will grieve, but tonight y'all need to tell us what you know."

Putney turned to the teamsters, "Chappy, there's a bolt of white cotton in the wagon you were driving," Putney said. "We can use that for clean bandages. There's also a box of liniments and wood alcohol."

"I'll get right on it," Chappy responded.

"Kenny," Putney looked at the burly, colored mule skinner. "You did all the cooking while we were on the trail. On one of the other wagons is a keg of beef and boxes of potatoes, onions, and such. Think you could work us up a big pot of stew." Kenny told Putney he would be glad to feed the people.

"Kenny, you and I will bring some blankets and dresses for Mrs. Forsythe and Dorsey," Putney said, addressing the last driver. "And Bill, as distasteful as it might be, I guess Javier and Jesus need to bring that jackass over here so we can all keep a watch on him and the brothers can know what's going on."

"Boy," said Bigfoot. "You're a natural at command."

As soon as the men had come back with the supplies and started their work, Brigid came to help. Putney gave her the dress and told her she should change first, and they would surely appreciate her help. Sinead wanted to know what to do. "Sinead," said Putney. "I think you could best keep those children comforted. You know Brendan and Breanna will need to know what has happened to their parents, and they will need you." Imogene also wanted to know what to do. "Sweetie," Putney told her. "Why don't you go help Kenny get the meal ready. We're all mighty hungry, and the quicker that gets done, the better off we'll all be."

Putney was surprised at the deft yet gentle hands of the big teamsters and Wallace while bandaging and patching up the wounded. Chappy ensured that he smeared the cauterized wounds with clean axle grease he kept under the seat of his wagon. "Keeps those burns from sticking to bandages," he said.

Jimbo worked cleaning Mark's cuts and bruises while Wallace and Brigid assisted Phineas. Kenny and Imogene made up a big pot of what Kenny called cowboy stew. Putney prepared pallets for the wounded. Sinead had fixed up a place for the children under one of the wagons. Putney knew she had told the children of the Fitzgeralds' deaths because he heard their crying and Sinead trying to comfort them with her soft singing. It was dark when everyone completed their work, and everyone had eaten. Putney and the other men gathered around to hear what had happened. Finally, each of the settlers had a chance to tell what they knew, and Putney started getting an idea in his head about what he would do.

21

In the morning, the Irish had heard some gunshots but didn't know where they were coming from. Jack, Sinead, and Erin had gathered the children and moved them to the brushy hiding place Putney had shown them. Alanis wasn't with the others, so Erin had gone to find her.

As they hid the children, a band of ten men wearing slickers and badges had ridden up to the camp. William Fitzgerald had been the first to see them and went to see what they wanted. The men told Fitzgerald that they were range detectives working for a rancher and that the Irish were illegally squatting on ranch land. William tried to explain that they had a grant from Santa Fe and that Putney had gone there to determine precisely where their grant was. He had told the men that when Putney returned, they would willingly move if they were in the wrong place. The leader said that wasn't good enough, and they had to move right then. When William tried to reason with the man, he pulled a gun and shot William in the chest.

All hell and confusion broke out. Phineas, Mark, and

Eileen retrieved pistols to come to William's rescue. Unfortunately, the outlaws were already tearing through the camp
before the three could stop them. Phineas shot at the
invaders and said he thought he had hit one. But, in his
excitement, Mark had forgotten to pull the hammer back on
his gun, and two men were on him before he could correct
his mistake. The two men beat him with their fists and
pistols, throwing him into the bushes and down the creek.
The men beat Mark so severely that he was knocked out and
didn't know anything until he came to in the camp.

Margaret had gotten the carbine but dropped it when
the men shot her husband. She was trying to help him
when one of the men shot her. Eileen had shot at the men,
but nobody knew if she hit any of them. One of the men
charged her, knocked the gun from her hand, and another
threw her to the ground. They both began stripping her of
her clothes. Where Eileen fell, the gun was in her reach. She
grabbed it and shot herself while one of the men was
forcing himself on her.

Brigid Forsythe had been by one of the wagons where
they had placed some tools. Two men came running at her,
and she picked up a hatchet in one hand and a knife in the
other. The men tried to grab her. Brigid swung the hatchet
down hard on one man's arm. She said she was sure she had
cut it half off as he stumbled away, holding on to it. But with
the action, Brigid had lost her grip on the hatchet. When the
other man grabbed her, she came up with the knife and, in a
swift action, cut his face. The man backed up a step and
came at her again, ripping her dress. That was when she
said she thought she nearly cut his ear off.

Sinead had said that Alanis had come into the hiding
place, but Erin was not with her. Jack asked where his
daughter was, and Alanis said some men had grabbed her.

Jack had the Walker pistol and ran up the hill. Sinead tried to stop Imogene, but she ran up the hill behind Jack. Two men were in the cabin and had stripped Erin naked. When Jack entered, he shot one of the men. The one they now held captive. The other man shot Jack five times. The man started toward Erin, and either didn't see or ignored Imogene. Imogene picked up the Walker from Jack's hand and shot the man. She kept shooting until the gun was empty.

Everyone believed that the leader had seen the settlers had not been such an easy mark. So he hollered at his men, and they all ran to their horses and rode away to the east. Nobody knew how long it was from when the outlaws left until Putney arrived, but they all agreed it wasn't longer than half an hour.

When Putney had heard the last bit, he cursed himself if *he hadn't stopped to eat breakfast. If he hadn't stopped to water his horse. He would have been there if he had just been in a bigger hurry. And he would have killed them all!*

When they had pieced together what the settlers had told them, Putney and Wallace walked over to where the Mendez brothers had their man tied to a tree. They both had tin plates full of cowboy stew and were teasing their prisoner by telling him how good it was. When he saw the two Texans walk over, he growled, "Tell these Mexes to get out of my face with that food!"

"You ain't in no position to be making demands," Bigfoot told him. Wallace sat cross-legged in front of the man and, with his big paw, grabbed the man by the hair and slammed it against the tree trunk. "This here is Nahum Putney. He has a hobby. He scalps Comanches for fun. Now he don't normally scalp white men, but he said, in your case, he might make an exception. Now we're going to ask you some questions, and you have one chance to answer straight. Else Putney here is gonna scalp you while you're still alive. Then I'm going to let these vaqueros finish giving you that shave they started. Comprehendo, amigo?" Bigfoot slammed the man's head into the tree a second time.

"I'll tell you what you want," said the outlaw. "Just keep that crazy redhead and them Mexes away from me."

"Tell me your name!" Putney demanded.

"Michael Rogers," said the man.

"Mike, who do you work for?" asked Wallace.

"The Montoya Ranch. We work for old man Hugo Montoya as stock detectives," Rogers said.

"Who was the man in charge here today?" was Bigfoot's next question.

"Man, if I tell you that, I'm a dead man," protested the prisoner.

"If you don't tell me that, you're a dead man," said Wallace. "So out with it."

"Hell," spat Rogers. "Lewis Musgrove, he heads us up. Ed Franklin is his right-hand man."

"I didn't ask you that, but thanks," Wallace told him.

At this point, Putney jumped into the interrogation. "Where were they headed from here?"

"I guess back to the ranch headquarters. How the hell should I know?" returned Rogers.

"Where's the Montoya Rancht?" Putney asked.

"South of here, about halfway between here and Fort Bascom," Rogers told him.

"Rogers," said Putney. "I'm going to go get a pencil and paper, and when I come back, you'll tell me the names of everyone riding with you today. And you're going to describe them. Except that bastard laying over by the cabin. I don't need his name."

When Putney returned, Rogers gave him the names of seven other men. After Putney had his list, he asked the Mendez brothers to provide Rogers with something to eat. Putney folded the paper, took a leather wallet from his back pocket, and placed the list inside.

"Hey," said Rogers. "I need to pee."

"Did you ever get caught in a rainstorm?" asked Wallace.

"Yeah," replied Rogers. "I got soaked, and I didn't like it. Why?"

Bigfoot grinned, "Well, your next soaking won't be near as cold."

22

P utney and the other men had spent the day digging graves for the dead in a nice patch down the river a few hundred yards. Sinead and Brigid, along with Alanis and Imogene, had worked to wash and dress the bodies. Because they didn't have enough lumber to build coffins, they wrapped the dead in cloth from the bolts Putney had bought in Santa Fe. Putney had given Sinead the silk dress with embroidered birds and asked her to dress Erin in it. Though still suffering from their wounds, Matthew, Mark, and Phineas fashioned some crosses for the graves. The men found a spot on the opposite side of the creek. Chappy and Kenny dug a grave for the dead outlaw and unceremoniously tossed the body in and covered it. They left no marker. As dusk settled in, everyone assembled at the grave site. Phineas read the twenty-third Psalm and said a few words about each of the pioneers who had lost their lives. He ended it with a prayer, and Kenny sang, "I am a Pilgrim."

After dinner, Sinead and Brigid sang some sorrowful Irish ballads, some in Irish and others in English. The songs

touched everyone so that even Bigfoot Wallace and the
other men shed a few tears for people they had never
known in life. Everyone, except Putney, whose eyes never
even grew damp. As the women were singing, Putney
stepped off to be alone. Imogene followed but kept her
distance. Putney lit a cigarette and blew smoke into the
bright stars as if trying to block out the twinkling specks of
light. Imogene finally approached the lone man. "Nahum,
are you alright?" she asked.

Putney raised his arm a little so Imogene could come
next to him and held her close. "I'm alright, sweetie," he said.
"Why do you ask?"

"I ain't seen you shed a tear. Not even one."

"I think, Imogene," pausing, he held her tighter, "I think
I'm too angry to cry." That's all."

"That's alright, Nahum. I don't mind crying for us both."
If Nahum Putney were going to cry, it would have been then.
He knelt beside his charge. "I have something to tell you,
sweetie. When I was in Santa Fe, I checked a registry of
missing people, and your name was on it. You have an uncle
in McKinney, Texas, that is looking for you. I didn't write
him. I thought you deserved to choose if you stayed with
these people or went home to your kin."

Imogene cast her eyes upwards, thinking of what to say.
She looked back at him. "I like Sinead and the others,
Nahum. Honest, I do. But the only reason I would stay is if
you was. But I know you're not." Putney wondered how a girl
so young had gained such foresight. "I would druther stay
with you, but I don't think I can, so I think I will just go back
to my family."

Putney hugged the girl with both arms. "We will figure it
out later," he said. "Right now, I have some more thinking to
do. You head on back. I'll be there shortly."

≈

WITH JACK CALLAHAN GONE, Putney considered Sinead to be the settlers' leader. He took her aside the next morning. "Bill, the Mendez brothers, and I are going to take that desperado to the Montoya ranch this morning," he told the widow. "I know there is no amount of money that will pay for what y'all have lost, but I need to make sure that payment gets exacted from someone."

"Don't do anything foolish," Sinead implored him. "Take him to the authorities. Let them handle it."

Putney didn't respond to her plea. Instead, he said, "When we get back, I will be leaving. I'm not sure where I will go, but I can't stay here." He handed her his passbook from the Stock Growers Bank, "There's a little over one thousand dollars in this account. When y'all decide what you're going to do, use that money."

Sinead didn't protest. She took the passbook and thanked him.

"The teamsters said they will stay until we get back. It shouldn't take us long," Putney told her. "Probably by tonight."

Before they left, Putney spoke with Imogene. "When I return, I'll see you get back to Texas, safe." he hugged the girl and sent her to help Sinead.

≈

"I AIN'T in no shape to ride," complained Rogers when the Mendez brothers brought him to a saddled horse.

"You can ride sitting up," said Javier. "Or you can ride on your stomach. It makes no difference to me." Given that choice, Rogers opted to ride sitting.

The Mendez brothers were familiar with Montoya's Ranch and guided the way. The ranch headquarters was a large adobe structure surrounded by an adobe wall eight feet high and about three acres. Inside the walls were the main ranch house, several outbuildings, a corral, and two barns. The wooden gates that protected the entrance through the wall were swung open, and the five men rode through as if they owned the place. A covered veranda went around all four sides of the main hacienda, and steps led up to the main door. The riders drew the ranch workers' attention, curious about the purpose of the strangers. Putney and the others rode up to the main entrance of the hacienda, where a tall, slender man stood. The man wore the clothes of a Spanish caballero.

"My name if Hugo Montoya. How may I help you men?" said the distinguished-looking Montoya.

"We brought one of your stock detectives back," answered William Wallace as he jerked a thumb at Rogers.

"You must be mistaken. I have no need of stock detectives," then looking at the man Bill had indicated, Montoya said, "No. This man does not work for me. He came here a week ago with some others. They said they were range detectives and wanted to work for me. I had heard of their kind before. A rancher like myself may find some cattle are missing and like that," he snapped his fingers. "Range detectives show up, looking for work. They are nothing more than cattle thieves themselves. I told them I did not want them on my rancho.'" Montoya continued. "I gave them a day to leave. I warned them that if mis vaqueros saw them on my property after one day, they would shoot the detectives on sight or hang them." Montoya used the term detectives derisively. "They left, and I have not seen them since."

Bigfoot glared at Rogers. Putney told Montoya what had

happened north of him, omitting nothing. "For this, I am immensely sorry, senores. I wanted that land, but the territorial authorities said they wanted to open the area to smaller settlers to grow the population. They need the people so that the government will consider us for statehood. I want this also; I would do nothing to jeopardize these people."

"Well then, Senor Montoya, we are sorry to have bothered you," said Wallace

Putney and the others started to leave when Montoya said, "If you would like, you can leave this man with me. I will make sure he gets taken to Santa Fe for the authorities,"

Bigfoot said it was alright, Rogers was their problem, and they would take care of it.

"Before you go," Montoya stopped them. "You tell your people how much I regret what has happened. Even though I bear no responsibility, I would like to help you as a neighbor. In a few days, I will send some people over with some cattle, including two milk cows. The people I send will also help to build some adobe cabins. That is something you will need before winter."

"That will be much appreciated, Señor Montoya," Putney told the rancher. "We will be sure to let the others know." The group left the Montoya hacienda and rode for fifteen minutes when they stopped. The four men surrounded Rogers and his horse on all sides as if they had planned it. "Well, Nahum," said Wallace. "You got that scalping knife because young Mr. Rogers here needs that haircut now."

"Whoa! Whoa, boys," protested Rogers, holding his bound hands up in surrender. "Alright, I see it wasn't smart to lie to you. I thought you would take me to Santa Fe, but I'll give you the truth. The plan was for us to head to Fort Dodge. Then was to go to northeast Colorado. There's some cattle ranchers up there, and they're having problems with rustlers, and we thought we could hire out to one of the big outfits" Rogers was talking fast, wanting to get everything out in hopes it could somehow save him. "We just happened on those immigrants. I thought we were just going to rob them. Then out of nowhere, Musgrove starts shooting them. I swear I didn't think it was going to go the way it did."

Bigfoot Wallace glared at the outlaw. "I suppose you were really trying to help that young woman you stripped." The menace in the giant grew with each word.

"That weren't me! Honest to God," swore Rogers. "That was all Jenkins. I was trying to stop him! Then that fella came out of nowhere and shot me!"

"Can we give him that shave now, Bill?" asked Javier.

"Si! It will be the closest shave he ever had!" said Jesus. Rogers started crying and pleading for them to take him to Santa Fe and turn him over to the Marshal there.

The whole time the others were speaking, Putney never said a word. He had only looked down at the ground, the wide brim of his hat keeping his face covered. Finally, he raised his head until his eyes could see the outlaw. "No. Nobody is going to shave this piece of trash," Putney's voice was just above a whisper, but something in it was so menacing it sent chills up everyone's back. "And we are not taking him to Santa Fe. It is too far. Bill, you, Javier' and Jesus go on back to the settlement. I will take Michael Rogers to Fort Bascom. They can hold him there until a federal marshal can pick him up. I will come back to the camp tomorrow."

"Do you think that's wise, Putney? Just you and him?" asked Wallace.

Putney glared at the big man with a look that was as black as a starless night. Wallace had seen that look in

Charlie Putney's eyes once before when they had come upon a baby with its head crushed by Comanches. As big and bold as Bigfoot Wallace was, he wouldn't have gone up against Charlie Putney then, and there was no way in hell he would go up against his son now. "Jesus, give him the reins to that horse. You' me, and Javier are going back to camp." Jesus Mendez did as Wallace had said, crossed himself, and turned his horse north. Javier followed Jesus. As Wallace started to trail the brothers, he gave Putney one more look and said, "Viaje con Dios, hijo."

As the three men rode away, Michael Rogers began pleading for them not to leave. He was crying, and spittle was running out of his mouth. He may as well have been shouting down a well. Putney tied the reins to the thongs on his saddle and started south. "I'll jump outta this saddle!" yelled Rogers.

"If you do, I will put my lariat around your neck and drag you to Fort Bascom," Putney's voice still full of menace. Rogers fell silent, and even his crying died to a near silent whimper. The two men rode toward Fort Bascom without another word.

After two hours ride, the men came to a small creek that flowed into a pond dotted with cottonwood trees. They crossed the stream, and Putney stopped the horses. Having gotten control of himself, Rogers asked why they were stopping. "Get off. I'm going to water the horses," was Putney's reply. "Go stand by that cottonwood. Rogers wasn't about to antagonize Putney, so he stepped over to the tree and stood watching Putney.

Putney put a loop around his horse's neck and looped the other end around another tree. He then took his cigarette case out of his pocket and extracted two Kinney's. Putney walked over to Rogers and handed one of the cigarettes to him. With his hands shaking, Rogers took the offer and put it to his lips. Putney lit the bandit's cigarette and then his own and walked off several feet and stared out at the rolling prairie.

When he had finished his smoke, Putney turned back to the horses. Reaching in his saddlebags, he removed a pistol and stuck it in the back of his gun belt. Putney walked toward Rogers and pulled his bowie knife out of its sheath. "I ain't gonna let you scalp me!" hollered Rogers. "I'll fight you tooth and nail, even as tied up as I am! You'll have to kill me first."

"Calm down," Putney said. "I am not going to scalp you. Hold out your hands." Rogers complied with Putney's orders. Putney twirled the big knife once, then grabbed Rogers' wrist with a grip like a bear trap. Then, slicing off the bindings, Putney said. "You'll want to rub those wrists and get a little feeling back in those hands." Putney walked off a few feet, so Rogers didn't act on a temptation to jump him.

Rogers didn't know what to think, but he was glad to have the thongs off his wrists. Jesus had tied them well, and even though Rogers had tried to slip them, all he accomplished was to strengthen the ties. Rogers rubbed one wrist and then another. Then holding his arms to his side, he shook his hands to get the blood flowing. Thinking he ought to say something, Rogers expressed his appreciation to Putney by saying, "Thanks, Red." Putney shot a look at Rogers as if the look alone could kill the outlaw. "Well," said Rogers, "I don't know your name."

"Callahan. Jack Callahan," said Putney, not knowing why.

"Well, thanks, Jack," Rogers hoped this sudden kindness was a good sign.

"Feeling better now?" asked Putney.

"Sure am. I don't guess I could have a drink out of that canteen, could I? I have an awful thirst."

Putney got the canteen off his saddle and tossed it to Rogers. "Thanks again, Jack," said the outlaw. "You ain't such a bad fella, after all." Thinking that his chance had come, Rogers thought if he tossed the canteen back to Putney, it would catch his captor off guard, and he would have the opportunity to pounce on him and get one of the pistols away. "Here ya go!" Rogers threw the canteen at Putney, who just side-stepped and let the canteen bounce on the ground. Rogers' ploy had failed.

Putney walked over to within arm's reach of Rogers. "That was a clumsy attempt, Michael Rogers," Putney said without emotion. "Here, try this." Putney reached back for the Colt tucked in his belt and dropped it in Rogers' empty holster. Then, not taking his eyes off his adversary, Putney took four steps back and unhooked the hammer loop from his gun.

"Are you crazy?" Rogers was confused by Putney's action.

"If I take you to Fort Bascom, they will hold you for a marshal, and he will take you to Santa Fe, where they will hang you. It may take a while, but there is no doubt about that outcome," Putney's voice was smooth as glass. "But I'm going to give you a chance at freedom. I'm no gunman, but I bet you style yourself as one."

"I ain't in no shape for no duel," claimed Rogers. "I ain't hardly ate. Them Mexican's kept me awake half the night. I've pissed myself. I ain't in no shape, I tell you. This is murder! That's what it is. I ain't got no chance!"

Putney's voice was flat as he said, "It's the only chance you are going to get."

Rogers measured the young man in front of him. Rogers

was no gunner either. Not in a straight-up fight like this, but he bet he had killed more men than this lanky ginger. Having made his decision, Rogers let his hand drop to the gun.

Putney had watched as Rogers had mulled over in his head what he was going to do. Finally, Rogers made his move, and Putney let his eyes follow Rogers' hand as it went toward the gun. Time expanded for Putney. He could see everything. The leaves and the grass became greener. The birds he hadn't heard before were all singing in his head. Putney could smell the saddles' leather and the horses' sweat. All these things were occurring at one time, yet outside of time. Putney saw nothing of Rogers, only the gun. The gun rose from the holster as if it defied gravity. The barrel leveled itself at Putney, and fire and smoke belched out as the projectile flew past Putney. Rogers was dead before the bullet ever left his gun. Time collapsed back on itself, and Nahum Putney looked down on the dead man without regret or remorse.

23

I t was just past dinner at the Irish settlement when Putney returned unexpectedly. Everyone thought he would return the next day. Imogene saw Putney, ran to him, and wrapped her arms around his waist. Sinead said they had some food left and told Putney to sit while she got him a plate. Putney was famished. Ever since he was fifteen and fended off an attack by robbers, he found he was always hungry after gunplay. Wallace sat beside him and asked, "Everything alright? Did you make it to Fort Bascom?"

"Everything is taken care of," is all that Putney would say. Sinead sat down near the two Texans. "Nahum," she said. "Phineas, Brigid, and I have decided to stay. Having our own land is a dream of all our people, and we want to see it through. We would like for you to stay."

Putney said, "I'm sorry, Sinead, I already told you I couldn't. Do you feel like you can handle being out here by yourselves?"

"Well, there's the good news, then," Sinead said. "Chappy and Kenny are going to stay until we get good houses built. And with Mr. Montoya's offer of help, we ought to be able to take care of that before it gets cold. Chappy said Jimbo can hook up all three wagons together and take them back to Santa Fe."

"That is good news," Putney agreed.

Sinead continued, "Jesus and Javier said they would like to stay, too, if it was alright with you and Mr. Wallace."

"I think it would be for the best," said Putney.

"What are you and Mr. Wallace going to do?" There was deep concern in the Irish woman's voice.

"I can't speak for Bill, but I'm going to take Imogene to Fort Dodge and see if I can arrange transport back to her family in McKinney," Putney told her. "I can't speak for Bill."

"I reckon I'm going to Fort Dodge, too," chimed in Bill. "I may head on back to Texas, myself."

"When will you go?" Sinead asked.

"In the morning," said Putney. "No need to tarry."

At breakfast, Sinead announced that Putney, Imogene, and Bigfoot Wallace would be leaving for Fort Dodge. Everyone tried to talk Putney into staying. However, he held them off by telling them he was going to get Imogene to her family. All the settlers approved of this idea but then harangued Putney for his return, to which he would only say, "We'll see."

Putney saddled the Indian pony for Imogene. It was smaller, and she would better be able to handle the animal. Sinead insisted that Putney and Wallace take one of the mules as a pack animal, which she and the others loaded with food and supplies. Sinead said that thanks to him, they were well equipped and could afford to spare the food and supplies.

Putney and Bill graciously thanked her and the others for their offerings. Then Putney called the teamsters and the Mendez brothers over to the side. He paid the teamsters what he owed them, plus a little extra for the return trip. Then he gave Jesus and Javier one hundred and fifty dollars each, the agreed-upon six-month wages. Both Mendez brothers wanted to know if Putney and Wallace needed them to go to Fort Dodge, but Putney told them it wouldn't be necessary. Putney said he believed all the outlaws would be gone from there by the time they arrived. Finally, he gave Kenny and Chappy an additional fifty dollars and told them that they would have to negotiate with Sinead if they needed more.

Before the three travelers could leave, everyone had to gather around to say their goodbyes. There were hugs and kisses all around. Bigfoot tossed a couple of the youngsters in the air and told them to be good and keep an eye out because they never could tell when he might return, just like old Saint Nicholas. All the children cheered and hugged him again. The youngest girl, Breanna, tugged on Putney's sleeve. "Imogene said you like peaches, so I made sure there were two cans in your stuff, just for you." He picked her up and kissed her on both cheeks.

Putney lifted Imogene onto her horse, then he and Bill saddled up. The people at the settlement watched them ride away until they could no longer see them. Imogene and Bill would turn once in a while and give another wave. Putney never looked back.

24

On the seventh day of their trip, just past noon, the trio found themselves looking at Fort Dodge. It wasn't an impressive sight. The Army had recently established the fort earlier in the year and hadn't had a chance to build it up. Some sod and adobe buildings made up part of the fort. The rest was tents, a corral, and some dugouts. A mile or so from what constituted the fort, a few buildings of the same type made up the settlement. There was no actual entry to the fort, except for one guard post that was a simple lean-to. Being familiar with the fort, Wallace led the group to the sentry and asked for the commanding officer. The guard directed them to the most prominent building atop a hill overlooking the rest of the fort. He told them to ask for Captain Pierce.

When Wallace had guided his wagon train from Fort Leavenworth to Santa Fe he had stopped at Fort Dodge and had met Captain Pierce. Wallace entered the quarters first and greeted a sergeant seated at a desk going over some papers. No doors divided the rooms, and Captain Pierce had heard Wallace ask for him. The captain came from a second room and greeted Wallace. Captain Pierce was a man of average height with brownish hair and sported a full bushy beard. Putney was impressed with how neat and clean the captain's uniform was. Bill introduced Putney and Imogene to the captain. He told Pierce how Putney had rescued Imogene from the Comanche. Bigfoot said they were now trying to return her to her family in Texas. Putney thought Captain Pierce would never stop pumping his hand and congratulating him on such an endeavor. The captain knelt in front of Imogene, taking hold of her by both shoulders went on about how brave she must be.

"I have to tell you, Mr. Wallace," said Pierce. "There are no transports from here to Texas, and there are no particular safe routes. The fastest route is through the Indian Nations. The Indians there are mostly tame." Then turning to the sergeant, the captain asked, "There was a Cherokee named White Owl here yesterday. Do you know if he's still here?"

"As far as I know, sir," said the sergeant. "He was supposed to meet a supply wagon sent by the Indian agent. I'm sure it hasn't arrived yet."

Again, addressing Wallace, the captain said, "That's your best bet, Mr. Wallace. White Owl should be picking up a wagon to take to the Cherokee Reservation. I'm sure he would take you along, for a fee, of course. He would at least get you as far as the Choctaw. You could pay a fee to pass their lands and end up in Denison."

"Do you know where I could find this White Owl?" Wallace asked both soldiers.

"There's a dugout between here and those traders south of here," the sergeant said. "The Indians usually stay around there. If the trading posts ain't real busy, they may go down there to buy some sweets, if they have money. If there's a bunch of white men around, they won't go down there. Too rough."

Putney spoke up for the first time. "Captain, we had trouble with some men over in New Mexico. They killed five people and wounded several more. We think they may have come over this way."

"Mr. Putney, I regret those circumstances, and I sympathize with you," said Captain Pierce, "But I'm not sure why you're telling me this."

"I thought if they were around here, you could arrest them. I have their names and descriptions."

"The problem, Mr. Puteny, is manyfold. First, the event happened in New Mexico, Not Kansas. And this is a civilian problem, and the nearest civilian authority is in Marion, a full six days from here. Lastly, You have presented no evidence of any warrants. Even if the sheriff from Marion came out here, there would be scant little he could do."

"So," said Putney in his low stern voice, "What you're telling me is that those killers could be standing right outside your office, and there would be nothing you could or would do."

"My hands are tied, Mr. Putney. I hope you understand."

"If they were outside here and I walked out and killed them all, you wouldn't do anything, then, either?" Putney asked.

"That would be another thing altogether, Mr. Putney," the captain was becoming impatient with being questioned by this civilian. "You would be committing murder on a military post which would fall in my bailiwick, and I would probably have Sergeant McIntire, here, shoot you. Now, if you found them down by the trading posts and killed them, that would be the sheriff's business."

"Come on, Bill," said Putney. "Let's go find that Cherokee." Then, taking Imogene's hand, Putney walked away from the captain.

It was a few minutes before Wallace exited the sod building and saddled up. "Putney, you need to calm down a bit. The captain only wanted you to understand his hands are tied," said Bill.

"Yeah, Bill," replied Putney. "Well, that's bullshit!"

The three rode down to the dugout the sergeant had indicated. There they found four Indians sitting outside on blankets on the ground. Wallace asked if they spoke English. "Better than you speak Indian," said one man.

"We're looking for White Owl. Is that one of you?" Wallace asked.

One of the men stood and walked into the dugout. In a minute, another man exited. He was a squat man with long black hair streaked with silver. The man wore a frock coat over a buckskin shirt and trousers, and he was wearing a bowler hat. "I am White Owl. What do you want with me?" he said.

Wallace introduced himself and explained their situation, and asked if they could hire White Owl to guide them down to Texas.

"Did you fight in the big war between white men?" asked White Owl. Wallace told the Cherokee he did fight in the war. White Owl asked Putney the same question, to which Putney said yes. "Which side?" White Owl wanted to know.

"We was both Confederates," replied Bigfoot. "Does it make a difference?"

"It does. I would not guide you if you were Yankees," said the Indian. "The Cherokee fought with the Confederates. But like in many things, we chose the wrong side. I will let you ride with me when the agent arrives with supplies. For that, I will take two American dollars each day."

"Can you take us through the Choctaw?" Wallace wanted to know.

"I will take you to a Choctaw village, and you can make your bargain with them," White Owl told him. "For that, I will want five American dollars."

"We can handle that," Wallace assured him.

"Good. You keep looking out for the agent. When he brings the wagon, we will leave." White Owl then turned and went back into the dugout.

"That was easy enough," said Bill to his companions. "Let's stake out a place to camp."

"I don't know, Bill," Putney said. "Look at those clouds in the north. It looks like it could rain. Maybe we could check out those two trading posts and see if they have any room." Putney suggested. "For Imogene," he added.

The first trading post was twice the size of Captain Pierce's headquarters and also made of sod. A thick wooden door was propped open to let out the oppressive heat of the cook stove in the back of the main room. The room had a small bar of planks set on two large oak barrels. Behind was a shelf that housed crock jugs of unknown spirits. Various sundries and hardware hung from the ceiling, like a child's mobile made of iron, steel, and tin. On the wall opposite the bar were shelves filled with canned goods, jars of tobacco, and more crock jugs. The shelves were bookended by barrels, presumably holding crackers, fruits, or salted meats. Hooks suspended hams and bacon on one side of the cook stove, and on the other side was a door made of thinner wood planks than the entry. Two cowhands were seated at one of the tables in the room. A short, wiry woman, either Indian or Mexican, was gently stirring a pot with the acrid smell of chili peppers. The room was smoky and dark due to lamps that the proprietors hadn't cleaned of soot often enough. From behind the bar, a bean pole of a man greeted them, "Howdy folks!" he said in a voice that sounded akin to an unoiled door hinge. "Welcome to Turk's Trading Post. Have a seat, and I'll be right over."

As they sat, Putney did not take his eyes off the two men stationed at the other table. Putney considered the descriptions Rogers had given of his cohorts. He dismissed what Rogers told him. He could make any man fit one of the descriptions, so they were practically useless except for Lewis Musgrove. Rogers was precise about his leader. Musgrove was a man nearly as big as Wallace with slate-colored hair and eyes as black as obsidian.

Soon the squeaky man was at their table with a jug and two glasses. "Here you are, gents," he said with pride, "Best whiskey in the badlands. We keep some milk cooled under the floorboards, and I'll bring out some for the girl," Then, before anyone could answer him, he spun on his heels and was back at his post, opening a trap door behind the bar.

Bigfoot Wallace uncorked the jug and started to pour whiskey into a glass. "I wouldn't drink that, mister," said one of the cowmen. "Unless all you have is a nickel. I'd spend the two bits and tell him to get some of that bottled stuff he hides behind the jugs." Wallace replaced the cork and nodded his head at the man.

"Who can I thank for probably saving my life and that of my young friend?" Wallace asked.

"Henry Sitler's my name, and this is my brother Thomas." The man told him. "We used to work for Jesse Chisolm down in Texas."

"Jess Chisolm!" there was a flash of excitement in Bigfoot's voice. "How is old Jess?"

"If you know him, then you won't take offense to me saying he's about as honery as ever," said Sitler.

"No offense, son! None at all!" Wallace gave out with a great guffaw. "What are you boys doing up here?"

"Well, the war didn't treat us none too good, even though we were on the winning side, Tom here lost a hand," Thomas Sitler held up his arm, showing a stump where his hand used to be. "We heard there was money in beef, so we went to Texas and learned that the only ones getting rich off beef are the ranchers. Or they would be if they could find a way to get their cattle up to Chicago."

"Ain't it the way," Wallace said in agreement.

"Y'all seen any other stockmen around here lately?" Putney inquired.

Both men shook their heads and said they hadn't. The squeaky voice showed up with a glass of milk and said, "Couldn't help but overhear. There was a bunch rode in a few days ago. Most of them left. There's been two hanging around at Croggins' place down yonder. They stayed around after Mamie Croggins patched them up. She said she had to stitch one of them boy's ear back on. It was near cut clean off. They said they'd been in a fight with Injuns. The other weren't much better. I guess one of them Injuns sunk a tomahawk in his shoulder. Mamie's the closest thing we got to a doctor, except at the fort, and he won't work on civilians. Mamie told them boys to hang around a while to make sure they didn't get septic."

Putney started to rise, but Wallace set his big hand on the younger man's arm. "Take it easy, Putney," keeping his tone low. "Let's get settled here and take care of Imogene first."

"Say, Turk, how about you bring us some of that good whiskey you have hidden away," said Bill Wallace, putting a dollar on the table, "And pour a drink for our friends."

"Oh, my name ain't Turk. That's my woman. But Turk

ain't her name neither. People just call her that because she's from Turkeyland. People call me Squeaky. I don't know why, though." Squeaky went to the bar, returned with a bottle labeled 'Samuels Kentucky Whiskey,' and poured a glass for all four men.

"Squeaky?" asked Putney. "Do you have any rooms?"

"Sure," said Squeaky. "We got two, not counting mine and Turk's, but these two gents took them."

"If you need a room for the girl, I'll give up mine," said Henry.

"That bed's big enough for me and Tom to share. But I don't think there's a bed made that's big enough for you, friend." Henry gave a jerk of his head at Wallace, and everyone laughed.

"That's kind of you, Henry. Thanks," said Putney.

"Say, I didn't get you fellas' names," said Henry.

That's William A. A. Wallace. The girl is Imogene Foster," said Putney.

"And yours?" asked Henry.

"Callahan. Jack Callahan," said Putney, and both Imogene and Wallace gave him disapproving looks. "Squeaky, what is Turk cooking?"

"She calls it chili stew. If you're going to eat any of it, I'll get you a glass of milk, too," Squeaky told him. "You'll need it."

⁓

IMOGENE DRANK three glasses of milk, trying to put out the fire in her mouth. The stew had beef and potatoes, beans, and carrots, but Putney could have sworn there were more chili peppers than anything else. He also drank a glass of milk to staunch the heat from the stew. Putney couldn't figure out how he did it, but Bill ate two bowls full without even asking for water.

By the time they had finished eating, Henry Sitler had moved his kit to his brother's room. Bigfoot went to take care of their animals while Putney got Imogene settled in a room. "Where are you going to sleep, Jack Callahan?" Imogene derided Putney.

"I guess I'll sleep on the floor," said Putney, aware of her contempt. "I've slept in worse places. Imogene, when Bill gets back, I need to take care of some business. I want you to stay here, no matter what. Understand?"

"Nahum, I don't want you to go over there," pleaded Imogene, "I'm afraid if you don't stay here with me, you won't ever come back."

"Don't worry about me, sweetie," he tried to reassure her. "You know I always come back."

"I'm afraid one day you won't," Imogene was in a huff. Seeing nothing would console her, Putney hugged Imogene and kissed her on the top of her head. He stopped at the door, gave Imogene a last look, and saw tears running down her cheeks. Knowing he had to go then or never would, Putney stepped out and closed the door behind him.

Wallace met Putney in the narrow hallway with bedrolls in his arms. "Where are you headed, pard?" he asked, his big frame blocking the hallway.

"You know where I'm going," Putney's voice was icy.

"I don't reckon I can let you do that, old son," Wallace told him.

"Are you going to try and stop me?" Putney became belligerent.

"If I have to, I will. But I druthered you listen to me and decide yourself," Wallace tried to reason with his young friend. "Nahum, you need to think hard about what you are considering doing. It's not going to change anything. No wounds are going to get healed. Nobody's coming back to life," Bill knew his argument was like spitting in the wind, but he had to try. "Son, I knew your Pa and your Ma, and I think I know what they would tell you, so I'm going to tell you now. Sure, your Pa and me and T.J, we chased down desperados, but it was for the law. Sometimes we had to defend ourselves, and people got killed, but we never did it for revenge." Wallace paused to see if what he was saying had any effect on Putney. Seeing it wasn't, he continued. "I didn't say anything about Rogers. I had hopes that it would make you sick, and you would have it out of your system."

Putney stopped him. "What do you mean about Rogers? What do you think happened?" Putney was angry because the big man had struck a chord in his conscience.

"Boy," Wallace's ire was also rising. "I ain't never treated you like you're stupid. Have the same respect for me. I ain't asking you what happened, I know. I knew what you were going to do when you left with that man by yourself. I'm to blame there because I should have rode with you. That's on me, but I ain't letting you go over there without you hearing me out."

Imogene had heard the men talking and had cracked the door to listen. Neither had noticed her until she butted in, "What are you talking about?" Imogene was confused by the conversation. "What did you do, Nahum?"

"Nothing, sweetie," he assured her. "Bill's just talking through his hat."

"Nahum, I'll go over there with you if your intent is to arrest them," Bill said. "Hell, we can put off going to Texas for a bit and take them up to the sheriff in Marion and let him take it from there. If they get froggy and jump, that'll be their bad luck. But if you have something else in mind, I won't go. You'll have to be on your own."

"I didn't ask you before, and I'm not asking you now." Putney was emphatic. "You stay and watch Imogene." Putney pushed past the big man and didn't look back, even when he heard Imogene calling for him.

≈

WHEN PUTNEY WALKED through the door, he saw Croggins' place was a smaller mirror image of Turks. The other difference was that someone kept the lamps clean. The room was as bright as possible, being night. Four soldiers poured drinks for themselves at one table from a crock jug. At another table sat two men, also drinking from a jug. One had a bandage wrapped around his head that covered his left ear, and he had a long cut down the same side of his face. The other man had his right arm in a sling. Putney walked up to the bar, which was tended by a bald man with a pot belly, wearing a shop apron. "Do you keep your good whiskey behind the crockery like they do over at Turks?" Putney asked.

The bartender grinned and said, "Sure do, mister." He shuffled some jugs and came out with a bottle also labeled 'Samuels.' This one still had the seal in place. The bartender broke the paper seal, produced a glass, and poured him a drink.

"Let me have four more glasses," Putney said, putting two dollars on the plank bar. As the bartender produced the glasses, Putney asked, "Do I call you Croggins, or is that your wife's name?"

"Yep, I'm Phil Croggins. My wife's name is Mamie," the owner affirmed.

Putney tucked the bottle under his arm, then stuck a finger in the empty glasses and, picking up his own, walked over to the table with the soldiers. He put the glasses down, uncorked the bottle, and poured out four drinks. "To the Union, boys!" he said and raised his glass.

"To the union!" the four soldiers said in unison and drank down their whiskey.

Putney could tell the four were drunk, he also saw they were wearing guns. *That's not good*, thought Putney as he walked back to the bar. When he got to the bar, he noticed Croggins was wearing a Patterson. The two outlaws didn't phase Putney, but the soldiers might try to get involved if shooting started. On the other hand, Croggins didn't look like a gun hand, and Putney figured he could probably prevent him from doing something stupid. But the soldiers concerned him until fate stepped in.

The soldiers all stood up and one announced in a loud voice, "Well, Phil, now that we know where you keep the good whiskey, and we've had a drink of it, we reckon we ought to get back to the post before the sergeant misses us. We'll all be on latrine detail for a month if he does" Then, looking at Putney, "And thanks, mister, for the drink, but next time come in earlier." The last line got a big laugh from the other soldiers, who all staggered out singing 'Jeff in Petticoats.'

With the soldiers gone, Putney believed he was evenly matched with the two bandits. Putney asked Croggins for two more glasses which he took to the men's table. He poured two drinks from the bottle and said, "It looks like you guys have had a hard time and could use a glass of good whiskey. Jack Callahan is my name." Putney returned to the bar, set the bottle down, and put another dollar on the planks.

The man with his arm in a sling said. "My name's Joe Sauder, and this here is my partner, Jim Walker. Yeah, we had a run-in with some Comanche. We may look worse for wear, but not as bad as those heathens."

With his voice as smooth as when he faced Rogers, Putney said, "Are you sure it was not a run-in with a group of Irish immigrants in New Mexico?"

"What did you say?" asked Sauder.

Putney turned his back to the two brigands and, so the others could hear, said to Croggins, "Phil, these two men got their wounds when they tried to rape a woman in New Mexico. What do you think should happen to such men?"

Croggins was visibly nervous, but he firmly said, "If it were up to me, they would hang."

"Well, I haven't got a rope," said Putney as he turned to face the pair of freebooters. "But if they will ride to the sheriff in Marion with me, they won't have to die tonight."

Sauder pushed his chair back and stood, and Walker followed his lead. "You're a God-damned liar," he hissed. Somehow Putney managed to focus on both men. Not so much the men as their guns. There was the sound of a clock ticking that Putney hadn't heard before. The lamps in the room showed brighter and emanated golden rays with blue fire at the tips that created a circle in their glow. The room grew broader and deeper, and the dark corners turned black. Each man's guns floated from their holsters, the men's hands barely touching them. Ribbons of black smoke wafted out of the guns' barrels and onto the room's heavy air. Then everything shrunk back to its original form.

Four bullet holes had appeared at Putney's feet and pistol balls had broken two jugs on shelves behind him. Putney turned to see Croggins, white as a ghost, with his hands straight up in the air.

"Have you got a pencil," Putney asked the frozen man. Croggins lowered his hands, reached in the pocket of his apron, and placed the pencil on the bar.

Putney pulled his case from his pocket and took a cigarette and lit it. Putney took a deep drag and exhaled a plume of smoke. Then he pulled the long wallet from his rear pocket, removed a twenty-dollar bill, and placed it on the planks. He then took the list of names from the wallet, picked up the pencil, and crossed out two names.

25

I mogene and Wallace found Putney sitting at a table in the main room at Turk's, eating a plate full of ham and eggs with biscuits, gravy, and potatoes. "Where have you been all night?" Imogene demanded to know. "I've been sick with worry!"

"Working," Putney said between bites.

"Working?" Wallace questioned him.

"Yes," Putney said. "Mamie Croggins made me do some digging."

Putney's companions sat at the table, and Squeaky came over with two glasses of milk. "Turk will have breakfast for you in a minute," Squeaky told the pair. "Reckon y'all heard of the to-do's over at Croggins' last night."

"No, we ain't and don't want to," Wallace shot Squeaky a look that made the proprietor decide to drop the subject. As he slinked away from the table, the door swung open, and in marched Captain Pierce, backed by Sergeant McEntire and two privates.

"Who in the hell do you think you are?" Captain Pierce barked the question at Putney, who looked up from his breakfast at the captain. Putney cocked his head and raised his eyebrows in what he hoped was a look of innocence. In the same tone, Captain Pierce continued, not buying Putney's feigned guiltlessness, "You killed those two men last night over in Croggins' place."

Putney's calmness contrasted with Pierce's excitement. Digging his fork into a pile of fried potatoes, he asked, "Excuse me, are you talking to me as the civilian authority?"

"Don't you quibble with me," the captain's voice grew a degree louder. "You put four of my soldiers in danger!"

"Are you talking about the four soldiers that were off-post without permission?" asked Putney without looking up.

"Whether they were there with or without permission is irrelevant!" Pierce's ire grew hotter.

Putney put down his fork, turned in his chair, and looked squarely at Captain Pierce but continued calmly, "Your soldiers were in no danger. They were gone well before anything happened. They were drunk and left singing. What happened after your men left Croggins' was self-defense. I'm sure you have already talked to Croggins, and he told you so. Since I didn't endanger your soldiers and this is a civilian matter, I'm not sure what you're doing here."

"I'm here to say you need to move on!" said Pierce, then added, "Today!"

At this point, Wallace broke in, "Are you declaring martial law, Captain?"

"Of course not." the captain sounded weaker.

"You told us yesterday that you had no authority to enforce civilian law," said Wallace, who was just as calm as Putney. "So, unless you are declaring martial law, you have no authority to tell Nahum or anyone else when or where to go. We will be here until the Indian Agent gets here, then we are leaving with White Owl. If that's not soon enough for you, I don't know what to say."

With all the wind taken out of his sails, Pierce ended by saying, "As soon as the telegraph is up, I will send a message to the sheriff in Marion." With that, he turned to walk out.

Before he could get out of the door, Imogene, believing that Putney needed defending, called after the captain, "If you had arrested those two yesterday, they wouldn't be dead today." Pierce paused as if to reply but instead stomped off with his delegation behind him.

After the captain had left, Putney cleared his throat, he had something to tell his companions, but he dreaded it because he knew what the reaction would be. "Bill, Imogene," Putney felt the words sticking in his throat. "I guess it's time to tell you I'm not returning to Texas. Not right now, anyway."

"What?" Imogene was genuinely shocked at the news. "You can't mean that!"

"Yes, sweetie," Putney told her. "I do mean it. I have things to take care of before I go back to Texas if I ever do."

Wallace said to Putney. "I said all I had to say to you last night, except this," with as stern a voice as he had ever used, Wallace continued, "If you continue down this path, it will be a wasted venture. There are consequences we can't even imagine. But, one thing is for certain. With every trigger pull, you will kill a small piece of your soul. And most likely, the only thing you will get out of it will be eight feet of rope with a ten-foot drop." Bill hoped this last effort would turn Putney around, though he knew it was falling on deaf ears.

"Bill," said Putney with all the reason and seriousness he could muster. "I've heard everything you have said. In my bones, I figure you're right. My Da said something similar, once. But tell me something. If I don't do something, who will ever make those men pay for what they've done. The law? You already know, if they don't see it, it may as well have never happened. This isn't a thing I want to do. It is a thing I must do."

"I've had my say," Bill told Putney.

"And I've had mine."

~

IT WAS another two days before the Indian agent arrived. There was little to do while they waited. Squeaky had scrounged up a checkerboard from somewhere. Putney and Imogene played a few games while she tried to persuade Putney into coming to Texas. Bigfoot Wallace spent most of his time whittling on a stick he had picked up. Eventually, the stick turned into a flute that he gave to Imogene. Wallace and Putney exchanged few words. But they ate meals together for Imogene's sake.

When the agent did show, he had two wagons instead of one. His drivers would not go into the territories. Wallace said he would drive one of the wagons but renegotiated his deal with White Owl. The Cherokee lowered his rate to one dollar a day and two dollars, fifty cents for an introduction to someone who would take him and Imogene through Choctaw country to the Texas border.

When the day arrived, Wallace busied himself stowing his and Imogene's gear on one of the wagons and securing the horses to trail it. Putney, for his part, took the mule and packed the equipment he would need. Squeaky had a coat Turk had made from beaver pelts that a trapper had traded. Fall was coming, and Putney knew the weather would be cold up north, so he bought the coat and a pair of wool mittens.

Imogene and Wallace were standing by the wagon when Putney came out of Squeaky's. Putney placed his latest acquisitions on top of his pack and walked over to send his friends off. The man, who had been a friend to his father and mother, wrapped his long arms around Putney. "I hope to see you again one day," said Wallace. "And for your sake, I hope you never find the men you're looking for."

"Thank you for being a friend, Bill," Putney's voice was filled with sincerity. "I have heeded everything you've told me. But I must find them because if I don't, I dread, I may never see home again."

Kneeling in front of Imogene, Putney drew her close and hugged her so tight he hoped she wouldn't break. But, of course, he knew she wouldn't. Nothing would ever break this girl. She was that strong. Putney felt her tears staining his cheek, then she pushed away and stood back to look at him. "I ain't crying for me," she said. "I'm crying for you and what you're going to do. I understand you can't turn from this any more than you could leave me with the Comanche. I love you for it, and I hate you for it. You were my savior, friend, and brother, but I fear I will never see you again." She hugged Putney once more and kissed him on his cheek, then turning to Bigfoot, Wallace said, "Let's go, Bill."

26

A t the end of August, Putney had made it to Fort Wallace in northwest Kansas. Putney could have made it to Fort Wallace sooner had he not been keeping a wary eye out for Indians. The only settlements between the two forts were Indian camps. Putney wasn't familiar with the tribes that roamed the area, Pawnee, Sioux, Cheyenne, and Arapaho, but he reasoned that they weren't any happier with white men than were the Comanche or Kiowa.

A white man alone in the vast wilderness stood no chance against these strong tribes. So he moved more cautiously than he might have if he had been in familiar territory. When he caught sight of a village or hunting parties, he would look for a good place to hunker down for a day or two, living on cold beans and corn dodgers he had gotten at Turk's before leaving Fort Dodge. That and dried beef were his staples. When he felt it safe, he would build a small fire, fry bacon, and cook coffee.

Fort Wallace was little more than a camp. Large A-frame tents, arranged in neat rows, made up the bulk of the fort.

There were a few stone buildings in various degrees of construction. However, the commanding officer, Major Edward Ball, had established his headquarters and living spaces in the only completed stone building. The structure's first floor housed an office with an ante room, designated by a rail around a sergeant's desk. There was also a kitchen and a room set as an officer's mess. Major Ball's residence was on the second floor.

The headquarters building was the first visit that Putney made when he arrived. Sergeant Williams, who manned the desk in front of the major's office, told Putney that the commanding officer was out, but he would see that the major received a note on Putney's visit. Putney had been around enough to know that was the sergeant's polite way of telling him the major wouldn't see Putney. He decided to ask the sergeant about the five men still on his list. The sergeant assumed Putney was a bounty hunter, and Putney did nothing to dissuade the soldier of the notion. But Putney was told that many people passed through Fort Wallace, going to the minefields in Colorado, and he couldn't be specific about five particular men. Putney thanked the sergeant and went into what was called a town.

The structures in the settlement ranged from temporary to semi-permanent, except for the livery, with a completed barn with a workshop. There were tents in assorted sizes and styles that housed a barber-surgeon, low-grade saloons, peddlers, a card house, and one had a plank with the words "Healing Arts" burned into it. Four establishments had put in plank walkways on their fronts and clapboard sides that were five feet high and topped with an "A" frame canvas structure to give them added height. Signs on these four showed two restaurants, a saloon, and a hotel. Apart from the other business was one set off from the rest. From the linens and clothes hanging on drying lines, Putney knew it was a laundry.

Having had meager meals while on the trail, Putney decided to try one of the restaurants. The food was standard fare for a frontier town. There were eggs, beef stew, pork or bacon, beans, potatoes, and other root vegetables. Putney ate pork that had been cooked on a spit over an open fire, beans, and potatoes, served up by a grizzled old man that did double duty as the cook and waiter. The food was flavored with plenty of salt, chiles, and black pepper. It wasn't the best Putney had ever eaten, but it was hot, which made up for any lack of cooking skill. After his meal, Putney walked to the large saloon on the other side of the street.

A sign hung over the swinging doors that read 'The Pequod.' Inside, the saloon was empty, which may have been the reason it looked larger than Putney had expected. It was undoubtedly more ornate. There was a polished oak bar with a brass foot rail and four brass spittoons spaced at equal intervals. The wall behind the bar was built up another five feet and had shelves. To Putney's surprise, there was a good selection of whiskies, if the labels were to be trusted, and several brands of rum and gin. On the top shelf was a whaling harpoon. A sturdy barman with a shaven head and an earring greeted Putney at the bar.

"I guess you're going to tell me your name is Ahab," said Putney.

"Ah, a literary man, I see," drawled the barman. "No. Name is Chandler. But I do have this,"

Chandler pointed behind the bar. Putney looked over and saw Chandler had a wooden leg. "Lost it sailing on the "Two Brothers' under Captain Pollard. A real Jonah, he was. Anyways, my brother, Tom Chandler, talked me into coming west and opening a saloon. Here is as far as we got when he died. Sos, I decided to plant here. Whiskey, gin, or rum?"

"Coffee," replied Putney and waited as the barman walked to a pot belly stove that stood at one end of the bar. He took a sip of the coffee, then, looking at Chandler, said, "This is good coffee."

"It's all in the roast, they tell me. Enjoy it while you can. That bag of beans is nearly gone. Don't know when I will get another bag in." lamented Chandler. "So, what's a well-educated man, like yourself, doing out here in the big middle of nowhere?"

Not wanting to tip his hand, Putney said, "Considering my options."

"There are only two options I see out here," said the bartender. "Go west and work the mines in Colorado, those that ain't played out, or go north up around Julesburg, Colorado and work the cattle ranches up there. Those ranches are feeding a lot of beef to Fort Laramie, and over to the new railroad they are building."

"The problem with either of those options is the word' work,'" Putney said.

"Ah," replied Chandler. "A man seeking action and adventure. There was a group of like-minded men through here a couple of weeks ago."

"What profession were they in?" asked Putney.

"Said they were range detectives. They were going to Julesburg, but they were going to Denver first," said Chandler. "One of them stayed here, though. Maybe you could ask him if they have need for another hand."

"That might interest me," said Putney. "Where would I find this man?"

"I don't know. There are so many places to look in this metropolis," a thick dose of irony in the barman's voice.

"I get what you mean," said Putney. "Reckon you could tell me what this man looks like and maybe his name?"

"Wayull," said Chandler in his New England drawl. "Don't rightly know his name, but he's a short feller with a bald nape if it's not covered by that John Bull Topper he wears."

"John Bull Topper?" Putney was unfamiliar with the term.

"Sure, it's like a stove pipe that's somebody cut in half," answered Chandler, "Kinda splays out at the top and has a short brim."

"Thanks," said Putney. "How much for the coffee?"

"On the house, this time. Come back and spend some money on whiskey later," Chandler said. "Maybe I'll tell you about the one that got away."

Putney said he would be back and left the saloon. He walked his horse and mule to the livery and paid the man there two dollars each for boarding the animals. He took his guns, bedroll, and saddle bags over to the structure with a sign that indicated it was a hotel. Inside the hotel was a counter built from rough-hewn planks and a man seated on a high stool, reading a worn-out newspaper. "Do you have any rooms?" Putney asked the man.

"If you want to call them that," the man said, barely looking up from his reading.

"I'll take one for two nights," Putney told him.

"One dollar," the clerk advised Putney. Then, after Putney put a silver coin on the counter, the man said. "Behind the curtain, Sign has the number three over the door."

"How about a bath?" Putney wanted to know.

"You'll have to go to the barber for that," then returned to his reading.

"Putney pushed a worn velvet curtain out of the way and walked down the hallway to find room number three. Door was a loosely defined word. Under the number three was a canvas curtain that hung from rings over a rod. Pushing the curtain open, Putney saw the term room was also loosely defined. It was an area six feet wide and ten feet long, surrounded by canvas walls. The interior walls that divided the space from the other rooms were about eight feet high. There was a small table with a wash basin and a lantern. Underneath sat an empty pitcher. Putney assumed one had to get wash water themselves. The bed was a wood frame with a duck mattress filled with feathers. A folded blanket on one end and a duck pillow on the other completed the room's furnishing. "Better than sleeping on the ground, I guess," Putney said in an outside voice. He spread his bed roll out and hung his slicker on a hook offered on one pole in the room. Next, he dug out two sets of clothes from his saddle bags, one dirty and one clean. Putney left the two Walkers and an extra Colt in the bags. Then, picking up his rifle, he left the hotel and went to the

the tent with a wooden barber pole propped outside. It was a large tent, probably fifteen feet square. Inside were two benches along one wall with a ragged-looking man sitting on one, studying the floor. There was a real barber's chair bolted to a raised platform that was big enough for the barber to walk around to ply his trade. A cracked mirror hung by wires on the wall opposite the benches. On the back wall, also hanging by wires, was a sign that read, 'Hair Cut - ten cents, Shave - fifteen cents, Bath - ten cents, Clean Water - twenty-five cents, Clean Hot Water – one dollar, Teeth Pulled – three dollars per tooth, Surgery – depends. A customer wearing a striped bib was in the chair. The barber shaving the customer stopped and looked at Putney. "What'll it be, mister?" he asked.

"Hot water bath and a shave," Putney told him.

"Buddy," the barber said to the man on the bench. "Go to the back room, drain and clean the tub. There's water on the fire out back. Fill up the tub and set out a clean towel," Then, turning to Putney, "It will take a few minutes. You want me to cut off that long red hair?"

"Did I ask for that?" Putney returned.

"No, I guess you didn't," replied the barber, directing his attention to the customer in the chair, said, "Surly, ain't he?' Putney sat on the one bench with a back on it, pulled a cigarette out of its case, and lit it.

After about fifteen minutes, Buddy returned and said the water was ready. Putney went behind the tent wall to find another tent attached. A copper tub with steam coming off the water was sitting on a slatted floor. On one side of the tub was a rack holding a towel and soap bar. On the other side was another rack for clothes and a chair. The warm water felt good on a man that had been two weeks in the wilderness. Putney soaked until he felt the water beginning to cool and began scrubbing himself down and washing his hair. When he had finished and toweled off, he put on his clean clothes, bundled up the dirty ones, and walked into the main parlor.

It took a few minutes for the barber to brush out the tangles of Putney's hair while muttering it would be easier if he just cut it all off. When the barber had finished his work Putney paid the required fee. Before walking out, Putney gave Buddy a dime and told him thanks.

Putney left the barber and walked to laundry. A boardwalk in front of the laundry tent kept a customer from walking in the perennial mud created by the washroom. In-

side he found a man and two women, one of whom was an
Indian. The women scrubbed clothes in large wooden tubs,
and the man dunked the soapy material in fresher water. He
left his clothes with the white woman who wrote down a
description of his clothes and his name. "We got an ironing
woman in the back tent. It will cost another two bits if you
want your clothes ironed." Putney didn't need his clothes
ironed but figured the business could use the two bits, so he
said to have them ironed. The woman noted his request and
told him to return the next afternoon if it didn't rain.

Putney returned to his room to check his gear against
theft, and he returned to the saloon just as darkness fell.
The room had a totally different feel. Men drinking various
spirits occupied most of the tables. Two men were seated in
a corner playing popular tunes on a fiddle and a concertina.
Four women were also in the saloon, all wearing little more
than sleeping shifts. An attractive colored woman and a
pretty but plump blonde with too much face paint were
dancing with two men. An Indian woman with a split nose
was seated alone in a corner, and a skinny woman was
sitting at a table with two men, drinking and laughing.
Evidently, Chandler's wares in the Pequod weren't limited to
spirits.

"Wayull, I see you made it back and looking fresh as a
daisy," Chandler addressed Putney as he walked up to the
bar. Putney asked Chandler if he had any whiskey worth
drinking. "It's all worth drinking, my boy. But some is worth
more than others."

"Then give me the one that's worth it the most," Putney
told the barman.

Chandler took a bottle from the shelf and poured a glass
for Putney, who was glad he had asked for the best. It was
smooth and went down easy. Putney wondered whether the

man they had discussed earlier was in the room. Chandler nodded at a bald man sitting alone at a table playing solitaire. Putney put two dollars on the bar and asked for a second glass. He walked over to the table and, placing the bottle and extra glass on it, said, "Jack Callahan. Mind if I join you."

"As long as I ain't paying for that bottle, take a seat," the bald man told him.

Putney sat, poured whiskey into the glass, and pushed it toward his host. The man picked up the glass, took a sip, and said, "Thanks. Claude Franklin," sticking out his hand to Putney. Putney had memorized all the names on his list. There was an Ed Franklin, but no Claude.

"Mr. Chandler over there said you might be looking to hire on a good man as a range detective," Putney told Franklin.

"I don't know where Chandler gets his information, but no, I'm not hiring anybody for anything," said Franklin. "I'm just waiting for a couple of men to show up here."

"He just told me you had been here with some others that said they were range detectives headed for Julesburg." said, Putney. "I told him I was looking for work. I guess he just thought you might be hiring."

"Nah, I came over this way to meet up with my brother. I got a letter from him while I was in St. Louis. He said he and another man had a group of men put together for range work," Franklin told him. "Ed told me to wait for two men who were supposed to come up from Fort Dodge. Ed said Comanche had attacked them in New Mexico, and these two were badly hurt. One almost had his arm taken off by a Comanche tomahawk. The other man was cut pretty bad in the face. Nearly lost an ear." Claude Franklin was a talkative type. So when he had said his brother's name was Ed, Putney knew he was on the right trail.

"These two men," asked Putney, "Their names wouldn't be Sauder and Walker, would they?"

"Yeah, how'd you know," Franklin asked back.

"I was down in Fort Dodge, myself," Putney told Franklin. "I met this guy named Walker with a bad cut across his face and his ear bandaged up. He said his partner, a man named Sauder, had his arm cleaved badly. He said a woman there had patched them both up, but septis got in Sauder's arm. It seems gangrene spread before anyone knew it and Sauder died."

"Is that so?" Franklin was genuinely interested in what Putney was telling him.

"Yes, sir," Putney assured him. "Walker said the army doctor wouldn't see any civilians, so he was heading to Leavenworth to see a real doctor and get patched up right before the same thing happened to him."

"Can't blame him," said Franklin reaching for the bottle and looking at Putney for approval.

"Sure, go ahead," Putney told him. He waited until Franklin filled his glass. He then took the bottle and started to rise. "Thanks anyway."

"Wait a minute," Franklin called for Putney to stay seated. "Look, I can't guarantee anything, but it looks like Ed and this guy Musgrove are going to be short-handed. So why don't you ride over to Denver with me? If they don't need you, maybe you can get on with some other outfit. Have you got any experience?"

Putney told Franklin that he didn't know what qualified but told him about his war experience, fighting Comanche and Kiowas. Franklin said he had been with the Union, but that was all over now. "Besides, from what I've seen, there

ain't no work for war veterans, Rebs, or blue coats. Can you
leave tomorrow morning?"

"I got laundry that won't be ready until tomorrow afternoon. Can we wait until the following day?" asked Putney.

"I don't see what difference one more day will make,"
said Claude Franklin. "Besides, if we finish this bottle
tonight, I won't feel like leaving tomorrow anyway."

"Deal," said Putney and stuck out his hand.

"Deal," said Claude, giving Putney's hand one strong
pump.

Putney had nursed his whiskey, letting Franklin drink
most of it. The last Putney saw of Claude Franklin that night
was when the skinny whore had walked arm in arm to the
back of the Pequod. Putney returned to his room and, after
lighting the lantern, studied his map. He figured the trip
would take eight to ten days. *I need to think about how Jack
Callahan will kill these bastards*. Putney thought as if Callahan
was a separate person from himself.

27

The journey to Denver was longer than either Putney or Franklin had estimated. They had not accounted for the rise in altitude. Although the terrain, in the early days, always looked flat, they discovered that the further west they traveled, the more their animals struggled. The situation applied equally to the men. When they struck the Smoky Hill Trail, the climb became apparent. The weather also had an impact. It would be warm in the sunlight. Then at night, the temperature would drop considerably. Putney was glad he had bought the beaver coat from Turk. It was warm and kept him dry enough that he let Franklin use his slicker for extra warmth.

At times Putney would momentarily forget that he was using Claude Franklin for his purpose of revenge. He genuinely liked the man. Claude told Putney of his time with the 1st Ohio Infantry and the numerous battles he had fought. Claude was a true believer and was among the first of the enlistees. At first, his letters home were full of righteousness that he was fighting on the right side and optimism that the war would be over soon. Claude never lost the faith that he was fighting for right, but Claude slowly became jaded and disillusioned at the truths of war. He saw his friends and comrades killed or terribly mangled with each battle. When rumors of a draft began, Claude wrote his older brother, Ed, telling him to go out west, beyond the reach of the draft boards.

Ed had taken his younger brother's advice. So when Claude got a letter from his parents that Ed had left for the gold fields in Colorado, Claude held a solo celebration by buying some homemade whiskey from a local farmer and getting drunk.

Miraculously Claude never even received a wound and was eventually promoted to sergeant. He received several awards and medals. But with the war's end, his promotion and acts of valor meant little to nothing. Returning home, he found little opportunity for work, so he traveled to St. Louis, hoping to find work. The job he found was working for a milk toast youngster whose family had been able to buy his way out of the draft. His employer had no respect for Claude's service or any veteran. That's where he had been when a letter from Ed had caught up to him telling Claude to meet his brother in Leavenworth, where he could have a well-paying job that guaranteed excitement.

Putney had told Claude how he was in San Antonio when the confederacy had started conscripting men and how he had managed to join the Texas Mounted Mountain Rangers, so he wouldn't have to go east. Claude had agreed that Putney had made the best decision. Of course, Putney left out anything about Captain Russell or anything that had occurred after he had left the command. When Claude asked what he had been doing since, Putney told him he had done a bit of cowboying but saw he wasn't going to get rich doing that, so he had decided to travel to Colorado in search of better prospects than chasing wild longhorns. It was only good fortune that had led him to Claude Franklin.

Because the trip was taking longer than either had expected, their provisions began to run low, but by that time, they were starting into the mountains where the game was more plentiful. It was nothing for one of them to take down a deer which meant more than mere meat and hide. They regularly met parties of others traveling to Denver with trade goods. Putney and Claude would trade fresh venison for coffee and tobacco.

Ed introduced Claude to Lewis Musgrove and the others at Fort Wallace. Musgrove became impatient waiting on the two from Fort Dodge. Musgrove decided that Claude, the newest to the group, would wait a few days for the other two and then meet the rest in Denver. Ed told Claude to check into a rooming house in Denver. Once they got settled, Claude and the others could find Ed at either Clodfelter's Saloon or Sloan's Billiard Parlor. It was afternoon in late September when Putney and Claude arrived in Denver. Unlike many frontier towns Putney had seen, most buildings in the middle of the city were built of brick or stone. He and Claude later learned that a great fire in 1863 had destroyed many of the wood buildings, and the city fathers had passed an ordinance requiring buildings to be erected with non-flammable materials. The pair found a place to stay at Docherty's Lodging House. They each got a room and, after stowing their gear, got directions to a nearby livery to board their animals.

Claude wanted to go to one of the establishments to find his brother, but Putney said he was going back to Docherty's for a bath. Claude laughed and told Putney he was the vainest man he had ever met. Putney agreed, then told Claude to meet him at Clodfelter's at nine.

Putney saw that even at night, Denver was a bustling town. It wasn't nearly as large as San Antonio or Galveston, but there seemed to be something happening in every saloon, shop, or hotel he passed. Putney went into a tobacconist shop on Broadway and found they had Kinney ready rolls, so he bought five packets. He also got directions to Sloan's Billiard Parlor and Clodfelter's Saloon. He walked a block, stopped at the Denver House Hotel, and went to their restaurant for a steak dinner.

After dinner, Putney walked to Clodfelter's and looked in the window. Claude Franklin was standing at the bar talking with another man. The saloon had a selection of gaming tables, including Faro, a wheel of fortune, roulette, and a dice table. There were three tables covered with green felt where men were playing cards. There were other tables where men were drinking. An array of women in colorful and revealing dresses strolled among customers or sat at tables. Putney supposed these women were prostitutes or drink pushers, neither of whom he had any experience. Guessing that none of the men in the saloon was his quarry, Putney walked in toward his friend.

Putney greeted Claude and ordered a beer from the barman who had taken his order. Putney learned that the man Claude was conversing with was a mining detective from Boulder named Lockwood Fuller. Fuller was in Denver looking to recruit men to work as detectives for a syndicate of large mining companies. Fuller said the mines were beginning to play out and that small prospectors were working claims and encroaching on the big companies' lands. The detectives' job was to ensure that the small miners had claims filed and were not poaching off the big mines. "You look like a young man that can handle himself, Callahan," Fuller said to Putney. "I've tried to convince

Franklin to come to Boulder, but he says he already has a job waiting in Julesburg."

Putney was about to answer when behind him, he heard someone yell, "Claude!" Putney looked over his shoulder and saw a group of men walking in. Claude, in turn, called out his brother's name and strode across the floor to greet Ed Franklin. The two men embraced and held each other at arm's length, then hugged again. Putney noticed six more men were accompanying Ed Franklin. One was taller than the rest and carried himself with the confidence of a leader. Five men gravitated to a table, but Ed and Lewis Musgrove walked with Claude to the bar, where Claude introduced Putney and Fuller to his brother and Musgrove. Seeing his recruitment wasn't going to be fulfilled at that moment, Fuller moved aside and made room for the additional men.

"Ed, this is Jack Callahan. He rode up with me from Fort Wallace," said Claude. "He's good company. I thought maybe you could put him on." Even though Ed was older than Claude, his face didn't tell it. It didn't have the premature aging etched on Claude's face by war and deprivation. The two could almost pass as twins if it hadn't been for that. Ed shook Putney's hand and said it was good to meet him, but before he could say anything else, Musgrove butted into the conversation.

"Weren't you supposed to wait for Sauder and Walker?" Musgrove's voice was cool. "Where are they?"

"Funny you should ask that," returned Claude, not sensing the danger in Musgrove's voice. "Jack here ran into one of them at Fort Dodge. What was his name Jack?"

Feeling Musgrove's eyes on him, Putney turned his head and looked directly into the outlaw's black eyes. Captain Russell had been a vain and greedy man, and the Missouri bushwhackers all had the look of meanness, but this was the first time Putney felt he had looked into the eyes of pure evil. Feeling a tiny shiver travel from the base of his neck down his spine, Putney took his time answering as he assessed the outlaw leader. Musgrove had jet black hair and a thick mustache that matched and grew past his lips to his jawline. Musgrove stood an inch taller than Putney and probably outweighed him by thirty pounds, none of which was fat. Musgrove wore all black down to the twin bracers with silver studs surrounding his wrists. As far as Putney could tell, Musgrove carried a single Colt in a cross-draw holster. "Walker," Putney finally said, the ice in his voice matched Musgrove's. "Jim Walker."

Turning back to Claude Musgrove asked, "Why ain't they here?"

"That was what I was about to tell you. According to Jack, Sauder's dead, and Walker's gone to Leavenworth to see a doctor," Claude said, unaware of the menace in the room.

Again, turning his face to Putney, Musgrove asked, "Is that so, Red."

"Just so," returned Putney.

"That's fine. Just fine," Musgrove's voice didn't sound like anything was fine. "Fact is, Red, we don't need no more help. It looks like you barked up the wrong tree."

Musgrove was using the moniker "Red" to try and gall Putney, but Putney wasn't taking the bait.

"It's fine with me, too," Putney's said, hoping to sound as hard as he had meant. "I already have another offer." Putney pushed his way past Musgrove and Ed Franklin and over to where Lockwood Fuller stood.

Musgrove took the two Franklin brothers over to the tables that the others of the gang had commandeered. Fuller, who was four inches shorter than Putney, ordered two whiskeys. When the drinks came, Fuller pushed one to Putney. "Do you know who that man is?" Fuller asked.

"They said his name was Lewis Musgrove." replied Putney.

"Well, sure, that's his name," said Fuller, "But maybe what you don't know is that he's a vicious killer. At least that's what they say."

Putney stared at the eight men at the two tables, memorizing how each man looked. Then, without looking away, Putney took the glass of whiskey and slugged the fiery liquid back. Setting the glass on the bar, Putney looked at Fuller and said, "I know who he is, and I know what he is. Now, how about that job."

28

N ahum Putney was already eating breakfast when Claude came in and sat across from him at the communal table. Claude was loading eggs and grits on his plate as he said, "Jack, I'm sorry about last night. I don't know what the deal was. Ed said that Lewis will make snap decisions like that."

"Don't worry about it, Claude," Putney told his friend. "I hired on with Fuller last night. I'll be headed up to Boulder next week." Putney hadn't wanted to go to Boulder, but his bankroll was shrinking. He didn't want to hit the Galveston bank again, so a job was necessary, at least through the winter.

"That's good. I'm glad things worked out for you," Putney appreciated the genuine tone of Claude's words. "We're headed up to Julesburg today. It looks like there is a lot of rustling going on up there. We'll be working for one of the big ranchers up there."

"Good for you, Claude," Putney said. "Just do me a favor and take care of yourself."

"Sure, I will, Jack. Maybe I'll see you back here some-time," Claude told him. "And you be careful, too."

Putney rose from the table, shook Claude's hand, and went to his room. It would be three years before Putney would see his friend again. Fuller had told Putney that he would be recruiting in Denver for the next week. Fuller told Putney to meet him at the Denver House Hotel, where he was staying. The Denver House was centrally located and close to shops and businesses, and it had its own stable in the back. Putney decided to move there himself. It would be easier to acquire new equipment and clothing. It also offered more privacy. After his move, Putney spent the day shopping. He went to a leather shop and ordered a new saddle holster rig for his Walkers and a gun belt with a straight draw right-hand holster and a left-hand cross draw for his French pistols with cartridge loops for pistols and his rifle. The weather was already cool and would soon be getting cold, so Putney bought clothing suitable for the oncoming winter.

Putney spent days relaxing, the evenings at the better restaurants and nights reading newspapers and books from the hotel's small library. His favorite book was a collection of poems by Edgar Allan Poe. The poems were dark, sad, and vengeful, all of which suited Putney. The fourth night in Denver was a Saturday, and the town was bustling with prospectors, cowboys, farmers, and merchants. Putney had eaten dinner and considered returning to the hotel and having them bring a bathtub to his room where he would soak, drink whiskey, and read Poe. But a nagging feeling pushed him to go to Clodfelter's.

Drinkers and men trying their luck at the gaming tables crowded the saloon. The girls in colorful dresses sauntered among the men. They sidled up to them, coaxing the men to

buy expensive wine. Smoke from cigars, pipes, and cigarettes hung in an ominous fog over the patrons' heads. It
was a boisterous and rude scene that held no appeal to
Putney. Then, just as he was finishing his beer and ready to
return to the hotel, two men entered the saloon and pushed
their way to the crowded bar. Over the din of the tavern, one
called to a bartender and ordered a bottle of whiskey.
Putney didn't know their names, but he knew their faces.
They had been with Musgrove, and Putney reasoned they
were on his list, but he had to make sure.

Putney ordered another beer and lit a Kinney while
watching the two men celebrate their Saturday on the town.
Putney needed to know their identities. He accepted that he
was a killer, but not a murderer. His mission was righteous,
and he would not sully it by killing men he was not certain
had been part of the raiders in New Mexico. Putney had to
bide his time. He had to be confident.

Putney didn't know how much time had passed when,
from the corner of his eye, he saw two men rising from a
card table, pitching their losing hands on the pile of money
in the center of the table, and leaving, disgusted with their
attempt to get rich, quick. His targets had also seen the table
open and, encouraging each other, pushed their way to the
table and took a seat. There were two men at the table with
the appearance of professional gamblers. Putney moved
deliberately, gently parting the ocean of men in the room
until he arrived at the table. He removed his hat and hung it
on a deer antler nailed to the wall for that purpose. Then,
pulling his wallet from his new frock coat, Putney sat and
asked what the game was.

"Stud horse poker," answered one of the card sharps. "Do
you know it?"

"I'm a quick learner," said Putney.

One of Musgrove's men looked up and said, "Look, Russ! It's that feller Musgrove wouldn't let join us. What did he call him?"

"Shoot Andy, that's ole Red," replied his partner.

Putney ignored the apparent intent to get under his skin, but not the men's names. Russell Horton and Andrew Bailey both names were on his list. Putney turned his attention to the two gamblers Putney introduced himself, "Jack Callahan," he said.

"Barton," said the first gambler.

"William Murphy," said the other.

"There you go, Russ," said Horton. "Red Jack Callahan. You reckon ole Red Jack here knows how to play poker? He looks mighty young."

Murphy fanned a deck of cards face down across the table.

"Draw for the deal?" he asked and began to reach for a card.

Putney put his hand on Murphy's wrist.

"Not to be rude, but I would like a new deck," Putney said in a manner that neither gambler wanted to contest.

"Certainly," said Murphy and called to one of the drink pushers to bring a new deck from the bar. The girl scooped up the cards and went to the bar. When she returned, Putney tipped her with a half dollar.

Murphy opened the new pack, threw away the jokers, and fanned the deck across the table. Barton won the draw. "Stud horse poker, gentlemen. Everyone know how to play?" Putney wasn't familiar with the game but knew he could figure it out as the game played.

"Shuffle the deck and deal," demanded Bailey.

Barton did just that, dealing one card down and one face up. When the betting started, Putney folded. He wanted to watch and understand how to play the game. Both Horton and Bailey played wild and loose. Murphy folded with the third card. There was another round of betting and another deal. Bailey started the betting with Horton and Barton calling. Another face-up card brought more wild betting. Barton hung in. With the last card, Horton passed the bet to Bailey, who bet twenty dollars. "You better be careful," said Horton. That's money Musgrove gave us to buy supplies.

"Shaddup," Bailey was sharp with his friend. Then to Barton, "You calling?" To which Barton silently folded his cards. "See Russ. The smart guys know when a man's got them beat." Horton also folded.

The game continued in the same manner, hand after hand. Bailey was always the aggressor. The more Bailey drank, the more aggressive he became. After an hour, Horton finally bowed out, saying, "I ain't losing any more money. I can't stay against you using the boss's bankroll. I'm going to go chat up one of the gals and see if I can get my noodle wet." Horton stumbled, getting up from the table, and staggered to the bar. The two professionals were treading water, neither winning nor losing. Putney played the game carefully until he had caught on to it, then he started losing, but only against Bailey.

It was midnight when the third hour started. Both Barton and Murphy were good players but had been reluctant to move in against a wild better like Bailey, so both bowed out. Bailey hollered, "Any more losers out there want to give me their money?" There were no takers. The men in the bar had watched as Bailey had gotten louder and more belligerent with each hand and figured it wasn't worth the aggravation. "Looks like it's just you and me, Red Jack. Have you got the stones to hang?"

All Putney said was, "It's your deal."

Putney changed his tactics and started winning as many hands as he lost. The longer the impasse went on, the angrier Bailey got. "I'm gonna take everything you got, Red, including them fancy damned cigarettes and the case."

The game went into the fourth hour, with neither man making headway. Putney had observed Bailey until he was confident he had the outlaw's pattern down. When Andrew Bailey was bluffing, he would keep both hands flat on the table and try to stare Putney down. When Bailey was holding a good hand, he acted unconcerned and always tugged on his left ear lobe. Finally, Bailey caught the hand that Putney wanted. Bailey was showing four hearts with a king. Then Bailey bet a hundred dollars and laid his hands flat on the table. Putney kept his eyes on the table. Putney looked at the cards in front of him, seven, nine, ten, jack, all different suits. Putney had been keeping track of Bailey's winnings and knew he had about four hundred dollars left. There were only fifty in front of Putney.

"What you gonna do, Red," Bailey taunted. Putney kept looking at the table. "You know I got you beat," Bailey spoke out again, this time but louder. Finally, people in the saloon started paying attention to what was happening at the table. As the audience grew, so did Bailey's audacity.

With the speed of molasses in winter, Putney reached to the inside pocket of his frock coat, pulled out his wallet, and counted the bills inside. He removed fifty to match what was in front of him and announced, "One hundred." pushing the money to the middle of the table. "And I raise," Putney counted eight fifty dollar bills, nudging them across the table and said in a barely audible voice, "four hundred."

There were a few gasps in the saloon. Everyone was paying attention, even the croupiers at the dice and roulette tables. Bailey's stare turned to a hate-filled glare. "There ain't no way you have an eight down," his voice was angry, but there was also a tiny quiver of fear. He knew what Musgrove would do if he lost the money. Horton had drifted back to the table and laid his hand on Bailey's shoulder, "C'mon Andy," he pleaded. "Just fold, and let's get out of here."

Andrew Bailey jerked his shoulder away and said, "There's no way I'm letting this bush popper bluff me." But he still did not call the raise.

Putney took a Kinney from its case, lit it, and blew a cloud across the table at his adversary. "That is as close as you will get to taking my cigarettes from me." Putney's voice was smooth and silky.

"God damn it! Call." Growled Bailey, counting out three hundred, ninety-five dollars.

"You are short," said Putney.

"It don't matter. I got you beat," Bailey insisted.

"I will let you owe me," Putney said as he took another pull off the cigarette. Putney reached out his hand and flipped over the eight of spades.

Bailey dropped his eyes and stared at the table. "You're a cheating son of a bitch." Andrew Bailey whispered so that only Putney could hear.

Russ Horton leaned over Bailey and said, "You gotta do something, Andy. Musgrove is going to whip us both if he doesn't flat out kill us."

Pushing back from the table, Bailey stood and repeated, but this time so everyone could hear. "You're a cheating son of bitch."

Men and women cleared to both sides of the room, knowing what was about to happen. Putney surprised everyone when he stood slowly, keeping his hands chest high with his palms facing out. With the tranquility of a sunset, Putney turned his back on Bailey, took his hat off the antler hook, and placed it on his head. Putney reached out softly and took one of the drink pushing girls gently by the arm. "You go scoop up that money off the table and take it to the bar. Keep fifty for yourself."

Everyone watched in silence as the girl did as Putney had said. Then, when he was sure she was out of harm's way, Putney turned back to face Bailey. "I did not cheat you. It is just that you are the worst poker player in Colorado." Putney watched as the saloon's walls pushed out twenty feet in every direction and took the people with them. The tobacco smoke floated through the ceiling and left the room glowing in the bright light of the lamps that hung down. Two glowing lead balls flew on either side of Putney. Finally, the saloon shrunk back to its normal size. Nahum Putney looked at the body on the saloon floor as blood seeped out of two holes in Andrew Bailey's chest.

Putney turned his body to face Russell Horton, who stood frozen with his hands above his head. "Don't shoot Callahan. I ain't making a move. If you shoot me, it'll be murder." Putney holstered his gun. "I am not walking around Denver waiting for you to slip in and shoot me in the back. You pull that Colt. You have one chance, and you had better take it now."

"I ain't going to Callahan. I can't match you, and I'm not giving you a reason to murder me," Horton pleaded.

"I already have a reason to kill you, but it will not be murder." Putney's voice was as hard as granite. "Now pull that God damned Colt."

Putney felt something touch his back, and he started to turn but thought better of it. "That's a smarter move, mister." The voice was a stranger to Putney. "You," the voice was louder. "The one about to piss your pants. Today is your lucky day. Get out of here and get out of Denver, or I may let

this red-headed bastard kill you just to make my job easier."
Horton could not make it to the door fast enough. "Now,
what are we to do about you, boy?" The voice asked. "I know,
first, put those fancy pistols on the bar, and be as smart as
you shoot."

Putney pulled the French pistols, walked to the bar, and
placed them next to his winnings. The voice then told
Putney to turn around. When Putney turned, he saw a man
with a shortened double-barrel shotgun pointed at him.
The man had a badge on his shirt. "I'm Marshal Wilson
Sisty, and you son are going to jail while I get this straight."
Then to one of the bartenders, "John, you pack up those
pistols and that money and bring them to the jail, and don't
let your fingers get sticky with that cash."

29

Putney was wakened by clinking keys and clanking steel doors on the second night of his incarceration. When he looked, he saw the jailer place a slender black man, about fifty years old, in the cell with him. The old man smelled from a mix of sour whiskey and piss. Putney rolled over on his side, away from the man.

"You ain't gotta be rude," said the old man.

Without turning, Putney replied, "I'm not being rude. I'm just trying to go back to sleep."

"My name is Lester Jones," the old man told Putney. "But most folk call me Oracle Jones. What's yours?"

Realizing sleep was not coming his way until he pacified Jones' curiosity, Putney rolled over and sat up. "Jack Callahan. Now, do you mind if I go back to sleep?"

"Like me, that's the one people call you, but that ain't your real name," said Jones.

"It's the name you're going to get," Putney was becoming irritated.

"Shore, shore," Jones said with a tinge of sarcasm. "Have it your way. They put me in here, regular 'cause I drinks a bit. And when I do, I start preaching and prophesying. It uncalms some folk, so they put me in here until I sobers up. So what are you in jail for?"

"I shot a man. Now, it's hard enough to sleep on this wood bunk, so would you mind being quiet for a while, so I can at least try," Putney said.

Jones stood and raised his voice so that other prisoners began waking up. " Dearly beloved, avenge not yourselves, but rather give place unto wrath: for it is written, Vengeance is mine; I will repay, saith the Lord. Romans twelve and nineteen," Jones nearly shouted. Other men in the block of cells started yelling for the old man to shut up.

Putney glared at the old man and growled, "What did you say?"

"You ain't deaf. You heard me. And hear this. Cease now, or you will feel pain like you never felt before, but it won't be pain of the body but the soul. Now, if you don't mind, I'm going to sleep," Jones laid on his bed and, within a minute, started snoring.

Putney didn't know whether he slept the rest of the night, but Jones was gone when the jailer brought around breakfast. Putney wondered if it had all been a dream.

∽

Do you know what I think?" Marshal Sisty asked of Putney, who had been languishing in the town lock-up for three days.

Laying on a wooden bunk with a mattress not much thicker than a blanket, Putney opened his eyes to look at the man that had control of his future. "I have no way of knowing what you think, Marshal. Enlighten me."

Marshal Sisty leaned over a spittoon, expelled a big wad

of tobacco into the receptacle, and then said. "I've spent the last three days looking into this killing you committed, and I came to some conclusions. First, I think for some reason that I can't suss out, you had a grudge against Bailey. Second, I think you purposefully joined that poker game so that you could face him. Further, from what Barton and Murphy told me, it looked like you set a trap for that man. Then you goaded him into pulling a gun on you. You knew that was what he would do, and you knew you would kill him."

"Marshal," Putney closed his eyes as he spoke. "I can't do anything about what you think."

"Do you even care?" Sisty wanted to know.

Putney sat on the edge of the bed and looked at the marshal through the cell's iron bars. "Do I care what you think?" Putney asked back. "No. What I do care about is what you can prove. What can you prove, Marshal?"

Marshal Sisty looked at Putney like his eyes were trying to drill into the young man's soul. Finally, he said, "What I can prove is that Bailey pulled a gun and shot at you. Twice. And miraculously, at that distance, he missed you both times. I can prove that you, in turn, somehow kept cool enough to return fire and put two bullets in Bailey, not more than an inch apart. What I can't prove is that you did all this with what the lawyers call premeditation. I can only assume that instead of being the cold-blooded murderer I believe you to be, you were so afraid that Bailey's third bullet wouldn't miss and that you believed you had to kill him to avoid that possibility."

"I believe," said Putney. "As you say, that is what the lawyers call justified homicide. When I go to trial, that will be my defense."

"Oh," said Sisty, as if surprised. "You thought there was

going to be a trial? No, we aren't going to the expense of a trial. The judge said we aren't going to spend money on a trial where you won't be convicted. That is unless you want to go to trial on charges of public nuisance and endangerment. We could make that case. Of course, you could pay the hundred-dollar fine and agree to leave Denver. We would be satisfied with that."

"I will be glad to pay the fine as soon as you let me get to my money you took up," Agreed Putney.

Marshal Sisty rose from his chair and left the cell block. It was a few minutes when the jailer came in and unlocked the cell, and led Putney to the outer office. All his personal items, except his guns, had been placed on a counter, and a piece of paper was next to the articles. "Make sure it's all there and sign the receipt," the marshal said.

Putney checked over everything, counted the money, then looked at the marshal sitting behind a desk. "Where're my pistols?" he asked.

Sisty spun around in his swivel chair and unlocked the doors of a cabinet behind the desk. Sisty retrieved Putney's guns and swiveled and placed them on the desk. Putney strapped on his gun belt and started to pick up the guns, but Marshal Sisty held on to them. "Son," said the lawman. "I know the war changed a lot of young men like you, and I'm sorry for all of you, but you have a choice to make. You're good at killing, and there's a market for that kind of talent. But in the end, it will ruin you. Either someone better or luckier than you will put you in the grave as you did, Bailey, or you will end up in some prison busting rocks twelve hours a day. Of course, you might miss both those events, but if you do and don't change, it will eat up your soul. Every life you take will eat a little more of your soul. Is that the kind of life you want?"

"I've heard this speech before," Putney's voice sounded sad. "And I will tell you what I told the last man. I've heeded everything you've told me." Putney reached out, picked up the guns, and met no resistance from the marshal. He holstered the pistols. Putney gathered the rest of his belongings and signed the receipt after putting them away. "Do I pay you the fine directly, or do I need to go to the court."

"You pay your fine here," said the marshal. "That will be two hundred dollars."

"What?" questioned Putney. "In the cell block, you said the fine was one hundred dollars."

"That's right," Marshal Sisty agreed. "But it seems the judge also set a fine for Bailey. Someone has to pay it, and since you are responsible for his death, it's only right for you to be responsible for his debts."

Putney counted out two hundred dollars while Sisty wrote out a receipt. The marshal counted the money and then handed the receipt to Putney. "You have a friend waiting outside for you. Get your business settled and go somewhere. Anywhere but Denver."

Putney walked into the daylight and smoothed his hair before putting on his hat. Outside, on a bench sat Lockwood Fuller reading a newspaper. Putney lit a Kinney and went to meet Fuller, who looked up from the paper. "You're famous. Did you know that?" Fuller asked, handing the periodical to Putney.

Putney looked at the paper and, in the left lower quarter in bold type, saw the headline. RED JACK SLAYS GAMBLER. 'Putney handed the paper back to Fuller. "I don't need to read it. It will all be bullshit, anyway."

"Maybe," Fuller said, "But it's a stroke of fortune for us both. They'll get this paper in Boulder, and this kind of reputation will only make the work easier."

"I suppose so," was Putney's only reply.

"Sisty told me he couldn't hold you," Fuller told him. "But I'll bet a dollar to a dime he gave you some speech about getting out of town before sundown or some kind of shit."

"He didn't give a time frame, but that's pretty close," Putney told him. "But I'm going to the hotel, get a bath, a good meal, and a night's rest. We can leave in the morning if you're ready."

"Oh, I'm ready," Fuller said. "I got three more men. I'm going to meet them tonight."

At the hotel, Putney stopped at the front desk and ordered a bath in his room. He had one foot on the bottom step of the stairs when he heard someone call out, "Mr. Callahan."

Putney turned to see a tall thin man standing straight as a rod. He wore a dark blue jacket with a slight military cut and trousers with creases so sharp they looked like you would cut yourself if you touched them. His face was gaunt and narrow, with thin lips and a nose as sharp as the creases in his pants. On his head, he wore a gray peaked campaign hat. He was staring directly at Putney.

"I'm Jack Callahan," said Putney.

"I know you are," the tall man replied. "I could hardly have been mistaken. The paper described you well, with your long red hair and your brace of French pistols. My name is David J. Cook."

"Nice to meet you, Mr. Cook," Putney said, sarcasm in his tone. "Now, I'm tired, I stink, and so if you will excuse me." Putney turned once again to ascend the stairs.

"You and I have business, Mr. Callahan," the man said.

Looking over his shoulder, Putney said. "Mister. I do not

know you, and I'm sure I have no business with you. If you think otherwise, come back and see me tomorrow."

"I think we need to conduct our business now," the stranger's voice was stern and commanding.

Putney stepped off the stairway and walked within three feet of the rigid man. "I can see you are an impatient man as well as rude," Putney told him. "So, whatever your business is, get it out so I can take a bath."

"I am remiss, Mr. Callahan," returned his vexer. "I told you my name but did not tell you who I am."

"Mr. Cook, if you don't get to the point, you can tell the hotel clerk who you are because I'm going to my room." A well irritated Putney said.

"The clerk knows I'm the sheriff of Arapaho County," Cook said.

"Marshal Sisty has already cleared me, so I don't know what business you have with me."

The sheriff spoke with an official voice, "I am sure that Marshal Sisty advised you that your prospects would improve outside the town limits."

"Why yes, yes he did," Putney affirmed. "It is my full intention to do so. After I have a bath, a meal, and a good night's rest."

Cook's voice lost its feigned politeness as he said, "I'm here to extend that advice to the limits of Arapaho County. Let me admonish you further. If you so much as shoot a rabbit while you are still in my county, I will dig a hole under the county jail and bury you under it. I hope I have made my intentions clear."

Taken back by the sheriff's sudden change in tone, Putney took a long breath and said. "Sheriff, it will be my pleasure to shake the dust of this town and this county from my sandals."

"Do not profane the Bible, you little shit." Cook's anger was rising. "I dealt with people like you during the war. I did not stand for their insolence, and I will not stand for yours. You have my notice. I expect you to be out of this county..."

Putney cut him off, then finished the sentence, "By sundown. I understood you the first time. I imagine that even in Arapaho County, insolence is no more illegal than arrogance." Putney turned to look at the desk clerk, who had a discernable look of dread in his eyes, and said, "I want that bathtub in my room as quick as possible."

30

G unplay had always caused Putney to have a nearly insatiable hunger ever since the first time he was confronted by a bandit at the age of fifteen. At the jail, the food had been barely fit for human consumption, and they fed only twice a day. Putney had eaten everything they provided, but it wasn't much, and that morning he still felt starved, even after the steak dinner he had the previous night. He ate four eggs, potatoes, a ham steak, biscuits, and jam. He finished off his meal with three canned peaches.

It was still early, so he decided to wait for Fuller in the lobby and read more poetry by Poe. He read *Eldorado*, which gave him pause, causing him to think about the past few months and wonder if he would ever find his Eldorado. He was lost in thought when Fuller came into the hotel. Three men that looked more like vagabonds than detectives followed. Fuller introduced Casper Jones, Cecil Roberts, and Phil Morgan. Morgan asked if Putney was the boss, and Fuller laughed, "No, he just dresses like that," said Fuller. "It boggles me where he gets the money."

"Are you an idgit or what?" Jones asked Morgan. "Don't you never read the papers? Fuller said his name was Jack Callahan. He's that gunman that shot down that poor feller in Clodfelter's."

"That's him?" returned Morgan. "He don't look that scary."

Disgusted with the talk of his fame Putney said to Fuller. "My gear's all packed on my animals out front. You ready to go?"

"Sure," replied Fuller. " If we leave now, we can make it to Boulder before nightfall. We need to meet with Calvin Ward tonight."

The trip to Boulder was an easy one. Miners and others traveling between the two towns had created a well-traveled road. At first, Putney had ridden up front with Fuller, but the constant chattering and vulgar talk wore on Putney, so he dropped back a few yards to be alone with his thoughts. He began to doubt his reasons for taking the job. He never really needed the money, especially after his winnings at poker. Putney had also thought about the start of winter and that even rustlers weren't so desperate as to steal cattle in snow storms. The job was taking him in the opposite direction of his objective. From the quality of his comrades, he was sure, with every mile, he had made a mistake.

It was sunset when they arrived in Boulder. To attract customers, saloon owners were lighting torches outside their establishments. The mining town consisted of saloons, gambling dens, and whore houses. Maybe in the bright daylight, there would be the mercantile shops and other respectable business, but at the time, Putney wondered if they existed. Traffic filled the streets with wagons, horses, and men on foot who made up their own rules. They had to pass single file to thread the gauntlet. A few hundred yards north of the town was a large three-story building Fuller said it was their destination.

There was a long hitching post in front of the building with a sign that read Niwot Mining Company. Fuller and Putney stopped on a long porch to brush off the road's dust. The other three didn't bother. Inside was an office with four men working at desks studying papers and maps. "Surveyors," Fuller said as they passed the men and walked through a door in the rear. In the next room was a well-appointed office with a desk set to one side, where an attractive middle-aged woman sat overlooking calendars and ledgers. Fuller cleared his throat to get the woman's attention. She looked up, and Fuller asked, "Is he in?"

"He certainly is Mr. Fuller, and he's expecting you," she said with a friendly smile. "Go on in."

The second office was extravagant. Finely woven oriental rugs covered the floors. A large, ornately carved desk with a green leather-covered rocker sat in the room's rear. In the center of the room stood a massive oval-shaped table surrounded by twelve chairs. Four plush velvet, wing-backed chairs arranged in a semi-circle in front of a grand fireplace completed the room. Two men, smoking cigars and drinking from brandy snifters, occupied two chairs. When the five detectives entered, both men stood, and Putney could see their clothes were well-tailored and expensive. One was tall but leaned to the portly side and had a head covered with thick, curly hair melding into bushy sideburns. The other was shorter but lean and had almost no hair except a gray halo around his nape. In addition, he sported a luxurious, handle-barred mustache. The mustachioed man exclaimed, "Mr. Fuller, we were talking about you and your recruits. I assume these are them."

"Yes, sir, Mr. Breath," answered Fuller. "This is Jones,

Roberts, Morgan, and Callahan. Boys, this is Mr. Samuel Breath, and this," pointing to the curly-haired man, "is Mr. Calvin Ward. They are part of the consortium that is hiring you." Neither of the gentlemen made an effort to shake the hands of their employees.

"Well met, men. Have a seat," Calvin Ward gestured to one end of the table. Fuller took the end seat. The others, two on each side, joined him. Ward and Breath sat at the other end, still smoking cigars."

"Men, this job is straightforward," stated Ward. "Mr. Breath, some others, and I own the largest mines in this area. The main part of our operations is located further north at Ward's Camp. We have made a heavy investment in these large mines. We have purchased equipment and machines that facilitate the mining of gold," he paused to puff on his cigar. "I shan't go into all the workings. That isn't anything you need to know. Suffice it to say, the amount of gold we pull out of these mountains steadily decreases. We find we need to expand our holdings, but we are having difficulties doing so," he puffed again. "You see, independent miners are hemming us in with their claims. They always think they are inches from making that big strike. But the truth is that they will be lucky to get a few ounces a year without proper equipment. But our equipment could make a tremendous difference, and we need those claims to remain profitable. I hope I have made myself clear."

Everyone at Putney's end of the table nodded. "Good," said Ward. "You will get two dollars a day plus meals and lodging. That is more than any town marshal or county sheriff in Colorado makes. And for all intents and purposes, you will be the law here. There is a town marshal in Boulder that will deal with the rowdies. That is not your job. You will be working directly for Mr. Fuller and alongside our surveyors. Your job will be to protect the surveyors as they do their work. Mr. Fuller has all the details and will explain them to you in the bunk house. I think the cook has a meal ready for you." That was the end of his speech and a blatant dismissal. Putney and the others rose to leave. "Mr. Callahan, we prefer you to stay for a few minutes. The rest of you may go with Mr. Fuller."

Ward and Breath walked back to the fireplace and signaled for Putney to join them. "Brandy, Mr. Callahan," offered Breath.

"Thank you, sir," Putney answered, wondering why they singled him out for special attention.

Breath poured a snifter of Brandy and placed it on a small mahogany table next to a plush chair. Breath opened a box of cigars, holding them open for Putney. "Thank you. I prefer to smoke mine if that's alright." Putney pulled out the tin case of Kinneys. Sitting, he lit a cigarette and waited. It was clear the two men were working up to tell him their plan for him.

"Lockwood sent us a telegram about you, Mr. Callahan, and we received the Denver paper and read of your exploits," Ward began the conversation.

"Yes," chimed in Breath. "And you are not of the same mold as the others. I, for one, am impressed with your manners and how you present yourself. What do you think, Cal?"

"I don't think we could have done better if we had got him from a mail-order catalog," replied Ward. "Mr. Callahan, you have a striking appearance and a way of carrying yourself that I wasn't expecting. Honestly, we thought just reputation alone would be all we needed. But I'm gushing. Go ahead, Sam. Tell him what we have planned."

Samuel Breath expelled a cloud of cigar smoke. "It will

be easy money for you, Mr. Callahan. First, we have arranged for you to stay at the McClancy boarding house in Boulder. It is off the main street and is preferred lodgings." Breath reached in his inside coat pocket and produced a silver badge. It was in the shape of a shield and read 'DETECTIVE' over crossed hammers then below 'WARD MINING DISTRICT.' He placed the badge on the table next to the snifter. "We have ordered a broadsheet to be posted over the district. It announces your arrival as a representative of the big miners. Then the only thing you need to do, Mr. Callahan, is to walk the streets of Boulder, letting the citizens see you. Let's say you will be our living advertisement."

"That seems mighty simple, Mr. Breath," Putney interjected. "I have to suspect there is some sort of catch."

"Oh, there is, Mr. Callahan. There certainly is," Ward told him. "But first let me tell you, your salary will be three dollars a day, with meals and lodging. Also, you may eat at any establishment in the town at no charge, as well as drinks in the saloons, in moderation."

"Mr. Ward, Mr. Breath, I've always been told that if something seems too good to be true, it probably is too good to be true," said Putney, "I think I must be blunt. In the end, you must be expecting me to kill someone, and I'm not a murderer."

"You certainly are not, Mr. Callahan," said Ward. "We would never expect you to kill someone for money. But, you see, it makes a difference. People may read about your exploits, but there will always be naysayers. They must be witnesses to be true believers. So yes, there will be someone killed."

"Not if I don't accept the job," Putney started to rise.

"Before you make a final decision, Mr. Callahan, allow

me to sweeten our proposition," Breath was speaking again. "You see, a man came into Boulder a few days ago. He got drunk and broke up one of the saloons. The town marshal had to arrest him. What little money he had was seized to pay for damages, but it certainly wasn't enough to fully compensate the owner. So tomorrow, this man will be released and set to work for the saloon keeper, to work off his debt."

"I don't see how this concerns me," Putney finished the brandy and rose to leave. He thanked the mine owners for their hospitality and the offer. Then, without another word, he walked to the door.

As Putney put his hand on the knob, Ward said, "Would it make any difference if this man's name is Russell Horton?"

Putney released the doorknob, walked back to the fireplace, poured some brandy in his snifter, lit another cigarette, and sat in the plush chair. Putney looked down at the side table and picked up the badge.

31

W hen Putney walked into the McClancy's dining room, three other men sat, eating breakfast. They all appeared to be laborers of some sort. They were all gathered around one end of the long table that sat eight. Putney took a seat at the opposite end. A young woman, about twenty years old, came through a swinging door holding a pot of coffee and filled Putney's cup. "Hi," she greeted Putney. "I'm Mandy. You must be Mr. Callahan." Mandy's long hair was the reddish-brown color of mink and tied at the nape of her neck with a long royal blue ribbon. She wore a light blue, high collared dress trimmed with ruffled ribbon the same color as her hair tie. The dress from the hips up was form-fitting that accentuated her well-proportioned torso. Most of the women Putney had seen had been in south Texas with brown suntanned skin, but Mandy's was a light tone and had the same silky look of fresh cream. Her eyes were bright and golden-colored. In short, she was one of the loveliest women Putney had ever seen.

· · ·

"Jack Callahan, Miss Clancy," said Putney.

"Welcome to our house, Mr. Callahan," said Mandy, her voice bright and cheery. "Mother wants to know how you want your eggs."

"Whatever is easiest," he said.

As Mandy walked back to the kitchen, she turned, "Sunny side up. Maybe it will bring a smile to your face." Just before entering the kitchen, Mandy sent Putney a coquettish smile.

When Mandy had left, one of the men at the table said, "My name's Smith. My partners here are Brown and Hill. We're surveyors working for Ward. Are you one of the new detectives he hired?"

Putney reached for a slice of fresh-baked bread sitting on the table with butter and jams. "I am," he said without looking up.

"We're headed up to Ward's Camp this morning," said Smith."Are you one of the men providing protection up there?"

Putney buttered his bread and reached for some jam. "No," said Putney.

· · ·

"You don't talk a lot, Mr. Callahan?" said Smith.

Putney looked up at the three men and said, "Not when I don't have anything to say." Smith's attempt at conversation ended. Putney took a bite of his bread.

Mandy returned to the room with one platter piled high with fried potatoes and another with bacon.

"You men load up your plates. I'll be right back with your eggs." The surveyors portioned out potatoes and bacon and were polite enough to leave Putney an equal amount. Brown passed the food down.

"Thank you," said Putney.

Mandy swooped back in and placed smaller plates of eggs in front of each man calling out the way they had asked for them. She then came to Putney's end and put a plate with three eggs on it. "Sunny side up for our cheery Mr. Callahan," she said as she set the eggs in front of him. "Now, Mr. Callahan, how about a smile?" Putney looked at the young woman and let a short smile crease his face, then it disappeared. "Well, that's a start," jibed Mandy. "We will have to work on that, Mr. Callahan."

≈

THE MERCANTILE AND GENERAL STORES, several specialty shops, saloons, and cat houses had been in Boulder since the 1858 gold rush. They had probably started in tents, but by late 1865 the establishments had all been converted to wooden structures. Wooden walkways ran the length of the businesses on the main street. The streets were mostly mud that never seemed to dry. Wide planks across the street were scattered at different intervals to help people cross without getting muddy. Most of the inhabitants didn't bother with the planks. Traffic on the road started at dawn and ran until eight or nine when decent folks were home, the miners were in their camps, and the less savory were in the saloons and whore houses.

A SLIGHT CHILL was in the air, and a dank mist hovered over the town. Putney wore his slicker over his other clothes, not being used to the cooler weather. Putney wore the detective badge pinned on the outside. Putney's first stop was at a barber's shop for a shave. Pinned on the wall where customers in the barber chair could see it was a colorful calendar with a picture of a scantily clad woman. Next to it was a broadsheet poster. In large capital letters was printed JACK CALLAHAN. Below the name in letters half the size, the sign read Famous Pistoleer of Denver. Below that was Newest Mining Detective. Two paragraphs in smaller print followed the headlines. Seeing the poster, Putney ripped it from the wall. The barber started protesting but then looked at Putney and remained silent. A customer was in the chair, so Putney sat under the calendar and read the broadsheet. It was a bloviated version of the already exaggerated newspaper version of the shooting in Denver. Putney wadded the paper and dropped it on the floor. Another waiting customer reached to pick it up when Putney stomped on it. When the barber finished with the customer in his chair, he signaled for Putney to take a seat. "Wasn't this other man here before me?" Putney asked the barber.

"WELL YEAH," said the barber. "But I thought you might be in a hurry."

"NO HURRY AT ALL," said Putney as he lit a cigarette.

AFTER HIS SHAVE, Putney promenaded up the south side of the main street. He peered into the near empty saloons and half full restaurants. Putney stopped in general stores and other mercantile to look around, not planning on buying anything. At a gun shop, he checked to see if they had any cartridges for his pistols. They didn't. When he reached the end of the street, he crossed and began walking in the other direction. The people showed no more deference to him than the next man. He guessed either people hadn't read the poster or hadn't connected him to it. The truth was it didn't matter to him. He was not comfortable with the idea of being a man of notoriety. Again, he reached the end of the street and crossed. He believed this would be the most boring job a man could ever have. At noon he walked back to McClancy's for lunch.

MRS. MCCLANCY WAS in the parlor when he entered the house. She met him in the hallway. "Mr. Callahan," she said. "The others have left, and we thought you would be eating at one of the cafes. We haven't prepared anything for lunch. We were going to have cold sandwiches in the kitchen."

"I DON'T MEAN to put you out, Mrs. Clancy," said Putney. "I can walk back into town."

"NONSENSE. YOU'RE HERE NOW," she said. "If you don't mind sandwiches and cold potatoes. Papa isn't back yet but will be soon. Mandy and I would enjoy the company. She's already in the kitchen preparing for dinner."

MRS. CALLAHAN WAS A THIN, diminutive woman in her middle age with a bundle of gray hair stacked on her head. She wore a plain gray wool dress with a white apron on top. Putney followed her to the kitchen, where she told him to take a seat. "Mandy, get that ham out and the potatoes left from breakfast," Mrs. McClancy directed her daughter. "Mr. Callahan is going to join us."

"OH, THAT'S WONDERFUL," said Mandy. "We don't get much chance to talk to people from anywhere but here in Boulder." Mandy scurried around and brought two plates covered with cheesecloth. "Oh, Mama, can we have some of that cheese Papa got from the store last week?"

"CERTAINLY, girl, bring that jar of Gulden's mustard and the bread." Her mother said. Mrs. McClancy started slicing the bread while Mandy fetched the cheese and mustard.

Putney had never had mustard, but he found he liked it a great deal. So, he promised himself to get some before he took to the trail again.

"MR. CALLAHAN," Mandy began the conversation. "Where about's, are you from? Originally, I mean."

"I WAS BORN in south Texas, Miss McClancy," he said. "I lived most of my life there until the war."

"OH," Mandy said, somewhat disappointed. "I guess you were a rebel, then."

"I GUESS," returned Putney. "Though I never went east. I stayed in Texas to protect settlers from Comanches and Kiowas."

MANDY BRIGHTENED UP. "So that means you didn't own any negroes?"

"NO, ma'am, I wouldn't have joined the army if it hadn't been for conscription," Putney explained. "If I hadn't joined, I probably would have been drafted and sent off to fight a war I didn't have any interest in."

. . .

"WELL, fighting Indians must have been dangerous, too," observed Mrs. McClancy.

"IT HAD ITS MOMENTS," he admitted.

THE SWINGING KITCHEN DOOR OPENED, and Mr. McClancy entered and turned directly to the kitchen counter where there was a wash basin. He didn't see Putney. Not looking around but talking to the wall. "You know what that damn Ward did to us, Mama?" he asked, "I'll tell you what he did." McClancy reached into his coat pocket with a wet hand, pulled out a folded paper, and tossed it over his shoulder. Mrs. McClancy picked up the paper and unfolded it as her husband continued washing his hands. It was one of the broadsheet posters. "Saddled us with a damned murder, that's what."

"UH, DEAR," said Mrs. McClancy, but her husband kept going. "I have a good mind to pitch him out on his ear," McClancy growled. Then, drying his hands, he turned to face the kitchen table and dropped the towel.

PUTNEY PUT down the remainder of his sandwich and stood. McClancy immediately broke out into a cold sweat and started stammering something unintelligible. "Mrs. McClancy, Mandy, thank you for lunch," said Putney. "I didn't mean to bring trouble to your home. I think it would be best if I start taking my meals at one of the restaurants for now. I'll shift my gear as soon as I can find a suitable place."

. . .

AS THE DOOR WAS SWINGING, Putney heard Mandy cry, "Papa! How could you?" She caught up to him before he got to the front door. "Mr. Callahan, please don't go away mad?" she pleaded.

"I'M NOT ANGRY, Miss McClancy. I just don't want to cause anyone embarrassment." Putney looked down into her golden eyes. "I wouldn't want to do that to you, especially."

MANDY'S FACE BECAME FLUSHED. "You aren't, Mr. Callahan, I promise. Besides, he didn't mean anything. He just talks before he thinks, sometimes."

"NO, ma'am. He meant it. And I don't blame him," said Putney. "Ward should have told him before he put me up here." Putney turned to walk out the door but stopped at the threshold. "Miss McClancy, it's important to me that you know that besides Indians, I have killed other men. But I want you to know I'm not a murderer."

PUTNEY STILL THOUGHT that righteous vengeance made a difference.

32

Putney walked back to the main street and began his tour of the boardwalks. When he was halfway down his course, a boy came running up to him. "Are you Jack Callahan, the pistoleer?" the boy said as he tried to catch his breath.

Putney said he was, and the boy said, "Marshal Swearengin wants you over at Strikers Saloon." Putney had made a mental note of all the saloons he had passed. Strikers was across the street toward the west end. Putney took his time going there. However, people stepped out of his way this time, women ducked inside stores and cafes, and a few men followed him from a respectful distance.

When Putney reached the saloon, the double doors were open wide, and as he entered, two men ducked out behind him. He had not met the marshal but saw a man with a six-pointed star sitting at a table just inside the door. Without going much further into the saloon, Putney said to the man, "I'm Jack Callahan. Did you want me?"

The marshal finished off the beer that sat in front of him and said, "Just doing what Mr. Ward told me," Swearengin said. "And I ain't sticking around for anything else. Your man's in the storeroom behind the bar. He should be out in a minute. There ain't no other way out of the saloon." Having spoken his peace, the marshal left.

Putney walked to the bar and asked the man standing behind it if there was any real bourbon. The barman said there was and produced a bottle and a glass and poured a drink. "If it's all the same to you, mister, I'm going now. Have as much whiskey as you want."

Putney shot his hand out and took hold of the bartender's arm before he could take one step. "It is not all the same to me. I need a witness, so you just back up, stay out of the way, and keep your eyes open." The bartender did as Putney told him and stood as still as a cigar store Indian. In a few minutes, the storeroom door opened, and out stepped Russell Horton.

Horton was carrying a crate of whiskey and didn't see Putney until he had put the box down. When he turned and saw Putney, he began to tremble. "Look, mister," he said. "I don't want no trouble."

Putney was silent.

"Mister, I ain't got nothing against you. Baily had it coming. I know that. He pulled first," exclaimed Horton.

"I know you have nothing against me," Putney's voice was low and flat. "Ask yourself what it is that I have against you."

"Mister, I never saw you before that night in Denver when you was talking with Musgrove." insisted Horton. "What could you have against me?"

"Do you remember a day in New Mexico two months ago?" Putney asked.

"Well, I was in New Mexico then, but I never saw you," Horton stopped, and realization began creeping in on him.

"Wait, you mean that thing with the settlers? I wasn't even there. My horse threw a shoe, and I had to walk back to Montoya's to get it fixed up. I met back up with them at Fort Dodge. That was when they told me what had happened. Honest, mister, I didn't have nothing to do with that."

"That is not what Rogers told me. He gave me a list of everyone that was there. Your name is on that list," said Putney.

"Rogers was wrong. I wasn't there. I swear to God I wasn't" Horton was getting louder as if the volume would convince the red-haired man standing in front of him.

"Where's your gun?" Putney asked.

"I ain't got no gun," Horton screeched. "The marshal took it. But, even if I did, I wouldn't go against you. I'm not crazy."

Without turning to look at him, Putney asked the bartender if he had a gun under the bar. The barman said he did keep one there. "Get it and put it on the end of the bar, then back away," Putney ordered. After the man put the gun on the bar, Putney asked, "How much damages does Horton still owe?"

"I guess about forty dollars. Why?"

"Because he is not going to be able to pay it," Putney said and reached in his coat for his wallet. Putney pulled out four ten-dollar bills and laid them on the bar. "Will that cover it?"

"I'm sure it will," the bartender's voice had nearly as much fear as Horton's.

Horton stuck his hands over his head and yelled. "I ain't picking up that gun. I can't beat you, and I would be a fool to try."

Putney slowly walked to within three feet of Horton. "Pick up that damn gun." He demanded.

Horton dropped to his knees. "Do what you're going to do, but it will be murder!"

Putney drew one of his guns and held the barrel against Horton's temple. Horton started crying, pleading for Putney not to kill him. Putney could feel the pressure of the trigger against his finger. Horton was blubbering. In the background, Putney could hear the barman begging him to stop. Just before Putney pulled the trigger fully back, he turned the barrel, and the bullet grazed across the back of Horton's head, taking a piece of his ear with it. Horton collapsed on the floor.

"Get up," Putney demanded. "You are not dead. Get up, damn it." Horton rose slowly to his feet. The tears had stopped, but his chest was still heaving. "Get the hell out of this town," Putney ordered Horton. "You find Musgrove, Franklin, and the others. You tell them I am coming."

Horton stumbled toward the saloon door. Before he could walk over the threshold, Putney called for him to turn around. Horton froze and slowly turned, fearing the worst. Putney glared at the broken man and said, "If you are with them when I catch up, you will not get a second chance. Whether you have a gun or not. I will kill them. Then I will kill you."

33

It was well past eleven o'clock before Putney returned to McClancy's. After his confrontation with Horton, Putney had gone to one of the cafes and had eaten a large meal. He had then returned to The Strikers Saloon and bought a bottle of bourbon. Putney sat at a table in the back, drinking the whiskey alone. The saloon started to fill up mid-afternoon, but everyone steered clear of Putney's table. The story of how Jack Callahan had shot an unarmed man spread through the town like wildfire.

Just after dark, Lockwood Fuller entered the saloon and sat across from Putney. "Mr. Ward and Mr. Breath are disappointed in you," he said. Putney just looked at him blankly. There was no questioning in his eyes, and there was certainly no concern about what the big miners' opinions were. "They expected you to kill this guy," said Horton. "To bolster your reputation."

"I told them I was no murderer," said Putney. "I would have killed Horton, but he wouldn't pick up a gun. So as much as I wanted to see him dead, I wasn't going to kill an unarmed man."

"It's alright," Fuller said. "I fixed it. I started a rumor that Horton was a small-time prospector and that you ran him out of town. I also told the bartender to tell the same story and forget about anything you said about New Mexico."

"Aren't you just the brilliant one?" Putney's words were thick with sarcasm.

"Look," said Fuller. "You aren't getting paid ninety dollars a month to live out some revenge. You do that on your own time, someplace else. Here your purpose is to scare the shit out of the small miners. Make sure you keep your mind on that task."

"I don't think that is going to be a problem," Putney said. "Most of the men in this bar are small-timers, aren't they?"

"Sure, they are, but I'm not certain what that has to do with anything," Fuller was confused.

In answer, Putney stood up quickly, pushing his chair back so it banged against the wall. Men hurried for the exit, jumped from tables against the walls or under the tables. Then Putney pulled his chair back to the table and slowly sat down. "That is what it has to do with everything."

Fuller was impressed as he watched grown men return to their respective places, still shivering with fear. "I guess you're right," he said. "Just keep it in mind what we are about here." Fuller rose from the table, doffed his hat at Putney, and left. Putney did not move except to fill his glass with whiskey.

Putney didn't know how he managed to find McClancy's, as drunk as he was, but he did. Someone left a lamp trimmed on a table in the entry so that light was barely glowing. Putney turned the key to raise the wick, and the hallway filled with light. He managed to make it upstairs to his room without waking the whole house. Putney sat the lamp on his bedside table, dropped himself on the bed, and fell asleep.

When he woke, Putney took his watch out of the vest pocket, but he had to blink several times to focus. It was past nine. He didn't remember the last time he had slept that late. His head was pounding, and his tongue felt wrapped in gauze. Putney stumbled over to the dresser where a pitcher of water and a glass were. He filled the glass and then filled his mouth, swishing the water around before swallowing. Putney drank three glasses of water before his mouth felt normal. What remained of the water he poured into the basin. He stripped off his wrinkled clothes, threw them on the bed, and began washing up. He put on fresh clothes and bundled up the ones that wreaked of whiskey and saloon smoke.

Putney was about to walk out of McClancy's when he heard Mandy's voice. "Mr. Callahan," she said. "Are you leaving before you eat breakfast?" The thought of food made Putney's stomach churn, and his head hurt more than it already was.

"I mean to move out today anyway, and it's late, and I figured everyone else had already eaten," he told her. "I didn't want to be a bother."

"Presently, you're the only guest. Papa spoke with Mr. Ward. They came to an agreement, and there's no need for you to move." Mandy told him. "Mama and I have biscuits, bacon, and potatoes already cooked up. All that's needed is to cook some eggs. You wouldn't want to see our food go to waste, would you?"

Putney didn't know if he could hold food down, but he didn't want to be rude, especially to Mandy. "I don't suppose I would," he said and sat his bundle of clothes on the table where the lamp had been the night before.

The hot coffee eased the roiling in his stomach and soothed the pain in his head. Mandy had gone to the kitchen and returned with his breakfast. Warm potatoes and biscuits were on the table. Mandy set a plate in front of him, and Putney saw Mandy had scrambled the eggs. Well done. "I thought scrambled eggs would match your temperament this morning," Mandy told him.

Putney didn't say anything in return. He ate his breakfast slowly, forcing each bite to stay down before attempting another. With a sip of coffee between each bite, he finished the meal without embarrassing himself. It was especially concerning that he did not puke since Mandy had chosen to sit across the table from him and watched, meticulously, as he chewed each morsel. When he had eaten the last bite, Putney thanked the young woman for the meal.

"There now," said Mandy. "I bet that makes you feel better." Putney could not fathom how she knew he was hungover, but he knew she was teasing him. Even the meal had been a sort of tease.

He rose from the table, thanking her for the breakfast, and walked toward the front door to retrieve his bundle. Mandy followed him, and as he was about to walk out, she said, "Mr. Callahan, I'm glad you didn't kill that man yesterday." Putney grimaced. He hadn't even considered that the story would have reached her, but then he realized, of course, it would have. Boulder was a small community; news of that sort wouldn't stay localized to the main street. "Though I wish you hadn't shot him at all," she said. "I'm sure he would have left without you shooting him. But at least you didn't kill him."

Putney wanted to tell her why he was in Boulder and what Horton and the others had done. For some reason, he felt it was important that she knew the truth. Instead, Putney said, "I regret your disappointment in me," as he closed the door.

34

The day had turned bitterly cold over the previous days, and Putney wished he had worn his beaver coat, but he wasn't returning. Instead, he took his clothes to a laundry business run by a German couple on a back street. Then Putney resumed his chore of walking up and down the main road. Occasionally, Putney would step inside a saloon where a stove burned to get warm. In the late afternoon, snow began to fall, and he decided to return to McClancy's. As he headed up the stairs, Mrs. McClancy stopped him. "Are you joining us for dinner tonight, Mr. Callahan," she asked.

Before he could answer, Mandy McClancy stuck her head out of the parlor door and said, "Of course, he is, Mama. He can't live on that meager breakfast he ate earlier." Putney nodded at Mrs. McClancy, confirming her daughter's answer.

Winter came early, it came hard, and it lasted a full five months before temperatures started staying above freezing for more than a day. The cold was nearly unbearable to Putney. He had grown up where freezing temperatures rarely lasted more than two or three days, and snow was even rarer. Almost as excruciating was his boredom. Every day, he would eat breakfast, walk around Boulder, find a warm place to sit for an hour or two and wander a bit more. The only good moments were when he returned to McClancy's, where they always had a good dinner, then they would sit in the parlor where Mandy, Putney, and Mrs. McClancy would take turns reading from works by Walt Whitman and Edgar Allan Poe. They would take turns reading chapters from The Last of the Mohicans, The Scarlet Letter, and Moby Dick. Mr. McClancy never took part in these activities. It was not something that remotely interested him. Besides, he still brooded over having Jack Callahan under his roof and knowing he could do nothing about it because Ward was paying the bills.

On Sundays, the McClancy family would attend church, regardless of the weather. Putney only went once, and it put the minister off his sermon so badly that Putney decided not to go again. Businesses stagnated due to the lack of supplies getting through. The weather prevented the smaller miners and prospectors from working their claims, and even activities at the large mines fell off so that many laborers were out of work.

As Christmas was nearing, Putney, making his usual trudge onto the main street, entered a general store and found they had an illustrated version of Jane Austen's book, Pride and Prejudice. He purchased it as a gift for Mandy. The McClancy house was beginning to feel like home to Putney, and his fondness for Mandy was ever-growing. But he knew it was futile. He knew that it would not be long before he would leave Boulder, and he knew the likelihood of returning was nil. On Christmas Day, the McClancys went to church, and as usual, Putney stayed behind. But that evening, the family and Putney sat down to a feast that Mrs. McClancy and Mandy had worked on for two days to prepare.

After dinner, everyone went to the parlor and exchanged gifts. Mrs. McClancy gave Mr. McClancy a new pipe and a tobacco pouch. Mandy gave her father a new belt and suspenders. For his part, Mr. McClancy gave his wife a new Bible and a set of pearl earrings. In addition, he gave Mandy a gold ring with a topaz set in it. Mandy gushed over the ring. But she raved even more over the book that Putney gave her. She said it was the best gift she had ever received.

After the gift exchange, Mr. and Mrs. McClancy announced they were retiring. Mandy said she would stay up a while longer and read part of her new book. When the parents had left, Putney stood and was about to excuse himself when Mandy asked him to stay a while longer. Putney agreed, sat back down, and was surprised when Mandy pulled a package from behind the cushion of the settee and handed it to him. He unwrapped it and found three packets of Kinney cigarettes. Putney was amazed. He had been out of the ready rolls for over a month, and smoking cigarettes, he rolled himself. But most impressive was a silver cigarette case, much finer than his own. On the front was an engraved scene of a ship on the ocean. It was exquisite work. But the surprise didn't stop there. When he opened the case, He found the words"To Jack, With Love, Madeline". Putney was stunned and didn't know what to say about such a precious gift.

Using his first name for the first time, Mandy said, "Jack, you have always been a perfect gentleman, and you have never tried to lead me on or even express one word that gave me hope. But I must tell you that I have fallen in love with you. I can't help it. I only hope someday you will feel the same about me."

Putney lowered his head and thought about what he could say, but he found the words came hard. Finally, and without looking at her, he said, "I cannot find words to express how fond I have grown of you. But I am a man with a past about which you know nothing. I must speak truthfully; I have a reputation that is not fitting for a woman as kind and gentle as you. As touched as I am, I must not. I cannot encourage your feelings."

"I don't care about the things people say about you," Mandy protested. "In my heart, I know you are not an evil man. But, somehow, you are trapped. You can't find a way out. I have seen how kind you truly are. I know we could go away from here. A place people have never heard of Jack Callahan. We could go and be happy."

Putney raised his head and looked deeply into Mandy's eyes. "I promise you that one day I will tell you everything. But for now, though it tears at my heart, I cannot be the man you need. I adore you for everything you are, but you must accept this truth. One day maybe things will change, and you and I could freely love each other. But for now, it is impossible."

Tears were beginning to flow from Mandy's eyes, and she knelt in front of him and held his face in her delicate hands. "I love you, Jack Callahan. Nothing will ever change that. I believe that one day we will be together. I will wait for that day, however long it may take." She gently kissed his lips, silently rose, and walked from the room.

35

The day following Christmas, Putney did not go down for breakfast. He could not bring himself to face Mandy. He wanted to. He had every desire to go and tell her everything about him. But then he would remember Erin and all the events surrounding her death, that of her father, and all the other evil deeds that had occurred that day. He had made a vow of revenge, and he had to see it through. Until he did, he could have no peace. Five men still had to pay for their crimes, and he was the only one who could bring the required justice.

Putney looked out the window of his room. A new storm came in, and snow blew almost horizontally across the landscape. He knew he couldn't avoid Mandy forever, but he hoped he could make it out the front door before anyone knew he was leaving. He wrapped a wool scarf around his head to cover his ears, then pulled his hat down tight. Finally, he donned his beaver coat and left his room. Putney managed to escape the house undetected. When he stepped off the porch, the wind rocked his body so that he had to stabilize himself before continuing. The walk to the main street was challenging as the cold sucked his energy.

He was hungry, but once on the boardwalk, he found every café was closed. The streets were empty, and he found most of the saloons were closed. He was about to return to the boarding house when he noticed light in the windows of Ballard's saloon. Ballard always had boiled eggs and cold cuts out for the customers, and Putney hoped there was something left there to eat. He fought his way with the wind as he crossed the street and was finally able to enter what he hoped would be his haven for the day.

Upon entering, he noticed six men huddled around the pot belly stove. Putney would have liked to sit next to the fire, but that wasn't possible. Instead, he walked over to the bar. Ballard was standing behind the bar with a mug of coffee in his hand. "Any more of that coffee left?" he asked the stubby barman.

"Sure," said Ballard, and he walked to the end of the bar where a smaller stove had a coffee pot sitting on it. Ballard returned with a mug and placed it on the bar. "Hungry?" he asked.

"Yes, I am," admitted Putney. Ballard reached under the bar and produced a tray with eggs and meats.

"I put it under the bar because those yayhoos weren't spending hardly anything and would have eat everything I had," Ballard told Putney.

Putney picked up a saltshaker, covered an egg with salt, and took a bite. It was good to eat something. Putney cast his eyes over to the group of men around the pot belly.

"They came in last night," said Ballard. "The wind blew their tents in, and they were out in the cold. So they came in here, and I didn't have the heart to throw them out. Too damned cold."

Putney was eating another egg when one of the men turned and looked in his direction. "Look here, fellers," he said. "God, all-mighty Jack Callahan has joined us. What do you think about that?"

Putting his left hand in his coat pocket, Putney made as if he hadn't heard the man. "You don't look so tough, Callahan," the man spoke louder to make sure Putney had heard him. Then, understanding it would be impossible to ignore the man further, Putney turned and faced the group. The man's coat hung open, and Putney saw there was a pistol hanging awkwardly in front of the man's belly. "Hell," the man continued, "with that big coat on, I've got the drop on you."

Having foreseen such a possible situation, Putney had long before cut a slit in the coat lining where the left-hand pocket was. Putney had already pulled the gun out of the holster and was holding it inside the coat. "What do you think, fellers?" asked the man. "You think I should cut down this killer before he comes after us?"

Putney glared at the man, his steel-blue eyes taking in every movement the miner made. "Mister, like you, I came in here for warmth, so let's just mind our business and keep ourselves to ourselves."

"What's the matter, bad man? Are you afraid now? You know I got you."

"Mister," Putney's voice was as cold as the blizzard outside. "Whatever you think, I am telling you, do not make a move for that pistol."

"This is my chance to put one of you mining detectives out of business, and you being the hardest case of them all, if I take you down, them others won't bother us anymore," Having set his course, the miner wouldn't back down. Then, he moved his hand to his pistol. Before he could get it halfway from the holster, Putney had his gun aimed at the man's heart.

"I am telling you again, mister," warned Putney. "Do not pull that gun any further. And if the rest of you are thinking of joining in, it will be the last thought you ever have."

The miner gulped hard and let his gun drop back into its holster. "Ballard," said Putney, still aiming at his adversary's chest. "Go over there and disarm this nitwit and then all his friends."

Ballard did as Putney said and brought all the men's guns and put them on the counter behind the bar. With his right hand, Putney unbuttoned his coat, reached inside his pants pocket, pulled out a quarter eagle, and put it on the bar. "That's for drinks on me," he told Ballard. "As long as I'm here, I'm buying. So, let's all settle down and act civilized. Everyone agree?" Nobody raised a disagreement. Putney stayed for about four hours, then decided he had best return to the boarding house, regardless of how uncomfortable it might become.

The first person to see him was Mrs. McClancy. "What in tarnation?" she said when Putney walked in covered with snow. "Why in the world would you be out in this kind of weather? Where have you been?"

Putney apologized for the snow he had brought in on his coat and hat. Mrs. McClancy tish toshed him, helped him out of his coat, and hung it on a peg in the hallway. "Now you come on into the kitchen where it's warm. Mandy's in there. She just put a roast in the oven. There's some peach pie left over from yesterday. You go on in there and eat a piece."

"I need to go to my room and put these up," Putney said, glancing down at his guns. Mrs. McClancy agreed and said she would be in the kitchen also.

Putney did not want to go back downstairs. He knew it would be awkward but also would be impolite, so he reluctantly took himself to the kitchen. But when he got to the kitchen, the only one that seemed uncomfortable was himself. Mrs. McClancy and Mandy chatted about the dinner the night before and the beautiful gifts everyone had received. They also talked about the revelations in the Farmer's Almanac that the winter would be hard and how it had been right so far.

Mandy never threw a knowing glance at him or accidentally touched his hand. Putney ate the piece of peach pie Mandy had served him and, before long, joined the conversation. The one thing they never talked about was Putney's occupation.

That was how things went for the next two and a half months, except for the glances, which became more frequent, and the secretive brushing of a hand. Soon, Putney found himself joining these little secret liaisons. The winter had become so harsh that Putney only went to the street a couple of times a week. It didn't matter. Few people would even notice. When Putney was in the house, Mr. McClancy kept to himself, except for mealtimes, and was still not friendly. Putney couldn't blame him. As March approached, storms became less frequent, and the temperatures began to moderate. By the middle of March, snow started melting off, and the people of Boulder became more active, as did Putney. Days would find Putney in a café, shop, or one of the saloons.

One late March afternoon Lockwood Fuller entered Ballard's and found Putney, alone, as usual. Lockwood sat and asked how Putney was getting along and other inessential small talk. Putney kept his answers short. "It was brutal up at Ward's Camp," Fuller told him. "Nothing to do but sit around and look at each other, play cards and listen to one of the surveyor's bad guitar playing." Putney made no effort to comment. Fuller reached to an inside coat pocket, pulled out an envelope, and passed it over to Putney. Last three months wages," he said, then, "Look, Jack, now that winter is blowing out, Ward wants us to step up our efforts. He was disappointed when he heard about your confrontation with one of the miners the day after Christmas. He had hoped something like that would heat things up."

"I wasn't going to kill a man just because he was stupid," said Putney. "He was never a real threat. Just tired and a little drunk."

"But that's the problem, Jack," Fuller told him. "See, most of the small-timers have sold out and moved on. Some didn't even bother to sell; they just abandoned their claims. They couldn't take the harsh winter. But this guy, Carl Beaker, that you faced down, he's a problem. Him and five or six others. They all have claims next to each other, and they're vowing to stick it out. Beaker's the leader. If you had taken him out, the others would have skedaddled by now, too."

Putney stared at Fuller across the table and said, "I have told you, and I told Ward and Breath, I'm no murderer. I have killed, sure, but I always had a reason. I had no reason to kill this Beaker."

"Alright, Alright," said Fuller. "Don't get your hackles up. Anyway, it's not going to be your problem. Ward wants you to keep doing like you are but keep your ears open. If anything pops up, tell the marshal. He'll get a message to us." Putney agreed, and Fuller left the saloon.

Putney settled into his regular humdrum of pacing the boardwalks and stopping in stores and saloons until one day in the first part of April. Putney was sitting at Strikers when

Casper Jones stumbled in. It wasn't even twilight, but Jones was already drunk. When Jones spotted Putney, he staggered over and plopped himself down, uninvited. "Well, looky here," Jones slurred. "If it ain't Jack Callahan, the man with the cush job. How you doing, ole buddy."

"You're drunk," replied Putney.

"That's right," said Jones. "Cooped up on that God-forsaken mountain with no hooch in sight. So I decided to come down here and get a snoot on. You got a problem with that, Jack?"

"None whatsoever," said Putney. "I just wouldn't let Fuller catch you."

"No problem there," Jones hollered to the barman for a bottle. "Fuller is up that mountain taking a gander at a mining camp and planning our little game."

This last statement piqued Putney's curiosity, so he pretended he knew about the game. "Yeah, Fuller told me something was up. So how's that going?"

"Couldn't be better. Them small-timers ain't moving, so night after tomorrow, me and Roberts and Morgan are going up there to make them see the error of their ways."

Wanting to keep Jones on the hook, Putney said, "And you're just the three that can do it. Are you going to burn them out?"

"Hell, no," Jones blurted out. Then lowering his voice and moving his head closer to Putney, he said, "We're going to kill Beaker and maybe a couple of others." Then holding his index finger to his lips, he let out a long, "Shhhhh."

"Absolutely," said Putney. "Nobody's going to hear it from me. Do y'all need help?"

"Nah," Jones was confident. "We got it handled. Fuller will be standing back if anything gets hot."

"Sounds like y'all got it down," Putney encouraged Jones. "Why is Fuller still checking things out?

"Aw, he's a worry wart, that's all," then yelling at the bartender. "Hey, where's my bottle?"

"Don't worry, Casper, I'll take care of this," Putney told the drunk detective. Putney rose and went to the bar and asked the bartender, "Have you got something that tastes like whiskey but will make that guy sick?"

"Sure, I do. I use it when I want people to get out of here," said the barman. "I have to get the swamper to clean up the vomit, but it makes it easier to carry them out."

Putney put a quarter eagle on the bar, "Take that guy at my table, a bottle, then send for the marshal. He's less apt to give the marshal any guff."

"You got it, Mr. Callahan," said the bartender as Putney left. He had returned to the McClancy's in time for dinner. He excused himself to go upstairs and wash up. While in his room, Putney wrote a note telling Mandy he had to talk to her alone. At the table, as was their custom, Mandy sat to his left and her mother to his right. Across the table sat Mr. McClancy reading the Farmer's Almanac. That night's dinner was ham and potatoes with green beans that the women had put up in the fall.

After eating, Mrs. McClancy asked if anyone wanted some stewed apricots. Mandy and Putney were eager for the treat, and Mr. McClancy just grunted, barely looking up from his book. When Mrs. McClancy left the dining room, Putney checked to make sure Mandy's father was still distracted, and he pushed the note under Mandy's plate. Mandy swept the paper into a pocket on her apron, then said, "I'll just clear some of these dishes." She scooped up several plates and carried them to the kitchen.

When the four of them had finished the stewed apricots,

Mrs. McClancy started to clear off more dishes, but Mandy stopped her. "Momma, Mr. Callahan has been with us long enough to start earning his keep. Come on, Mr. Callahan, pick up some dishes. You can help me with the washing." Mrs. Callahan smiled knowingly. Evidently, the little secret Mandy and Putney thought was theirs only wasn't unknown to everyone.

As soon as they were in the kitchen, Mandy asked him about the note. "Let's get these dishes taken care of first. I don't know if I can stop once I start."

As soon as they had finished, Putney peeked out of the kitchen door to make sure nobody was in the dining room that could overhear. Then, he took Mandy to the kitchen table and sat her down. "Mandy, I have to leave tomorrow, and I don't know when I will be back," He began. Mandy started to interrupt him, but he held his hand up. "Please, I have to get this out. Tomorrow night some of Ward's other detectives are planning on murdering one or maybe more of the small miners. I have to leave to find the camp and stop them. I can't let men kill others so a rich man can take their claim. Once I stop this thing, I won't be able to stay because Ward will send men to kill me. I can't stay here and endanger you and your family."

"Oh, Jack," said Mandy taking his hands and squeezing them tightly. "I always knew you weren't a killer."

"That's not true either. I have a lot to tell you. You may want nothing to do with me when I'm through," he admitted.

"Jack, it can't be as bad as all that," Mandy insisted.

"It can, and it is. My name isn't Jack Callahan. It's Nahum Putney, but you must never tell anyone that, do you understand? Never." Putney said. "Whatever I have done or whatever I will do, for now, it must be under the name of Jack Callahan. My real name must stay clean."

"Certainly, Jack, I mean Nahum. Oh, I don't know what I mean," Mandy was trying not to let her confusion get the best of her.

"Don't worry about that. you must know my story." Putney began telling her everything that had happened to him since he left Captain Russell's camp. He left out nothing. It took him an hour to tell everything, and when he had finished, he was exhausted. He rested his arms on his knees and hung his head. "That's all. You know everything about me."

Mandy took his face in her delicate hands and lifted it so she could look into his eyes. "Nahum," she said. "I am so sorry all this has happened to you. I'm sorry you felt the need to do what you have done, but I understand. I truly do. But it can stop now, and you don't have to do this anymore. I will go back with you to Texas. There we can start over, and none will know the difference."

"But Mandy, you must understand. I cannot let this evil thing happen to men who are just trying to eke out a living." he told her. "If I don't stop it, nobody will."

"What about Mashal Swearingen?" Mandy asked. "He could stop it. All you have to do is to tell him."

"You're not listening, Mandy," said Putney. "The marshal is up to his hip pockets in all of this. He's as corrupt as the rest. No. If there were any other way, I would take it. But there isn't. I need you to understand this."

"Once you stop it, where will you go? What will you do?" Mandy needed to know.

"I've thought about that," Putney said. "I'll have to go north into the Wyoming territory for a while to shake anyone Ward sends after me. Then, I'll go to Julesburg and get a job working on a ranch. I will write you and let you know where I am. You can let me know when everything cools down, and I will come back." Putney knew he wouldn't be working as a cowboy. He knew he would still have to hunt down Musgrove and his gang, but he could not tell her that. She wouldn't understand. Even if he decided not to go after Musgrove, if Horton had found the outlaw, then Musgrove would eventually come after him.

"Alright," she said. "And if things don't cool down, I will come to meet you." Putney agreed, even though he knew that could never happen either.

Mandy lifted her face to meet his and kissed him long and tenderly. Putney longed to take her in his arms, hold her, and wash everything away. Instead, he said, "I have to go now and pack. I have a lot to do tomorrow." He kissed her again and left the kitchen in fear that if he didn't leave, he never would.

Putney had stowed all his gear and clothes in the large packs he kept. He left out a set of clothes and his beaver coat. Items like his bedroll and canteen were with his saddle in the stables, so he was finished and ready. He would leave first thing after breakfast. Putney had just laid down and pulled the covers up when he heard a scratching on his door. He walked across the room and slowly opened the door. There stood Mandy, wearing only her night dress. She pushed him aside, closing the door and turning the key as quietly as possible. She threw her arms around his neck and kissed Putney with a passion he had never known.

36

M andy was able to rise and get downstairs to help start breakfast before her parents figured out where she had spent the night. An hour later, Putney was up, shaved, and dressed. He announced at breakfast that Fuller summoned him to come to Ward's Camp. Also, he told the McClancys that he had already packed his things and would leave after he had eaten.

"You don't have to take everything," said Mrs. McClancy. "We will keep your room locked. That won't be necessary."

"Thank you," returned Putney. "But I don't know how long I will be gone. At least a week, I'm sure. I don't know what I may need. It's better this way."

Mrs. McClancy was surprised that her daughter hadn't protested, but she let it go. The smile on Mr. McClancy's face said all anyone needed to know. He was glad to be rid of this killer. Maybe they could get some respectable boarders now. Something that hadn't occurred in a long time.

When Putney finished eating, he went to the barn to saddle his horse and pack mule. Then, he came back to the house to get his things. Mandy went to the barn as he was loading his mule. She had a bundle in her hands, " I told mama I had packed some food for your trip," she said. Mandy put the bundle down and threw her arms around him. "I'm going to miss you so very much." Then she kissed him deeply. It was all Putney could do to pull himself away.

"When it's safe, I will return," he promised. "Go on back to the house now. It will be easier for both of us." Mandy kissed him again and ran to the house's back door, tears streaming down her face.

Putney rode quickly out of Boulder. He needed to get to Ward's Camp and locate the Beaker camp before dark. As Putney rode up the main street, he thought he heard some people clapping. He didn't give a damn.

Putney rode as fast as he could, but the muddy road from the spring thaw kept his animals bogged down. When he saw Ward's Camp looming, the sun was lowering over the mountains. Putney hadn't allowed for the early sunset and now had to hurry to find Beaker and his cohorts. So Putney didn't ride into the big camp. It wouldn't do for anyone to see him somewhere he wasn't supposed to be.

Since he hadn't seen anything that looked like a small mine camp on his way up, Beaker's group had to be on the other side of Ward's Camp. He rode around. The rough terrain and forest cost him valuable time. Dragging the mule didn't help, but he couldn't leave it behind, hoping to pick it up later. After doing what was needed, he would have to make a beeline to Wyoming. It took him an hour to skirt Ward's Camp, and night had fallen. He hadn't heard any gunfire, so he hoped that he wouldn't be too late. A half-hour later he saw the flickering of a campfire. Putney headed straight to it, trusting it was the right camp. He didn't believe he had time to hide and tie up his animals in the trees, so he rode in without stopping. He knew he had hit it lucky when the campfire showed Beaker stand up and shout, "Whose there?" Identify yourself or be shot."

"Hold your fire," called Putney. "I'm a friend."

"Ride in but keep those hands where we can see them," yelled Beaker.

Putney obeyed the command, holding the reins high so everyone could see he wouldn't pull on them. Soon the fire light lit up his face, and everyone stood and stepped back. "Callahan," exclaimed Beaker. "What the hell are you doing here? If you come to kill us, it's six against one."

"Calm yourself," said Putney as he dismounted and tied his horse to a nearby stump. "If I had wanted to kill you, I would have done it the day after Christmas. Y'all have any coffee?" Nobody answered, so Putney walked to the fire and saw a coffee pot and an empty cup. Using his neckerchief as a hot pad, he squatted and poured himself a cup of coffee. Looking around at the group, he saw two old men, a boy of about sixteen, Beaker, and another man about Beaker's age who wasn't wearing a gun. Maybe Beaker could hold his own, but it was obvious to Putney that the others were woefully ill-prepared. "There are going to be three or more show up here shortly," said Putney. "They won't ride straight in like I did. They'll sneak up on you. They intend to kill all of you. They will probably claim you started it, and they acted in self-defense. Since Ward, Breath, and others have the law in their pocket, it won't be a hard sell. My advice to y'all is to get up in the rocks and hide until morning. When you come back, if I'm dead, y'all need to find a new occupation. If I'm not here, you'll be as safe as you were sitting by the old home fire."

"How do we know this ain't some kind of trick to say we abandoned our claims? How do we know any of it is true?" Beaker wanted to know.

"You don't," said Putney. "But I can tell you that I'm leaving if you don't go to the rocks. Whatever happens then will be on your head." Putney looked up for the first time and pointed directly at Beaker.

"We ought to go, Beaker," said one old man. "It's better to believe him and live another day."

"Shut up, Cal," ordered Beaker.

"Shut up yourself," said the other old man. "I ain't getting my grandson and me killed." So he and the boy started up the mountain, followed by Cal and the other man. Beaker stubbornly stood his ground.

"Get out of here. Now," barked Putney. Beaker's resolve melted away like the snow in the valley. It wasn't five minutes before there was no trace of the six men at the camp.

Putney poured another cup of coffee and waited. He didn't have to wait long before hearing the first twig break. Putney stood and walked to the side of the fire opposite the direction he had heard the noise. In a few minutes, Jones, Roberts, and Morgan stepped out from the cover of the trees. They stood stock-still at the sight in front of them. Finally, Jones said, "Callahan. What in the hell are you doing here?"

"Having a cup of coffee," a calmness had come over Putney. "Care to join me?"

"You son of a bitch," snarled Jones. "Where's Beaker and the others?"

"Gone, for now," Putney's voice was low and cold.

"Ward promised us a hundred dollars a head bounty on those bastards," Jones' anger was at a fever pitch.

"Maybe he will pay you that six hundred for me," Putney postulated.

"Maybe he will!"

The light from the campfire grew intense, lighting up Putney's full view. The three men reached for their guns to draw them from the holsters. To Putney, time ceased to exist. He watched as long, blue tongues of flame exited the barrels of the three men in front of him. The campfire flashed even brighter. Putney heard the dull roar of his French revolver as it jerked in his hand. He pulled the second gun with his left hand and fired three more times. Pistol balls crashed in the trees behind him or sputtered in the dirt in front of him. The light from the fire fell back onto itself like a waterfall. Putney looked at the trio of bodies lying on the earth before him. "Maybe he won't," Putney said to nobody and holstered the pistol in his right hand, keeping the other gun aimed to his front. "Step on out, Fuller," he called to the trees.

Lockwood Fuller stepped from his cover. Both hands held open-palmed in front of him.

"God damn it, Callahan," swore Fuller. "What the hell have you done?"

Mocking his boss, Putney said, "It seems kind of plain to me. It should you, too, since you watched it all from behind that tree. That was smart of you."

"Boy, I don't think you realize what you have done," Fuller told Putney. "Ward's bound to swear out a murder warrant for you."

Putney walked straight through the fire and within inches of Fuller. He reached to Fuller's belt, pulled a Colt out of his holster, and threw it over the fire behind him. "You tell Ward what you saw here tonight. Then you tell Ward this for me," Putney whispered. "If there is one single piece of paper hung on me, I will come back here, and I will kill you. Then I will kill Ward, Breath, and all the other members of the consortium. After I have killed them, I will kill every member of their families, down to their second cousins. Women and children included. The same goes if I learn that any of these poor miners die of anything other than natural causes. You need to understand and believe what I am saying. You must also make it as clear to Ward and the others as I'm making it to you now."

Putney turned his back on Fuller and walked to his animals, climbed on his horse, and started up the steep hill. Crossing over the mountains took Putney three weeks to reach Fort Laramie.

37

P utney traveled up to Fort Laramie to shake anyone that might have been trailing him. Crossing over the mountains seemed the best way to travel, even with Putney's unfamiliarity with the terrain and the difficulty it presented to the animals. Traveling alone gave him time to think. He thought about Mandy and if he would live to see the day they could be reunited. He also thought about Erin Callahan and what she would think of the person he had become. The person who had taken her father's name to exact vengeance upon Musgrove and his gang. But the words he said to Lockwood Fuller kept Putney awake at night. Had he meant what he had said? And if he did, was he becoming like the men he hated? What would his mother, father, and sisters think?

When daylight came, Putney would banish the ghosts that haunted him. He had to remain clear-headed and vigilant. Besides keeping watch for somebody following him, Putney always kept a wary eye out for Indians. He was not familiar with the Indians in the Wyoming country and wasn't sure what reaction his presence might bring, but it most likely would not be good for him. As Putney got further north, he found broad flat valleys that made the travel much easier, and the lower altitude helped his animals. After three weeks, he found himself riding into Fort Laramie. He skirted the fort in favor of a small settlement that had cropped up near the military post.

The Army established Fort Laramie to protect westbound pilgrims and was a main stop on the Oregon and Mormon Trails. Due to the traffic of settlers, Fort Laramie was a busy, if small place. The warm spring weather had brought the first trains of people seeking their fortunes in the west. There were two groups camped outside the town, and a variety of people sought to trade or buy services. The hamlet was a wide spot in the prairie with a couple of trading posts, a livery, a few saloons, other assorted businesses, a telegraph office, and a stage depot. The town had once been a stop on the Pony Express line, but the telegraph had killed that business. Settlers stopping at Fort Laramie needed repairs of various wagon parts, making the livery the busiest place in town, so much so that they employed three smiths, two saddlers, two farriers, and half a dozen general livery workers.

Putney rode to the livery to stable his animals and asked if there was a place a man could get a warm bed for the night. The stable worker laughed and said he could get a warm bed at Sue Landon's, but he would have to pay by the hour. Putney didn't laugh at the crude joke, which caused the man to reevaluate his customer, and he told Putney that Johnson's saloon had a bunkroom in the back with six or eight bunks. Since he didn't want to carry all his gear, Putney asked if the livery had a place he could lock up his packs. "For four bits a night, we can lock your stuff up during the night in the tack room," the man told him. Putney paid for stabling and securing his equipment for two nights, then went to Johnson's Saloon, seeking lodging.

The man at Johnson's told Putney the bunkroom was full and that he could try at Sue's. "If business is slow, Sue will sometimes rent out a room and maybe even throw in a bath," the bartender had told him. It seemed Putney was not going to be able to avoid Sue's, so he asked directions and was told the third building down, the bartender indicated by jerking his thumb in the general direction.

At Sue's, a woman of ample proportions told him she would rent a room for five dollars a night. The amount was five times what Putney typically paid for a room in an out of the way place like Fort Laramie, but he was tired of sleeping on the ground, so he said, "Throw in a bath, and you have a deal." Sue agreed and said she would even change the bedding. He was welcome to go to the Johnson's or one of the other two saloons for an hour or so while she got the room vacated and straightened up.

Putney couldn't go to sleep until the early morning hours due to the noise made by soldiers and girls of the line trouncing up and down the stairs. That noise was nothing compared to the havoc that must have been going on in the rooms. He found himself disgusted at the noise of the iron beds banging against the walls and the sounds the men and women made, like two deer rutting in a cage. He thought of his night with Mandy. It was the first time making love for either of them. It had been soft, tender, and loving. It did not seem possible to him that what he was hearing could be remotely the same as what he and Mandy had done.

When most of the ruckus started dying, Putney fell

asleep like an anvil falling. He slept hard and dreamless until the noise of cattle awakened him. Looking at his watch, Putney couldn't believe he had slept until ten that morning. The last time he had slept that late was when he had gotten drunk in Boulder. He had packed some clothes in waxed canvas to keep them dry, so he donned the fresh clothes and left his room to look for a laundry. He asked Sue where he could take his clothes, and she told him to just leave them with her. The girls had to wash sheets, towels, and under-garments daily and would wash his clothes with theirs, except his frock coat, which she said she would give a brush-ing. Of course, all this would cost him another five dollars, but he agreed so he could have some clean clothes. Before he left, Sue told him that if he wanted, he could come back around one o'clock for the bath he paid for if he desired first dibs at the clean water.

Down the street from Sue's, Putney found a sort of café. It was the top of a tent supported by four poles on the corners and a longer one in the center. At the rear was a long pit over which two "A" frames suspended a long spit from which hung various cast iron pots. A grill with cast iron frying pans was on one end of the pit. A wagon backed up to the fire on the other side. A man was using the tailgate as a chopping board and was slicing a ham. Under the tent were four long tables with benches on each side. Nobody was under the tent, so Putney walked over to the man slicing the ham. "Is it too late to get some breakfast?" he asked the cook.

"Not at all, friend. What would you have?" the cook asked in return.

"I'm not particular as long as I can have some eggs and coffee," said Putney.

"Have a seat. I'll bring over something," The cook smiled and waved a two-pronged fork toward the tables. The cook placed a blue ceramic coated tin cup filled with coffee in front of him. Putney sipped the hot coffee and looked at the muddy street in front of him. The cook brought over a blue-coated plate filled with three eggs, a good portion of ham, some fried potatoes, and a biscuit.

"Biscuit's a might cold, but it'll do for a pusher," the cook told him. "That'll be six bits. Putney pulled a coin purse out of his vest pocket, put a dollar on the table, and told the cook to keep the extra two bits.

"I heard somebody driving cattle earlier. What was that all about?" he asked the cook.

"This time in the spring, outfits down in Colorado will drive some cattle up here to sell to the fort," said his host. "After a long winter of dried beef, ham hocks, and beans, them soldier boys are ready for some fresh meat." The cook sat down across from Putney with his own cup of coffee. "I set up here, every spring, myself. Down in the holler over that way, I raise some hogs and grow a few crops. You know potatoes and onions and carrots, to put in stews. I get a lot better price for ham, bacon, and pork roast by cooking it than I can for selling a hog." Putney was getting more information than he wanted. He didn't even care about the cattle. He had just been making small talk. But he didn't have anything else to do except pick up some supplies and get another night's sleep in a bed before he headed down to Julesburg and began hunting for Musgrove and his gang. "Now most of those ranchers down there, they have a contract to deliver so many beeves a month. I reckon it's the same with other forts around. On them cows, there's a set price per head. But once in a while, a bunch will push the

cattle through and then dicker with the Army Quarter-
master on the price. And you can bet every dollar in that
purse of yours, them cows have been reived. The Army don't
mind 'cause they get the cattle at a better price, and them
reivers don't mind 'cause the cattle didn't cost them anything
but the work-stealing them and pushing 'em up here."

Putney was amused at the term reivers. It was a term his
Scottish father had applied to cattle rustling. He remembered his father telling the old stories about how cattle
thieves in Scotland would raid across the border and return
with cattle from Northern England and how the Northum-
brians would do likewise. The old cook had kept talking
while Putney was musing. "and that's why I know this bunch
of cattle was legal because I saw H. L. Newman. He's a
rancher down in Colorado. Not a great big one, but big
enough, I reckon."

Confused for a moment, Putney said, "Huh?" then, "Oh,
yeah. Thanks for the lesson."

"Reckon, I'll let you finish in peace," the cook said and
walked to the other side of the fire pit to continue slicing
ham.

When Putney had finished eating, he took his dishes to
the table nearest the cook and thanked him again. Then, he
walked out to the street and looked for the nearest trading
post. Spying one, Putney walked to it, and there he bought
canned beans, some tinned meat, matches, tobacco and
papers, a loaf of black bread, some cheese, and other items.
Putney paid a young man fifty cents to carry the box of
supplies to his room.

Sue's place had a porch with some chairs, so he waited
outside until Sue told him the bath was ready. Since he had
eaten breakfast late, Putney didn't want lunch, so after his

bath, he took a walk around town just to kill time. Putney passed a few soldiers that were wandering between saloons. Several of the settlers from the wagon trains were doing business at the trading posts, and he saw a couple of trappers that had brought in pelts from their winter up in the mountains.

Late in the afternoon, Putney decided to stop in a saloon for a beer. The double doors were propped open, letting in the fresh spring air and sunshine. It was a rustic place, not even matching the standards of the ones in Boulder. Putney sat at the table fartherest from the door, with his back to the wall. The place was half empty. At one table were four soldiers playing poker with a card sharp. A couple of other soldiers were sitting at tables sharing bottles of whiskey. A few of the pilgrims were standing at the bar. At one table sat two men drinking beers and looking at a map. These men looked like ones that had traveled along the western trails many times. They both wore fringed buckskin coats with gun belts strapped around the outside. It was a friendly crowd, putting Putney in a congenial mood. He rose to go to the bar for another beer when a man he recognized hurried in the door, straight for him. Putney started to pull his guns on Russel Horton, who, seeing his mistake, threw his hands up and shouted, "Callahan! Don't shoot!" Putney saw he was in no immediate danger and returned to his table.

"What the hell are you doing here, Horton?" Putney demanded to know.

"I was with an outfit that brought fifty head of cattle to the Army. After my run-in with you, I went to Julesburg and found Musgrove and Franklin, as you told me. I gave them your message and told them you were after them for what they had done in New Mexico. Then I parted company with them. I found a job working for Mr. H. L. Newman. We just finished rounding up cattle, and he chose me and two others to come up with him. I'm telling you all this because you have to believe me. I quit the outlaw ways."

"Alright," said Putney in as cold a tone as he had ever used. "You told me, now leave me alone."

"I saw you walking around town, and I meant to keep clear of you," Horton told Putney.

"Well, why the hell didn't you?" Putney demanded to know.

"Because I came to warn you," Horton was talking fast. "And I didn't want you to think I was with 'em. You can ask Mr. Newman."

"With who?" Putney felt his muscles growing taut.

"Crawford and Carlson," Horton told him. Putney immediately recognized the names of two of the men on his list.

"What about Crawford and Carlson?" Putney was growing impatient with Horton.

"I saw them over at the fort," said Horton. "They was hanging around the sutler's store talking to a couple of soldiers. I know Musgrove's been rustling, and I figure they're here setting up a deal for stolen cattle. But you have to believe me. I ain't with them."

"Where's this H. L. Newman you're supposed to work for?" Putney asked.

"Him and the other two guys are across the street at a café. I saw you come in here, so I told them I saw somebody I knew and wanted to say hey. I told them I would catch up with 'em. I just wanted to warn you."

"Fine," said Putney. "Let's go see Mr. Newman."

Horton was glad that Putney wanted to talk to Newman because he had been telling the truth and wanted Putney to know it. Putney followed Horton out the open doors and into the street. Horton seemed in a big hurry, but Putney kept his pace slow. When Horton had nearly reached the other side, Putney heard someone shout Horton's name. Putney turned and saw two men he recognized from Clod-felter's Saloon in Denver. He knew the men recognized him when he heard one yell, "Callahan! What the hell?"

This time Putney had no sense that time had changed. There was no change in the sun's color or the street's width. He didn't hear the roar of the guns or see the smoke billowing out of the barrels as he felt his flesh burning and ripping simultaneously. All around him, men were yelling, and women were screaming. Putney fell to his knees but managed to keep enough wits about him to pull a pistol. He fired wildly and knew his bullet had disappeared some-where over the town. Putney concentrated, when firing the second time. He knew his aim had been better because he saw his target double over. Now the sun was starting to hurt his eyes as he tried to focus on the second assailant. This man was shooting at Horton. Again, Putney concentrated through his pain, trying to aim at the gunman whose atten-tion was focused on Horton. When Putney fired, he knew something was wrong because the bullet hit the mud yards in front of his target. The miss drew the shooter's attention to Putney, and he felt a blow to his left shoulder that hurt more than when Leaping Antelope had clubbed him.

With all the pain he was now feeling, Putney could barely stay conscious, much less concentrate. The best he could do was to fire three times as rapidly as possible. Luck had taken over where skill had failed him, and Putney watched as the man's skull exploded from the impact of his bullet.

Putney was about to succumb to his pain when he saw the first man stumbling toward him, hunched over but pointing his gun. Putney believed he was about to die when he heard three loud booms though he couldn't tell from where. Putney's would-be murderer spun, lurched forward two steps, and fell face down in the mud seconds before Putney did the same.

38

A t first, Nahum Putney could see only white, hurting his eyes. Then, after a few moments, colors began to drift into his vision which was still blurry. About the time things started to come into focus, he heard a woman scream, "Sue. Sue. He's awake." In no time, he heard footsteps in the hallway, and the door flew open. The large woman with huge breasts burst into the room.

"Well, Lord. It's about time you woke up," bellowed Sue Langdon, "The girls and me were all worried about you."

Putney tried to rise and felt a sharp blast of pain shoot through his lower abdomen. Then he remembered what had happened as he collapsed back down on the soft mattress. He closed his eyes tight against the pain.

"You sure were lucky the Army doctor was inside Bohannan's Trading post," Sue told him. "Some cowboys and wagon train scouts carried you up here, and that doctor patched you up. Me and the girls have been taking turns nursing you."

With his eyes still closed and his voice croaking like an

injured bullfrog, Putney said, "I thought Army doctors didn't look after civilians."

"I don't know about that, but this one looked after you," said Sue. "He said we were to send for him when you woke up." Then Sue bellowed again, "Mary Lou get in here, right now."

"I'm right here, Sue. Been looking in when I heard Linda holler," a girl said.

"Get some decent clothes on and go over to the post and tell that doctor that Mr. Callahan, here is awake," Sue ordered, then to Putney, "The doctor said you could have some broth. Would you like for me to send for some?" Putney must have nodded because she said to someone in the room, "Linda, go to the café across the street and see if they have some chicken or beef broth. If they do, bring Mr. Callahan a bowl."

"Yes, ma'am," Putney heard another girl saying. The pain from his abdomen had begun to subside. Putney opened his eyes again in time to see a girl with long blond hair leave the room.

"You've been here two days and nights," said Sue.

"I can pay," Putney told her.

"Lord, I wouldn't hear of it. I'm just proud we can take care of you," Sue told him. "And you ain't been no trouble. Well, maybe some girls lost a dollar or two, but they can make up when we get you healed."

"How long will that be," he asked.

"Well, Lordy. How would I know? I ain't no doctor. But he'll be here soon enough, and you can ask him," said Sue." The large woman rose from the chair. "I'll send Linda up when she gets back with the broth, and I'll send Betsy to help her."

Though the pain in his gut had slowed, Putney was now feeling pain in his left shoulder. *Damn,* he thought to himself, *take this as a lesson Edward Nahum Putney. Never let your guard down.* The day of the shooting started replaying in his mind, and he wondered if Horton had set him up. But that didn't seem right because they had been shooting at him, too. He wondered if Horton had survived. He was pretty sure the other two hadn't. He also wondered who had shot the man coming at him just before he went out. Then his mind wandered to Mandy. He realized if someone had killed him, she probably would have never heard about it. This thought reminded him, again, to never let his guard down.

Before long, the door creaked open, and he heard a girl say, "Mr. Callahan, it's me, Linda. Are you asleep?" He told her he wasn't. "Good," she said. "Betsy is with me. She brought some extra pillows to help prop you up. And I brought some beef broth from across the street."

The two prostitutes managed to get him in a sitting position, almost. Betsy soaked a cloth in water from a wash basin in the room and patted his head to keep him cool. The broth that Linda fed him was tasty, and its warmth felt good going down his throat. For the first time, Putney saw these ladies as real people and wondered what misfortunes had led them into such a life. Out of politeness, he didn't ask them.

Linda had finished giving him the last spoonful of broth when the door opened, and a man in an Army uniform entered. He put a small bag on the bedside table and sat in Betsy's chair. "Look at you, living in the lap of luxury and tended by angels. I'm Doctor Birdsong," the man said by way of introduction. "How are you feeling?"

"Sore," said Putney.

"I suspect so," said the doctor. "You had a bullet pass through your abdomen, just above your hip. It went through the top of your large intestine and came out the back. You were lucky it didn't hit any other organs."

"I guess so," returned Putney.

"Tore up some muscle, though. Same with your shoulder," Birdsong continued. "That bullet ripped through nothing but muscle and missed an artery." Putney nodded to indicate he understood. "I was able to stitch up the intestines before much leaked into your body. The ladies here told me you haven't been running much of a fever. That tells me you don't have septis from anything spilling out of your gut."

"How long is it going to be before I can travel?" Putney asked.

"Son," said the doctor. "This is no splinter in the finger we're discussing. I estimate you'll be able to get out of bed in about a week if you follow my instructions. With rest and mild exercise, I guess you ought to be able to mount a horse in about six weeks. If you don't follow my instructions, that intestine could tear open, and we might not know about it. If septis set in, it could kill you."

"Six weeks is a long time," Putney said.

"True," said the doctor. "And death is forever. I want to listen to your heart and lungs." The doctor pulled his stethoscope out of his bag. "You're young and strong. You should heal without any problem. For the next week, you can sit up in bed. Eat broth and soup for a couple of days. Then you can start on soft food like mashed potatoes and such. By the end of a week, you can start on more solid food." The doctor was going through his instructions by rote. "You can sit up in bed, but no walking about, just yet. Try not to move that left arm too much, and don't put any weight on it." The doctor pulled a small bottle out of his bag. "Here's some laudanum for pain, if you need it. Take a couple of drops in a glass of water but take it easy. I won't give you more."

"Thanks for everything, doctor."

"Thank me by doing what I tell you. Whatever you have going on in the world can wait. I'll be around to see you from time to time. If you need me, send one of the ladies." The doctor closed his bag and left the room, patting Betsy lightly on the rump. Sue, who had been standing in the doorway, gave the doctor a disapproving look.

Feeling a little stronger, Putney asked Sue to come in and the other girls to leave them alone for a bit. When Linda and Betsy left, Sue sat down and asked Putney what was on his mind.

"First," he said. "I don't mean to be rude, but could you tell me where my wallet is?"

"Ain't that just like a man," said Sue. "Here you are, just stepping out of death's door and worried about your money." She stood and walked over to a wardrobe, took his wallet off a shelf, and brought it to Putney. "It's all there. We may be whores, but we ain't thieves."

Embarrassed, he said, "I'm sure you're not, and I meant no offense. I know you said I didn't have to worry about the cost of things, but if I'm going to be here for six weeks, I think it's only fair to pay you something." He did some calculations in his head. "You said five dollars a night. For six weeks, that comes to six hundred and ten dollars." Putney opened his wallet, pulled out that amount and fifty more, and handed it to the madam.

"My Lord," Sue nearly fell from her chair. "Where did a roamer like you get that kind of money?"

"Lucky at poker, I guess," said Putney.

"Well, I told you before, we ain't doing this for money," Sue told him.

"I know," said Putney. "And I truly appreciate it, but there is something else you should know that may change your mind. I need to ask you, what happened to the other three men?"

"Oh, they're deader than door nails," Sue said.

"That's one good thing," Putney said, almost to himself. "Sue, two of those men were looking to murder me, and they aren't the only ones."

"You ain't wanted for anything, are you, Hon," Sue asked.

"No," Putney wasn't sure if he was, but Sue didn't need to know that part of the story. "They were outlaws that knew I was looking for them. There are three more, and if they hear about this and that I'm not dead, they may come to finish the job. That's why I want you to accept this money, because I may be putting you and your girls in harm's way. You might want to use some of it to hire somebody to watch you and your girls. Whatever. I want you to take it. And I need my guns. I want to keep them close by."

Sue counted the money, put half of it in her bodice, and returned the rest to Putney. "The original price was for a healthy man," she said. "I ain't charging a shot up man full rate. That's my deal. Take it or leave it." Then Sue went to the wardrobe and brought the two pistols with their gun belt. Putney checked the chambers and reloaded. One gun he left on the side table, the other he tucked under his pillows.

You have a deal, thanks, Sue," he told his hostess. "Now, I think I would like to get some sleep."

In the evening, Sue knocked on his door, poked her head in, and asked if he was awake. She told Putney there was a man, one of the cowboys who had helped him and wanted to see him. Putney tucked his right hand under his pillow, then nodded, and Sue allowed the man to enter. The cowboy was a tall but heavy-set man and looked to be in his late forties with a weathered face. Time had peppered his beard and short, cropped hair with gray. Looking at the man's hands reminded Putney of his father. They were hands that had seen plenty of hard work in their time. The man gestured at the chair near Putney's bed, signaling for permission to sit. Putney nodded.

"I'm H. L. Newman," the man said, "I take it your name is Jack Callahan."

Putney said nothing. He only nodded.

"I'm returning to Colorado, but I didn't want to leave until I knew you were doing alright," Newman told him.

"The doctor thinks I'll make it," said Putney.

"That's good, I wish I could say the same for Horton. I have to tell you. I'm slightly curious about how you knew Horton and what those other two had against him."

"I knew Horton only in passing," Putney saw no sense in giving Horton a bad name to the man that had trusted him enough to hire him for an honest job. "Those men weren't after him. They were after me. Horton knew that and came to warn me. I'm sorry he got killed in doing so."

"I see," Newman scratched his chin and mused a moment. "I guess they must have had some grudge against you."

Putney was silent. He wasn't about to tell this man; he didn't know it was the other way around. Putney certainly wasn't going to say that if he had seen them first, they would have been dead, and Horton wouldn't.

"Are you running from the law or something, Mr. Callahan," Newman asked.

Putney shook his head. He wondered what Newman was getting at and wished he would get to the point.

"I don't mean to get too personal, Mr. Callahan, but I have a reason for asking," continued Newman. "I have a cattle ranch a little north of Julesburg, Colorado. Since the war, there has been a high demand for beef. Right now, is a good time for me, but it might not be for long. I've heard quite a few of the cattlemen down in Texas are looking to bring their stock up to Kansas rail lines. If they do, naturally, that will affect the price of my cattle. But I have a problem. Rustlers. Whenever those bastards steal one of my cows, my profit margin goes down. And believe me, they are stealing more than one at a time."

"What does all this have to do with me?" Putney asked.

"Well, it's this way, Mr. Callahan, I saw the way you handled yourself out on that street. If they hadn't bush-whacked you, I don't think they would have stood a chance. And if you aren't an outlaw, like you say, then I could use a man with your skills and cool head."

"Go on," Putney urged.

"If I can ask one more question, do you have any experience in tracking, Mr. Callahan?" asked the rancher.

"I do," Putney answered. "I was a scout for the Confederates during the war, but I was with a unit in Texas that protected settlers from Indians. My job was scouting out where renegades were so that we could prevent attacks."

"Excellent," said Newman. "I think you're just the man I need. The governor has given me a license to hire a cattle detective to hunt down and bring these rustlers to justice. And when I say bring them to justice, I don't necessarily mean bringing them to the local sheriff if my meaning is clear."

"I've heard there are plenty of cattle detectives running

around Colorado. Why don't you hire one of them?" asked Putney, then added, "And no, your meaning is not clear. You will have to say it in plain English for me."

"Alright," declared Newman. "Julesberg is full of them, and each one is a damned cattle rustler himself. I can't trust any of those men saying they're cattle detectives. I need one that I know and I hire. I'm willing to pay you fifty dollars a month and a bounty for every cattle thief you bring in, or their ears, whichever is most convenient to you."

"I'll tell you like I've told others. I'm no murderer. I just happen to be good at killing. But I've never killed a man that didn't try to kill me first, and I've never killed an unarmed man." Putney's eyes bored into the other man's. "Besides, the doctor says I'll be laid up for six weeks. So I couldn't come now if I wanted to."

"That's alright, Mr. Callahan. I'm willing to wait for the right man." Newman told him.

"Then my fee is the fifty dollars a month you offered and a two-dollar bounty on every cow, bull, or yearling with your brand I bring in. Plus, a dollar bounty on every head I bring in that has another rancher's brand or no brand at all." Putney told Newman. "And the bounty is payable whether or not I bring in a single man."

Newman sat silent for several minutes as he thought about Putney's offer. Then, finally, he stuck out his hand and said, "You've got a deal, Mr. Callahan."

Putney gave Newman's hand a weak shake, then said, "and I want a written contract, agreeing to those terms before you leave here."

"You are a savvy man for your age Mr. Callahan," Newman complimented Putney. "I'll bring a contract around tomorrow."

As Newman was leaving the room, Putney asked him if

he had killed the man that was coming toward him in the end.

"No," said Newman. "That was one of those wagon train scouts. They pulled out the next day."

Putney couldn't believe his luck. This deal was going to put him right where he wanted to be. With the contract and the governor's license, he could go anywhere he wanted in Colorado. Even Cook couldn't stop Putney from going to Denver if he needed.

That night Mary Lou sat at his bedside while the other ladies worked. There were six girls in all. Each took a turn off the line one night of the week, and Sue took the seventh. Putney later learned that the two and a half dollars a night he had paid for the room, Sue gave to the girl that sat up with him. The first week, Putney lived in a state of near-perpetual embarrassment because if he had to relieve himself, one of the girls had to help him by placing a pan under him as he stayed in bed. After the first week, the doctor had allowed Putney to sit up in a chair part of the day, and he took the opportunity to use the chamber pot on his own. He also began eating more solid food. By the end of the second week, Putney was feeling well enough that it was no longer necessary for the girls to sit up with him, which relieved him greatly.

As usual, the nights were raucous, and Putney slept little until the early morning hours. But he came to begrudge the girls' activities less and less. Everyone in the house, including Putney, would sleep until noon. One of the girls would bring in breakfast, even before eating her own. After they had eaten, the girls would take care of chores, then before the night began, one or two were always stopping by his room just to sit and talk. A couple of the girls offered him "free ones" if he wanted, but he would politely decline, citing his health as the reason.

Slowly Putney began to improve, and the doctor allowed him to go downstairs for his meals. He tried to move around as much as possible and exercise a little. He made it to the livery by the fourth week to check on his gear. Putney paid what he owed there. He took the two Walkers and rented a horse and buggy, which he took a few miles from town to get some practice shooting. He used the Walkers because he had plenty of powder and ball, and he didn't want to waste the cartridges for the French pistols because that ammunition was hard to come by. On the fifth week, Putney bought two boxes of ammunition for the Henry and took them out for practice. He was feeling stronger and was happy his time convalescing was nearly at an end.

He had grown fond of the girls, and they had of him. He did, however, feel sorry for their circumstances, and one day, when it was just Sue and him, he finally broached the subject of why the girls would take up the trade. She told him that, for her part, she owed it all on a no-good husband. He had been a gambler but not a very good one. So one night, to pay off a gambling debt, he pimped her out. When he learned he could make money off her, he kept doing it. She said she would have left him, but the fact was she enjoyed it. The problem was they kept getting run out of so-called decent towns and moving further west. Along the way, he picked up two other girls, and they finally ended up at Fort Laramie. He caught pneumonia the first winter they were there and died.

That was when she took over the business. With the fort nearby, she had a steady stream of customers, and within one year, she built a house instead of working out of the big tent they had. Sometimes, a father from a wagon train would catch his daughter with some beau and kick her out, telling her she could make her own way. Most had been beaten badly by their father. She felt sorry for them, but at least when she took them in, they had a roof over their head and meals to eat. Sue said she never forced any girls into it, but they all seemed resigned to their fates. So she clothed and fed them and let them keep some of their earnings. Sue also put back a little of what each girl earned and had it ready anytime they wanted to leave, which two had.

Putney decided that, like him, these girls were only trying to make their way the best they could. Life on the frontier was harsh and unforgiving. But, here at Fort Laramie, the girls were safe from Indian attacks, and Sue didn't allow any mistreatment by any of the men that came to her establishment.

Finally, the day came when the doctor said Putney was fit enough to travel, as long as he didn't take it too roughly or go too far at a time. All the girls hated seeing Putney go and begged Sue to throw a going-away party for him. Sue agreed and closed down the brothel that night. The only man besides Putney that Sue invited was Doctor Birdsong. The girls had baked a cake, and Sue had brought food from the café. There was drinking and dancing, although Putney limited his exercise of both. Before the party was over, Sue gave one final toast. "To the best gentleman that ever visited our house. Here's to you, Red Jack Callahan." Putney couldn't have known, then, that the moniker "Red Jack" would follow him from Fort Laramie.

The next morning Sue and the girls all gathered to say goodbye. He thanked them for all their kindness and said if he ever came that way again, he would look in on them. The girls all gushed over that statement. Finally, he went to the livery, paid what he owed, saddled up, and left Fort Laramie —not realizing that he would, one day, return.

After Putney left, Sue went to clean Putney's room. On the bedside table, she found six sealed envelopes with each girl's name and one with hers. She took the envelopes to the breakfast table and passed them out to her girls. Inside each was a twenty-dollar bill, except hers. In Sue's envelope was fifty dollars and a note she never allowed anyone to read.

39

A long with the contract Newman had provided Putney, he included a map with directions to the ranch. Putney had decided to follow Doctor Songbird's recommendation and traveled slowly, taking his time and resting well overnights. Putney had purchased enough supplies to last at least two weeks. It was a good thing because it wasn't until the fourteenth day that he came in sight of the ranch house and surrounding outbuildings.

THE HOUSE WAS a large two-story clapboard house with four gables and a covered porch surrounding three sides. In addition to the main house, there was a barn with a corral attached, what looked like a bunk house, and several smaller outbuildings. Putney rode directly to the front of the main house and tied his horse and mule to one of the three hitching posts. As Putney was hitching up, Newman stepped out on the porch and greeted him. "I've been watching you for the last half hour. I have a telescope in my upstairs study to watch people approaching. How was your trip?"

"UNEVENTFUL," said Putney.

"WELL, THAT'S A GOOD SIGN," said Newman. "At least the Indians aren't acting up yet. Come on into my business office and have a drink." Putney dusted off his clothes and followed his employer into a room just off the main foyer. Newman had furnished the room with a large pine desk. In an arch in front of the desk were five knotty pine chairs with cushions covered in cow hides. To one side of the desk was a shelf with several ledgers; on the other was a sideboard with an
     assortment of bottled spirits. "What will it be?" asked Newman.

"I SEE you have a bottle of Maritime Malt, Scotch," remarked Putney. "That was my father's favorite."

AS NEWMAN WAS POURING a glass of whisky for Putney, he asked, "So, are you a Scotsman, Mr. Callahan."

"NO, SIR," Putney said politely, "American."

.   .   .

NEWMAN LAUGHED AND REPLIED, "Well said, Mr. Callahan. Well said. So, I suppose you have given up your southern loyalties."

"I NEVER HAD ANY," Putney said truthfully. "I only joined the Mounted Mountain Rangers to keep from getting drafted. Otherwise, I'd probably be a San Antonio lawyer by now."

The comment brought another laugh from Newman, who handed the glass of whisky to Putney. Newman sat in one of the chairs in front of his desk instead of the cowhide-covered rocker. He motioned for Putney to do the same. "So, how are you feeling?" Newman wanted to know.

"VERY WELL, THANK YOU," said Putney. "I took the doctor's advice and took my time getting down here once he said I could go. I wanted to ensure I was as fit as possible before I got here."

"EXCELLENT," said Newman. "So, you're ready to get started, then?"

"Yes, sir," said Putney.

"BEFORE WE DO, it seems you have built yourself up quite a reputation over the past year," said Newman, who then handed Putney a copy of the Rocky Mountain Times with a small article circled in red pencil. The article read:

·   ·   ·

'A MAN NAMED Callahan survived a deadly attack by three gunmen on the streets of Fort Laramie township. We later determined the full name of the survivor to be Red Jack Callahan. Is it possible this is the same Jack Callahan that killed one Andrew Barton in Clodfelter's Saloon last spring, or the same Mining Detective Jack Callahan who killed three mine jumpers near Ward's Camp earlier this year?

UNDOUBTEDLY IT IS. Just as certainly, we expect to hear more about Red Jack before much longer. A man like this can't keep from publicity.'

READING THE ARTICLE, Putney immediately knew two things. The first was that Ward had feared him enough to keep from bringing charges against him. Ward must have doctored the reports to make it look like Putney had done a service to the community. Also, Putney was now confident that Mandy knew he was safe. He was glad of that. However, he was less pleased about the notoriety. It was probable that the Franklin brothers, Mark Farnsworth and Lewis Musgrove, were well aware of him also. At least they didn't know he was working as a stock detective. Putney laid the paper on the desk and asked, "Do you want to end our contract then?"

"ARE YOU SERIOUS?" asked the rancher. "This was the best thing that could happen. I was in Julesburg right after this article came out. I let people know that I had hired you as my Range Detective. That got quite a few tongues wagging, I can tell you."

. . .

SHIT, though, Putney. *And the tongues wagging the most would
be those he had sworn to kill. They knew from Horton who I am
and now Newman had told them where I would be."*

"IS IT A PROBLEM FOR YOU?" asked Newman.

"NO, NOT AT ALL," lied Putney.

"GOOD, now let me give you the layout," Newman said,
taking him over to a large map on the wall by the door.
Newman showed him the ranch's boundaries but explained
that Putney wasn't limited to staying within those boundaries. Putney could look for and pursue rustlers anywhere in
the general geographic area he chose. Newman described
the bunkhouse and said Putney could sleep there if he
chose. Newman also said a large dining hall was in the back
of the house for his ranch hands. They ate there, except
during a cow gathering. In that case, meals got prepared
where the work was. Newman also said he kept a hog farm,
run by an old Mexican, about two miles away. There was a
smokehouse on the property; they smoked their own hams
and bacon, and the cook made fresh sausage.

PUTNEY TOLD Newman that if it was all the same, he
preferred staying out on the range. Putney said he would go
out with a week worth of supplies and would come in every
week to report to Newman unless, of course, there was

something of note before that. Since he didn't entirely trust
Newman to do the right thing, Putney said he would take
any cattle thieves he caught to the sheriff in Julesburg.
Newman at first balked at this information, then reconsid-
ered it. Finally, Putney insisted that he receive a notarized
copy of the license the governor had given Newman to hire a
stock detective. Putney explained that if he had to kill any
rustlers, he wanted to be covered by the contract and the
license. "I'm saying," Putney was thinking of the Musgrove
gang, "that if it is necessary, I want a license to kill."

40

T hat night Putney stayed in the bunkhouse at Newman's ranch. He and Newman planned to go into Julesburg the following morning to get the governor's license copied and notarized. He wanted to get one or two good nights' sleep before starting his duties as a range detective. Besides, his animals could use the rest, and a few days in a barn with good feed would be to their benefit and his.

CALVING season was near its end and rounding up the cattle for branding wouldn't begin for a couple of months, so only three other men were sharing the bunkhouse. Newman introduced Putney to the three full-time hands. John Finch was the range boss who did the hiring of cowboys for the cow gathering. Finch had a separate room with a small desk, as one of the privileges of the boss. Raul Vasquez and Joe Blackman tended the barn, remuda, and milk cows. They also kept up repairs on the outbuildings and corrals and tended the vegetable garden.

. . .

AFTER PUTNEY HAD PUT away his animals and stowed his gear, the four men went to the dining hall at the back of the house. The cook served up roast beef, potatoes, carrots, and green beans. The cook rounded out the meal with plenty of coffee and apple pie. Newman nor his family ate with the hired help. When the men returned to the bunkhouse, Putney found and scanned through a stack of old newspapers. He found two articles that garnered his attention. The first article was about the appointment of Uriah B. Holloway as U. S. Marshal for the Territory of Colorado. There was no particular reason this article should have interested Putney; it was only something that caught his attention. However, the second article did have significance to Putney. It was an article about Julesburg, and in it, the reporter claimed that the town was the wickedest in the west, having more outlaws than even a city the size of Denver. How many towns west of the Mississippi the reporter had been to wasn't mentioned, and Putney put it down to a tendency of reporters to exaggerate their experiences with the people they met and places they had been.

AFTER BREAKFAST THE FOLLOWING DAY, Putney and Newman rode a wagon into Julesburg. They were going to take the governor's license to a print shop to be copied, then to the County Courthouse to get the copy notarized as an authentic copy. During the ride to town, Newman told Putney that the only law out there was the sheriff. The sheriff had a hands-off policy as far as criminals were concerned. The sheriff believed that if a man hadn't broken the law in his county, they hadn't broken the law. "So it is

wise you decided not to try and bring anybody into Julesburg on your own," said Newman. "Chances are neither
them, nor you would make it to the sheriff's office."

IN PUTNEY'S MIND, it wasn't bad that Julesburg was as
lawless as purported. He believed that many outlaws meant
more competition between them, so it was unlikely one
gang would rule the roost. But, on the other hand, since
Newman had advertised that 'Callahan' would be working
for him, Putney would be a target for every would-be
pistoleer in the area.

WHEN THEY HAD FINISHED their business at the courthouse,
Newman said he had to pick up feed and supplies for the
ranch. Putney said he had seen a gun shop as they were
coming into town, and he went there. Putney and Newman
agreed to meet at the café near the general store. Putney was
much more cautious in Julesburg than in Fort Laramie. The
town's reputation as a haven for scofflaws would have been a
good enough reason, but combined with the fact that there
was a probability he could run into Musgrove or any of his
gang certainly caused Putney to be more aware of his
surroundings.

WALKING PAST THE STORES, shops, and saloons, Putney kept
his vigilance high, keeping an eye on every man he passed
and men on the other side of the street. Whenever he
would come to a cross street or an alley between buildings,
he would stop and look both ways before continuing.
When Putney finally entered the gun shop, he maneuvered

himself to see both the front entry and the opening that led to the back of the store. Putney told the shopkeeper he needed powder and ball for the Walker's and to know if any cartridges for his pistols were available. The shopkeeper said he would have to look in the back for cartridges because the French guns were a rare item. While the man was in the back, Putney saw a rifle in a glass case high on the back wall of the shop. It was a new rifle with a similar look to his Henry, but it had a shiny brass receiver. When the store owner returned, he saw Putney gazing at the rifle and said, "Ah, I see the new Winchester has caught your eye. Many a man has looked, but few can afford it. Would you like to take a closer look?" Putney said he would, and the owner pulled a folding ladder over and climbed to the second rung to unlock the case and get the rifle down. "It uses the same cartridge as the Henry. You load it through this port on the side instead of the magazine in the stock."

THE OWNER HANDED the rifle to Putney, who admired the quality of the workmanship.

Putney tried the action and said, "Much smoother than a Henry, too."

"YES, IT IS," said the owner. "And with the loading port on the side, you can load it five times as fast as a Henry. With a little practice, you could even load it while riding."

PUTNEY TRIED the action again and asked how much the gun cost. "It just came out this year," the owner told him. "Not many in circulation yet. I expect the price to go down as more are available."

"How much?" asked Putney.

"Seventy-five dollars," the owner told him. "That includes a box of shells."

"I'll take it," Putney told the man.

Smiling, the shopkeeper said, "I have the cartridges you wanted, along with the powder and ball. Do you need anything else?"

"That will suffice," said Putney.

"You hold on to the rifle. I'll get the other stuff boxed up for you," the salesman told Putney. As the shopkeeper added the total of the purchases, the door opened, and Claude Franklin stepped in. Feigning surprise, Franklin said, "Jack, Jack Callahan. I never expected to see you here."

"I don't know why you wouldn't," said Putney. "I saw you when I passed that saloon a few doors down."

.   .   .

"You got me," Claude's laugh was uncomfortable. "What brings you to Julesburg?"

"Let's not fling cow dung at each other, Claude," Putney said. "My bet is you know good and well why I am here. H. L. Newman has hired me as an honest stock detective."

"Well, I reckon that's fine, just as long as it isn't about that cock and bull story Horton told us," said Claude.

"Horton's dead," Putney told Franklin. "I don't know what he told you, but if he said I mean to kill Musgrove, Farnsworth, and your brother, that was no cock and bull story."

"Musgrove and Farnsworth are your business, Jack," said Claude. "But I don't see how I can stand by and let you kill my brother Ed."

The serious turn of the conversation made the store owner nervous and hoping to break the tension, he spoke up, although with uncertainty in his voice, "That'll be a total of ninety-two dollars and fifty cents." Without looking away from Claude, Putney reached in his vest pocket and pulled out his coin purse. He took five double eagles and placed them on the glass counter.

. . .

WITH SADNESS IN HIS VOICE, Putney said, "Claude, I like you, and I regret deceiving you at Fort Walton, but by now, I am sure you know my intent. Musgrove, Farnsworth, and your brother are villains of the worst degree. So, I am asking you to get away from them. Go to Denver or back to Saint Louis or anywhere."

"IF IT WERE JUST MUSGROVE, I would, Callahan," replied Claude. But I can't desert my brother."

"I TRIED. I've said all I will say on the matter," said Putney, scooping up the change the clerk had laid on the counter.

"IF THAT'S all you got to say, that's all you got to say. Adios, amigo," said Claude as he turned to leave the store. But instead of reaching for the doorknob, Claude's hand went to his pistol. Before either man could make another move, a loud boom and smoke filled the room. Because both Putney and Claude had focused on each other, they had disregarded the little shopkeeper. Looking in the little man's direction, they both saw him holding a sawed-off, double-barreled shotgun. Smoke drifted from one barrel. "I don't know what your beef is with each other, and I don't give a God damn. But the first man that reaches for a gun gets the next barrel." said the small man.

CLAUDE GLARED AT THE SHOPKEEPER. "You know," he said. "If you pull that trigger, whichever one of us you don't get will most likely get you."

. . .

A WOMAN CAME from the back room with another shotgun raised and aimed. "I doubt that," she said. "You, near the door, get. And you, mister," directing her attention at Putney, "Pick up your purchases, and you get, too. What you do in the street doesn't concern us. But there will be no gunplay in here."

FRANKLIN FROWNED AND SAID, "I didn't want to see how this played out anyway." Claude left the store, and Putney waited a moment.

"I MEAN IT, MISTER," said the woman, "You get out of here and don't bother coming back. Take your business else-where from now on."

SAYING NOTHING, Putney picked up his package and the rifle and left the store.

41

The following day Putney asked the cook to pack up a week's worth of food. Newman and Finch met him at the back of the dining hall. "John is going to ride out with you and show you around to some of the places most of the cattle graze," Newman told him. "We will join with other outfits for a gathering in a couple of months. Anybody you find out there probably shouldn't be, unless they're just counting cows, so if you find anybody and they say they are with another ranch, bring them here. John and I know all the permanent hands in the area. If they don't belong, we'll handle them from here. Anybody doing any branding or anybody you catch with a running iron will be thieves. How you handle them is up to you. John will head back around mid-day."

Putney and Finch saddled up and rode out. Finch told Putney he had been in Fort Laramie and seen the shootout. "Sure hated to lose Horton. He was a pretty good hand," Finch said. "It was a sight, how you handled yourself, though. They would have probably killed me. I ain't no gun hand, like you."

Putney accepted the compliment without comment. The rest of the morning, Finch showed Putney around. Putney was impressed by the number of cattle he saw. Newman had a sprawling ranch. There was good grass and plenty of water. "When H. L. started this ranch, people said the cattle couldn't survive winters up here," said Finch. "I guess he proved them wrong. Now I reckon there will be cattlemen from all over to start ranches here and in Wyoming. Maybe even Montana."

"How many cattle are you able to sell up here?" Putney had asked.

"Quite a few," Finch told him. "We drive some over to Denver regularly and have contracts with the Army forts around. But the rustlers are starting to hurt us. They ain't out any cost, and if they can get cattle to the forts, they can undercut our price. So that's why it's so important for you to get a handle on this."

"I'll do my best," Putney said.

"In a year or two, the business ought to pick up," said Finch. "That new Trans-Atlantic Railroad will be passing nearby. Once it's up, we can start shipping beef to Chicago by rail. That's when the real money will be coming in. They say cattle buyers are paying as much as thirty-five dollars a head to ship to Chicago."

Putney thought back to the ranches in Texas. Before the war, they were lucky to get two dollars a head. But people didn't eat as much beef back then. In the east, people used cows for milk, not meat. The war had changed all that. Both armies needed meat, and there just weren't enough chickens and hogs. So men in Missouri, Kansas, and Texas started raising beef to supply the troops. After the war, soldiers had developed a taste for beef, and when they returned to the big cities, they created a demand. But thirty-five dollars a head boggled Putney's mind.

After Finch had shown Putney where he could find most of the cattle, he took Putney to a few draws and small canyons where rustlers could push the cows and do the branding, unseen unless somebody was looking. "There's more places like these around," said Finch. "I reckon an experienced scout like you won't have trouble finding them. One thing you should know, though. You may see some Indians gathering up cattle. Let them be as long as it's just four or five cows. H. L. would rather lose a few head than start some kind of war with the Indians."

"A wise decision, I suppose," said Putney.

"Damn straight it is," said Finch. "Why, did you know them Indians burned down the whole town of Julesburg a little over a year ago?"

"What?" Putney asked in surprise.

"Sure," Finch assured him. "The town wasn't where it is now. Did you hear of the Sand Creek Massacre in '64?"

"No," said Putney. "We didn't get much Yankee news down in Texas."

"Well," began Finch. "Back in '64, some Cheyenne, Arapaho, and Lakota had made a winter camp up on the Sand Creek. I never heard any reason for it, but the Army attacked the camp and killed nearly half them Indians. A couple of months later, the Indians came and raided Julesburg. Most of the town folk made it to Fort Rankin. The Indians carried off all they could but left the town like it was. Then, a month later, the Indians came back and carried off anything of value that was left. Then they burned the whole town to the ground."

"Sounds like they had good reason," Putney said.

"I reckon," said Finch. "Anyway, the people all got together and rebuilt the town where it is now because it was closer to Fort Rankin."

"That's quite a story," Putney was duly impressed.

"Yep. That's why H. L. don't mind if the Indians take a few head. As long as they don't get greedy," Finch told him. "Say, look at the time. Let's have a bite to eat, and I need to start back."

Putney agreed, and the two men shared some cold ham and biscuits. Before he left, Finch wished Putney luck. "Don't get killed out here," he told Putney. "H. L. said if anything happens to you, he might give me the job, and I don't want it."

∾

PUTNEY SPENT the next week roaming the countryside, familiarizing himself as much as anything else. He didn't see a living thing except cows. He did make out signs of wolves and coyotes, but he never saw any. During his trek, Putney took regular landscape notes and drew little maps indicating unusual formations. Around the edges of the ranch land were some forested areas, and Putney would camp in a few yards. If there weren't any wooded areas around, he would find one of the arroyos and camp up in there. The days were warm but nothing like the summers in Texas, so Putney wasn't much bothered by the mild heat. The nights were cool, but with his bedroll and beaver coat, he could stay plenty warm with just the coals left over from any small cook fire he built.

Putney liked the solitude of his work. It reminded him of when he had scouted for Russell before the captain went rogue. He returned to the ranch on the seventh day to restock. Putney reported to Newman that he had seen no activity. He spent the night in the bunk house and played checkers with Vasquez, Blackman, and Finch. Vasquez and Blackman proved to be much cannier players than Finch or Putney, so the two retreated to Finch's room and drank a couple of whiskeys before turning in.

The next day, as he headed out, Putney determined to put his skills to work. The previous week he had concentrated on getting to know the area. Now was the time to start his work in earnest. Still, the first two days, he saw no sign of rustlers. *Maybe*, he thought, *it was all in Newman's mind, and that rustling wasn't the problem either Newman or Finch had said.*

About noon on the third day, however, he changed his mind. Putney came across tracks that indicated several cows headed east. It was hard to tell how many cattle there were, but it was at least a dozen or more. He did find three distinct sets of horses' tracks. Shod horses left the tracks, so there wasn't a chance Indians had left them. Putney followed the tracks for half an hour until he came on some cow dung. He tested the dung and found it was fresh and relatively warm. He knew they couldn't be more than two or three hours ahead of him. Putney referred to his notes and maps. If he had been accurate, he knew there was a small cut between two hills about four hours from where he was.

Putney had worked a lot of cattle in his life and knew that unless spooked, a man could get cows to move only so fast. He reasoned that if he rode north for about two miles, he could cut back southeast and arrive well ahead of the cattle. Putney could stake his animals out of site and take the high ground above the cut. He would be in place long before his quarry got there. That was if they headed where he had predicted.

It took two and a half hours for him to reach the area of the shallow gorge. He rode to the top of a hill to get his bearings and ensure he was where he thought he should be. After confirming his location, Putney looked around. The hill was covered with late spring wildflowers the best for his purpose, being ones that grew in little bushy clumps about two feet high with purple flowers. He could use those flowers for cover. Putney took his horse and mule back down the hill and staked them out. With his animals taken care of, he ate some ham and biscuits, then took the Henry, the Winchester, and a canteen of water back up the hill and waited. Putney wished he had his spyglass, but he lost that to Quanah. He decided he would buy a new one the first opportunity he had.

Putney laid in the sun for two hours, the little bushy plants providing almost no shade. Finally, he heard the low mooing of cattle. He waited half an hour before seeing the first rider, a tall man on a bay. As the man entered the arroyo, Putney counted the cattle that followed. There were twelve cows, five calves, and what looked like a yearling bull. Two more men followed the cattle. The cut ended in a rise steep enough to keep the cows from trying to climb. That's where the rustlers herded the cattle. When the men had the cattle pinned against the rise, they took to the open end and staked out their saddle horses and one pack horse, forming a kind of equine fence. Several more feet toward the opening, the men made camp. Putney checked his watch. It was four-thirty.

The men settled in about forty yards from the top of Putney's hill. Well within the range of both rifles. Putney

waited as the men built a fire and put on a pot for coffee.
Putney figured they planned to wait until morning to start
rebranding the cattle. They would take turns on watch
throughout the night, mainly to keep the cows calm. Putney
decided to wait until they prepared a meal and started
eating. They would all be gathered around the fire then.
That was when he would make his move.

It was five-thirty when the men started dishing up their
food. As they shoveled the first spoonsful into their mouths,
Putney aimed in with the Winchester. He exhaled slowly.
When he had exhaled sufficiently, he held his breath and
gently squeezed the trigger. The rifle report boomed in the
wilderness, and the coffee pot flew. The men jumped to
their feet, spilling beans and bacon on the ground and into
the fire. As they stood, they all drew pistols, which would be
mostly ineffective against Putney at that range. Putney
worked the lever and squeezed the trigger a second time.
Their horse started whinnying, and one of the saddle horses
reared, pulled up its stake, and ran toward the men, who
scattered to keep from getting trampled. Now the cattle
started getting skittish. The men scanned the hilltops, trying
to see who was shooting. The next shot from Putney hit a
few feet from the horses, causing them to spook even more,
but the stakes held. One of the men shot wildly at the top of
the hill opposite Putney. They were spooked as well. Two
men started to their horses, but Putney placed another
bullet between them and the horses and sent them skit-
tering backward.

The cattle were ready to panic, so Putney decided to egg
them on by firing twice in rapid succession at the hillside
that barricaded them in. It was enough. Unable to climb up,
the cattle turned and started moving, slowly at first, toward
the men. Then the yearling broke into a run, and the cows

and calves followed him. The horses became terrified, broke their tethers, and took off ahead of the cattle. The three men scampered to the hills' sides to avoid the stampeding of animals. The grassy soil had kept most of the dust down, but enough started rising, obscuring the men from Putney's sight for several seconds. One man had figured out where the rifle fire was coming from and that he had a moment's cover. He started scurrying up the hill, firing his revolver as quickly as possible. He never realized his strategy was flawed. Putney hurried his shot. Instead of it hitting in front of the man, the bullet clipped the ankle. The man fell crashing into the hillside, face first. The other two men kept cooler heads and hid behind the sparse foliage on the hillside as best they could.

The fight was not over, but Putney knew he was far ahead. So, he called out to the men below, "Throwdown!" he yelled. "Throw down now, and nobody else has to get hurt."

"Who are you?" hollered back one of the men. Putney could not tell which.

"Jack Callahan. Stock detective for the Newman ranch," Putney yelled out, then again commanded, "Throw down now."

The wounded man called out, this time, "Mark, I lost my gun. This guy has me pinned. Throwdown, for God's sake."

"To hell with that," yelled the man that Putney supposed was Mark. "This son of a bitch means to kill me."

Mark Farnsworth, thought Putney. *You're damn right I do.* Putney called out again. "You. The one that's wounded. What's your name?"

"Duggan. Sanford Duggan" came the reply.

"And who is the one that's not Mark?" Putney questioned again.

"That's Niles Hill," Duggan shouted.

Putney hollered again. "Niles Hill. Duggan has already lost his gun. I'm out of your range, and you can't hit me without getting a lot closer. If you try that, I'll kill you. Throw your pistol out where I can see it. I promise to let you and Duggan go.

"Niles," yelled Duggan. "Do like he says. He's got us cold anyway."

"To hell with you, Duggan," yelled Mark. He fired a shot in Duggan's direction and missed.

From his position, Putney could no longer see the man he guessed to be Farnsworth, so Putney took a chance and stood. As he did, another shot came his way but hit about twenty feet short. "Hill," hollered Putney. "This is the last time I'm going to ask. Throw out your gun. You and Duggan can get out of here."

This time Hill finally answered. "If I throw down, Farnsworth will kill me."

"You're choice," hollered Putney. "Take your chance he won't, or take your chance I will."

For a long minute, the only answer Putney received was silence. Then, Putney saw a pistol fly toward the campfire from the man's position. "There, I done it," yelled Hill.

"Good," Putney called to Hill. "Now come collect Duggan. I'll make sure your safe from Farnsworth." The man Hill started crawling up the side of the incline toward Duggan, but Farnsworth stood to aim at him. Putney fired his rifle in Farnsworth's direction, causing him to duck back behind the foliage. Hill hesitated, then started his climb again. When he reached Duggan, Putney called out again. "Bring him up the hill. I'll keep Farnsworth down, but make sure you don't come close to me."

Hill reached Duggan and pulled the wounded man to

his feet. The two struggled up the incline but angled away from Putney. When they had reached the top, Putney told them to take out in the direction of their horses, and the two outlaws obeyed his command. Putney watched until they were out of sight, then called to Farnsworth. "I'm guessing Horton told you who I am and what I intend to do."

"Look, Callahan," yelled Farnsworth. "I'm not the man you really want. You already got Bailey. We got word that it was you that killed Crawford and Carlson. I know you got Rogers because he was the one that gave our names. My bet is you killed Sauder and Walker, too, since nobody's heard hide nor hair from them."

"What's your point?" Putney asked.

"Look," said Farnsworth. Putney saw Farnsworth throw his gun out in the open. "I ain't armed no more. You wouldn't kill Horton unarmed, so I reckon you won't kill me. I'm willing to tell you where you can find Musgrove and Franklin. Just don't kill me."

Putney weighed what Farnsworth had told him. It was true Musgrove and Franklin were the leaders. They were the men responsible. If Farnsworth would give them up, Putney could end this business. He could go back to Boulder and get Mandy. The two of them could go back to Texas, and he could start his life over again.

"Come on up," Putney said. "I won't shoot you."

Farnsworth stood and started climbing towards Putney. Keeping his eyes on his enemy, Putney shifted the rifle to his left hand. Farnsworth climbed until he was about twenty feet away from Putney when he stumbled and fell. As he stood again, Farnsworth had a derringer in his hand. Farnsworth brought the pocket pistol up to aim at Putney. But it was too late. When Farnsworth had stumbled, Putney had drawn his gun and already had the villain in his sights. Two bullets flew from Putney's gun, striking Farnsworth in the chest. The derringer fell from Farnsworth's hand as he fell and slid halfway back down the hill. Putney walked down to where the unfired derringer lay. He picked it up and put it in his vest pocket.

42

P utney went to the outlaw's camp and gathered their guns. When he was a boy, his father had given him advice about run-ins with outlaws. Following his father's advice Putney didn't bother with Farnsworth's body. He began the ride back to the ranch headquarters to report his run-in with the three rustlers. On the way, Putney came on Duggan and Hill. They had bandaged Duggan's ankle as best he could, but they were having a hard time. They hadn't gotten more than half a mile from where the skirmish had occurred. Putney rode past them without a word even though they called to him for help.

About a mile further, Putney came on two of the rustler's horses where they had stopped when the fear had been exhausted. Against his father's advice, he gathered up the horses. Searching the saddle bags and other gear, Putney found no weapons, so he tied the horses to his mule and returned to where he had left the struggling bandits. The two were sitting in the wide open, giving Duggan a rest. When he arrived, Putney didn't dismount. "Untie these horses," Putney said to Hill, who was going overboard with gratitude along with Duggan. "Don't go back to Julesburg," Putney ordered. "If I find you there, y'all won't get a second chance. Am I clear?"

"It's the closest town," complained Duggan. "I need to get someone to take care of my ankle. Where are we supposed to go?"

"Go to Denver for all I care," Putney told him.

"What about Farnsworth?" asked Hill

"Farnsworth stays where he is," Putney told him. Pointing west, Putney said, "Denver is that way. Wyoming is that way." Putney pointed north. "Now, get moving before I change my mind and shoot those horses." The rustlers mounted and spurred the horses west.

The work continued in much the same manner for the next two months. Putney would go out, always taking notes and adding to or improving his hand-drawn maps. He ran into small-time rustlers but never any large operations. The reivers all operated as if they were working out of an instruction book. There would be two to four men stealing ten to twenty head of cattle and moving them into a box end gulch or small canyon where it was always easy for Putney to get the high ground and catch them off guard. Most gave up without a fight. Those would bargain for a clean getaway, which Putney would allow. Occasionally a group would try to fight it out. In those cases, someone would lose their life or be seriously injured enough that the others would surrender. They were always surprised that one man would be able to take them. Except for that first time, if Putney had to use force, he always took the offenders to the ranch and turned them over to Newman. Every time, Putney expected to run into Musgrove and Ed Franklin, but he never did.

After two months, word had gotten around that rustling cattle on or near Newman's ranch was not gainful employment. His efforts and the round-ups cut cattle thieving to nonexistence. Except when he was confronting outlaws, Putney was enjoying himself. He also enjoyed the confrontations more than he ought if he told the truth. He liked demonstrating his prowess against the thieves. His only disappointment was never seeing any sign of Musgrove and Franklin. Even those he captured would deny knowing the whereabouts of the two men.

One day, after the round-ups had started, Putney noticed a rider coming. He held up his horse and put his hand on his Winchester if it became necessary to use it. As the rider got closer, Putney relaxed when he recognized it was a young cowboy named Marv Chalmers. Putney wasn't close to any of the working hands, but the few times Putney had been around Marv, Putney found he liked him. When Marv was close, Putney said, "Hey, Marv, how are you doing?"

"Good, Jack, how are you?"

"I'm well, Marv. What brings you out here?" Putney was curious why the young cowboy would be out where there were no cattle.

"Finch sent me to look for you. Mr. Newman wants to see you at the ranch house."

"Did he say what for?"

"Nope. Finch just said to find you and tell you Mr. Newman is stoked up to see you."

He thanked Marv and asked him if he wanted to ride along with him a piece. "Sure, Jack. I mean, I can't go all the way to the ranch house, but I wouldn't mind a little company. I'm not thrilled about being out here by myself."

"It's not so bad. You get used to it."

"Say, is it true, Jack, that you were a reb?"

"It's true. I didn't want to, but it was join or get drafted. And I got to stay in Texas."

"They say you fought Comanches."

"True and a few Kiowas and Wichitas. Maybe others. Sometimes they would band together, and I never thought to ask who was who." With that, Putney laughed.

Marv also laughed at Putney's little joke. He had heard that Jack Callahan never joked and was a little proud to be privy to the jest.

The two men rode along and passed the time about matters of the day, nothing significant until they reached a point that Marv had to peel off and get back to the camp. Putney rode the rest of the way, wondering what was so crucial that Newman would send especially for him.

As he arrived at the ranch headquarters, he saw there was a landau carriage with matching black mares pulling. Loitering around the carriage were four men that would never be mistaken for cowboys. Dusters hung over the hitching rails of the main house so that anyone could see their sidearms. At the watering trough were four horses saddled with rifles hanging on them. Maybe they were more stock detectives. Instead of riding up to the house, Putney guided his horse and mule to the corral.

He unsaddled and unpacked the animals, then dusted himself off and looked toward the house. Propping a boot on a rail of the corral fence, he took out tobacco and papers and rolled a cigarette. He smoked and watched the men watch him. When he had finished his smoke, he ducked under a rail and started to the house. Putney got around the landau and started to the fence gate. One of the men stepped in front of him and put his hand on Putney's chest. The man was about as tall as Putney. He had a day's growth on his unshaven face that was so black and thick it looked like a fully grown beard. Putney looked down at the large hand covered with black hair on his vest. The dark man spoke in a growling voice, "Who are you, and where do you think you're going."

Putney looked directly into the black eyes of his assailant and said, "If you like that hand, I would strongly suggest you remove it."

"And if I don't?" The dark-haired man asked.

Putney thought of breaking the man's thumb. But, being outnumbered, he decided to give a warning. "If you don't, I may have to break your thumb, and then I'll end up shooting at least one of you. Then the others will shoot me. I bet that this event would not make your boss, whoever that is, very happy."

"I don't think any of that will happen," said the dark man, as he stepped in closer and took a wide stance in front of Putney.

Striking like a rattlesnake, Putney brought a knee up into the man's groin as hard as he could. Then, with almost the same motion, he twisted, drawing a revolver before the other three had a chance to move.

"Callahan," Putney heard Newman yell from the porch. "My instructions were for you to come see me as soon as you got here."

Putney carefully eyed the three men, standing stock still while their companion was writhing on the ground moaning. "Any of you fellas named Callahan?' he asked. None of the men answered. "Well, I guess he means me then. Excuse me, gentlemen," Putney said as he stepped over the dark man, swung open the gate, and walked to the porch.

"What the hell was that all about?" Newman demanded to know.

Putney looked over his shoulder at the men helping their comrade to his feet. "Rude behavior needed dealing with," said Putney.

Newman showed a slight grin and said, "Never mind. I have some men I want you to meet." Putney followed Newman to the office. He had just walked over the threshold when he stopped. In the office sat a man so straight one would think he had a board down the back of his coat. A dark blue coat with a slight military cut to it. On the desk next to him was a peaked military campaign hat— Sheriff *David J. Cook of Arapaho County. Shit,* Thought Putney.

Newman had no idea that Cook and Putney were already acquainted when he said, "Jack, this is Sheriff Cook of Arapaho County." Putney nodded at Cook, who in turn seemed to look through Putney. Newman said, "And this gentleman is United States Marshal, Uriah Holloway." Indicating a stout man with receding curly hair and a long, full beard.

Holloway took a step toward Putney, holding out his hand. Putney took the man's hand. Holloway's grip was firm, and Putney could feel the power in the man's arm. "So, you're the tracker Newman's been bragging about so much lately." Said the Marshal.

"I'm a tracker, but I don't know about Mr. Newman's bragging," said Putney, to which the Marshal laughed. Then, over his shoulder, Putney heard a "harumph" come from Sheriff Cook.

Newman had poured a whiskey and handed it to Putney, telling him to sit. The only available chair was between Marshal Holloway and the one occupied by Cook. Putney was uncomfortable sitting so close to Cook. He became even more uncomfortable when he realized that he had just had a confrontation with Holloway's deputies. Or Cooks. Or both. *Shit,* he thought a second time."

"Well, Jack," said Newman. "The truth is I have been

bragging on you a bit, but not exaggerating. Gentlemen, Jack here has tracked down so many rustlers around here that the activity has come to a near halt."

"It's no chore to track a dozen or so cows and a few riders," Cook said, not hiding his contempt for Callahan. "Just like it's no chore to shoot down a half-drunk cowboy over a poker game."

Putney thought of making a retort but refrained. Newman and Holloway had confused looks on their faces.

"Gentlemen, I'm not confident that Mr. Callahan is the sort of man we want to hire. He's a would-be gunman. He killed a man in Denver over a card game, and I hear he killed three men in Boulder, then another three in Fort Laramie."

"If he has killed that many men," replied Holloway, "I don't think you could call him a would-be gunman. More like a damn good pistoleer. Even so, perhaps you're right."

"Just a minute," interjected Newman, "I don't know about Denver and Boulder, but I can tell you firsthand that he did not kill three men in Fort Laramie. Two men attacked him. One of which killed one of my ranch hands. Callahan did manage to kill one of the assassins, but a wagon train scout killed the other. I should add that Jack sustained severe wounds in the fray. Anything he did there was in self-defense."

"That does make a difference, David," Holloway said to Cook, who harumphed again. "Let's get down to why we came here. Mr. Callahan, we are trying to hunt down two men and their gang terrorizing parts of Colorado. This gang has been waylaying stagecoaches, mostly in Arapaho County but others. They have been robbing passengers, stealing bank cash transfers and U. S. Mail." Holloway paused to take a drink of whiskey, and Cook took over.

There are one or two smaller gangs," said the sheriff. "But the most notorious and violent is a gang headed by two men, Lewis Musgrove and Ed Franklin. These men have pistol-whipped passengers, shot drivers and guards, and violated more than two women."

Putney now knew why he hadn't encountered Musgrove and Franklin stealing cattle. Putney wanted to tell the men that the obvious solution was to arrest them, but he resisted. So instead, as the three powerful men looked at him, all he could think to do was shrug his shoulders.

"We need someone that can track these bandits," said Holloway. "Newman tells us that you are the man for the job. Tell me, other than tracking rustlers, do you have any other experience tracking."

Putney looked from one to the other of the men before answering. He didn't know about Newman, but Cook had already told him how he felt about Confederate rebels, and Putney figured that it was likely Holloway had also been in the Union Army. But he decided what the hell. Let the chips fall where they will. "In the war, I was a scout, and I tracked Comanches, Kiowas, Wichitas, and others," he said, adding, "Which were much more difficult than tracking a dozen cows and a few men."

"A rebel," groused Cook. "I knew it."

"That doesn't matter now, Cook," said Holloway. "We're all one country now. Besides, if he was tracking Indians, it's not likely he had much contact with our soldiers. That would be right, wouldn't it, Mr. Callahan?"

Putney nodded.

"Do you think you could track these men?" Holloway asked. Putney couldn't believe his luck. A U. S. Marshal was asking him to track down the men he had sworn to kill. *Damn straight, I can do it,* he thought. *And when I do, I'll kill them both.* But out loud, he said, "I'm sure I can."

"Good. Good," said Holloway. "Now, if you don't mind, stepping out for a moment, we may have some more to discuss before we make an offer."

Putney stood, walked out of the office carrying his whiskey, and closed the door behind him. The door muffled the conversation, but Putney heard the words "insolent rebel," and he could guess who had spoken. After about five minutes, Newman opened the door and beckoned Putney back. "Mr. Callahan," said Holloway. "We have reached a decision. We want you to track these outlaws for us. The U. S. Government will pay you twenty dollars a month, with another ten coming from Arapaho County. Mr. Newman has assured us he will make up the balance of the pay you would otherwise be out. In addition, the stage companies offer a sizeable reward, of which you would have an equal share. Would you accept this offer?"

Putney thought a minute before he said, "I have a question. Will I be working with those men outside?"

"Most certainly," said Holloway. "They are our deputies." He waved his arm, indicating Cook.

"Well, I'll take the job," said Putney. "That is if Mr. Newman will let me have a bottle of that good whiskey. I have a feeling I'm going to need a peace offering."

43

P utney had moved to The Planters House Hotel in Denver and enjoyed a clean room, good meals, and hot baths. He had also taken the opportunity to replace some of his worn clothing by visiting some men's clothing shops. Putney bought Kinney's at a tobacconist. But he was starting to get anxious about Musgrove and Franklin. What if they had decided to quit the robberies? They had made enough loot to live pretty well in a place like Fort Leavenworth or maybe even go to St. Louis. They may not need to run the risk anymore. Putney's doubts ended when a message from Sheriff Cook about the robbery of a Holladay stage. The stage and passengers were stranded about fifteen miles east of Denver. Putney was to start immediately as his and the marshal's deputies had already left.

Putney had just sat down to lunch in the hotel's restaurant when the message came. Putney decided he didn't need to hurry. By the time the posse and he arrived, it already would be too dark to start tracking. So Putney finished lunch, went to his rooms, and picked up his already packed gear. Putney was on the road to Julesburg by one o'clock, trailing his mule behind him. He kept a good pace without wearing out his animals and caught up with the posse before they got to the stage. They were stopped on the road, letting their horses rest. Cook was livid, wanting to know why Putney hadn't caught up with them sooner. Cook became more incensed when Putney said he hadn't seen the necessity of wasting a good lunch or his animals. The sheriff was angry because he knew Putney was right. It took Marshal Holloway to calm the sheriff down by saying it didn't matter because Callahan was here now, and they needed to get on to the stage.

The attack on the Holladay stage had been brutal. To stop the coach, the bandits shot the lead horse, then the driver and the guard, killing the guard. A passenger tried fighting back, and the outlaws killed him for the effort. Then, the gang broke into the strong box containing five thousand dollars intended for a bank in Denver. It was unknown how much money the mail bags held or what the passenger had. The most heinous part was the rape of two female passengers.

To make a clean getaway, the bandits drove the team of horses off. A former soldier with a lame arm walked until he found the horses and rode one to Denver to report to Sheriff Cook.

By the time the posse reached the stage, it was an hour past sunset. It was impossible to begin any tracking until the sunrise. The passengers huddled around a fire, waiting for a rescue. Sheriff Cook sat at the fire and began questioning the victims to get as much information as possible. Deputies and civilian posse members gathered to listen. Putney stood away from the crowd, believing this manner of questioning would accomplish nothing. Putney thought a better method would be to question each victim privately. He also thought it was cruel to ask the female passengers about being raped while fifteen men stood around, eager to hear the lurid details. But that was not Putney's job. Besides Putney, the only persons not attending the interview were the man from the stage depot and Marshal Holloway.

Putney was leaning against a tree, enjoying a cigarette, when Holloway stepped over and said, "This is awful business. We must put a stop to this right away. I got a wire the other day saying people are starting to fear coming to Denver. Some are even opting to stay in Julesburg. Julesburg, for Christ's sake. That's how desperate they've gotten. Now with this attack, I just don't know." Putney said nothing, so the marshal continued, "Do you think you can track these bastards, Callahan?"

"It depends," said Putney. "On how much of a mess all these posse members have made. More than one rode their horses all around before finally lighting. I may have to work further out from the coach to pick up tracks that make sense. That could take a while. You could help, though."

"Tell me what you need, and it's yours," said the marshal.

"Have everybody keep their horses in one place and keep their milling around to one area, too. That way, I may be able to find tracks," said Putney. "The other thing is that tomorrow, I need to check each horse's hooves and shoes."

"Why do you need to inspect the horses' hooves,' Holloway wanted to know.

"Each hoof and shoe are different," Putney told him. "They pick up cuts and marks that you can distinguish. Each farrier has a different style, too. So if I can look at all the shoes, I can probably decipher which prints are posse and which are outlaws'."

"That all makes sense," said Holloway. "I'll see to it."

"One other thing, Marshal," said Putney before Holloway could walk away. I need someone to help me. Someone that can read and write, so they can make notes for me and just help in general. Then, when we hit the trail, I want the posse to wait half an hour so that we can get out ahead tracking. I'll send your man back if there's anything important. Otherwise, we'll put up markers, especially if the tracks take a turn."

"I'm going to give you your head on this," Marshal Holloway told Putney, then ended with, "This time."

Cook had finally finished his interrogation of the victims and had the depot man load up and take the passenger to Denver. He assigned some posse members to wrap the dead men in tarps and secure them to the rear boot.

Putney was not popular with the deputies, so he chose to camp apart from the main bunch. In the morning, a young man came to where Putney was sitting alone, eating dried beef and bread. "Marshal Holloway says I was to report to you." The voice was familiar, and Putney saw Marv, the young cowboy from Newman's ranch.

"What in the hell are you doing here?" Putney asked.

"Well, there ain't no future in cowboying," Marv told him. "I heard you had hired on to work for the marshal, and I decided I want to be a lawman, like you."

"I'm no lawman. I only hired on to track until Musgrove and Franklin are caught'" Putney informed Marv.

"You're a range detective, aren't you?" Marv asked. "And I heard you had worked as a mining detective, too."

"Do you know what a range or a mining detective is?" Before Marv could answer, Putney added, "They are nothing but paid assassins to do the killing for the wealthy. Neither the mines nor ranchers care if I arrest someone or kill them. That's no lawman."

Marv Chalmers stood dumbfounded by the bare truth Putney had just given him. Putney felt sorry for the young man's naivety and said, "You may as well sit. "Have you eaten yet?"

"No, sir," Marv said.

Putney reached in a burlap bag and produced a tin cup. "Pour yourself some coffee and have some of this dried beef and bread," Putney told him. "And don't call me sir. I'm not more than three or four years older than you." Marv nodded and filled the cup with the hot brew. Putney reached behind himself for his saddlebags and pulled out a notebook and pencil. "We'll get to work after eating. I'll want you to take notes for me."

What are we going to do?" Marv asked.

"We're going to make notes about the horses' shoes and hooves," Putney said. Marv looked confused. "Don't worry. You'll understand when we get started." It was just a few minutes until they had finished, and Marv followed Putney to the horses. He inspected each horse's shoes, telling Marv to keep notes in the order Putney looked at the hooves. There were seventeen horses in all, not counting Putney's.

After the inspection, Putney told Marv to follow him. The depot man had taken the coach and passengers to Denver the previous night, but where the coach had been easy to see due to the lack of horse tracks. Putney told Marv to stay behind him and be ready to take notes or refer to the notes about what Putney saw. Then Putney combed the earth for tracks. Putney started in one spot, walking in a counterclockwise circle, widening the arc as he worked. Many of the tracks he could remember from the inspection of the horses, but he frequently asked Marv about a track. Marv would thumb back through the notebook until he found the one Putney had asked about, then they continued. Finally, Putney started seeing tracks where one horse had stepped over the tracks of another. Again, he would ask Marv to check the notes. The tracks on the top always corresponded with the notes. Putney had expanded the circle until he identified an unknown track. Then Putney began working in small clockwise circles and gradually increasing the size of his arc. He finally identified the direction of several unfamiliar tracks. He straightened his line but zig-zagged back and forth. Marv remarked that he couldn't tell one track from the other or even decipher the direction because there were so many tracks.

Putney stopped and, squatting next to a particular track, told Marv to come closer. Marv bent over to see what Putney wanted to show him. "You see this track here?" Putney asked and, with his finger, drew a circle around an obvious track. Marv said he did. "Now, look closer and tell me what you see."

"It looks like there's a V-shaped notch here in the front of the print, but kind of off to the left," said Marv.

Putney moved to another track. "Now, what do you see?"

"This one has the same V notch, but the track doesn't seem the same. It looks larger." Said Marv.

That's right," Putney told him. "That's because the second track is a front hoof and the first one is the rear hoof, but they're both from the same horse. The farrier cut the V notch. That way, if a man comes and tells him he didn't put the shoe on right, he can tell whether it's his because of that notch. Did we note any notch like that from the posse horses?"

Marv scanned his notes. "No."

"There you go," Putney congratulated him. "That's one of the outlaws' horses. Now look over here."

"Well," said Marv, "I don't see any marks like you're talking about, but it's deeper."

"I'll make a tracker out of you yet," said Putney. "That tells you that either the horse is bigger, the rider is substantially large, or the horse is carrying more weight, or maybe all three. In this case, the horse is larger. Follow me." Putney took two steps. "See, the stride is longer, so the horse is bigger. It would be a good guess that a big man would ride a big horse, but not necessarily. You understand?"

"I do," said Marv.

"Good. These two sets are the ones we are going to follow. Get your horse saddled. I'll be right with you."

Putney went to speak with Cook and Holloway. "There are several tracks I made out. They're all going the same direction, but there are two that are going to be the easiest to keep up with," Putney said. "They headed that direction," Putney continued and pointed to the northwest of the wagon road. "Marv is saddling up now. Give us thirty minutes after passing that big cottonwood up there after we are on our way. Then follow that direction. I will leave markers along the trail. Shaped like an arrow if we're on them or in a heap if we've lost the tracks.

"Alright," said Marshal Holloway. "And Callahan, keep that boy safe."

Putney nodded and went to saddle his horse. Marv was securing his bedroll when Putney threw the blanket on his horse. He stopped and looked at Marv, then walked around Marv's horse and inspected the saddle. "Is that Colt the only gun you have?" Putney asked the young man.

"Yeah, I can't afford more right now," Marv said sheepishly.

Putney didn't say anything. Instead, he saddled his horse and secured the saddlebags and bedroll with the beaver coat rolled up in it. Lastly, he secured his Winchester in the sheath to his saddle, under his right stirrup fender. Then he picked up his Henry carbine in its sheath and took a pistol from his saddle bag. "Here," he told Marv. "Tie this carbine to your saddle like I did my Winchester. And take this pistol and tuck it somewhere secure so you can get to it."

"Thanks, Jack," Marv was exuberant. "I'll give them back after we track these criminals down."

"Don't thank me. I gave them to you out of pure selfishness. If you can't defend yourself, it means I will have to defend you, which puts me at risk," Putney said brusquely. "I can't believe you would come out so ill-equipped for a job like this. What did you think we were doing, going on a church picnic? Do you even have a slicker in that bedroll?"

Marv started stammering, saying, "Er, uh." Until he finally got it out that he did have a slicker.

"Well, thank God for minor miracles," barked Putney. "Now mount up. Tie my mule to your saddle." before they got to the cottonwood, Putney held his horse up. Marv had been following behind because of the upbraiding Putney had given him. he waved for Marv to come abreast of him, then reaching inside his bags, he pulled out a box of cartridges for the Henry. "The carbine is fully loaded but keep this box just in case. And don't worry about giving the guns back to me. I have plenty," he said. Then Putney added, "And don't get yourself killed."

〜

AFTER THE GANG split up the loot made from the robbery, Musgrove told them the association was over, and they needed to go their own way. One outlaw, a burly man, asked where they should go. Musgrove said, "I don't care, as long

as it is no place near Franklin and me." There was some
grumbling by the other men as they were preparing to
mount their horses, so the burly man decided to challenge
Musgrove.

"If we have to split up, we think we should get another
share of the haul," he said, standing with his feet apart,
prepared to reinforce his defiance. Without hesitation,
Musgrove pulled his sidearm and shot the burly man, who
dropped like a sack of grain.

"You all can have his share," Musgrove told the others.
The bandits dismounted and stripped their fallen comrade.
They took his portion of the robbery, his guns, boots, and
everything else. They immediately started arguing about
who would get the horse, saddle, and other gear that had
belonged to the dead man.

Musgrove and Franklin got on their horses and
continued northwest toward Wyoming. Both men road
good mounts they had stolen from ranches in Utah.
Franklin rode a gray Steelduster that was tall and sleek,
while Musgrove, rode a shorter but much heavier and
muscular Morgan. Both steeds were fast and had served
them well when evading lawmen or competing gangs. This
day was no exception, but now they didn't have the burden
of thick-headed louts. The pair figured they had managed
to get the band at least a day ahead of any pursuers. Now
the oafs would have to make it on their own. They would
also split up if they were smart, but the two leaders knew
they wouldn't. Privately Musgrove bet Franklin that the
bunch of them would be in jail before a week was out. But
now, it was time for Musgrove and Franklin to get moving.
They hoped the split with the other outlaws would confuse
the posse, and the lawmen would go after the large group.
They were near the Wyoming line and meant to make it to

their hideaway in the Medicine Bow range as quickly as possible.

What the outlaw chiefs hadn't figured on was Jack Callahan. Even if they had thought that Callahan was among their pursuers, it would have only been that he had joined in hopes of continuing his revenge. But they had given Jack Callahan no thought at all. It was their big mistake. Because of Putney, the posse was only a half-day behind the bandits.

≈

PUTNEY AND MARV were sitting by a small fire drinking coffee when the rest of the posse caught up with them. Holloway and Cook, in the lead, dismounted and walked to where their tracker was relaxing, leaning against a tree. "What's going on here?" Cook demanded to know. "There's still a couple of hours of daylight."

"Have a cup of coffee," Putney suggested. "Then look behind that fallen log yonder." Putney pointed to a large fir tree that had fallen twenty feet from the trail. Cook chose to look behind the tree first. He found the body of a man stripped to his long johns. Coming back to the fire, Cook told the others in the posse to dismount and take a rest.

"I don't suppose you know how that body got there," said Cook.

"I don't know for sure," Putney replied. "But I can guess. Marv and I concentrated on two horses, even though I figured out there were eight by yesterday evening. Over in that little opening," Putney pointed to the area he meant. "There was a falling out. At least that's my guess since that guy is dead from a bullet in the heart. After that, five men rode away to the southwest. Two others kept northwest."

"Hell," exclaimed Holloway. "What do we do now?

Cook sat cross-legged on the ground, reached for the empty cup near the fire, and poured a cup of coffee for himself when a thought hit him. "We will have to split up the posse," Said Cook.

"Well, obviously," a vexed Marshal Holloway said. "But we only have the one tracker, so which group do we go after?"

The sheriff sipped at the hot brew and said, "I think we should concentrate on the larger group."

"That's not what I would do," said Putney.

"Oh. Is that right?" Cook wanted to know. "And pray tell what would the great Callahan suggest?"

"As Marv and I were tracking them, there was always two in the lead. Sort of like you and the Marshal," Putney couldn't resist the jab. "If this is the Musgrove and Franklin bunch, the bosses are the ones that separated. Those two horses are moving northwest. And like I said, the others are riding southeast. If they were smart, they would split up. But my bet is that they all have the same thing on their minds. They will go to Boulder because it's the nearest town for drinking, gambling, and whoring. You don't need a tracker for that. Send half your men there. Because these desperados will be spending money like it was on fire, they will probably be easy to spot. The town marshal there will be keeping tabs on them. He's not honest but knows Ward doesn't want this sort of trouble in his town. The other half, along with Marv and me, will keep on the trail of those we think are Musgrove and Franklin. I believe we have closed the gap on them by about half a day. With luck, we could cut that even more. I reckon we could catch them in two days, at the outside.

"What makes you think the two-headed northwest are Franklin and Musgrove?" queried Cook.

"One set of tracks belongs to a heavy horse. Probably a Morgan or something like that." Putney told the lawmen. "I met Musgrove once. He's a big man and would like a big horse. If I'm right, then the other is going to be Franklin. One thing I know about these two is that Franklin will be wherever Musgrove is. It's these two that you really want."

"How is it you know so much about Musgrove and Franklin?" Cook asked.

"Because that's who Newman thought was behind all the rustling on his place," Putney said. So, I made it my business to learn about them."

"Hmmm," pondered Holloway. "Callahan has given us something to think about, Dave. Why don't we tell the others to go ahead and set up camp? Then, you and I can discuss the situation, and we'll figure out what to do."

"That's good with me," said Cook.

"While you're doing your planning, there is one more thing you should know," Putney said to Holloway and Cook.

"What would that be?" asked Cook.

Putney poured another cup of coffee, rested against a tree, and lit a cigarette. "First thing tomorrow, I'm going after Musgrove and Franklin."

44

As he had predicted, it was noon two days later, when Putney and Marv spotted two riders in the distance. It didn't appear that their quarry was in any hurry as they were walking their horses. Putney told Marv to ride back to the main posse. "Tell them we sighted Musgrove and Franklin. Tell them I will lay back so they don't see me, but I will keep checking on them once in a while until the posse catches up," Marv said he understood and turned his horse and headed back to the main body. Every bone in Putney's body wanted to set off after the two bandits, but these were the most dangerous men he sought, and he knew he wouldn't stand a chance. So Putney stayed back a safe distance, fighting the urge for revenge, never letting the outlaws see him.

Putney was waiting on the side of a hill where Musgrove and Franklin couldn't see him when the posse came thundering up. The Marshal and sheriff asked Putney where the robbers were, and Putney told them. Sheriff Cook abandoned caution and ordered the posse after them. It was a

reckless move. The posse could have outflanked the two
fugitives, giving them no place to run. Instead, the posse
drove their horses, hell-bent for leather. Putney would be
damned if he was going to let someone else beat him out of
his revenge.

Musgrove and Franklin were within a mile of their hideaway, a dug-out cabin set in the side of a hill near Elk Mountain, when the first shot rang out. Looking over their
shoulders, they saw half a dozen or more men coming after
them. They began whipping up their horse and split off in
different directions. Whoever had fired that first shot had
done them a good turn because the posse was still a good
quarter of a mile behind. Neither man doubted that they
could outrun the posse, nor did they look to see what the
other was doing. Splitting up in the event of lawmen coming
after them was always their plan.

Putney was livid about whoever fired that shot. No pistol
ball could travel the needed distance. Riding at their speed,
it would have been a futile shot even if the man had a
Sharps. Nevertheless, the deed occurred, and there was no
use worrying over it. Putney knew the outlaws were on
faster steeds, but the pony he had gotten from Leaping
Antelope had the stamina to outdistance them if only he
could keep them in sight. Putney loosened the riata that
kept his mule tied to his saddle. The pony shot forward like
an arrow, and Putney urged the pony faster, passing
everyone else. But the errant shot had warned the outlaws,
and they spurred their horses in two different directions.
Putney chose to pursue the man he believed to be Musgrove
and leaned forward on the pony, hoping he could get more
speed, but though he led the rest of the posse, he was not
gaining on Musgrove. Suddenly, another man, John Cronin,

rode past Putney as if his horse had wings. It wasn't a few seconds before Musgrove, and the other rider were increasing their lead on Putney.

Musgrove was whipping his Morgan to its limits when he heard hooves pounding behind him. Musgrove removed his pistol from its holster and fired behind him without looking. The outlaw's purpose was not to hit his purser, but hoped the rider would veer off, even a little, allowing Musgrove to increase his distance, however, his luck did not hold. He had looked behind him to see where his stalker was and never saw the hunk of sandstone his horse stepped on. The Morgan stumbled and fell to its knees sending Musgrove sailing through the air. When Musgrove hit the ground, he lost control of his pistol, which skidded across the grassy plain. In the next second, Cronin was on him like a duck on a June bug. Realizing escape was now impossible, Musgrove sat on the ground and put his hands on top of his head.

When Putney arrived at the scene, Cornin had tied Musgrove's hands behind his back with a leather thong. Putney reined his horse in and scowled down at Musgrove, who looked at Putney and laughed heartily. "This is one murder you're going to miss out on, Callahan," the outlaw was still laughing. "I may dangle at the end of a rope, but it ain't gonna be you that finishes me."

The other man looked confused and asked Putney, "What the hell is he talking about?"

"Outlaw gibberish," said Putney. "How the hell should I know?" Putney then asked how Cornin had managed to pass him with such speed. Cornin said he had once been a Pony Express rider on the eastern leg of the express. They all rode thoroughbred horses, and ever since, Cronin trusted only in the power and speed of thoroughbreds.

Musgrove laughed again, then said, "I don't know who you are, partner, but I can tell you that if young Callahan had caught up with me first, I'd be cold meat."

By then Sheriff Cook had caught up with his two posse members. "Good work John," he said. "And you, too, Callahan."

"I didn't have anything to do with it," admitted Putney. "It's all Cornin's doing. I don't think I've ever seen a man ride a horse so fast." Then, turning his horse back the way he had come, Putney said, "I have to go catch my mule."

Nahum Putney was disgusted. Musgrove had been half right. If Putney had caught him first, one or both would be dead by now. Putney consoled himself that Musgrove was going to meet his end on some gallows. If he admitted the truth, Putney was glad he hadn't caught Musgrove first. Putney was sick of killing. When he killed Rogers in New Mexico, he added seven more men to his death score. Though he would never admit it to anyone else, each death weighed heavily on him. Big Foot Wallace and Oracle Jones had been right. Putney had never lost sleep about Comanches he had killed. It was not that Putney thought less of them as humans. Instead, they had always been in battle and were kill or be killed situations. Every man he had killed in Kansas and Colorado, Putney had goaded into a fight, knowing none of them stood a chance. They were either drunk or wounded, or both, and in the case of the three mining detectives, just plain stupid. The killing in Wyoming hadn't bothered him as much because that time, he had been the one with the disadvantage and was lucky to come out alive.

Putney figured his mule wouldn't wander far, but the prairie was large, and the mule could have roamed anywhere. It took Putney an hour to return to where he had left the mule and find where it had wandered. Putney found his animal in a prairie half a mile from where he had left it. The mule was calmly grazing along with the other pack mules that posse members had left. Putney gathered the animals, tied them in a train, and started back to the trail where they had seen Musgrove and Franklin. By the time he returned to the trail, Cook and Cornin were arriving, with Musgrove walking in front. The Morgan Musgrove was riding had broken its leg, so Cook had dispatched it where it laid. Putney met Cook where the two parts of the posse had split off.

Cook told Putney, "Callahan, I may have misjudged you. You did a superb job of tracking these two villains. Now we will wait here until Marshal Holloway gets back with Franklin."

"Unless Ed's horse met with an accident like mine, ain't nobody going to catch ole Ed," spewed Musgrove. "Not unless somebody else has one of them thoroughbreds." Then directing his words to Putney, "Looks like another man you won't get to murder anytime soon, Callahan."

"Shut up, Musgrove," ordered the sheriff. "Or I'll have Cornin shove a gag down your gullet. Callahan, there's a little copse of trees over yonder. We'll make camp there. Holloway may indeed be back late. A fire will guide him to us."

"Mr. Cornin," said Putney." "Would you untie those other mules from mine, please?"

"Why?" asked Sheriff Cook. "You can guide them over there."

"I'm not going over to those trees," Putney informed the Sheriff.

"What? Where are you going?" the sheriff demanded to know.

"I have done my job," said Putney. "I tracked Musgrove and Franklin here. If y'all miss Franklin, it's no fault of mine. When I see you next, I'll collect my wages and share of the bounty in Denver. Right now, I'm headed to Boulder."

45

Three days later Putney arrived on the outskirts of Boulder. He was reasonably confident nobody in the town would challenge him, but he waited until after dark to ride to McClancy's boarding house. Putney noticed a light in the parlor window, ascended the steps, rapped on the door, and waited. Mr. McClancy answered the door. "Oh, it's you," said McClancy. "I thought we had seen the last of you."

"I was hoping I might see Miss McClancy," Putney said.

Now, why on God's green earth would I let you do that?" McClancy demanded to know.

Before Putney could answer, he heard Mrs. McClancy's voice say, "Who is it, Pa?"

In a belligerent tone, her husband answered, "It's that killer. You know Callahan."

"Well, he hasn't killed anyone here," Putney could hear the woman's voice grow closer. "Tell him to come on in."

Before her husband could object, Mrs. McClancy reached past her husband and pulled Putney in the house. "My, you're as thin as a rail. Didn't they feed you anything in

Julesburg?" Putney guessed that Mandy had told her mother of his letters. "We've finished dinner, but some potatoes and cold roast are left. Come on to the kitchen," she said and pushed her husband aside to let Putney through. As she guided Putney to the kitchen, she stopped at the stairs and yelled, "Mandy! We've got company."

When Mandy came through the kitchen door, she said, "Since when do we see company in the kitchen?" Putney had been sitting at the kitchen table with Mr. McClancy glaring at him while Mrs. McClancy was dishing up some food. He stood when Mandy entered the room. Her mother nodded in Putney's direction. When she saw him, Mandy jumped into his arms and planted a long kiss on Putney.

"Young lady, what do you think you're doing?" Mandy's father was appalled. Then to Putney said, "Bad man or no, Callahan, you get your hands off my daughter."

Putney had been too shocked even to return Mandy's embrace. He was at a loss as to what to do. Finally, he put his hands on Mandy's shoulders and gently pushed her back. "Your father is right. This isn't proper."

"Oh, pshaw," said Mandy's mother. "Kiss him again, then let him sit down and have something to eat." So Mandy did as her mother had said.

"There better be an explanation to this, Callahan," McClancy said. "Or I'm going to get my shotgun, and it won't be to march you to the preacher."

Having just taken a mouth full of cold beef, Putney waited until he swallowed to answer. "There is an explanation, Mr. McClancy, and it's a long story," said Putney.

"Let the boy finish his dinner, Pa," Mrs. McClancy broke in, then he will tell us everything."

I hope not everything, Mandy thought to herself.

Putney was in as much a hurry to get his story out as the

McClancy's were to hear it, so he ate hurriedly but kept his manners, as his mother had taught him. After eating the last bite, he thanked Mrs. McClancy and took a big drink of milk before starting. For some reason, he was more scared facing Mr. McClancy with his story than he ever had been fighting Comanches or outlaws.

Putney started by telling the McClancy's that his real name was Nahum Putney. Then he told them almost everything, from when his parents died until he knocked on their door that night. Tactfully, he left out anything about the night before he left. Putney also left out the part about telling Lockwood Fuller what would happen if Ward swore out warrants on him. Putney said that Ward and he had reached an agreement and part of that was that Putney would leave town. Otherwise, he had not withheld any significant fact. He told them about the men who had met death at his hands and the reason. Finally, he looked at Mr. McClancy and then at Mrs. McClancy and said, "Except for the time I spent in your house, the two years since I left New Mexico have been the worst in my life."

"You mean to tell me those men weren't claim jumpers like Ward told everyone," said Mr. McClancy. "He even sent a story to the Rocky Mountain News about them."

Putney just nodded his head.

"Well, I'll be," said Mrs. McClancy. "Those men worked for Mr. Ward, and he was just using them to run off honest miners?"

"That was the job," said Putney. "I'm ashamed to say."

"Those poor Irish people in New Mexico," said Mrs. McClancy. "It was right of you to seek out justice, Mr. Calla-han. I mean Mr. Putney."

"If I had sought justice, Mrs. McClancy," said Putney,

"You might be right. But I didn't want justice. I wanted revenge. And now, the truth of it may serve me poorly."

"Why did you come back here to tell us all this?" Mr. McClancy asked.

"There's only one reason, Mr. McClancy," Putney cleared his throat, dreading the moment. "The truth is I wanted to ask your permission to marry Mandy if she will have me."

McClancy jumped back as if there had been a rattlesnake on the floor. In doing so, he tumped his chair over and fell to the floor. Mandy jumped from her chair to Putney's lap, kissing him again. The action was so sudden that the two of them fell to the floor also. Mrs. McClancy roared with laughter while at the same time trying to help her husband to his feet. Putney and Mandy extricated themselves from each other and climbed back into their chairs. When everyone was seated, and Mrs. McClancy had managed to get her laughter down to an occasional snicker, Mr. McClancy said, "That's impossible. Even with what you have said, everyone around here knows you as Red Jack Callahan. You have a reputation all over this part of the state. No one would hire you except for your ability with a gun."

"I know that, Mr. McClancy," said Putney. "What I haven't told you yet is that I want to take Mandy to Texas with me. When my parents died, Mr. McKinney took care of their ranch with his. Everything we made we split down the middle. Most of that money is in a bank in Galveston, probably around six thousand dollars. When I joined the Confederacy, Mr. McKinney bought out my ranch. I have ten thousand in gold and silver in a bank security box in San Antonio. I have four hundred left on me, and Sheriff Cook in Denver owes me a couple hundred."

Both Mr. and Mrs. McClancy's jaws were gaping open,

and Putney didn't quite know how to interpret their expressions, so he continued. "I want to take Mandy to Texas. There nobody knows of Jack Callahan. I could start another ranch or some business in San Antonio with that money. I'm only asking if we can get married here, using my real name. then we will go to Denver for me to get a few things settled."

"Yes! Oh yes, Nahum," said Mandy leaning over to kiss him again. "Please say yes, too, Pa."

"Well, I don't know, Mandy," said her father. "Texas is a long way off."

"Oh, pshaw, Burt," said Mrs. McClancy. "We came all the way out here from Pennsylvania, didn't we? And you were only hoping to make the kind of money this boy already has. Scratching in the dirt for gold. If I hadn't made you buy this house from the little you found, we would have nothing."

"But she's my little Mandy, Maude," Burt said. "We might never see her again."

"They're building train tracks all over the country, Mr. McClancy," said Putney. "In a couple of years, you can probably ride from here to San Antonio in just a few days instead of weeks. And I promise as soon as possible; we will visit you often."

"Oh, please, Papa, please," begged Mandy. "I've known about Putney since before he left, and he wrote me often. I love him, Papa. And I know he loves me."

Burt McClancy put both elbows on the table and dropped his head into his hands. He rubbed his temples for a while before looking up into Mandy's hopeful eyes. "If it will make you happy, then yes. You can marry him."

46

Putney and Mandy arrived in Denver one week after he had returned to Boulder. They had been married in a small ceremony at the McClancy's house. The only people, other than the McClancy's, that were privy to the Putney's secret were the parson at the church the McClancy's attended and his wife. In addition, there were two boarders at the house, drummers who had just recently arrived and were also present. Since they were living there, it would have been challenging to have a wedding ceremony without them knowing. But they only knew Putney by his real name and no knowledge of Jack Callahan.

Putney had stayed in the house the entire time he was in Boulder, so he would not meet people who knew him. Burt sold Putney's pony and bought a used wagon and three mules with the money. Maude spent the week altering her wedding dress to fit Mandy. Mandy was taller than Maude but not as busty and had a thinner waist, so Maude had to take the dress in and add lace to the hem. It was a simple dress, but Mandy glowed in it. Maude also cleaned and pressed Putney's best frock coat and embroidered vest. Mandy herself baked and decorated her own wedding cake. The wedding was a simple affair at noon. After the ceremony, everyone enjoyed a wonderful beef meal and various roasted vegetables prepared by Maude. The cake was light with white icing and several rosettes made of sugar. The couple left in the mid-afternoon. Mandy had changed into a traveling outfit her parents had bought at the general store. It was a full skirt made from maroon taffeta topped by a wine-colored bodice made from satin and buttoned up the front. Over the bodice, Mandy wore a maroon jacket with gold brocaded flowers. The jacket had a high collar, and the front was open, with each side ending in points over the skirt. The wedding ended with Maude and Burt crying, the pastor and his wife throwing handfuls of rice, and the two peddlers consuming what was left of the cake as the newlyweds drove away. Burt had sent a telegram to the Planters House Hotel, giving the date Mr. and Mrs. Jack Callahan would arrive and reserving the best suite available. The couple had to use the alias because the staff already knew Putney by that name.

Putney and Mandy arrived at the hotel at ten o'clock that night. Besides the clerk, there was still a bellman on duty. The two men were all aflutter over the newlyweds and greeted them with as much elegance and grace they could muster. The bellman helped Putney retrieve a large trunk and two carpet bags from the wagon. The chest filled with various items that the McClancy's had bought over the years for Mandy's trousseau, along with two Army Colts, a Remington, and Putney's Walker pistols. It was heavy and required both Putney and the bellman to get it into the hotel lobby. The bellman said he would take the wagon and team to the livery behind the hotel and get the liveryman to help haul the heavy trunk to the second floor, where the hotel had prepared a suite for the couple.

The clerk carried the two carpet bags and escorted Putney and Mandy to their suite. Putney lifted Mandy in his arms, and as they passed the threshold, Mandy kissed him on the cheek as he did. After setting Mandy down, Putney gave the clerk a silver dollar for bringing the bags. The clerk thanked him profusely, then quietly closed the door.

The suite consisted of two rooms, both well-lit with modern gaslights instead of oil lamps. The first room was a sitting area with a red velvet sofa and two matching armchairs. In front of the couch was a low mahogany table on which sat a bowl of fresh fruit, a bottle of champaign, and two long-stemmed glasses. Putney surveyed the bedroom. It had a large four-poster bed made of mahogany covered with a burgundy-colored chinch bedspread. On each side of the bed were mahogany tables. There was also a large wardrobe and dresser with a large mirror. The walls were covered with burgundy and gold flocked wallpaper.

Mandy had never seen such elegant rooms and was delighted that the furnishings matched her dress. She flung herself on the bed and laughed with glee. "Nahum," she said. "Have you ever seen such a beautiful room?" Putney said he had not, and this was the truth. Even though he had stayed at the Planters House before, his rooms were plain compared to this one.

Putney opened the bottle of champagne and poured them both a glass. "To Mr. and Mrs. Nahum Putney," he said, handing Mandy a glass. He raised his own. The bellman and his helper brought the trunk just as Putney and Mandy finished their second drink. Putney tipped them both with a silver dollar.

When the two had left, Putney pulled Mandy close and

kissed her deeply, his tongue exploring her open mouth. They could not contain themselves. Soon clothes flew off until they were both lying naked on the chenille bedspread. The first time they had made love, the room had been dark, and they could not see each other. In the brightness of the gas lamps, this was the first time either had seen the other without clothes. Putney wondered at the beauty and perfection of Mandy's nude body. Her sun-tanned face and hands belied the whiteness of her naked body, so white that it made the pink rosebud of her nipples stand out like a winter rose on a snow-covered hill. Mandy also was surprised at how fair Putney's body was except for the red scars where bullets and knives had left their permanent impressions. Mandy felt each blemish so lightly with her fingertips it made Putney shiver. "Do they hurt?" she asked her husband.

"Not anymore," he told her and softly kissed her eyelids, making her entire body ache with desire. Putney moved his lips over her cheeks and down to her body. With her strong hands pressing on Putney's muscular chest, Mandy pushed her husband away a mere inch. "Nahum?" she said in a half-whisper.

"Yes, my love," Putney returned.

Mandy sighed, not wanting to press the issue that weighed heavily on her, but still knowing she must, Mandy said, "Promise me that you will have no more business with guns."

Putney had expected his wife's request and had already considered it in his mind. "Dearest," he said. "I have already planned to sell all my guns tomorrow, except for the Winchester rifle and my father's Walkers. Those we may need to defend ourselves on the trail to San Antonio. But I swear on my sisters' graves, you will never see me raise a gun in anger or retribution."

Mandy pulled the man she loved close to her and whispered in his ear, "Make love to me. Now."

When they made love, it was as gentle as the first time, even though they had no need to worry about her parents or anyone else hearing them. The slow rhythm of bodies was like the soft ripples on a mountain lake as the wind blows across it. Mandy felt herself drown in the waves of pleasure that came over her body. The pleasure was more than she could have ever imagined. After what seemed like eternity to Mandy, Putney's body shook violently as his hips made one final thrust. Their bodies collapsed as if there was no more life in them even as they breathed in unison. "Do it again," Mandy moaned.

Light laughter escaped from him. "I don't think it works quite that way," he said. "We may have to wait a little while." Putney found himself craving something to eat. Not unlike the food cravings he had felt at other times. Violent times. The feeling worried him, but he shook it off as he rose from the bed. Naked, he walked into the sitting room, opened the carpet bags, and pulled out their white linen nightgowns. Mandy followed him, took her gown, and pulled it over her head.

"I'm starving," she said and chose an apple from the fruit bowl on the table, then poured them another glass of champagne, emptying the bottle. She bit into the crisp freshness of the apple and, having swallowed, said, "Let's stay here forever and do nothing but make love, eat fruit and drink champaign."

"Forever is the time we have together," Putney said in return. "But I may need a little red meat to keep up my strength during that eternity." They both laughed, and Putney chose a pear and bit into it.

When they had finished, Putney led her back to the bedroom and turned down the covers. They stood on opposite sides of the bed and shucked their gowns simultaneously. Mandy jumped in the bed and, bouncing up and down, said, "Let's do it again. Now."

Putney felt the urge growing in him and climbed onto the bed. They kissed again as they both knelt on the bed. Suddenly Mandy pushed Putney back on the pillows and sat straddling him. This time their lovemaking was not so quiet. Now Putney knew why he had heard all the noise at Sue's house in Fort Laramie. Their bodies drove against each other as if they had no will. With animal-like passion, Mandy pushed Putney against the headboard, then sat up and arched backward until her head nearly touched the bed behind her, as she let out with, "Oh, God!" Then as she sat straight up again, Putney pushed with such force that he thought he would throw her to the ceiling. Putney flipped them both over and attacked with such ferocity he thought he might hurt Mandy, and he consciously made himself slow down, but then Mandy yelled, "No! Don't stop!" They made such passionate love for at least an hour, and finally, they collapsed again. This time Mandy was certain she had died because nothing she had ever known felt like this. Putney pulled her back to him and gave her one more ardent kiss. Then they both fell into the deepest sleep either had ever known.

47

Waking first, Putney rose from the bed and went to the dresser, poured cold water from the pitcher into a matching porcelain basin, and washed his face. The cold water quickened his body, and he was suddenly fully awake. Putney opened the large chest, found a thick knitted robe for Mandy, and laid it softly across the foot of the bed. Then he got dressed and went downstairs to the hotel's restaurant. He ordered a large breakfast of eggs, bacon, potatoes, biscuits, and coffee to be placed on a tray he could take to Mandy. While the cafe prepared the meal, Putney asked the hotel clerk to send hot water to his room so that he could shave. Mandy was waking when Putney came into the room with her breakfast, which he took to her in bed.

"Have you eaten already?" Mandy asked.

"Not yet," Putney replied. "I have some business to take care of this morning. So you just lie in while I'm gone. I'll get something to eat afterward. This afternoon we'll go shopping for clothes for you."

The hot water came, and Putney shaved before gathering up all his extra guns and putting them in a satchel. He was putting on his holster with the brace of Belgium revolvers when he noticed the look on Mandy's face. "Don't worry," he told her. "I'm going to sell these, too. It's just easier to carry them this way."

Mandy sighed with relief. "Just be careful," she told her husband.

At the gun shop, Putney got a fair price for his guns and started back to the hotel. About halfway to the hotel, a man called out for Jack Callahan. Putney reached to where he usually would have been wearing his pistols. *Shit*, he thought, *I hope whoever is calling me isn't looking for gunplay because I am done for if he does*. Expecting the worse, Putney turned slowly, hoping he could move in time before a bullet came ripping his way. Having about-faced, Putney saw the man he knew as Niles Hill, one of the rustlers who had been with Mark Farnsworth. Putney waited for Hill to near him and start talking or go for a gun.

Hill walked toward Putney. "Do you remember me?" asked Hill. Putney remained silent. He was waiting for the man to try and kill him. "It's me, Niles Hill. You done me a good turn, and I want to do one for you in return." Hill was nearly in striking distance.

"I remember you," spoke Putney, while wariness made his whole body tingle. "What is it you want?"

Hill took another step forward and, in a quiet voice, asked, "Can we step in that bar, yonder?" Hill indicated a small saloon on the other side of the street. "I don't want to take the chance of someone overhearing me."

Putney said they could talk in the bar, and the two men crossed the street to the small bar. The saloon was a long narrow affair with a bar nearly as long as the establishment itself. There were only half a dozen tables, and Hill selected to sit at the last one. Putney ordered two beers as the pair walked past the barman. Hill said as the two men sat, "Look, since that time you let me and Duggan go, I've turned around. I got me work over at the Denver stockyards pushing cows down the shutes to the slaughterhouse. It don't pay much, but it beats getting shot at." The bartender came and put the beers on the table, and Putney fished out his coin purse from the left pocket of his vest, gave the man two bits, and told him to keep the change. Hill continued, "I read in the newspaper that you were one of the men that tracked down Musgrove but that Ed Franklin got away."

"Alright," said Putney being as evasive as he could.

"Franklin sent word out around the area, from Boulder to Idaho Springs to Pikes Peak, to break Musgrove out of jail," Hill told Putney. "There's probably twenty or twenty-five thugs hanging around Denver, right now, waiting on word from Franklin on when to move. I wanted to tell somebody, but I didn't want anyone to see me going into the sheriff's office. They'd kill me, for sure, if they thought I had shopped out information to the law. But when I saw you, I thought if I told you, then you could pass it on to the sheriff."

"And, of course, you're telling me this out of the goodness of your heart," Putney was being snide.

"Well, I mean," Hill stammered, "If the sheriff wanted to pay for the information like I said, working in the stockyards don't pay all that great."

"Where's Franklin?" asked Putney.

"There's the point, Callahan," Hill had decided to be coy.

"There's a hundred-dollar reward on Franklin's head. If I tell you and you tell the sheriff, you get all the reward, and I get nothing."

Putney reached for his purse again, produced two half and one-quarter eagle, and laid it on the table.

"That's only a quarter of the reward," complained Hill.

"That's right," Putney said. "You get twenty-five percent for the luxury of not being seen going directly to the sheriff."

Scooping up the coins, Hill said, "Sure, that's fair. Franklin is hid out in a hotel in Golden, along with Duggan. You remember Duggan, right?"

"Does he still walk with a limp?" asked Putney.

"Yeah, and he's still pretty angry about you tearing up his ankle, but not angry enough to come looking for you," Hill said. "You've got quite the reputation as a gunman. Duggan ain't got the guts to go up against you again."

"Alright," said Putney. Then giving Hill a glare that nearly burned the ex-outlaw, Putney said, "And never approach me again. No matter the reason."

Hill assured Putney that he would give Red Jack Callahan the widest birth possible were he ever to see him again. Hill finished his beer and left the bar. Putney rose and walked over to the man tending bar. "Do you know who I am?" he asked the man.

"I got a good idea," returned the bartender.

Putney produced another dollar and laid it on the bar. "Then," he said, "You know I have never set foot in your establishment."

"Mister," said the bartender. "I didn't even come to work today."

Putney left the bar and walked back toward the gun shop, which was in the opposite direction of the sheriff's office. He walked two blocks past the gun shop and turned to go a block over. Then, when he felt nobody was following him, Putney walked to the sheriff's office. Sheriff Cook was not overly joyful at seeing Putney but greeted him cordially. "What can I do for you, Callahan?" Cook wanted to know.

"I'm leaving Colorado within the week," Putney advised the sheriff. I want to pick up my pay and the share of any reward on Musgrove I have coming."

"I've put in a requisition to the Board of Commissioners," Cook said. "I will have the money for you in two days."

Hold on to it because you may owe me more," Putney said.

"Oh, and how's that?" the now irritated sheriff asked.

Putney told the sheriff about his information, leaving out Franklin's location and anything about Duggan. "If this pans out, I want half of the reward on Franklin. You can just add it to the amount you already owe me."

"Wouldn't you like to come with me?" asked Cook. "Just to make sure you reap your reward."

"I'm through hunting men," Putney told Cook. "Now, do you want to know where Franklin is or not?"

Sheriff Cook agreed to split the reward by halves if he found Franklin. Putney told the sheriff the information he had on Franklin. "He's with a man named Duggan. You will know Dugan by his limp from where I shot him in the ankle."

Putney left the lawman's office and headed back to the hotel. He had been gone too long, and Mandy was probably starting to worry. His suspicions were confirmed when Putney entered the room and saw his wife was fully dressed and pacing the floor when he entered. Mandy flew into his arms. "Oh, Nahum," she exclaimed. "You were gone so long. I was afraid something had happened to you."

Speaking gently in her ear, Putney said, "There, there. I'm sorry that I worried you. My business took a little longer than I expected. But I'm here now."

Mandy hugged Putney with all her strength. "Nahum," she said. "When can we leave for Texas? The sooner we're out of Colorado, the happier I'll be."

"A few days, yet," Putney told her. "I still have to wait on a payment from the sheriff. And Mandy, remember until we get through Kansas, I'm Jack. Jack Callahan. We don't want anyone here knowing my real name."

"Oh, yes, Na..., I mean Jack. I will remember. Promise" vowed Mandy.

"Now, let's go shopping," Putney said.

Putney and Mandy started with lunch in the hotel's restaurant and went to several shops and stores around the Denver business district. Putney bought his wife two new, fancy dresses and three dresses meant for day-to-day wear. He also bought two new flannel shirts in his size, two for Mandy, and two pairs of dungarees each. Mandy complained about the rough cotton pants and woolen shirts, but Putney explained that it was more practical to travel across the frontier and that cold weather would soon prevail. When presented with his reasons, Mandy agreed but pouted about it still. Putney also bought her a boy's corduroy coat that had a quilted lining for warmth and then two pairs of leather gloves with long cuffs for each of them. Next, they went to the tobacconist where Putney had previously bought Kinney's. To his surprise, the shop had ten packets. The shop owner explained that after Putney had bought the ones he had, he started ordering more, and they had become trendy. Putney bought all ten packets.

After their day shopping, Putney took Mandy to Pemberton's Restaurant for an early evening meal. They returned to the hotel before dark. They had agreed that it was best. It was unlikely any man in Denver would challenge Putney in broad daylight, but cowardly men will take chances under the cover of night. Putney asked the clerk to send up two bottles of champagne and more fruit at the desk. Once in their rooms, the young couple waited barely long enough for the deliverer of wine and food to leave before they threw themselves into their amorous adventures of the previous night.

~

ON THE MORNING following the receipt of Putney's information, Sheriff Cook and two deputies left for Golden to locate Ed Franklin. Before leaving, the sheriff brought in extra deputies against the possibility that the gang might try to break Musgrove out of jail. After Cook left, one of the part-time deputies began spreading the word about the possibility of a plan to help Musgrove escape. Before lunchtime, the word possibility had dropped from the rumor. Then by mid-afternoon, the entire town of Denver was abuzz with the imminence that an army of outlaws was on their way to conduct an armed assault on the county jail. By late afternoon the rumor was fueled by members of the County Board of Commissioners and the Mayor of Denver.

Putney and Mandy were on another shopping spree when the word was spread through the general store. Putney knew the rumor was far from the truth, and he was sure that no attempt to break Musgrove out of jail would happen without Franklin leading the charge. But, fearing a mob would begin gathering, Putney insisted that he and Mandy return to the hotel. At the hotel, he ordered a meal for their room. Putney told Mandy that he was the one that had passed the information to Sheriff Cook. Word had already begun spreading that city and county officials were talking of taking the law into their own hands in the absence of the sheriff. Fear grew in Putney that if a mob successfully removed Musgrove from the protection of the jail, the outlaws would gather and try to free Musgrove, even without Franklin's leadership. Putney told Mandy that he needed to do what he could to stop anything of the sort from occurring. Mandy pled with him to stay at the hotel, but her pleas were futile. Putney had sworn not to continue his bloody path of revenge, but he would be damned if he was going to see justice fail because of the hysteria that was building in Denver. Mandy finally relented, and Putney quickly left the hotel for the sheriff's office.

Putney was too late. The head of the Commissioners and the Mayor, accompanied by City Marshal Sisty, had ordered the deputy sheriffs at the jail to release Musgrove to their custody. Putney stood apart from the crowd watching a deputy exit the prison with Musgrove and handing him over to Marshal Sisty. Sisty, with the encouragement of the mob, dragged Musgrove down the steps of the jail. As the throng passed Putney, Musgrove said something to Sisty, who stopped the procession. Sisty quieted the crowd telling everyone that Musgrove had something to say. A hush fell on the crowd, and Musgrove stood erect, displaying his full height. Then he called out, "Jack Callahan! I see you there, you bloody bastard. It's you they should be taking to a gallows tree instead of me. But know this, you son of a whore, it won't be you that murders me."

It wouldn't have seemed possible, but for a short moment, the mass of men and women fell quieter than before. Then some man in the horde yelled, "Let's get on with our work! The crowd marched Musgrove down Larimer Street to the bridge that spanned Cherry Creek. Putney waited until the mob had passed before returning to the hotel. Before going to his room, Putney stopped at the hotel bar and bought a bottle of whiskey. Upon entering the room, before even speaking to Mandy, Putney plopped himself on the sofa, broke the seal on the bottle, and poured himself a

drink. Sensing that something dreadful had occurred, Mandy sat gently on the sofa and, stroking his long red hair, asked her husband what had happened. He told her everything that happened, then said, "It's odd, Mandy. I spent the better part of two years tracking the man down. I do not doubt that I would have killed him myself if I had caught him. But to watch these men, whose duty is to uphold the law, to watch them pervert justice the way they have, I feel sorry for the man I had sworn to kill. I can't understand why I would feel that way."

Mandy took his face in her tiny hands and turned his head to face her. "Because, darling husband," she said, "you are a good man."

48

The night Musgrove was killed, neither Putney nor Mandy felt in the mood to make love. Instead, Mandy went down to the restaurant and ordered a meal of cold meats and bread. Putney ate very little. They retired early, but neither got much rest. To Mandy, Putney must have been having nightmares most of the night. His sleep was so fitful. Putney tossed and turned and spoke in his sleep, though the words were so muffled, Mandy couldn't make them out. Just before dawn, Putney finally fell into a deep and dreamless sleep. Mandy cuddled close to him, and soon she was fast asleep.

The couple did not wake until noon. It was Mandy who woke first. Looking at the clock on the mantle, she couldn't believe it. She had never slept that late in her entire life. Mandy took care of her morning needs and gently roused Putney from his sleep. As he stretched and rubbed his eyes, Mandy told him the time. He smiled and told her it was alright. They were on their honeymoon, after all, and they deserved to be a little decadent. Putney rose from the bed and washed up. When he finished, he walked back to the bed, where Mandy was sitting, and leaned over to give her what he meant to be a slight peck on the cheek. It was two in the afternoon before the couple started dressing.

Mandy was wearing one of her new dresses of a deep violet color. The dress had a low collar but wasn't close to being overly provocative, but the fit hugged her body, leaving little doubt of her striking figure. It had tightly rolled shoulders, giving her the appearance of having much broader shoulders than she had. In addition, a slight bum roll made her hips look a bit larger than they were. It was a one-piece dress, and luckily for her and Putney both, it buttoned up the front. If it had required Putney's help, they probably wouldn't have made it downstairs until dinner time, and Mandy was famished.

Mandy ordered roast chicken for her late lunch and tea. Putney, for his part, ordered two pork chops and coffee. While waiting for their meal, the dining room manager came to their table with a newspaper in his hands. He excused himself and asked Putney if he had seen the paper, which he had not. The manager left the daily with Putney.

The front page had two main stories. The first was naturally about the illegal hanging of Musgrove and the other about a confrontation between Sheriff Cook and deputies with Ed Franklin. Cook and his men had located Sanford Duggan, but another outlaw had started shooting at the lawmen. Cook and deputies had hit the other outlaw, a man called Burly Smith, but Duggan had managed to escape in the fight. In return for quick medical assistance Smith told Cook where Ed Franklin was hiding. Cook left one deputy with Smith while a local citizen searched for a doctor. The sheriff and his remaining deputy went to the hotel where Franklin was staying and burst into Franklin's room, catching the outlaw unaware. Instead of surrendering to

Cook, Franklin reached for a cocked pistol on the table beside the bed. The two lawmen fired their guns in unison, and Ed Franklin was dead. What bothered him about the story, and it was now obvious why the restaurant manager had pointed it out, was that it had mentioned him.

"Your intrepid reporter has it on good authority that Sheriff Cook received information on the notorious Edward Franklin's whereabouts from a source nearly as notorious as the outlaw himself. A source, whom this writer shan't reveal, said it was none other than the infamous pistoleer, detective, and tracker, Red Jack Callahan. It may lead you, dear reader, to wonder what connections, if any, the red-haired Texan may have with the villainous Musgrove and Franklin faction."

"Well, shit," Putney said loud enough for anyone in the dining room to hear. Mandy was slightly embarrassed at her husband's language, but not as much as it was late in the day and there were few other diners present.

"Language, Jack," The young Mandy reprimanded her husband.

"What?" he asked. Then, realizing the words had not remained in his head but had been spoken aloud, in mixed company, Putney apologized.

Putney had finished his first pork chop when Marv Chalmers, his protege, entered and stood at the couple's table with his hat in his hand. Putney stood, shook the younger man's hand, and introduced him to Mandy. "Pleased to meet you, Mrs. Callahan," Marv said.

Putney could not miss the badge pinned to Marv's short jacket outside. "You still working for Holloway?" Putney asked Marv.

Marv smiled proudly and said, "Only part-time, but it's

enough for me to keep a nice boarding room and buy a few odds and ends."

"I don't expect you came here just to pass the time, did you, Marv?" he said to the young man.

"No, Jack," Marv answered. "Marshal Holloway sent me to tell you, I mean to ask you, to come over to his office as soon as you can."

Putney swallowed a bite of pork chop. "My bride and I have other plans for the day," Putney said. "What's so important it can't wait until tomorrow?"

"He didn't say, Jack. Just that I should find you and ask you to come along," Marv was feeling embarrassed about even making the request.

Turning to Mandy, Putney asked, "What do you think, Hon? Should we comply with the Marshal's request?"

"It might be important, Jack," said Mandy. "I can wait here until you return."

"Nope," Putney was emphatic. "We either go together or not at all. I've spent enough time away from you these past few days."

"Then I think we should go," said Mandy, who was privately excited about being summoned to see such an important man.

"Do you think it will be alright if we finish our meal, Marv?" Putney teased.

"Well, sure, Jack. I don't think the Marshal would want to disturb your meal," Marv was innocently sure of his remark.

"Then sit and have a cup of coffee while we finish," Putney told him.

～

A CLERK politely escorted Putney and Mandy into Marshal Holloway's office, with Marv following close behind. Putney bristled when in one of the high-back chairs in front of Holloway's desk sat Sheriff David Cook, straight as a rod. Marshal Holloway rose, walked around his desk, and introduced himself to Mandy. When Cook realized a woman was in the room, he rose, embarrassed he hadn't done so sooner. "Thanks, deputy," Holloway told Marv. "Go on, now and serve that process I gave you earlier."

Chalmers told Putney and Mandy goodbye, remarking what a pleasure it had been to meet Mrs. Callahan. Holloway pulled another chair over to the front of the desk for Mandy and asked everyone to sit. "I guess you're wondering why I sent young Chalmers to find you."

"We wouldn't be here if we already knew," said Putney.

"It is really David here that wanted to see you, so I guess I'll let him get to it," Marshal Holloway gave the floor to the sheriff.

Cook cleared his throat and started, "Callahan, I owe you an apology." Putney was surprised to hear the stiff-necked Cook coming close to admitting he may have made an error, though he wasn't sure where Cook was going. "I guess you've read The Rocky Mountain News." Putney nodded, indicating he had. "I don't know where the reporter got the information, but I sincerely apologize that he put your name out to the public like that."

"I guess worse things have been said about me," Putney replied. "Some of them by you."

Cook's neck stiffened even more until Mandy said, "Now, Jack, Sheriff Cook is being nice, so you be, also."

"I had asked Marshal Holloway to have you come to his office, Jack," this was the first time Putney could remember the sheriff using his first name. "The thing is, I didn't want to bring you to my office for fear that some busybody would leak it to the newspaper again."

"I appreciate that, David," Putney couldn't help himself from using the sheriff's first name.

Cook cleared his throat and continued, "I wanted you to know that I have your pay for your tracking services and your portion of the reward on Musgrove." Cook pulled an envelope from his inner coat pocket and handed it to Putney. "I also submitted for the reward on Franklin, and there was a twenty-five-dollar reward on Smith. I will get that money tomorrow. I will send it to your hotel here, so you don't have to come to my office. And you should know I'm only giving my deputies a quarter of the reward. The rest I'm giving to you. I'm not taking any for myself."

"Why would you do that?" Putney inquired.

"Let's just call it a wedding gift, shall we?" Putney nodded.

"Well, Jack," said Holloway. "That's mighty generous of the sheriff. So, are you and Mrs. Callahan planning on staying on in Denver?"

"No, Marshal," Putney said. "As soon as we have our money, we are heading to Texas. Mandy wants me to return to university in San Antonio and read law."

"Excellent idea, Mrs. Callahan," Marshal Holloway said.

Putney could read the relief on both lawmen's faces.Then in an offhanded remark, Sheriff Cook said, "I don't know what I'm going to do about those commissioners and the mayor concerning the lynching of Musgrove."

Nobody quite understood why he would have brought the subject up. Finally, Putney touched Mandy's elbow, and they both stood. "Thank you, gentlemen," he said with some sincerity. "Oh, and Sheriff, maybe you should just tell them

to get out of your county like you told me the first time we
met."

~

PUTNEY AND MANDY spent the rest of the afternoon
shopping, but this time for supplies and staples they would
need for their trip. At each store, he told the proprietors that
they would pick up the order in two days. Then he and
Mandy returned to the hotel for a late supper and
adjourned to their room with two bottles of champaign.

The following morning the couple rose and went down
for breakfast. The couple was ravenous after eating what
fruit remained in their room. Putney ordered three eggs,
potatoes, a ham steak, pancakes with butter and honey, and
a bowl of peaches. Mandy went slightly lighter with two
eggs, bacon, and pancakes. She said she would share
Putney's peaches, which made him smile. They were both
reading different sections of the newspaper while they ate.
He was mostly scanning his section, looking for more refer-
ences to himself, while Mandy was perusing the society and
entertainment sections.

"Oh, look," said Mandy. "Tonight is the last night of
Burlesque Theater, Na... I mean Jack" Putney looked at his
wife curiously. "I mean, this is the theater performance all
the way from New York. They say it's hilarious." Still looking
at his wife as if she had two heads, Mandy continued. "Can
we go, Jack?"

Finally understanding, Putney said, "We talked about
this, you remember. It may be dangerous for us to be out at
night. I think we should stay in the hotel. Besides, there will
be bigger and better theaters and performances in San
Antonio."

"But that's weeks, probably months," Mandy put on her best pouty face. "And you bought me that beautiful yellow gown. I won't be able to wear it forever."

"Mandy," Putney started but was interrupted when Mandy took his hand and gave him a cow-eyed look.

"Puhleeese," she moaned.

He broke out in laughter and relented, saying, "Alright, since this is our last night, too. Why not."

Mandy gave out a yelp of glee and reached out and hugged her husband until Putney was embarrassed by the looks they were getting from other patrons. "Calm down, Mandy," he said. "I'll order one of those small coaches to take us and pick us up. It should be safer that way."

Mandy was ecstatic over the chance to go to a theater. She had never been before. The only entertainment they had in Boulder was the dance hall girls in the saloons; she had certainly not been allowed to go near one of those. "Can we eat at Billy William's, too?" she asked. "I read they serve oysters that have been smoked and canned in Massachusetts. I would like to try smoked oysters at least once."

"Sure," said Putney. "I've read oysters are good for later in the night." With that, he gave Mandy a wink, but she didn't quite understand.

Before they finished their breakfast, Putney noticed an insipid little man in a brown suit wearing a brown Derby and spectacles pinched on the end of his nose. As meek as the man appeared, Putney was surprised when he boldly walked directly to their table. "Do I have the pleasure of addressing Mr. Jack Callahan?" the little man asked.

"It would depend on who is asking," Putney replied.

"My name is Joseph Atwater. I work for the Rocky Mountain News." said the man in a nasally voice.

"Are you the one that referred to me in that article on Ed Franklin?" asked Putney.

"Yes, that would be me," Atwater was proud of the fact and felt that Putney should be proud he had gotten a mention in the newspaper.

"Mr. Atwater," said Putney, even as Mandy touched his arm, trying to calm him. Mandy could see the anger boiling in her husband. "My wife and I are trying to enjoy our breakfast, so for my wife's sake, I will politely ask you to remove yourself from our presence and never approach my wife or me again."

"Mr. Callahan," Atwater spoke with impudence and arrogance. "I have the power of the press. I can use that power to make or break men. Now, if you allow me a minute of your time, I think I can make you more famous than infamous."

Putney reached over and took Mandy's hand and removed it as delicately as he would an egg, then he stood, towering over Atwater by at least eight inches. "And I, Mr. Atwater, literally have the power to break a man like you in half. So, for the sake of my wife and the other patrons here, I asked you politely to leave us alone. You now have one second to do so before...."

"Jack," Putney heard a familiar voice call his alias. Putney's rage focused on the little man so much that he had not seen Claude Franklin enter the dining room. "Jack," Claude repeated. "Don't worry yourself or your wife about this insignificant ant. Let me do it for you." With that, Claude Franklin took Atwater by his belt and collar, lifted him, and carried him out of the hotel with no more trouble than if he had been ejecting a dead mouse. Claude returned to the table, barely breathing hard, and stuck out his hand to Putney, who took it warmly. Putney introduced Claude to Mandy and asked him to sit and have coffee with them.

Putney had only invited Claude to join them since Claude had gotten Atwater out of his hair, but Claude's presence made him feel ill at ease.

Claude finally broke an awkward silence: "Jack, I want you to know I don't blame you for what happened to Ed. It wasn't your fault. Ed knew the path he had taken, and he had to know how it would end."

"It is a relief to hear you say so, Claude," Putney returned. "There was a time I would have gone after him, myself, but I could see I was on my own path to destruction. I could no longer live the way I had."

"We have both made some bad decisions," Claude agreed. "But stealing cattle and horses was one thing, but when Ed and Musgrove turned to banditry and murder, I had to wash my hands of the business. So I'm going back to Ohio. Back to farming."

"It looks like we both are returning to what we know. Mandy and I will be heading out for Texas," he told his friend. "Mandy wants me to become a lawyer."

"Well," said Claude, rising from the table, "I wish you both the best of luck. Goodbye, then."

Both Putney and Mandy said goodbye to Claude and hoped the best for him, too. When Claude had left, Mandy asked Putney if he would have killed Ed Franklin. "There was a time, Mandy, that I would have killed him and Musgrove and not bat an eye. But those days are past," Putney meant what he was saying. "An old friend of my father told me that revenge would take its toll on me and if I kept on, I would eventually pay a horrible price."

"But those days are gone now, aren't they?" Mandy asked.

"I have things to look forward to, Mandy," he said. "You are the one that gives me the strength to become something better than I have been.

49

Mandy and Putney had spent the day with their usual pursuit of shopping and purchasing things they would need for their trip. While they were out, Putney hired a coach to take them to dinner, then to the theater, and back to the hotel. It would have been an easy walk for both of them, but Putney felt better about being in a coach. He believed it was safer for Mandy.

They returned to the hotel early to prepare for their big night on the town. Mandy wanted to wear the evening gown that Putney had bought her. The outfit had an underskirt with an attached bodice. The skirt was made from yellow silk, and the bodice was cream-colored and made of fine linen with shallow ruffles on the front. A long flowing gown made of satin that had been purposefully died to match the bodice covered the dress. The gown had a collar embroidered with gold flowers and green leaves. Matching embroidery ran down the entire edge of the overdress, and the cuffs also matched the collar. Mandy had never felt so elegant. She couldn't believe that only a few days prior, she had been cooking and cleaning in her parent's boarding house. Now, she was dressed like a queen. Soon she would be eating dinner and going to the theater in the company of some of Denver's finest.

To compliment his wife's dress, Putney had bought himself a yellow satin vest embroidered with small green leaves. The two stood in front of the mirror and admired themselves. They knew it was pure vanity, but they also knew they would be the most handsome couple in Denver that night.

The coach was at the front door of the hotel waiting on them. The well-dressed driver helped Mandy in the small coach and then offered to assist Putney, who declined the help. Just as Putney was stepping in the coach a hand grabbed his arm. Putney spun around, ready to do battle when he recognized Oracle Jones. "Well, Howdo, Mister Not Jack Callahan. Reckon you could help a poor friend out?"

Relieved that it wasn't someone with malintent, Putney reached in his vest and pulled out a five-dollar coin. "Sure Jones, don't drink it all in one place."

"Thank you that will pay for my prophecy," Then Jones leaned in and with his foul breath whispered, "But it don't pay for yore sins." Jones went away dancing as he sang "The Battle Hymn of the Republic".

Putney got in the coach and Mandy asked him what that had been about, and he passed it off as a drunken old coot. Putney worried about Jones' cryptic message but soon put it out of his mind as they pulled up to Billy William's Restaurant. The restaurant indeed served smoked oysters. Mandy could not think of anything she had ever eaten, like smoked oysters. She wondered aloud what fresh oysters would taste like and made Putney promise to one day take her somewhere she could eat fresh oysters.

At the theater, Mandy outshined all the other women

present, and there were quite a few side glances, envious of the beautiful young woman. There were also many whispers about the notorious Jack Callahan accompanying her. However, if Mandy heard the whispered gossip, she never let on. Putney, on the other hand, was conspicuously under-dressed. The other men wore evening dress with long-tailed coats that cut away toward the waist and revealed their starched shirts and silk vests. But Putney didn't mind. He was, after all, with the most beautiful woman in town. Putney swore to himself that there would be many nights like this in San Antonio.

The show was delightful, if bawdy. The entire cast were women dressed in tights and close-fitting garments that showcased their voluptuousness. It was all quite daring. The songs and skits were ribald and naughty. The audience didn't seem to mind and roared with laughter at every jest. There was an intermission; the ladies drank champagne and cackled about the show while the men smoked cigars and drank whiskey. Putney got Mandy a glass of champagne and himself a whiskey, but they stood apart from the rest of the crowd. From its case, Putney produced a cigarette. Mandy told him she was feeling a little naughty and asked him if she could also have a cigarette. Putney didn't see why she couldn't, so they stood apart, sipping their drinks and smoking cigarettes. If tongues hadn't been wagging before, they certainly were now. Mandy was enjoying every minute of it. She delighted in being the scandal of Denver and promised herself she would repeat it in San Antonio.

The crowd spilled out onto the front walk when the show was over. Some, like Putney and Mandy, waited for their carriages while others took a leisurely stroll toward their homes. A rough-looking man pushing his way through the crowd caused the people to part aside. There were gasps from the women and comments about the rude oaf from the men. Putney and Mandy were at the tail of the line waiting for their coach when Putney caught the noisy commotion of the gentlefolk.

Looking for the cause, he saw coming toward him Claude Franklin. Claude had been drinking but not so much that he didn't know what he was doing. When Claude came within a few steps of them, he spoke loud enough for the entire crowd to hear. "Jack Callahan," said Claude, adding to the name, "Bloody Red Jack Callahan. You killed my brother, sure as if you had been there yourself."

Putney used his left arm to guide Mandy behind him. "Claude, you're drunk. I don't know what's got into you, but your brother's death is on his own hands. He could have given himself up, but he chose not to. You said as much this morning."

"This morning?" slurred Franklin, "You fell for that malarkey? I was sizing you up. Now I know you've gone weak. I know I can take you now, and I'm going to."

Putney knew Claude was trying to build up his courage but believed he never would. It wasn't in Claude's nature to kill another man in cold blood.

"Claude," said Putney as he stepped a fraction closer to his one-time friend. "This is the whiskey talking." Putney inched a little closer to Franklin. Putney noticed that he wasn't the only one that had gotten closer. The crowd that, at first, had backed away from the two men came closer. They wanted to see this show. They wanted to see Jack Callahan killed or Jack Callahan killing. It didn't matter to them which man died. What they were watching now was a better show than the one they paid to see.

Putney was nearly within an arm's length of Franklin

and said, "Claude, you're not going to be able to do this. I won't let you."

"You won't let me," Claude laughed in Putney's face. "Well, let's see you stop me." With those last words, Claude dropped his hand to the Colt he was wearing. His drunkenness gave Putney the edge. As Franklin pulled the pistol from its holster, Putney stepped in and, striking Claude's gun hand, deflected the gun just as it went off. Putney had kept Claude from killing him. That was when Putney heard the women screaming. Putney turned and realized that instead of staying behind him, Mandy had stepped out, just a little, to see what was happening.

A deep red spot was growing on the yellow gown, obliterating the golden flowers. Putney fell to his knees beside his wife and cradled her gently in his arms. He looked into her dark eyes, and he could see the life oozing out of them.

"Nahum," Mandy's voice was as clear and strong as any time he had known. "Nahum," she said again. "I love you and am proud to be Mrs. Nahum Putney."

"And I'm proud you are my wife, Mandy. I love you, Mandy," Putney's voice was weak.

"Nahum, remember your promise, Nahum," Mandy said.

"I don't know, Mandy. I'm not as strong as you," his voice was beginning to crack.

"Nahum, I love you," Mandy had spoken her last words.

Putney cradled his wife in his left arm. He bent over and kissed his love one last time. Putney looked up to see Franklin standing over him, the Colt still in his hand and pointing at him. Putney's focus grew sharp. The crowd around them floated backward through no power of their own. The air grew thick with the smell of cigar smoke and French perfume. Putney saw that Franklin no longer had his finger on the trigger. Putney knew that Claude Franklin had finished murdering this night. Putney reached in the right pocket of his vest and extracted the derringer he had taken off Farnsworth. Other than his father's Walkers, the only pistol he had kept. Nahum Putney, Bloody Red Jack Callahan lifted the derringer and placed two forty-four bullets in Claude Franklin's forehead.

PART III

50

I t had been a cold morning when Imogene Foster had climbed aboard her uncle's wagon to ride into town. Sherman, Texas, was the county seat of Grayson County and a trip into town was always exciting, even in the middle of January. It certainly was better than staying in the five-room farmhouse caring for her young cousins, just to stay warm. Imogene had bundled up by wearing her mackinaw over a heavy sweater, a knit cap over her ears, and mittens over doeskin gloves. Her uncle was not a talkative man, except when it came to farming. Then he would talk the ears off a rabbit. But the silence allowed Imogene time to think. An extravagance when one considered the racket her three young cousins were always making.

It had been nearly five years since a Comanche raid on her family's farm had left everyone dead except her. The Indians had kidnapped Imogene. They had ridden for days with hardly any rest and finally came to a camp in west Texas, south of Llano Estacado. There she was nothing more than a slave, beaten daily by the women of the tribe. She would have remained that way until forced to marry one of the men of the tribe if it hadn't been for Nahum Putney. She thought of him often and wondered whatever had happened to him. The Nahum Putney she had first known as brave and kind and loving. This was the man Imogene thought of most. Rarely did she think of the dark, angry, hateful man Nahum had been turning into after the outlaw's raid on Callahan's Irish settlers in New Mexico. He had changed overnight and vowed vengeance on the evil men who killed his friends and his fiancé. The last time she had seen him, she begged him to come with her and Bigfoot Wallace back to Texas. But he was determined to exact justice on the vicious band of criminals.

In Sherman, her uncle had bought feed for the cows, horses, and mules that would have difficulty finding fodder in January and February. Imogene purchased fabric for her aunt and her to sew dresses for the two girls. She bought a pair of dungarees for herself and her male cousin, who was three years her junior. Imogene would like to have a pretty new dress for the spring. She desired to promenade in the streets of Sherman and flirt with the boys in town. But Imogene knew it would make no difference. She was pretty enough, that was sure, and it wasn't her vanity that told her so. A few times, boys traveling through Sherman had remarked on her beauty and whistled at her, but it wasn't long before someone told them Imogene had been a Comanche captive. Once informed, someone always followed up with "Who knows what all she did to survive?' or a similar comment. No, frilly dresses and picnics with beaus weren't in the cards for Imogene Foster. At least not for a few more months, when with some luck, she could leave the farm and move to Dallas, where she wanted to attend Center University, an all-girls college. Maybe in a big town like Dallas, which boasted nearly fifteen thousand people, the stigma of having been a captive would cease to haunt her. Imogene pushed the thought from her mind and continued shopping for the odds and ends her aunt had asked her to pick up.

Her uncle had finished shopping for feed and supplies and had started talking with a couple of other farmers who had come to town. Imogene was glad because it gave her time to finish buying what her aunt wanted and some candy for the children. Next, she bought a book for herself, a copy of <u>The Poetical Works of Elizabeth Barrett Browning</u>. Imogene wanted to start reading it immediately but forced herself to wait. Instead, she would read one poem every night after the children had gone to sleep. That way, she could make it last longer.

Her uncle could talk longer than the other farmers wanted to listen, and when there was nobody else to talk farming to, he told Imogene it was time to leave. With the wagon loaded up, Imogene's uncle pulled a blanket from under the seat, saying it seemed to be getting colder and they might need it. Imogene was daydreaming about what wonderful poetry she would read in her new book. Something caught her eye as the wagon passed the last saloon on the main street. At the end of the boardwalk, huddled up against a rain barrel, sat a man in a long, ragged beaver coat. The man had the collar pulled up, hiding his face but out of the top stuck a mop of thick red hair. "Stop, Uncle Stop," Imogene demanded and had jumped from the wagon before her uncle could rein in the mules and set the brake. Imogene stooped over the huddled figure and pulled back the collar to reveal a long, shabby red beard. Her action had not roused the man, who was sleeping or passed out. She gave the man a gentle shake and said, "Nahum? Nahum Putney? It's me. Imogene Foster." The man's eyes opened slowly to reveal steel blue eyes buried in bloodshot lines. He blinked a few times as if trying to focus. "Nahum? Imogene Foster. You remember, don't you?"

Life slowly crept into the emaciated eyes of Nahum Putney. "Imogene?" he croaked. He had a short coughing fit and said, "You can't be Imogene. She's just a little wisp of a girl."

"No, Nahum," tears were welling up in Imogene's eyes. "That was nearly five years ago. I'll be eighteen in three more months. Oh please, Nahum, please say you recognize me."

Nahum pulled his near-frozen hands from his coat pockets, rubbed his eyes, then said, "By God, that is you. Little Imogene Foster. What are you doing here?"

Imogene's uncle had tethered the mules to a hitching post by this time and was standing over her. "Imogene," he said, "Get away from this drunk. Come on back to the wagon." Her uncle took her by the arm to guide her away.

As fast as a striking rattlesnake, the beaver coat flew open, and Imogene's uncle was staring, wide-eyed, down the barrel of a big Colt Walker. "Let go of this girl," Nahum growled between clenched teeth. "Or I'll drop you where you are, you son of a bitch."

The uncle immediately released Imogene's arm, afraid the man would kill him anyway. "No. Nahum," Imogene pleaded. "This is my Uncle Bob, Nahum. You remember the uncle Bigfoot was bringing me to?"

"Uncle Bob?" confusion was flying around inside his brain, but slowly his memory returned. "That's right. Bigfoot and you and some Indian left Fort Dodge to take you to your uncle." Nahum lowered the pistol. "And this is him? Where the hell am I?"

"Why, you're in Sherman, Texas, Nahum," said Imogene. "That's where you are."

∾

Nᴀʜᴜᴍ ʟᴏᴏᴋᴇᴅ ᴀᴛ Dᴇɪᴅʀᴇ O'Nᴇɪʟʟ. She thought it may have been the most despondent look she had ever seen on any man's face. "So," he continued, I stayed with the Fosters for nearly three months. There wasn't much room in the house with the three younger children, their parents, and Imogene. I slept next to the fireplace for three days, but I was always underfoot and felt uncomfortable around the folks. They were so kind, and I wasn't used to being treated kindly, not for three years. But I don't want to go into all of that now. Just know those years were dark, and I did many things I am not proud of. If I end up going to hell, it will be because of those years."

"Bob and Imogene helped me fix up space in the barn's tack room, where I could be alone when needed. We used old newspapers to fill any cracks in the walls, to keep the cold out as much as possible. Bob made an extra trip into town to buy ticking, and Imogene and her aunt Mary sewed it together. We stuffed the ticking bag with straw for a mattress. They put a table and a lantern in the room and another table for an old metal wash basin they had. It wasn't the most comfortable place I ever stayed, but with the extra blankets and quilts the family had, it was serviceable."

"I never spoke with Imogene's aunt and uncle about the track my life had taken for nearly five years, but I told Imogene everything. She cried when I told her of Mandy. She cried so much; I think it made up for the tears I never shed. I was too angry for tears."

Nahum rubbed his bleary eyes, and Deidre thought for just a moment maybe he had let some tears well up in his eyes. "The Fosters are good people. They treated Imogene as if she was their own. They never scorned her for her situation. Their goodness also extended to me. They bought me new clothes and a horse, saddle, and tack before I left. I know it put a strain on the budget, with planting season coming up, but they never groused."

The telling of the story and his memories of those years had exhausted Nahum. He shook his head and stretched to keep himself awake. "At the end of March; I left the farm for T. J. McKinney's ranch. When I had been there a few days, I told T. J. I needed to go to San Antonio. I needed to get some money from my safety deposit box."

"I opened an account at the bank in Imogene's name, then I wired her, telling her she could draw on the account to pay for college in Dallas and repay Bob and Mary for the money they had spent on me."

"And," said Nahum, "that's about all. Marshal Parnell wants a written report about Jack Callahan on his desk by three this afternoon. Here it is six in the morning, and we haven't even slept."

"Don't you be worrying about that, now," Deidre said to her lover. You get yourself back in the bed and sleep. I'll wake you at noon. You will have plenty of time to write your report after that."

"How?" asked Nahum. "It took me six hours to tell you the story. So how can I possibly write a report in less than three hours? And what difference will it make? In the end, he will know the legend of Jack Callahan, and I will be out of a job. I think it may be best for me to go ahead and resign."

"Now don't you dare be talking like that," Deidre demanded of Nahum. "If you give up, you're not the man I think you are. And if you were someone different, I don't think we could continue." Deidre's famous Irish anger was on a slow simmer. She got her purse off the bedside table and took out a small paper packet. Deidre poured powder from the package into a glass and filled it with water. "Here, now," she told Nahum, "The doctor gave me this to help me sleep. You drink it down. I'm going to get dressed and have breakfast. I will wake you at noon."

Nahum was tired. Too tired to resist this woman who had so much will. He drank the draft and laid down on the bed. He was asleep before Deidre finished dressing. It was tricky dressing with her injured shoulder, but Deidre managed. She looked herself over in the mirror and approved of how she looked. In the hotel restaurant, Deidre only took the time to eat a scone and drink two cups of black coffee. After her meager breakfast, she left the hotel and managed to find a cabriolet to take her to the federal courthouse, where she asked directions to the Marshal's office.

She found the door with gold lettering that read "Office of United States Marshal John Parnell." She marched through the door and found a weaselly-looking clerk at a desk. Deidre told the clerk she wanted to see Marshal Parnell, and he retorted that the marshal wasn't available if she didn't have an appointment. The clerk wasn't quite sure what Deidre meant when she said that if the clerk didn't admit her, she would rip his goolies off and stuff them in his mouth. Whatever she meant, the clerk was sure she would do it, and it seemed like it would be an uncomfortable event. He asked her to wait a moment and entered the marshal's private office.

"Er, Marshal," the clerk said to his boss. "There is a woman outside who is very insistent on seeing you."

"Did you tell her I was busy?" asked Parnell, even though he wasn't.

"I did, sir," the clerk told him, "But I'm afraid she is on the verge of hysteria, and to be quite frank, if you don't see her, I'm afraid she will raise a ruckus."

Exasperated with the clerk, Parnell said to admit her. He figured he would placate the woman, whoever she was, then send her on her way.

The clerk returned to find Deidre with arms folded and tapping one foot, a sign which he believed said she was running out of patience, if she ever had any, to begin with. "Marshal Parnell will see you now," the clerk said weakly.

When Deidre entered the office, Parnell rose from his desk to greet her but then froze, and a look of dread came over his face. For Deidre's part, her look of determination turned to surprise. *Well, well, well,* she thought, *isn't this just grand.* Deidre had come to the Marshal's office to demand he lay off Nahum, but she had no real plan of how she would enforce her demand, but now she knew exactly how.

Marshal Parnell quickly overcame his anxiety and met Deidre in the center of the room. "Good morning, miss," he said cordially. "I'm Marshal John Parnell. How may I be of assistance to you."

"Oh, ho ho, isn't that good," said Deidre. "So, it's John Parnell, now, is it? That's funny because it's not the name you used in New Orleans."

"I'm afraid I don't know what you mean, Miss, er Miss?" Parnell's speech was halting.

"Oh, and here I am remembering a Mr. Paul Madison that visited me several times at Madame Isabel Beaumont's house in New Orleans. Maybe you remember me better by the name I was using then. Aisling Flanagan? Remember?" Deidre said.

Parnell ran a finger around his shirt collar and insisted he didn't know what Deidre meant. "That will not do, Mr. Madison," Deidre emphasized the surname. "But let me help your reticence. The secret of Mr. Paul Madison can remain right here in this room, or I can go down the street to the Daily Austin Republican newspaper offices."

"I will deny it," said Parnell. "It will be your word against mine.

"And will you deny that birthmark on your chest, in the shape of a heart, just over your left nipple?" asked Deidre.

Parnell walked back around his desk and sat down in his chair, defeated. "What do you want, Miss...?"

"O'Neill. Deidre O'Neill,"

"Ah, I see now. I should have guessed. Did Putney send you to blackmail me?" asked Parnell.

"Nahum doesn't know I've come here, and I prefer he never knows," said Deidre. "It will be another little secret we share. What I want is very simple. All this speculation about somebody named Jack Callahan must stop. Nahum is a good man, and I won't bear to see his name dragged through the mud by association with a myth."

"So, what you are saying is that Jack Callahan is the alias of someone we both know," Parnell was delving for an admission.

"I said nothing of the sort," it angered Deidre that Parnell was trying to twist her words. "I can tell you that Jack Callahan is dead and has been for years. As long as you and I are in agreement over those two small facts and that Nahum will retain his position, then our business is complete."

"And I have your assurance that you will never repeat the name Paul Madison outside of this room?" asked the Marshal.

"It will never pass my lips. That is my promise," Deidre pledged. "Nahum will bring you his report this afternoon.

But, whatever he says, you are to let it pass, and none of this ever needs to be spoken of again."

Marshal Parnell stood again, walked around his desk, and held out his hand to Deidre. "Agreed, Miss O'Neill"

Deidre shook the Marshal's hand, and as she walked out the door, she said, "It was a pleasure speaking with you, Mr.," and she paused for a heartbeat. "Parnell."

Deidre made it back to the hotel at half-past eleven. She entered the restaurant and ordered a large meal of cold cuts and beer sent to the room. Deidre had a few minutes to relax before twelve, and she sat on the couch and let out a long breath. She couldn't believe the luck. She didn't know what she would have said to Parnell to convince him about Nahum's trustworthiness, but fortune had shone on her.

The food and beer arrived at the room at precisely twelve. Deidre had the boy leave the food on the low table and fished in her purse for a quarter to give him.

Deidre walked to the bed and, bending over, gave Nahum a light kiss on the forehead and a gentle shake. It's time to wake up, dear," she said.

He groaned, then stretched before opening his eyes and asking, "Is it twelve already?"

"It is, dear," answered Deidre. "I have some food ready for you, and you need to get your report done and wash up."

"Yeah, my report," he breathed. "I'll have to think about that."

Nahum put on a robe that the hotel furnished and walked down the hall to the privy to wash up. When he returned, he sat and slathered two pieces of bread with hot mustard and stacked on Swiss cheese, ham, and salami for a sandwich. Along with the sandwich, Nahum ate two hands full of Saratoga chips. Then Nahum dressed in the finest day clothes he had, complete with a red vest embroidered with blue thread.

By the time he had washed, eaten, and dressed, it was a quarter until two in the afternoon. Nahum sat at a writing table, opened the drawer, and pulled out two pieces of paper, an ink well, and a pen. In the center of one paper, he wrote "Jack Callahan is dead" and signed it. In the center of the second paper, Nahum wrote: "I am Jack Callahan" and signed it also. He waited for the ink to dry, folded each piece in thirds, and placed them in separate envelopes. Each addressed to Marshal Parnell.

"If either of those is your report, they seem mighty short," Deidre remarked, sitting on the couch where she had been eating and drinking beer. "Are you sure they are not resignations?"

"Neither are resignations," Nahum stated flatly. Nahum stood from the table, crossed the room, put on his gun belt, and dropped his pistols in the holsters. He donned his frock coat with the badge on the left lapel, looked in the mirror, and approved of his image.

Deidre handed him his broad-brimmed hat to put on. She adored his look with his long red hair that came to his shoulders and his luxurious red beard. Of course, he was not wearing a tie. At that moment, Deidre decided that, without a doubt, he was the most handsome man she had ever known. Nahum kissed Deidre and said, "I should be back no later than five." It was exactly two o'clock when he left the room.

As Nahum walked onto the hot Austin street, he looked at his watch and decided to walk to the courthouse. He took his time, looking in shop windows and saying hello to strangers he passed. He walked tall and proud. Whatever Parnell decided, Nahum was not going to be ashamed. He would either walk back to the hotel with a badge or without, but he would not slacken. When he arrived at the federal courthouse, he checked his watch, which showed twenty minutes until three, so he sat on a bench near the entrance and smoked a cigarette. When he finished his smoke, it was ten until three, so he slowly ascended the stairs and walked to the Marshal's office. Rechecking his watch, Nahum walked through the entrance at five minutes to three. "I think Marshal Parnell is expecting me," he said to the clerk who told him to go on in.

Parnell was sitting at his desk when Nahum walked in, strode over to the desk, and set the two envelopes in front of the Marshal. "What's this?" Parnell quizzed his deputy.

"My reports," Nahum purposefully kept his comment short.

"Are they duplicates or what?" Parnell wanted to know.

"No, sir," said Nahum. "They are two different versions, but both are the truth. You choose which one you want to read."

Marshal Parnell picked up an envelope in each hand and remarked, "They both feel mighty light."

"Either tells all there is to tell," said Nahum.

Parnell put one envelope back on the desk and pushed it toward him, which Nahum retrieved and placed in his inner coat pocket. Parnell opened the other envelope, unfolded the paper, and read it. The Marshal folded the paper back and put it in the envelope.

"I guess that's all there is to it," said Parnell. The Marshal opened the humidor on his desk and selected a cigar. He rolled it between his fingers, clipped off the end, struck a match, and lit the cigar. As the match burned, he took the envelope, lit it afire, and watched as the envelope and the paper inside turned to ashes. He looked at Nahum and said, "Now don't you have some criminals to find?"

Nahum said, "Yes, sir. I do." Then walked out of the office. Nahum Putney sat on the same bench he had left not more than a half-hour before. He opened his cigarette case, extracted a Kinney, and lit it. He pulled the unopened envelope from his coat pocket, looked at it then put the match to it. He held it until it burned his fingertips.

Nahum Putney finished his cigarette and returned to the hotel.

THE END

EPILOGUE

Nahum Putney woke and had to blink his eyes several times to get them to focus. The first thing he saw was only a blank white wall in front of him. Thinking he still hadn't focused, Putney blinked several more times, shut his eyes hard and this time looked above himself. Again, he saw only a blank white ceiling. Putney was confused and wondering what had happened to him. He attempted to rise, but the pain in his chest reminded him of what had happened. Someone had shot him. Things start to make sense as Putney realized he was in a hospital. He attempted another look, but this time only raised his head. Now he could see a doorway that led to a hall, but he saw nobody. Suddenly Putney was very thirsty. He decided to call out to see if he could get someone's attention, but his voice was hoarse and croaky. Putney could barely hear himself, let alone make anyone else hear him. He laid his head back down in futility. He would try again in a moment.

Putney must have fallen asleep because the next thing he knew, sharp pain in his chest brought him to immediate consciousness. Opening his eyes, he saw a man about his age, wearing a white smock. This man had his hands on Putney 's chest and seemed to be probing around, trying to cause Putney pain. "Stop it," Putney croaked.

The man in the white coat jerked his hands back, but gathered his wits quickly, then said, "Oh, I see you are awake, Mr. Putney."

"Water," Putney said in little more than a whisper.

"Certainly," said the man, who by now Putney had figured out was a doctor. Then, speaking to someone Putney could not see, the doctor said, "Nurse, get Mr. Putney a glass of water. Maybe crank up the bed first so he can drink." Past his feet, Putney saw a starched white hat set on a head of dark brown hair, and he heard a groan from the same direction. Putney felt the upper portion of his body rise a little, and he felt the pain in his chest again. When the nurse positioned him where she thought he could drink, she disappeared from sight but soon returned to his side. The nurse lifted him slightly with one hand as she placed the rim of a glass on his lips. Putney took a few sips, then she let his head back on the pillow.

Putney watched as the doctor replaced the nurse in his vision. "There," he said, "Is that better?" Putney nodded. "I'm Doctor Adams. I guess you're wondering why you're here."

"Somebody shot me," said Putney as if it were an everyday occurrence.

"Yes, and they nearly killed you," Adams made it sound as if it were Putney's fault. "The bullet passed very close to your heart. You're a fortunate man to have survived. But the bullet did puncture your left lung, collapsing it. You will be here sometime until that lung heals and you can breathe well."

"What about Deidre?" Nahum was less concerned about his lung than what had happened to Deidre.

"Miss O'Neill? She's well, but I think she could do with some rest," Adams said. "I asked her to step out while I examined you. She will be pleased to know you're awake. I'm about through here, anyway," Then, speaking to the nurse, the doctor said, "Miss Carter, be sure that someone changes this bandage every six hours until the wound stops seeping. I don't want an infection setting in and causing more problems than we need."

"Yes, doctor," said Miss Carter.

Returning his focus to Putney, Adams said, "Mr. Putney, I am restricting you to soft foods for a while, soup, porridge, that kind of thing. We will look in a few days and see how you are progressing. And please don't try to get out of bed. You need to heal."

The doctor didn't need to tell him not to get out of bed. Putney felt like he couldn't get out of bed if it were on fire. It wasn't a few minutes after the doctor left that Deidre came into the room. "There you are, then," she said, trying to sound cheerful. "I saw the doctor; he said you were on the mend."

"Yeah, that's his story," Nahum was not feeling Deidre's cheerfulness.

"Well, I know you. You'll be up and around in no time," Deidre said to him.

"Sure," said Nahum. "That's me. Nothing stops me." He did not believe his own words, and it showed. "What happened? Who shot me? Was It Courtwright or Russell?"

"Neither it was some cowboy by the name of Ned Blakley is what they said," Deidre told Nahum. "Have you ever heard of him?"

Nahum started to laugh, but it caused a coughing fit.

Deidre got some water and let Nahum have several sips. When the coughing calmed, Nahum said. "I know him. Remember, years ago, when I told you about Jack Callahan?"

"Yes."

"Blakely was the Missouri Bushwhacker I left nearly naked on top of that mountain," Nahum told her.

"Oh," said Deidre, "Just one of the many enemies you've made in your life."

"I guess some people can't let go of a grudge. What happened to him?" Nahum asked

"He's dead" Deidre didn't offer anything else. "I thought you were going to die too. And you would have if it hadn't been for an Indian."

"Who was he?" Nahum asked.

Deidre shrugged her shoulders. "I don't know. An Indian, tall and dressed like a white man. He saw everything that happened. When he saw you on the ground, he rushed over, picked you up, and took you to a wagon across the street. From what I heard, he drove those two horses like the devil was after you both to get you here. I haven't seen him since. But he most likely saved your life."

"I guess I'll have to thank him one day," Nahum posed. "Surely somebody knows him."

"No matter, all that," Deidre told him. "The important thing is you're going to be alright. I was afraid I had lost you."

"You can't lose me. I'm like a bad penny. I always show back up," Nahum joked.

"You could turn in that badge and live here, in Fort Worth, with me," Deidre knew her plea would fall on deaf ears. She had tried to get Nahum to give up being a lawman and settle down, but he always refused. To him, it was like a religious calling to atone for his prior sins.

Nahum gave Deidre a look as if saying, "Please don't go there again." But instead, he said, "I'm tired. I think I'm going to sleep a little. You go on back to your restaurant. You can bring me up some soup later. I'm sure it will be better than what they have here." The request was Nahum's way of avoiding the conversation about him taking up residence with Deidre.

"Sure, darling," Deidre knew Nahum's looks and how to read what he meant rather than what he said. "I'll have the cook make up some beef broth with barley."

"Thank you," Nahum said and closed his eyes. He really was tired and in pain. Nahum just wanted to rest. Before leaving, Deidre bent over the bed and kissed him on his forehead.

～

THE NEXT TIME PUTNEY WOKE, he was startled by what he saw. Standing at the foot of his bed was an Indian, almost as tall as he. The man wore a brown tailored suit and a hat with a tall round crown and wide brim. "I see you managed to live again, Eka Toyatuku. I thought maybe this time you might die." Quanah Parker had a grin on his face.

"You could have let me. I guess it was you that brought me here," said Putney.

"I did bring you here. I was surprised to see you, but I was going to come to speak with you when that man attacked you. I needed you to live so you could see my prophecies come true. So I rushed you here, to the railroad hospital," Quanah said.

"What are you talking about? What prophecy?" Putney queried.

"I told you one day I would be a great chief among my people, and you didn't believe me. You also said my mother was famous, but I was not." Said Quannah. "Do you remember that?"

"It took you a while, but I guess you finally made it." Said Putney, "but not before I kept you from buying guns from Joaquin Doyle."

"Yes, our paths have crossed often, and sometimes I hated you," Quannah was blunt. "But I have read about you, and I have come to respect you."

"I have read about you, too, and I see that you are also famous and have done well for yourself and your people. And I want to say thank you for saving my life," Putney was being his most sincere.

"That was to fulfill the second prophecy," Quanah said.

"I don't follow," Putney said.

"Remember, I told you one day I would hold your life in my hands," Quannah reminded Putney.

"At the time, I don't think you meant it quite that way," Putney, in turn, reminded Parker.

"Prophesies are funny that way. They don't always occur as you believe they will. We live in a strange world. Things happen for a reason, but who are we to question the ways of the Great Spirit?" Quannah said. "But now you owe me a life, and someday I will collect."

"And I will gladly pay," Putney said. "That is my word, and you know I have never lied to you."

"This is good, Eka Toyotuku," replied Quanah. "And that woman with the fiery hair. She is fierce. You should do right by her."

"Now, what are you talking about," Putney was getting tired, and Parker's ways were wearing on him.

"When that man came from the alley and shot you, you fired at him once," Quanah told Putney. "You hit him. I think because he fell also. But I don't know if you killed him. The woman with you, she picked up your gun and shot him five times. I think maybe she wanted to make sure he was dead."

"Thanks for telling me that. I don't remember anything after being shot," Putney said.

"You do right by her, Nahum Putney. Like you did for that little girl so many years ago." With that, Quanah Parker left the room. There was no goodbye. He was just gone. Putney thought to himself that it is indeed a strange world.'

$\sim$

Two DAYS after he had awakened, Nahum was feeling much better. He was staying awake longer and even passed the time reading the local paper. In the newspaper, an article reported how another Comanche chief named Yellow Bear, who was visiting Fort Worth along with Parker, had died because of a faulty gas lamp in his hotel room. Nahum was saddened over reading about Yellow Bear, but he was glad it hadn't been Quanah.

Deidre had been visiting but had returned to her business, and Nahum was secretly glad. He loved when she came, but Deidre always fussed over him that sometimes it tired him out. It had been the same with Mary Johnson when she came to visit. Mary was constantly fluffing his pillows and filling his water glass, which he then felt obliged to drink, then she would refill it again. Brutus and Caesar came once, and unlike the women, they mostly heckled him about getting shot in the first place. He always liked seeing the twin giants. They were good company.

There was a gentle knock on the door, and the nurse opened the door and told Nahum that a lady outside wanted to see him asking if she should admit her. Nahum was tired. He couldn't think of who it would be. The last time Nahum had been in Fort Worth, Everett Jackson and Margaret Swenson and him had arrested five members of the Knights of the Rising Sun, one of which was Captain Montague Russell. The others had been up and comers in Fort Worth politics, so he hadn't left Fort Worth with a lot of friends. As far as Nahum knew, Meg was living in Paris, Texas, with a lawyer she had married. That had been fourteen years ago, and he couldn't think why Meg would even know he was in Fort Worth.

The nurse admitted a beautiful young woman wearing a well-tailored traveling suit. The jacket was light brown tweed with fur collar and cuffs. Fur also trimmed the bottom hem and stopped at her hips. The skirt was a darker brown tweed that matched the fur trim of the jacket and was a newer fashion with no bustle. It was long and fit tightly to the mid-thigh, flared out slightly to give a long bell appearance. The hem of the skirt was also trimmed in brown fur and swept a mere two inches above the floor. The lady's hair was blond, hung down to the center of her back, and topped with a fur hat that matched the rest of the fur trim. It had been long since Nahum had seen the woman who now must be in her mid-thirties, though she looked ten years younger. Nahum was pleasantly surprised that Imogene Foster should visit him.

"Well," Imogene started. "If we don't see each other often, and it seems when we don't, there's trouble. Now, look at you."

Nahum took Imogene's admonishment as a good-natured jab, then said, "It is wonderful to see you again, Imogene. I have to say you look stunning. Much better than the first time we met."

"Thanks to you, of course," Imogene replied. "I dread to think about what I would have become if you hadn't rescued me. But now, here I am to look in on the famous Nahum Putney. How are you, Nahum? What happened? Why aren't you in Austin or San Antonio instead of Fort Worth?"

"The doctor says I'll mend alright," Nahum told his young friend. "you know I always mend. I have a little pain still, but I'm ready to get out of this place. All the nuns running around make me uncomfortable."

"I imagine so," Imogene said. "From what I read, you're lucky you don't need a priest. So, why are you here? What happened?"

"You know I've told you about Deidre O'Neill," started Nahum.

Imogene interrupted, "Oh, her," she said. "I should have known that the infamous Miss O'Neill would be involved."

"Don't start that, Imogene," said Nahum. "I'm wounded, and I shouldn't have to listen to your opinion of Deidre,"

"I'll let it pass this time," Imogene relented. "But only because you're an invalid, so go on. What happened?"

Nahum started again. "She and I were taking an afternoon stroll around town when Ned Blakely ambushed me. You remember, before Quanah captured me, I told you about the Missouri bushwhacker I had left on that hill. It was him. Evidently, he has been carrying the grudge all these years. He saw me somewhere. And, true to his back-shooting nature, took advantage when I was most vulnerable. How did you know I was here?"

"Do you think something like you getting shot wouldn't

make the Dallas paper?" asked Imogene. "Hell, you're as famous as Wyatt Earp or Bat Masterson. Didn't you know that?"

"I don't pay much attention to the newspapers. Most of what they write is fiction anyway," said Nahum. "I mean, all the stories about Luke Short would have you believe he's ten feet tall. I met him a few nights ago, and he's not as tall as you."

When the door opened, Imogene was about to say something, and Deidre swept in like she owned the place. At first, she ignored the other woman in the room as she went directly to Nahum and kissed him long and passionately. It wasn't until Imogene cleared her throat that Deidre looked up and saw her. "I see, Mr. Putney, another one of your many women, has come to visit."

"Hardly that, Miss O'Neill," Imogene said, truthfully, although she would give almost anything if it were so.

"Excuse me, have we met before? I don't remember if we have," Deidre was getting ready to bare her teeth.

"No, Miss O'Neill," said Imogene. "I've just heard a lot about you from Nahum."

"All good, I'm sure, Miss...."

"Imogene Foster,"

"Oh," said Deidre. "I've heard about you, too. "It's nice we finally meet. We are the two most important women in Nahum's life. It would seem. He's always bragging about you and how well you've done. And how prim and proper you are," she soaked the words prim and proper with sarcasm. "But I must say I respect your accomplishments. Especially being one of the only women to graduate from the Saint Louis School of Law."

"Thank you, Miss O'Neill, and I too have heard a great deal about you," Imogene could barely hide her disapproval. "You are quite a successful woman yourself, in your way."

Nahum could see that things were about to go upside down, and he was in no condition to stop a cat fight. "Deidre! Imogene! Stop, both of you," he demanded. "You are both special in my life, in different ways. I will not put up with you sniping each other." Both the ladies took seats on either side of Nahum's bed. To Nahum, it was like two boxers going to their respective corners. Resting, but prepared to come to the middle of the ring as soon as the referee signaled.

Deidre took Nahum's hand and said, "You're right, dear. After all, it is you we both worry about."

Not to be outdone, Imogene took Nahum's other hand and was about to speak when there was a loud knock, and a tall young man walked in, bold as brass. He didn't look to be more than twenty years old. He was wearing a six-pointed star of a sheriff on his coat lapel and carrying a gun.

To Nahum, the entrance was rude, and he made a point of it, saying, "Do you always barge into rooms unannounced, boy?" Putney asked. "And wearing your hat and all. Does this look like a barn or a saloon to you?"

The young man jerked the hat from his head and stood, turning it in his hand by the brim. "No, sir, Mr. Putney. Excuse me."

"Don't excuse yourself to me, son," Putney was intent on his lesson in manners. "There are two ladies present here. You should be apologizing to them and introducing yourself as well." Even severely wounded and lying in a hospital bed, Putney was still an imposing figure.

"Yes, sir," The young deputy sheriff was nervous in the presence of such a notorious lawman. Finally, addressing the women in the room, the deputy said, "My name is

Hubert Forsythe, sir. Excuse me, ladies, for bursting in and for my ungentlemanly manners." Both Deidre and Imogene nodded that they accepted his apology.

"Now, Deputy Forsythe," said Putney. "I suppose you have business here."

"Well, uh, yes, sir," stammered the young lawman. "You see, Sheriff Maddox sent me over here with a warrant for murder."

"Why did he send you and not come himself?" Putney quizzed the youngster.

"The sheriff said you might have pistols in your room, and you would be less likely to shoot a novice, like me, than an older man," said the young deputy.

So, somebody had the gall to swear out a warrant on me for shooting a bushwhacker, thought Putney. "Well, since I'm not likely to get out of this bed at the moment, go ahead and read your warrant. When the doc allows me, I'll come to the jail and turn myself in."

"Oh, no, sir," said Hubert. "You don't understand. The warrant isn't for you."

"Well, son, then why are you here?" Putney demanded to know.

Gathering up all his courage, Deputy Hubert Forsythe announced, "Miss Deidre O'Neill, I'm here to arrest you for the murder of Ned Blakely."

Made in the USA
Monee, IL
31 January 2024